"UNDOUBTEDLY THE BEST COURTROOM NOVEL I HAVE EVER READ."
LAWRENCE BLOCK

"Everyone who liked PRESUMED INNOCENT, will love REASONABLE DOUBT."
The Flint Journal

"If you like complicated plots, twists, finely chiseled courtroom dialogue and a very interesting story, you'll get them in this book."
Lincoln Journal
Lincoln, Nebraska

"Friedman handles the game of legal chess with the kind of authority and suspense that will keep you reading well past your normal bedtime. . . . This is Friedman's fourth thriller, and his best. He may be on his way to joining the major leagues."
The Commercial Appeal
Memphis, Tennessee

"REASONABLE DOUBT provides a wonderful opportunity to get inside a lawyer's mind. . . . A novel that, once started, must be read to its conclusion."
Booklist

"If you are a mystery fan, try this one. It breaks new ground in development of plot and character, and the subtlety of clues that come to play significant roles in what the evidence reveals."
John Barkham Reviews

Also by Philip Friedman:

RAGE
ACT OF LOVE, ACT OF WAR
TERMINATION ORDER

REASONABLE DOUBT

Philip Friedman

IVY BOOKS • NEW YORK

Ivy Books
Published by Ballantine Books
Copyright © 1990 by Philip Friedman

Library of Congress Catalog Card Number: 88-45381

ISBN-0-8041-0749-1

This edition published by arrangement with Donald I. Fine, Inc.

Manufactured in the United States of America

First Ballantine Books Edition: November 1990

This book is dedicated to
the people whose faith and love and support
enabled me to write it,
and especially to Sylvia and Sam.

In those days they shall say no more,
The fathers have eaten a sour grape,
and the children's teeth are set on edge.

JEREMIAH 31:29

Many people gave generously of their time and their expertise to help me with this story. I thank them all. Special mention for their unstinting willingness to educate me in areas where I was ignorant is due Mary Corrarino and Craig Kaplan, and also Sasha Chavchavadze, Philip Olivetti, Jake Rosen, and Lynne Bundesen. They, and the many others who helped—prosecutors, defense attorneys and nonlawyers alike—deserve the credit for what is accurate in these pages. For the mistakes, the fault is entirely my own. My gratitude goes as well to the New York State Association of Criminal Defense Lawyers and the New York City Medical Examiner's Office, and to William Smart and the staff of the Virginia Center for the Creative Arts, where much of this book was written.

PREPARATION

1

FACE TO FACE WITH THE WOMAN ACCUSED OF MUR-
dering his son, Michael Ryan felt remarkably calm.

He had barely noticed the dark figure emerging from a limousine
as he entered the building where his law firm had its offices, had
not realized who it was until she stepped into the elevator with him.
Before he could react the doors had slid firmly together, locking
them in with three other people.

When the elevator finally let them out on the thirtieth floor he
stood his ground in front of the firm's broad glass doors. If he could
not avoid a confrontation at least he could keep it out of the office.

His daughter-in-law was pale under her makeup, the elegant
planes of her face puffy from too little sleep and too much crying.
Her blue-gray eyes held his.

"I didn't do it, Michael, I swear." The words came in a controlled rush. "I'm not guilty."

The plea was no surprise, only that she would make it to him.

"Guilt is for the jury." He turned away from her.

"Please, Michael. Just give me the benefit of the doubt."

"What difference does it make what I think? We barely know
each other."

A pained hesitation. "That's not how I wanted it."

"Then whose fault is it?" His anger breaking through. "Mine?
Ned's?"

"No, I didn't mean . . ." Her composure dissolved. "I'm sorry,
Michael, I'm not doing this right."

"You said what you wanted to. Let's leave it at that."

He got to his office with no awareness of walking the long corridors past partners and associates, paralegals and secretaries. It
took him a while to remember why he was there.

He stacked some file folders on his desk, work he could do while

3

he was away from the office if he felt up to it. He buzzed his secretary. "Tell Mr. Legler I'm ready for lunch when he is."

"There's a rumor Jennifer was here this morning," Legler said, his bulk parting a way for them through the lunch-hour crowd clogging the lobby.

"It's true. She waited outside in her daddy's limo and cornered me in the elevator."

"Why? What did she want?"

"To tell me she's innocent."

"What do you think?"

"Guilty as charged. Assuming the prosecutor doesn't screw up."

"Have you talked to him?"

"Him, and his boss."

"Franky Griglia?"

"The man himself."

Legler dredged his memory. "That's right. You're old friends."

"We go back a long way."

"What did they tell you?"

"Mostly what's been in the papers."

The story had been soaked up by the press like a rainstorm in a desert. The murder of Ned Ryan was a crime straight from a soap opera, a crime that people could enjoy without feeling guilty about it: passion and jealousy among the overprivileged. Ned and Jennifer Ryan's marriage had been in trouble. They had gone to a glitzy art-gallery party where Ned had reportedly flirted with the guest of honor openly enough to provoke Jennifer into a tirade that had turned violent. Ned had been found in the gallery owner's private study, bludgeoned to death.

"That's all the prosecution has, or that's all they're telling?"

"They're pretty sure they can tie her to the murder weapon."

Legler whistled. "That should do it."

"You know what convinces me they have her nailed? This is the first big press case since Franky was appointed Acting D.A. It has to be a winner. He'd never let his people risk a charge that might not stick, not on this one."

Legler turned off Madison Avenue toward the modest French restaurant where the two of them had their bi-weekly lunches.

Years before, when Ryan had been starting out at the U.S. Attorney's office, Bob Legler had been his mentor. They had kept in touch after Legler left, and when Ryan had been feeling pressed by Ned's upcoming college bills Legler had argued that private practice was the answer to Ryan's problems, and that Pane, Parish, Eisen &

Legler was the place to be. Ryan had taken him up on it and for his first seven years there Ryan had been busy and successful, a mainstay of the firm's substantial corporate litigation practice. The last three years had been a different story.

The restaurant was crowded but the maitre d' greeted them warmly and led them to a table in the corner, out of the bustle of traffic. Legler asked for imported water with a slice of lime; Ryan ordered a double shot of Irish whiskey. He saw Legler's eyebrows go up but did not care.

"You know," Ryan said, "it sounds crazy, but for a moment there I was sure Jennifer was going to ask me to defend her."

"Crazy doesn't begin to cover it."

"The funny thing is, after Ned's funeral I decided she was the closest thing I had to family and I ought to get to know her better."

That perfect June day Jennifer had caught up with him as he walked alone toward the grave. She had taken his hand, unexpected intimacy from a woman he hardly knew. They had stood together for the short service over Ned's ashes, Ryan comforted by the human warmth of his dead son's wife leaning against him. Maybe I've misjudged her, he had thought as together they shoveled the first dirt into the grave. Maybe it would do us both good if we could find a way to share our grief.

Only four days later that fantasy had been demolished by a tabloid front page shouting SOCIALITE NABBED IN HUBBY'S DEATH. Below the headline had been a picture of Jennifer Kneeland Ryan on her way into the courthouse for arraignment. There were more pictures on the inside pages, including one of her father, H. Robertson Kneeland, looking at once enraged and bewildered. A subhead said $-MILLION-$ BAIL.

Ryan had been furious with himself. Share the grief! Any fool knew the first rule in cases like this. It was always the same, and it wasn't The Butler Did It.

The two lawyers talked office politics over lunch—ways to defeat a renewed push by some of their younger partners to add criminal defense work to the firm's repertoire. It was a point of pride for both of them not to be among the ex-prosecutors who switched sides when they went into private practice.

Legler sat back while the busboy cleared the table and the waiter gave them their coffee.

"You said you had a problem."

Ryan drank coffee. Legler waited.

"Ned named me executor."

"And?"

"I'd have to spend every day for months studying the ins and outs of Ned's life. *And* dealing with Jennifer."

"I assume you're not asking for the obvious. But here it is." Legler inclined his head the way he had for two decades of pronouncements. "You can always hide from this kind of thing if you want to badly enough. It may save you some pain today but in the long run you'll feel a lot worse."

They sat in silence.

Legler said, "There's more to it, isn't there?"

Ryan had never liked talking about his personal problems; whenever he made the mistake of thinking it would help, he promptly regretted it. At this point there was nothing he could do but go ahead.

"I'm worried about what I'm going to find."

Legler considered it. "I know how hurt and angry you were that Ned kept you out of his life all those years. Making you his executor, he invited you in."

"Too late to do any good."

"You won't know that until you try."

It was the hardest kind of advice to hear: the advice you've already given yourself and don't want to take.

"Marion wants to know when you'll come out for dinner again," Legler said.

"Soon."

Twice bereaved now, Ryan was armed against some of the ironies of his situation. Though mostly he wanted to be left alone he knew his friends would insist on keeping him company and offering him solace. The last time he had been to the Leglers', Marion had compared him to Job. "Worse than Job," she'd said. "At least Job didn't lose his wife."

The next morning Ryan woke up clammy with sweat. An unremembered nightmare floated just out of sight like wisps of poisonous fog. He stretched and rolled over to go back to sleep.

A part of his dream reappeared—Alison's car racing off the road and into the bridge abutment, as clear as if he had been there. He sat up breathing hard.

He made himself get out of bed and walked himself into the bathroom for a shower. He was determined not to let himself start another long slide into despair like the one after Ali's death. Being in motion helped. The water streaming over him helped more, the way it always did.

He made coffee and called the lawyer who had drawn up Ned's will.

"I've decided to go ahead with it."

"Good. I'll fax the papers over for you to sign. It'll be a few weeks before they issue your Letters Testamentary."

"Just let me know."

After he had signed the papers to start the probate process Ryan rented a car and drove north through Westchester and then northeast into Connecticut for his planned week in the country. The morning's panic had confirmed how badly he needed to be away from familiar people and places. He took a room at an old inn near the Massachusetts border.

He paid almost no attention to the files he had brought with him from the office or the books he had thought he wanted to read. Instead, he took long walks in the woods, his eyes on the spongy mat of brown needles underfoot, dappled with tree-filtered spring sunlight. It was cool here, and it was quiet, free of the crowds that would soon descend. Ryan did not see the trees. His mind was occupied with other images.

He had expected to be full of thoughts of Ned. He was not prepared to be thinking so much of Alison. After all, he'd had three years to absorb the shock of her death.

And yet it made sense. How could he think about Ned—about their estrangement and about the many ways he did not know his son—without thinking of Alison?

The day of the accident they had all been at the groundbreaking for Ned's first solo real-estate project, a commercial building in northeastern New Jersey, small as those things went but a source of justifiable pride for a young man just past twenty-four. In a tailored suit Ali had looked more like one of Ryan's corporate clients than the high-school English teacher she was. Her soft blonde hair had been cut shorter since he had last seen her, blunt and even with the determined line of her jaw; she had used some kind of rinse in it that had turned the pale gold almost orange. And her blue eyes were bloodshot in a way he had not seen before. From what he had heard, the red in her eyes, like the red in her hair, came out of a bottle.

After the ceremony, with the late-afternoon sky threatening rain, Ryan had asked Ali to have dinner with him. She had been reluctant; he had kept after her until she finally gave in.

He had hungered to be with her that day; he hadn't thought he'd had anything more than that in mind. As things had turned out he had pressed her to let him come back home, promising yet again to work hard at being a full-time husband. And meaning it, as he did every time.

Ali had been drinking vodka gibsons: small metronomic sips that added up with surprising rapidity. The alcohol had not softened her assessment of his repeated promises. "Your work will still come first," she had said. "It always has and it always will."

He had come back with a version of his usual response: "The only reason I work so hard is for you and Ned." Meaning that, too.

The argument had rapidly disintegrated into a rehash of all their old grievances, Ali accusing him of deserting the family, Ryan feeling unappreciated and misunderstood. Their barbs were sharpened by frequent use; every sentence drew blood. Finally Ali had stalked out into the rain. Eighteen miles down the road her car had hit a bridge abutment at high speed.

Ryan had been in no shape to make funeral arrangements. The service had been organized by Ned and his new girlfriend, Jennifer Kneeland, seven years Ned's senior and his boss's daughter. After a eulogy by the pastor of the church Alison had been attending for the past year, Ned had walked firmly to the podium, head up, looking calm and self-possessed, older than his twenty-four years. He had stood before the small roomful of people and compared his mother to the Bible's capable woman, her worth above rubies. His love for her had shone through the grief.

And then his expression had darkened and he had begun to talk about the emotional turmoil of his mother's last months and the tragedy of her premature death.

"Alison Ryan was loved by many many people," he had said. "She earned that love and she gave it back with her whole heart. But the tragedy of her life was that there was one person she loved more than anyone else"—he had glared at his father, his voice a rough whisper—"and that man killed her. He drove her into that stone wall just as surely as if he'd been behind the wheel."

Ned had stood there, hands clamped on the lectern, eyes fixed on his father, until someone had broken the stunned hush and led him to a seat.

People had told Ryan that he should not take it to heart, that Ned had been too upset to realize what he was saying. Ryan knew better.

One of the daily tabloids had thought enough of the incident on a slow news day to give it a front-page headline: SON SAYS DAD KILLED MOM.

For Ryan, three years had not muted the pain.

2

LATE ON THE FRIDAY NIGHT AFTER HE CAME BACK TO the city Ryan stopped into Kelly's Shamrock, his first time since the Friday he'd gone from there to the morgue to identify Ned's body.

Since Alison's death the Shamrock had been a refuge, a place where Ryan could shut out the world and be just a guy who didn't say much and have a couple of beers and a double shot of Irish whiskey every Friday night.

Jimmy Kelly drew him a beer and a short one for himself. Raised his glass to Ryan. "Welcome."

"Good to be here."

There was a call for service at the other end of the bar. The Shamrock had been crowding up nights since the new luxury apartment houses opened on Broadway. The regulars, Ryan among them, were not pleased.

Unlike most of the others who hung out at Kelly's after the local dinner crowd was gone, Michael Ryan was no Irishman. The name had been a present to his grandfather from an immigration officer with patience only for the short and simple. No one at the Shamrock had ever questioned the donated name, or Ryan's seemingly black-Irish looks, and he had quickly become as much a part of the place as anyone.

"Eddie O'Neill left tomorrow's paper," Kelly told him. "You seen it yet?"

"Nope."

Kelly put the folded paper on the bar and went to deal with the clamor.

Ryan unfolded the newspaper.

JENNIFER INDICTED! the tabloid headline read, over a picture taken months before at a charity costume ball where Jennifer had appeared as Diana the Huntress, looking anything but chaste.

Ryan knew better than to attach much significance to an indictment. Grand juries heard what the prosecutor let them hear, and mostly they did what the prosecutor told them to do.

Somehow the knowledge did not dilute the impact of this particular indictment. It banished any doubt Ryan had that his daughter-in-law had killed his son. "Guilt is for the jury," he had told Jennifer, yet even then he had been sitting in judgment on her, as he had since his first conversations with Franky Griglia after the arrest.

Ryan wondered if Jennifer had testified for the grand jury. It was her right, and in some cases it could be a smart thing to do. The downside was that the more often you testified the more likely you were to contradict yourself. Better to save your testimony for the trial, if you were going to testify at all.

The old warrior dies hard, Ryan thought. Here I am, it's my son's murder and I'm trying to guess the defense's strategy. As if it were *my* case to prosecute.

There would be plenty of time to see what happened, when it happened. For now, nothing to do but wait. The grand jury had spoken, and the trial might not be for a year or more, depending on how successful the defense was at delaying. And assuming there was no plea bargaining.

Suppose there was a plea bargain? How would he feel about that? No mystery there. He could feel his face heating up just at the thought. He did not want to see Ned's murderer returning to a normal life after spending only a few years in jail.

Ryan had lost all opportunity to bring Ned back into his life, all chance to make amends to his son for past mistakes. Ned had lost more. Ned had lost everything.

Whatever provocation Jennifer had had—and the media had been full of speculation about Ned's sexual escapades—taking his life was no answer. There was no justification here. Only the maximum penalty would do.

It was something to talk to Franky Griglia about.

"Michael!" the D.A. said. "What can I do for you?"

Ryan did not trust Griglia's hearty good fellowship. Too much had changed since the two of them had been law-school buddies and then aggressive young prosecutors—one federal, the other state—meeting in noisy bars to trade war stories and gripes about their bosses.

He got straight to the point. "I'm assuming your man Becker is going to hold out for murder."

"That's what the indictment says. Murder in the second degree."

Griglia was dodging the question. Ryan pressed harder. "Maybe I'm not being clear. I don't want to see her pleading to some lesser offense."

"I don't either, my friend, but I've got four hundred ambitious lawyers working for me, and I can't be looking over their shoulders all the time. Not even on a case I care about, like this one. I don't have the time, and they wouldn't put up with it if I tried."

"You're the boss, aren't you? You made the decision to arrest her before you went to the grand jury."

"Sure. A high-profile arrest like that and I've only been Acting D.A. a couple of months, I wanted to make the call on when and how. I figured there was a fair chance she'd decide to take a long vacation someplace far away. She can sure as hell afford it. So I decided arrest first, indict later."

"And that's why the million dollar bail."

"Hell, we asked for no bail at all, straight remand, throw her in the clink. But the defense argued she had strong ties to the community, by which he meant her old man. The judge probably figured H. Robertson Kneeland cares too much about his status to let his daughter skip out."

"Twenty-five to life is a pretty good reason to embarrass your father."

"And a million bucks is reason to stay. Let's hope so. Who knows—maybe she wants to clear her name. She says she's innocent."

"Her and every other defendant in history."

"I didn't say I believed her."

"Just so you make sure she gets what she deserves."

"It's like I said, from now on the ball's in Joe Becker's court. He's a good man. Eight years on the job, a lot of major felony experience. If you're worried about this, talk to him. And listen, I never had a chance to say this but I was kind of disappointed when you left the government. I used to miss those public pissing contests we had."

In a pig's eye, Ryan thought. Public pissing contests! As if that told it all. As if Joey Baldasaro had never lived or died. As if Franky

Griglia's headline grabbing had not cost Ryan a year's work and a stack of important convictions.

"You take care of yourself, you hear?" the D.A. said.

The court officer at the reception desk took Ryan's name and called upstairs to make sure he was expected.

"Eighth floor," the officer said, and gave Ryan a gummed-paper visitor's badge to stick on his suit jacket.

Joseph A. Becker turned out to be a medium-size man in his early thirties wearing a white shirt and a tie pulled loose at the neck. There were bookshelves on both long walls of his shoe-box shaped office; two wooden chairs for visitors faced the civil-service metal desk. Ryan saw mismatched file cabinets, file envelopes lined up on the floor, piles of transcripts on a long table. Either Becker liked his work or he had too much of it.

"It's a pleasure finally to meet you in person, Mr. Ryan." Becker went to sit behind his desk, waving Ryan into a chair. "I'm told you were with the U.S. Attorney's office for ten years. Is that right?"

"A long time ago."

"Head of the Criminal Division for the Southern District, I heard."

"Nothing so grand. I put in a little time running the Frauds Unit, and Organized Crime before that. Basically I was an assistant, like you."

"You're very modest, based on what I heard about your conviction record. I don't know what I can tell you. You've got a lot more trial experience than I do." The A.D.A.'s voice was tense.

"Look, Mr. Becker . . ."

"Joe."

"Fine. Joe. Let's get something straight right from the start. I don't want to run your case for you. All I ask is that if you're sure you've got the right defendant you get a conviction. A conviction and the maximum penalty. How you do it is your business."

Becker relaxed. "Mr. Ryan, I'm glad you said that, because I'm going to be honest with you. I was kind of worried about what role you wanted to play in this. The thing is, I'm happy to talk to you about the case, a man with your experience. But, you know, victims, victims' families, sometimes they have pretty definite ideas, and it can be a problem, get in the way, and your being a prosecutor yourself, ex-prosecutor, I have to admit I was worried you'd want to be in here every minute with an opinion about everything we were doing, meaning well I'm sure, but you're very close to the case . . . I want to assure you, we're going to do our best with this.

We've definitely got the right defendant. It's like I told you when we talked on the phone, we wouldn't have come this far if we didn't. I guess you know the story, reading the papers.''

"Actually, I do my best to stay away from them, but it's been a hard story to avoid.'' What mattered to Ryan was that his son was dead and that the murderer be punished. Everything in between was a pointless source of pain.

He let Becker take him through an overview of the prosecution case, listening only closely enough to get a sense that Becker had things under control.

"So we've got motive,'' the assistant district attorney concluded, "and we've got the murder weapon—a piece of sculpture, happens to be made by the very woman he was flirting with who provoked the argument, which is maybe not such a coincidence, actually. We can definitely place the wife at the scene and the preliminary tests confirm that she handled the murder weapon, the way I told you. That's since I talked to you last, and it's still for your ears only. Next to an eye witness and a confession, it's about as good as you can do.''

"How's the police work?''

"Real solid. I know that can be a problem sometimes, and even when it's not the defense tries to make it one, but I think we're okay on that.''

"Good. Then I can leave you to build the strongest case you can, get a murder conviction and twenty-five to life.''

"Whoa. Hold on a minute.'' Becker was smiling uncertainly. "I guess you're kidding, or—not kidding but . . . I know you know it doesn't go like that: wham bam thank you ma'am. I mean, we'll go in there and I'm not saying we won't get a murder conviction, because I happen to think we will, but I can't *promise* it, and you know I can't.''

Ryan did not like what he was hearing. "What are you telling me?''

"All I'm saying is if you expect murder, and twenty-five to life, you may be disappointed. I don't know how it is in federal court, but here it's never smart to rely on getting the highest count on the indictment plus the maximum sentence. You said a conviction. Okay. If we're talking about manslaughter one and a sentence of eight-and-a-third to twenty-five, then I'm pretty sure you'll be satisfied. And you might end up pleasantly surprised, because we could do better.''

"As long as you don't let her off easy to buy a plea.''

Becker's pleasant expression disappeared. "Look, Mr. Ryan, I'm not here to let people off easy."

"That's what I wanted to hear."

"Right. But you have to understand, the party line around here is trials are expensive, we've got more trials than we can handle, kill the backlog. Somebody says, we'll hand you this one on a platter if you back off a little, we're supposed to take it and say thanks. I mean, don't get me wrong, nobody walks out of here with less than they deserve, but all the same, you go into court there's always a chance they walk—the jury thinks they're cute, something like that. A plea bargain means we don't have to worry about that, so it's worth something giving them a little less jail time. I'm talking generalities here, I mean you did this yourself, you know how it goes."

"I know the theories. I don't see how they apply here." Ryan fought to keep the anger out of his voice. "It's not as if she had accomplices—you don't want her to turn somebody else in, or co-operate in some other way. You're talking about someone who took a human life, acting alone and out of pure malice, and you're talking about a crime that has already been the subject of major public attention. The only theory I see operating here is the public's right to see justice done in a prominent and serious case. As for this need to kill the backlog, as you put it, there are a lot better ways."

"Hey—I'm on your side. I mean, look, I'd be crazy if I wanted to plead this one out. Where else am I going to get another case this big?"

Hooray for dedication to the law and the search for justice, Ryan did not say.

He stood up. "I don't care about your reasons. I care about results."

3

—

AS SOON AS RYAN'S LETTERS TESTAMENTARY WERE IS-
sued, making him officially Ned's executor, he had his secretary
call Jennifer to set up a time to inventory Ned's belongings.

Going to Ned's apartment was one thing, going there alone was
another. Ryan called his accountant and at three minutes before
Ryan's four o'clock appointment they were both on the stoop of the
brownstone where Ned had lived.

The curtained glass-and-wrought-iron door swung open.

"Yeah?"

The challenge came from a tall, broad man in a mud-brown suit
stretched tight across his shoulders. Ryan guessed he had been
hired to keep away reporters and cranks.

"Michael Ryan, to see Jennifer . . ."

"Who's your friend?"

Ryan half turned to include the precise, silver-haired man next
to him. "This is Mr. Kaplan. He'll be working with me."

The bodyguard looked doubtful, then said, "All right."

He opened the door no more than wide enough to let them in
and led them down a short corridor paneled in oak. An inner door
admitted them into a bright, airy high-ceilinged room.

It was Ryan's first visit to the place that for more than two years
his son had called home. Ryan's mouth was dry and his hands felt
cold. He looked around, seeing a blur of furniture, fresh flowers
and potted plants. The pinkish off-white walls were bare, but large
and small rectangles of clean, unfaded paint marked the former
location of whatever used to hang there.

Except for Ryan and his accountant, brown-suit was the only
person in the room. Ryan was glad to be spared an encounter with
Jennifer.

Before he could ask if she'd left instructions, she came down the stairs from the duplex's second floor.

"Hello, Michael."

His breath froze in his chest.

"Michael, can't you please hear me out? That's all I ask."

He turned away.

"Sorry," she said stiffly. "I know that's not why you're here. There's a note for you on the mantel and a set of keys. I'll leave you to do your work."

He found her note in a white business envelope propped against a crystal vase over the fireplace: The apartment was his to explore for as long as he needed it. She had no desire to stay in it alone and be reminded of Ned. She was especially eager to have Ryan remove the artwork Ned had collected—she had stacked all the paintings in the spare room and put all the sculpture into boxes. She had looked through Ned's papers for the most obviously important items; they were on the dining table. Ryan was welcome to look through the apartment for more. She had taken only some of her clothes and a few personal possessions. Aside from the clothing and jewelry she had left behind, and the furniture she had specified on an enclosed list, Ryan should assume everything in the apartment was Ned's.

Kaplan had already discovered the papers on the dining room table. He was leafing through a business checkbook.

"Is it what you need?" Ryan asked him.

"It's a start."

"The place is ours as long as we want it." He handed Kaplan Jennifer's note.

While the accountant continued to look through the checkbooks and other papers on the dining table, Ryan explored. He had made a full circuit of the apartment—living room, dining room, powder room and kitchen on the first floor; bedroom, guest room and study upstairs, each with a bath—before he realized that he was seeing everything through a haze. He went back to the living room and sat down on a generous wing-back chair and closed his eyes.

All right, he told himself, this is a job. You have to think of this as a job.

"Michael?"

He opened his eyes to see Kaplan standing in front of him, briefcase bulging. "I couldn't see any reason to go through these here so I stuffed them in my bag and I'm going to take them to the office, unless there's some reason not to."

"As long as we have a list of what you're taking."

"I left it on the table."

"You go ahead," Ryan heard himself say. "I'm going to stay here."

For a long time he did not move. The chair was vantage point enough until he could absorb the fact of where he was and why he was there.

This was Ned's house, Ned's living room. The son he did not know, the son he had never understood. The son who, against all logic, had named the father he would not talk to in life to be executor of his estate. Invited him in, as Legler had put it.

If Ryan was ever going to come to terms with all that, to find out what he had missed, to get to know the man who had been Edward Ryan, the journey began here.

He was glad there was a guest room. He did not think he could have slept in Ned and Jennifer's bed.

Once he had made up his mind to stay, Ryan felt better. He wandered through the living room. Gradually, he began to assimilate what he was seeing. The furniture was all old, antiques, he supposed, rich woods with the soft patina of age. The upholstery was a mix of deep solids—midnight blue, dark burgundy—and old-fashioned prints on pale backgrounds. Jennifer's taste, judging by her list, or her family heirlooms.

He had never understood her. From the little he had learned about her at the beginning she had seemed just one more example of the bad choices Ned was already making. No one could argue with her looks, but Ned had never had trouble finding good-looking women his own age. Ryan could only guess that her special attraction for Ned had something to do with her father, and with the Kneelands' being part of a circle whose glitter and show beguiled Ned, though to Ryan it seemed transparently phony.

Jennifer's earliest contact with Ryan had been a clumsy attempt to patch things up between him and Ned. It had not warmed Ryan to her.

She had called the day after Alison's funeral to say she was worried about leaving things the way they were between father and son. "I suppose it isn't really my place, but I'm afraid if I don't say something, no one else will. I'm sure Ned's mother would have wanted the two of you to make peace. It hurt her that you and Ned didn't get along with each other."

Ryan had been amazed. Could she think he didn't know how Ali had felt about him and Ned? At a distance of three years it was still hard to believe that Jennifer could have missed completely that he had tried over and over to find some common ground with Ned.

"I appreciate your concern," he had told her, "but you're right, it isn't really your place."

She had persisted anyway. "In case you change your mind, Ned is having lunch at the Gotham at one o'clock on Tuesday. He'll be alone, and you're welcome to join him."

Ryan had had no choice but to go. He had not expected anything from it; he had not even been sure that Ned would show up. But when Ryan arrived Ned was already there. For a time neither of them had spoken. In the end Ryan wished they had left it that way.

They had fought from the first word, Ned accusing him again of causing Ali's drinking and her death, blaming him for everything bad in the marriage.

"You moved out on her. How in hell could you do that?"

"She *ordered* me out. You know that. You and I had this out then. You said I should have refused to go, and I said it wasn't that simple. You said get her to take you back, all she wants is for you to stop being a stranger, and I listened to you. I did my best."

"Your best! Some flowers, some phone calls. You broke dates with her. Your own wife."

"I had to be in court."

"Wonderful—you had to be in court. Your answer to everything."

It had gone rapidly downhill from there, until Ned had stood up, knocking over his chair on his way out. Watching him go Ryan had wondered how Jennifer could possibly have imagined this meeting would succeed.

He had next spoken to her a few months later, after the wedding he had not been invited to. She had suggested dinner, so they could get acquainted. "I know you and Ned aren't speaking to each other right now, but I'm still your daughter-in-law."

The meal had been impossibly strained, Jennifer trying too hard to make an impression that Ryan had been too angry and too much on guard to decipher. They had parted knowing they had made no contact.

Just as well, he thought now.

He decided it was important to see everything in the apartment, to absorb it all. He wanted to do it gradually, to build up to the point where he could handle the inevitable unpleasant surprises. He assumed he would be safe as long as he stayed on the first floor. Living room, dining room, and kitchen were neutral territory. It was the study, upstairs, and the bedroom, that he was worried about.

Opening the wide, shallow bottom drawer of the dining room sideboard, he was unprepared to find it full of photographs, thrown in helter-skelter. Photographs of all sizes, from machine-made passport pictures to studio portraits grand enough to hang on a boardroom wall. He knew as soon as he saw what was there that he should close the drawer. Leave it closed until tomorrow, or next week, or next month. But fascination overcame good sense. He reached in among the memories fixed in silver and pulled one out. He could not have done worse.

The picture was a black-and-white snapshot Ryan had not seen in years, though seeing it now he could not think of a time when it had not been fresh in his mind. Alison, lovely Alison, sat with her knees gathered under her on a picnic blanket, smiling radiantly enough to make the gray tones of the print seem alive with color. The object of her pleasure was a young, brave Michael Ryan, smooth of skin and bright of eye, on one knee beside her, one arm around her shoulders, the other stretched out in front of him, palm up. Riding his cupped hand, chunky legs on either side of the fingers, hips snug against the upraised thumb, was the beaming baby Edward Michael Ryan.

Ryan knelt by the sideboard, on a less flexible knee than had supported him then, frozen in the present looking at the frozen past. Only a growing awareness of pain in his knees prompted him to stand. Stiffness kept him from getting up as quickly as he might have, but it was still quickly enough to turn his vision gray and make him grab at the sideboard for support. When his head cleared he went looking for a glass and a bottle of whiskey.

He drank himself to sleep sitting in the wing-back chair, the photograph propped on its arm.

Sunlight slanting through the tall windows opened his eyes. He took a long cold shower in the guest room bath and dressed in the clothes he had slept in. Downstairs, he could not bring himself to disturb the kitchen. He went out for coffee and found that he was reluctant to go back.

This is ridiculous, he told himself. He had to face it, sooner or later. He went back, but he did not stay.

Another time, he rationalized—no need to do this part of it right away. There are other ways to follow Ned's trail, to get to know who he was.

4

THE APARTMENT BUILDING WAS NOT FIFTH AVENUE'S oldest or grandest; in a thunderstorm early on a summer evening there was little to distinguish its broad limestone facade from the gray faces of its neighbors.

"Yes, sir?" Unknown visitors did not prompt the doorman to graciousness.

"Michael Ryan to see Mr. Kneeland."

The doorman checked a list on a clipboard. "Yes, sir." Acknowledgment, but hardly acceptance. "Go right up." Lifting a receiver to announce him.

Ryan marched across the oriental rugs, past the marble columns. The elevator man admitted him into the wood-paneled car and sped him skyward without a word. The car slid smoothly to a halt and the elevator door opened on the apartment's entrance gallery. No long hallways dotted with gray-steel apartment doors here: this was the land of one apartment to a floor. Or, in H. Robertson Kneeland's case, one apartment to two floors.

Ryan stood alone in the gallery—as big as his own living room and twice as high, its walls hung with a museum's worth of modern art—and listened to his umbrella dripping water on the marble floor.

Kneeland appeared in the archway at the other side of the gallery, wearing a lightweight sweater and worn khaki trousers, a tall man with gray hair and round metal-rim glasses, the kind of man who looked fifty before he was forty and then did not appear to age a day for the next quarter century.

"It was good of you to come all the way over here in the rain," Kneeland said.

Ryan did not think he could match his host's insincerity; he did not try.

A maid in uniform came to take Ryan's umbrella.

"We'll be more comfortable in here." Kneeland turned and walked away from him.

Ryan followed, down a long hall and into a wood-paneled, book-lined room.

"Before we start," Kneeland said when they were sitting on matching leather wing chairs flanking a dead fireplace, "I have to tell you—Jennifer is devastated by what happened."

Ryan said nothing.

Kneeland went on. "She says that she never in her life would have or could have hit Ned, not even with her hand."

He stopped, again as if he was waiting for Ryan to acknowledge what he had just said. When Ryan again said nothing Kneeland added: "Hearing her say that is enough for me. I believe her."

"She's your daughter."

"And Ned was like my son."

The words shattered Ryan's artificial composure. There it was, out loud, in so many words: *Ned was like my son.*

"Mr. Kneeland, I understand your concern for your daughter, but that's not what I came to see you about."

"You want to talk about Ned, and his businesses."

"Exactly."

"Is there something in particular?"

"Why not start at the beginning?"

"All right." Kneeland crossed one knee over the other. His hands rested on the chair arms with men's-club ease. He talked about meeting Ned when he was working for a developer Kneeland was doing a deal with. Ned had been performing impressively, Kneeland said, in a difficult job working for an impossible boss.

"And he had the kind of charm a lot of people can't resist. His best qualities were wasted where he was. I made him an offer and put him to work on some real estate deals. They worked out well for both of us, well enough so that Ned could begin generating deals of his own. At first it was small things, individual buildings here and there, small businesses. Nothing that took much money, and I was usually happy to be part of it. I don't know how many deals we did that way. He was always up to something. He had tremendous energy and he learned very quickly.

"When he came to me with an idea that needed serious financing, I was ready to listen. It was an area I knew nothing about, private medical clinics and pharmacies, but he had a partner who was a doctor, and it sounded interesting. The best part was that they weren't looking to the profitability of the clinics to make their money. Since you can't know how hard any of the doctors or pharmacists are going to work, you don't want to rely on them to generate your revenues. The idea was to establish enough of these clinics to be a captive market for a company that would supply the clinics with everything they needed to stay in business, from paper towels to prescription drugs. The numbers said they could make a good profit that way, even if the clinics themselves were doing barely enough business to stay open.

"As far as it went, it was a good idea. The problem was, he hadn't thought it all the way through. It's one thing to get these people to say they'll buy everything from you, but it's something else to hold them to it. He didn't have any workable way to keep them from buying from other suppliers. Luckily, I had some ideas about how we could beat that problem, so I was able to say all right, let's try it. And it worked."

Kneeland looked off into some private distance. "That's how it started. Once we were in business that way, the rest of the details were up to Ned. And my lawyers, of course, and all the other people who get involved in deals before you're done. If you want to know more about it, I think you'd do better to talk to Ned's partners. He came to me for money, and he came to me for advice when things were going badly, and we celebrated when things went well. I'm willing to answer your questions, but I'm afraid I don't have the kind of details you need."

Kneeland's words echoed in Ryan's mind. *He came to me for advice when things were going badly, and we celebrated when things went well.* Exactly the kind of relationship Ryan had wanted to have with Ned but had never been able to create.

It was another week before Jake Kaplan was ready to present a preliminary report on Ned's business affairs. Ryan scheduled it for after his meeting with an observer from the state tax department to open Ned's safe-deposit box.

Ryan was expecting to find bonds or stock certificates. There were none. Instead, there was a large manila envelope containing Ned's birth certificate, some high school report cards and other bits of personal history, and a photograph of Alison that Ryan quickly turned face down. Another manila envelope held what looked like love letters and photos and audiotape messages from old girlfriends. There were also three fat bricks of hundred dollar bills.

Ryan watched a bank officer count the money with rapid precision for the benefit of the observer from the state tax department. Each brick of bills contained at its center a currency-size slip of paper with a hand-written note on it. The bank officer dealt them to Ryan without breaking her count. When the tally was complete and the tax papers filled out and signed, Ryan asked to open an account for the estate. He didn't want to be carrying around eighty thousand dollars in cash, even to bring it to another bank.

For a few minutes he was alone with the money and the hand-written notes. He propped each note against its stack of bills. Strings of numbers which were not the amount of money in the stacks. Bank-account numbers was the easy guess, but that did not make it right. And it said nothing about where all the cash had come from.

Kaplan registered the news with his usual sour acceptance. "At least it wasn't wrapped up in an old sock behind a drawer in the bedroom. There's too much damn money floating around these days."

He looked at the list of numbers. "I don't deal with Swiss banks, but I'll have a colleague of mine look at these for you. Meantime, you ready for the show?"

"That's why we're here."

Kaplan waved a hand at the stacks of papers covering the top of the conference table. "A lot of this is thanks to Mr. Kneeland, whose lawyers sent over enough undigested files to bury the poor kids I've got working on it. Ned himself didn't keep records as mere accountants understand the term. There seems to have been a lot of cash flow, money in and money out, but most of it was probably OPM—other people's money. It's hard to tell how much of it stuck to Ned as it passed through his hands."

"So you can't put a value on any of it."

"Not until we learn more. There's whole collection of small businesses, and one big one—the medical clinics. We can start wherever you want."

"Let's save the clinics for last."

More unsettled by the lumps of cash than he had let on, Ryan was not eager for any more hints of shady activity, and medical clinics were a potential danger zone. In the U.S. Attorney's office he had seen a stream of cases involving Medicare fraud, a quick way to bilk the government, so common that most districts had minimum dollar amounts they would prosecute, to avoid being swamped. For some U.S. Attorneys the threshold was fifty thousand dollars.

Kaplan picked up a file folder from the top of one of the stacks. "All right: one inventor of surgical instruments, financed through the good offices of Edward Ryan. That's the simplest."

Simple as it was, it took them an hour to get through the details. Next was a computer software consultant, a deal something like the one with the inventor.

The rest of the day was more of the same. Some small commercial buildings in Brooklyn and Queens. More real estate ventures, residential this time. The afternoon was over before Kaplan got to the files on Ned's medical clinics.

"We'll have to leave that for next time," Kaplan said.

"No hurry," Ryan told him.

5

THAT FRIDAY RYAN SHOWED UP AT THE SHAMROCK just after ten, a good hour earlier than usual. The dinner lights were on and half the tables were still occupied. He hardly recognized the place.

Kelly put a mug of beer on the bar in front of him.

"You're early tonight."

"Nobody's perfect."

Kelly grinned. "You're one weird Irishman, Michael Ryan."

"You don't know the half of it."

Kelly went to serve a customer, leaving Ryan to his thoughts.

While he nursed his beer the last of the diners straggled out and Kelly turned down the lights. Ryan preferred it that way. The dimness suited him.

His brooding was interrupted by Kelly's hearty "Yes, ma'am, can I help you?" It was aimed at someone behind Ryan, near the door.

"I'm looking for Michael Ryan."

The voice was the last one Ryan would have expected to hear at the Shamrock.

"Looking for Michael Ryan are you?" Kelly challenged. "And who might you be?"

"It's okay, Jimmy," Ryan said, and swiveled on his bar stool. "Over here."

Jennifer was standing just inside the door, all in summer black, with a floppy-brim hat that shrouded her face.

"How did you find me?" he asked as she took the stool next to him.

She hesitated. "A friend helped me."

It took him a moment to translate. "You had me followed?"

"Well . . ."

"You had me followed," he repeated, not a question now.

"It was a friend, not a detective or anything. I really had to talk to you."

"What do you want to drink?"

She seemed surprised by the offer.

He said, "I'm not going to run away from you forever. If our last conversation wasn't enough, let's really get it over with this time."

He waved Kelly over.

"Yes, ma'am, what can I get you?" Kelly was being formal, waiting for Ryan's lead.

"I'd like some orange juice and club soda, please."

Kelly poured the juice from a jug of fresh-squeezed he used for mixing and squirted it with seltzer. He garnished the glass with an orange slice and put it on a napkin in front of her.

"Patrick Jameson Kelly," Ryan said by way of introduction. "Jennifer Kneeland Ryan."

Kelly started to hold out his hand and then the name registered. "How do you do," he said in a voice slightly strangled, and then quickly, "I'll let you two talk. Shout if you need me."

"All right," Ryan said to Jennifer. "What's all this about?"

She sipped at her drink, reluctant to start. "This is harder than I thought it would be."

Waiting, watching her precise, regular features framed by wings of dark hair, her eyes shadowed in the dim bar, Ryan felt strangely detached. He was not aware of any anger, only coldness.

"My lawyers want me to plead guilty."

Ryan, finding it perfectly commonplace, waited for more.

"But I'm innocent." With a touch of outrage.

"So you've said. Apparently the police and the district attorney don't see it that way."

"But I am."

"Why tell me?"

"I've been trying to tell you from the beginning."

"You called me around the time you were arrested."

"Yes. You didn't call me back."

Did she expect an apology? "Why did you call?"

"Because I wanted to tell you my side of it. Before your mind was poisoned by the official story and the press reports." She tried to smile, succeeded only in looking forlorn. "I didn't make it, did I?"

"I still don't see why you'd care what I thought."

"Because I think of myself as part of the Ryan family. I never accepted that you and Ned wouldn't find a way to get together. I told you when we had that awful dinner together—I'm your daughter-in-law. That's how I still see it."

"And that's why you called, and that's why you waited outside my office."

"I had to tell you I was innocent. I didn't kill Ned."

She stopped to take a handkerchief from her shoulder bag and wipe her tears and blow her nose. Ryan reminded himself that the profession this woman listed on her resume was "actor."

"The police think you did. Did you tell them your version of what happened?"

"No."

"Did you make any statement at all?"

"When they told me about Ned, that he was dead, I sort of fell apart. Inside, I mean, I didn't get all hysterical or anything. They wanted to talk to me but I told them to get out and leave me alone and I'd talk to them in the morning." The blue-gray eyes, visibly reddened even in the bar's dim light, filled with tears. Again she stopped to use her handkerchief. "Anyway, when the police left I sat there. I guess I was in shock. I didn't call anyone, I didn't go to sleep, I just sat there. Eventually I dozed off for an hour or two. The first thing I did in the morning was call my father. I was upset and scared and I didn't want to talk to the police by myself. I got him on the car phone and he came right over."

"So your father was with you when you talked to the police."

"He got me a lawyer."

"Who?"

"His name is Hamilton Bishop."

Ryan tried not to wince visibly.

"Do you know him?" Jennifer asked, picking up on Ryan's re-action.

"The Hamilton Bishop I know does corporate litigation and white-collar crime." He had been among Ryan's co-counsel on the Gibson case, the major lawsuit Ryan had humiliated himself on immediately after Alison died. Bishop had taken over as lead counsel when it became apparent how badly Ryan was screwing up. "He's about sixty, white hair."

"I guess it's the same one. Very distinguished and courtly, with a million years' experience at whatever he does, but I got indicted anyway. I fired him and got somebody else, a man named Jeff Rosen."

"But Bishop was with you when you talked to the police."

"Yes. He told me not to answer any questions except to say Ned and I had been to the party and had an argument, but it was just married people yelling at each other, and then I left."

"And that's where your story and the police story part company. You say when you left Ned he was alive, and they say you picked up a statue and beat him to death with it."

"Yes . . ."

"And Jeff Rosen thinks you should plead guilty."

"Yes, but I'm *innocent*."

Ryan drank some beer. "I guess we're going to have to talk about that. Why should I believe you? Why should anyone believe you?"

"Because it's true. Ned was fine when I left him."

"Do you have any kind of proof?"

"Just my word. I'm telling the truth."

Ryan had dealt with too many champion liars to buy her earnestness. "Who do you think killed him?"

She shook her head. "I don't know."

"No idea?"

"People were jealous of him. He beat them in business. I don't know. All I know is it wasn't me."

"Do you know what the prosecution is offering? What charge they want you to plead to?"

"I'm not sure they're *offering* anything. Jeff said he convinced them to consider a plea. I don't know why, because I never told him to do it. All I know is he wants me to plead guilty. I'd have to go to jail for years." The idea brought an edge of panic to her voice.

"Killing people is a serious crime."

"I didn't kill him!" Her eyes widened at the volume of her own words. She glanced down the bar to see if anyone had heard.

"Did he tell you how much jail time?"

"He says if I'm lucky it could be something like eight years. Can you believe it? Eight years!"

"I'm surprised they're offering you any deal at all." Surprised and not pleased.

"Jeff said he was surprised, too. Right after the indictment Hamilton Bishop said if you can get a deal take it. So I fired him. And now this one is doing it, too."

"Has it occurred to you that two experienced lawyers gave you the same advice because they both, independently, think it's best for you?"

A flash of anger. "I'm innocent, so you'll excuse me if I don't think it's in my best interest when people give me advice that goes—say you're guilty." She took a breath. "I understand that eight years in jail is better than twenty-five. Or fifteen, or whatever the minimum is if I get convicted in a trial. But nobody listens when I tell them that spending *any* time in jail—and telling the world I killed my husband when actually I didn't—is no solution to anything. I mean, I loved Ned." Her face crumpled for an instant, then recovered. "It's true we used to fight, not only that night, other times, in private and, I'm sorry to say, in public. But it's also true that I loved him."

Her words set Ryan's mind going. They fought in public. Could Becker get testimony about it admitted as evidence? To prove motive? Maybe intention. That was better: claim you were using it to show that she had formed the intent to kill long ago.

"You've already fired one lawyer," he said. "Fire this one."

"I plan to."

"Then why . . ."

"I need another lawyer."

"You don't need me for that. Everybody knows lawyers." Could that be why she had pushed so hard to see him? For a referral? "I'm sure your father knows some criminal defense lawyers."

"Yes, Daddy knows some criminal lawyers," Jennifer said. "He recommended the ones I tried so far."

"Maybe he knows some others."

"I've had enough of my father's lawyers, thank you. I want to find my own."

Ryan finished his beer. "There are plenty of prominent criminal defense lawyers. They don't hide from potential clients, and if they're not right for this, they'll know who is."

"I already know who I want."

That stopped him. "Then why talk to me about it?"

"Because I want you."

"You what?" The words made no sense.

"I want you to be my lawyer."

It was ridiculous, of course. It didn't even bear discussing.

"That's it?" he managed to say. "That's what you had to tell me?" He wanted to be out of there, to be anywhere else.

Her hand was on his arm, as if to hold him there. "You're the only lawyer I can trust."

Mercifully, Kelly's antennae were up. He appeared on the other side of the bar. "How're you folks doin'?"

"We're fine, Jimmy. I've got to go, but give the lady whatever she wants."

In parting, Ryan said how surprised he was by her request, and that he doubted it was ethical.

"I'll call you," he said to her. Anything to get away.

For the first couple of blocks after he escaped he was oblivious to everything, and then he realized he was striding along like one of the weekend racewalkers in Central Park. He made himself slow down.

Incredible. He had been right thinking she had some such bizarre idea in mind that day she cornered him in the elevator.

And he was also right thinking it was ridiculous. Every instinct told him so. A million reasons. Unethical was only the beginning.

He had a sudden antic picture of himself in court with Jennifer. "Your honor, I object," he shouted, rising at the defense table wearing a black suit symbolically rent, the dried tracks of tears staining his cheeks. A black-bordered portrait of Ned hung from a chain around his neck.

That was it, of course. As the father of the deceased victim he would bring all the weight of his bereavement into court with him. It had to be what Jennifer had in mind: not the quality of her defense but an attempt to overbalance the scales with the jury by having that weight on her side.

But in the final analysis it did not matter what her motives were. Even if he said yes, no prosecutor in his right mind would stand still for it.

6

THE NEXT DAY HE THREW HIMSELF INTO HIS WORK IN a way he hadn't since Ned's murder. It helped keep his mind off Jennifer and her outrageous request.

At home after work that evening he pulled a couple of packages from the freezer and popped them into the microwave. While he waited for them to heat he wandered into the study and glanced over the miscellany of law books on the top shelves. Books left over from old cases, books from the library at Pane, Parish he had forgotten to return. Treatises on federal practice, mostly. Product liability, maritime law, securities law. Not necessarily areas he had practiced in—books that had followed him here for want of a proper home, books he had intended to read, books he had consulted once that had stayed on the shelves for reasons unremembered.

On the top shelf, *Problems of Trial Advocacy*. A prize for winning a mock trial competition in law school. Had he known it was there? He climbed onto the kickstool and put one foot up on a file cabinet, reached and pulled the book down. It bore a gray blanket of dust that he blew off in the general direction of the window, creating a momentary cloud of sparkling motes in the waning daylight.

He wandered back into the kitchen, glancing down the table of contents. "Problems of Representation." He checked the microwave, took out a plate and silverware and set himself a place at the dining room table. Book face down next to the plate, splayed open to the page he had found. A kitchen mitt and a serving spoon: he ladled out scallops in some kind of pink sauce, rice and a grim sprinkling of wrinkled peas and tiny soggy carrots. Poured himself a beer and sat down to eat and read.

"Defense Counsel's Obligation as a Member of the Legal Profession," one heading read. Skimming down the page his eye was caught by an excerpt from the Bar Association oath of admission.

"I will never reject for any consideration personal to myself the cause of the defenseless or oppressed."

Jennifer Kneeland was hardly oppressed, and despite her fears she wasn't defenseless, either. Ryan took a forkful of scallops and promptly burned the roof of his mouth.

He slammed the book closed and drowned the wound in beer.

What the *hell* was he doing? He couldn't be taking this seriously.

He pushed his fork around in the congealing scallops. By the time they were cool enough to put safely in a human mouth they would be too gluey to eat. He waited until they were cold and ate them anyway. He washed them down with another beer and a shot of Irish.

He sat by the living room window in the dark, looking out at the starless summer sky, sipping another whiskey and trying not to think. When his glass was empty, he called Jennifer.

"What do you know about me?" he asked her.

"I know you were a famous lawyer."

"I used to get my name in the paper. Because of who I was prosecuting, not how good I was. It was office policy—it's good to have the public know you're getting the bad guys."

"You're being modest."

"I'm telling the truth."

"No. I know. Ned used to talk about you. About the big cases you won."

That stopped him. "Ned used to talk about me?"

"Yes. He, um . . . yes."

"About what a great lawyer I was."

"Yes." A hesitation. "I don't want to give you the wrong idea. It wasn't like My Father The Great Man, or anything. He could be very bitter about you. But usually in the middle of it there was all this about how hard you worked and what a big hero everybody else thought you were."

That was more like what he'd expected.

"Two things about that," he said. "One, he was probably exaggerating or you're making more of it than he did. And two, even if I was this big hero lawyer, that was a long time ago. I left the U.S. Attorney's office ten years ago. More."

"I know."

"I haven't been in a courtroom in nearly three years."

"I didn't know that." She was silent a moment. "Isn't that when your wife died?"

"Yes. I was about to try a case when it happened. And even though I was in no shape to do it, I went ahead."

He paused, remembering the compulsion that had driven him and the mental blindness it had produced. Blindness to his own mistakes of law and strategy and tactics, and blindness to the bigger mistakes he was making dealing with his colleagues.

"What happened?"

He found himself telling her. "It was my first time as a defense lawyer. I'd been a prosecutor for ten years, and then I'd worked on civil suits in federal court, not criminal cases, big corporations suing other corporations. This time I was on the other side, defending a corporation and its officers who were being sued by the Justice Department. It was an enormous case, a lot of lawyers, and I was lead counsel. And I screwed up. If the other lawyers hadn't insisted on replacing me when they did everybody would have gone down the tubes. Our side won, but it took months longer than it should have, and it cost the clients hundreds of thousands of dollars in extra legal fees. If we had lost, some of the corporate officers might have been criminally liable, too. And you know who saved the day? Your friend Hamilton Bishop. So if you don't think he's good enough, don't for a minute expect better from me."

"What went wrong? If you were so good."

"I underestimated how bad off I was emotionally and how it affected my ability to try the case."

"Because of your wife."

"And because of what happened at her funeral."

After a silence in which neither of them seemed able to speak, Jennifer said, "Maybe I don't care about all that."

"You'd be crazy not to."

There was another silence.

"You want to know why I want you to represent me." A statement more than a question.

He waited.

"I think you believe me. I think, maybe in spite of yourself, you believe I'm innocent."

"*Listen to me*. Lawyers don't want to know if you're innocent or guilty. All they want to know is can they make a better case than the prosecutor. Proved or not proved is all that matters."

"That's what the others told me."

"It's no help believing your client is innocent. Just the opposite." It was beyond his experience, but it was what they all said.

"Then why are people defense lawyers, if it isn't to get innocent people acquitted?"

"To get *people* acquitted. Everybody is presumed innocent until the jury says different."

"It doesn't feel like that to me. Everybody treats me like I'm guilty."

He changed tactics. "Why do you think I believe you're innocent?"

"Because you're talking to me."

"I talked to you at Kelly's because I knew that if I didn't you'd keep after me forever." And if I didn't hear you out I knew I'd always have doubts, he did not say. "And I called tonight . . . I'm not sure why I called tonight." Because I've had too much to drink. "Except maybe to tell you how badly I screwed up my last case, so you'd know that you weren't missing out on such a great thing, not having me represent you."

"You wouldn't be talking to me like this if you thought I killed your son."

"For God's sake! This is nuts. I don't think you're innocent."

Silence, then she said, "You must. I know that you and Ned didn't speak to each other, but I also have an idea how much it hurt you that you didn't. You wouldn't even say hello to someone you thought was his killer, much less sit around on the phone talking strategy."

"That's nonsense." He could not tell if she meant it—that she thought he thought she was innocent—or if she was acting.

For a while she did not say anything, then her voice erupted theatrically.

"I won't plead guilty to something I didn't do!"

More silence. He considered hanging up.

She spoke again, calmer now. "Michael, suppose, just *suppose*, someone else killed Ned. Not me. If that's true and I plead guilty, what happens to the real killer?"

And of course there it was—the unspoken underside of pressing too hard for a plea. When an innocent person pleads guilty, the real culprit gets away with it.

"How do you feel about that?" she prodded. "Is that all right with you? That if I'm innocent and I plead guilty, the person who killed Ned gets to laugh at all of us the rest of his life."

Ryan felt a million years old. This was not some game of What if? They were talking about his son. His dead son. And this woman was the accused murderer.

"At least think about it." Imploring. "Please."

"All right, Jennifer—enough for now. Good night."

"Good night, Michael. Thank you for listening."

He hung up and finished getting drunk.

7

RYAN'S HANGOVER THE NEXT MORNING WAS NO
worse than he deserved. He discovered that he only had one clean
shirt and remembered that he had to look for a new housekeeper
or start keeping track of his own laundry and cleaning. This is no
way to live, he thought, with no expectation that it would change.
He drank as much coffee as he could stand and hurried out of the
house with a bundle of laundry to drop off on his way downtown.

There was a fax at the office from Jake Kaplan. Ryan got the
accountant on the phone.

"You're looking at the loan activity of a group of companies,"
Kaplan told him. "Ned was working for them as a broker or a
collection agent or both. The loans add up to about sixty million
dollars over twenty months. So far we can't tell where the money
came from. I didn't want to start playing investigator without permission."

"Sixty million dollars," Ryan repeated as he glanced over the
list. "That's an awful lot of money."

Nothing on the list jumped out at him. It looked like a catalog
of ordinary real estate deals. Shopping centers, industrial parks, a
couple of motels, residential housing developments. A low of half
a million, a high of eight.

"You think Kneeland's the money man?" Kaplan asked.

"Could be." But Ryan did not believe it. Robertson Kneeland
was the kind of hustler who lived by moving money around, getting
the maximum leverage out of it, not tying it up in mortgages.

"Let me look it over and we can decide how to handle it from
there." Ryan's face felt tight; he had to form the words carefully.
The federal prosecutor who still lived in his head, primed by the

chunks of cash in Ned's safe-deposit box, told him that if the capital for the loans was not coming from Kneeland, it was that much more likely to be coming from someplace illegal. Drug dealers were the usual suspects these days.

Ryan braced the phone between shoulder and ear and scanned the list again. "What about these interest rates? They look ordinary enough."

"Right. Market rates. Some of them are higher."

"Not lower."

"Why should they be? I assume the lenders want to make money."

"Most of the time." Except when people were so eager to get the money into legitimate circulation they didn't care what interest rate they got for it.

Easy credit terms would not have been courtroom evidence that Ned was lending out dirty money, but they would have certainly raised suspicions. By the same token, high interest rates like these might mean the money was clean after all. Ryan hoped it was not too little reason for him to feel relieved.

"If it's easy credit you're looking for," the accountant offered, "the place you'll find it is Ned's medical business. Shible Medical Suppliers. Shible, I don't know what that is, people's initials mixed up, maybe, except his partner's name is James Morris."

Shible, Ryan thought: Circassian god of thunder, war and justice—highest in the old-country pantheon so dear to his father. Ned had been fascinated by George Ryan's embroidered tales of the Caucasus the few times they had seen each other. They had made quite a duo, Ned and his Grandpa George, closer in some ways than the father-son pairs either of them made with Ryan.

"Tell me about easy credit."

"Right now, the numbers I have say Shible Medical Suppliers had very generous credit terms. Customers got at least ninety days to pay, a hundred twenty in some cases. That's three or four times as long as most people usually get. Which would be okay, except that the interest rates are so low. In effect, they're lending money to their customers for less than they could get just putting the money in a bank."

"That's one way to keep your customers loyal."

"Yeah, great, except Shible has to pay interest to whoever financed their inventory. If the interest coming in is lower than the interest going out, they'd eat up their profits, and maybe more, just to stay even. It's like that old joke: I lose a little on each transaction but I make it up on the volume."

Not if they got their inventory financing from someone who didn't care how much interest he got, Ryan thought.

"So, what do you think?" Kaplan's voice said in his ear.

"It's pretty complicated for a twenty-seven year old." Avoiding the real issue.

Kaplan seemed to sense his discomfort. "Ah hell—you know, these days, the way people make money pushing paper around, kids some of them, it's a different world from the one we grew up in."

"I suppose. Myself, I've always figured things don't change much, underneath the surface. Good and evil are pretty much the same from year to year."

He had Kaplan send him a copy of the papers on Shible Medical Suppliers and its clinic customers and spent most of an afternoon going over them. Kaplan had laid out the cash-flow patterns and Ryan was surprised to see how much money was involved, well over a million dollars a month, altogether.

He thought about the bundles of cash in Ned's safe-deposit boxes, and the sixty million dollars in mortgages and the millions being cycled through the pharmaceuticals supplier on easy, low-interest credit terms.

How had Ned, in less than four years, got so tangled up in so much money? And whose money was it?

In the morning Ryan decided that looking at pieces of paper was not enough. He called a car-service company and by eleven o'clock he was in the backseat of a radio-dispatched sedan heading across Central Park at Eighty-sixth Street and then uptown on Third Avenue. To the north loomed the pale bulk of the state office building and the brick towers of subsidized housing projects. After about a mile the driver turned onto a street lined on both sides with townhouses. Once solid middle-class residences, they had been battered and begrimed by decades of poverty and exploitation.

In mid block a white metal sign stretched across the faces of two former townhouses: CENTRAL HARLEM MEDICAL CENTER. Ryan could see two lines of people, one leading up the front steps to a door next to the main entrance, the other leading to a door below the stairs. When the driver pulled up in front of the building, Ryan read the sign hanging from a bracket over the understairs door. PHARMACY, it said in large letters. PRESCRIPTIONS FILLED. MEDICAID HONORED. The legend was repeated in Spanish. Over the other door a similar sign said DIAGNOSIS AND CONSULTA-TION. NEW PATIENTS MUST SEE THE DOCTOR FIRST.

Most of the people waiting to get into the consulting rooms and the pharmacy looked poor and undernourished. Their clothes were faded and worn, some clearly scavenged. Many of the people Ryan saw were young, and many of those looked as if they might be on drugs.

The picture was all too familiar, Ryan thought as the driver pulled away and headed east to the Triborough Bridge. If they fit the pattern, the clinic and the pharmacy would prescribe and sell as much medicine as they could, more than anyone needed or could use, all paid for by Medicaid. The "patients" resold their legal drugs on the street and used the money to buy the illegal drugs they preferred. It was a scam practiced with local variations wherever there was a public medical-insurance bureaucracy to be defrauded. And this example of it was part of Ned Ryan's legacy to the world.

Ryan's next stop was a bleak industrial corner of Brooklyn. A pair of white trucks with SHIBLE lettered in black on their flanks stood in the loading bay of a long cinder-block warehouse. Ryan could make out a few people behind the blinds of the small front office. He did not stop in to say hello.

On the ride home he thought again about the money swirling around his son in such quantity. Ned had moved quickly once he got hooked into a source of capital. Maybe in the process he had crossed somebody he should have played straight with. Somebody mad enough and bad enough to kill him.

Though the possibility was not enough to raise any real doubt in Ryan's mind about Jennifer's guilt, it confirmed his antipathy to a plea bargain. At this point the police would be ignoring Ned's money connections and the potential murder motives they implied. They would only be followed up thoroughly if a good lawyer was working on a defense for Jennifer. A plea bargain meant that would never happen.

He wondered if Jennifer had given him the real goods on the plea deal. Could Jeff Rosen really be pushing her that hard to take it? And if he was, why was he?

The car had a back-seat phone. He called Jennifer.

"I want to talk to your lawyers. Both of them, Bishop and Rosen."

"Sure. Anything." She sounded excited.

"Don't jump to conclusions. I want to hear how they assess the situation, and I want to hear about their conversations with Becker." Maybe she had it wrong. Maybe the pressure for a plea bargain wasn't as strong as she thought. "You'll have to tell them it's okay to talk to me."

"I'll call them right away."

8

AT RYAN'S SUGGESTION JEFF ROSEN MET HIM FAR-ther uptown than most business lunchers ventured, at a place in Ryan's neighborhood where they could have a decent-size table and a reasonable amount of privacy.

Ryan remembered the younger lawyer as hearty and athletic looking, full of youth and enthusiasm. Rosen was ruddy and balding now, the extra weight camouflaged by a custom-tailored three-piece suit. He greeted Ryan with: "You know, I still remember that time I was second seat for Denny Flanagan and you blew us out of the courtroom. *United States v. Klein*. It must be . . . shit, ten, twelve years ago. And twenty pounds for me, at least. I learned more watching you prosecute that one case than I did in a year toting Flanagan's briefcase."

With only minor prodding from Ryan, Rosen told stories about himself most of the way through lunch. He had stayed with Flanagan for a few years, then left to form a small partnership: four lawyers who specialized in criminal defense work and, Rosen said, had built a thriving practice.

"We know how to keep prosecutors honest. And we make them work for everything they get. It's amazing how many times that's all you need to do." He moved a spoon around in his coffee cup. "I admired you enough years that I wasn't going to turn down a chance at lunch. But I'll be frank with you, I don't know why we're here. All Jennifer said was that you'd be calling and I should talk to you."

"She didn't tell you why?" Ryan asked, not happy about it.

"No, she didn't."

"She doesn't want to plead. She thinks you're pressing her too hard."

"That's no surprise. She tells me that herself. Why involve you, of all people?"

Ryan waved to the waitress for more coffee and waited while she refilled their cups before he spoke. "She says she wants me to represent her."

Rosen said nothing at first, then: "That's a joke, right?"

"That was my reaction. I told her I was sure you knew what you were doing."

Rosen stared into his coffee.

"I told you how much I respect you. That doesn't change. But you understand the only thing I can do now is call my client."

He came back ten minutes later, a study in puzzlement. It made him look a decade younger, the wide-eyed associate Ryan remembered.

"Live long enough, you see everything. Okay. I talked to her. She says tell you what you want to know." Rosen took a sip of his cold coffee, made a face. "My problem is I can't really do that. I mean, attorney-client privilege or not, you're the victim's father, and whatever anybody says I don't see you standing up in court for the defense. So I have an ethics problem here."

"Don't even think about my taking the case. I've only got one thing on my mind. I don't want her pleading guilty if there's any chance she isn't."

"Maybe I can make this easier for both of us. I'll give you the ten-cent tour, mostly public-record stuff. They've got motive—he was cheating on her, and she knew it. She yelled at him in public, plenty. And they had a spectacular fight immediately before the murder, in front of all kinds of people. Opportunity—he stormed out of the party, she followed him, a dozen people saw them. Nobody saw him alive after that. Means—the murder weapon is a statue, sculpture, maybe a foot and a half high, metal, weighted at the bottom. Lots of his blood on the heavy end, which is no surprise. But it looks like they've got her blood on it, too. Some of this is from the arraignment, some I'm guessing from the materials they've delivered so far. Best I can tell, they've got no eyewitnesses, no accomplice testimony, no confession. You tell me."

"It still sounds pretty strong. You haven't found any holes?"

"Well, you never know where you can trip them up till you really look. I've had an investigator out. So far, nothing."

"Tell me about the blood on the murder weapon." Becker had only hinted at it.

"They found a small amount of blood on what you might call the handle of the murder weapon, and they wanted a blood sample from Jennifer. Her blood type matches the blood from the weapon, so they're moving on to more definite tests—genetic markers, maybe DNA. They wouldn't go ahead like that if they weren't pretty confident."

"So they have a good case and they want to plead it," Ryan said. "Why, when they could have all the glory of a big juicy trial? Becker as much as told me he was dying to get this one in front of a jury and I can certainly see why. It's always nice to put away some rich white person for a change, with an audience of millions every step of the way."

"Yeah, that's sure how I'd feel. But I hear Becker's not a risk taker. Robertson Kneeland has friends at City Hall who'll be embarrassed if this drags on, and Franky Griglia wants a good, clean victory. Suppose Becker sees the plea as a way to make some points with the bosses for wrapping it up fast and cheap, and at the same time get himself nearly as much credit in public as for a conviction if he plays the press right. And that way he doesn't have to worry that anything will go wrong in court."

Rosen had worked up a good head of steam. He stopped abruptly. "Shit! I get carried away. Here I'm talking to you like . . . I'm showing off, is what it is—how I've got the A.D.A. figured out and how I can get this defendant a reasonably attractive deal. And then I think hold on just one sweet minute—I'm saying these things to the victim's father. The victim's *father*. It's like Alice in Wonderland or something. It makes me nuts."

"To tell the truth it makes me a little crazy, too." Ryan gave it a moment, then said, "The rule is innocent until proven guilty."

"Sure, but . . ."

"And she says she's innocent."

"You ever see one who didn't?"

"No, but I was a prosecutor. You'd be a better judge than I am whether to believe her." Pushing him to see where he'd go.

"All I can say is, I think she ought to take the deal. You said just now you don't want her to plead guilty if there's a chance she's innocent. I can understand that. If she's innocent and she pleads guilty, your son's killer goes free and you don't want that. Okay, sure. But I have to look at this as her lawyer and I say, innocent or guilty she's taking an enormous chance if she goes into the courtroom. I'd be doing her a serious disservice if I didn't make that crystal clear to her."

* * *

After lunch Ryan took a subway down to the southern edge of his old stomping grounds, where the courthouses and the federal and municipal office buildings gave way to the beginnings of the Wall Street skyscrapers. His conversation with Hamilton Bishop was formal and subdued, in offices of a stateliness so extreme even the computer desks were antiques. Bishop made no reference to their experience together on the Gibson case. About Jennifer he was discreet to the point of being moribund. The only thing he and Jeff Rosen had in common was their opinion that Jennifer was likely to be convicted if she went to trial. That, and their unwillingness to speculate aloud on her guilt or innocence.

Ryan and Jennifer met in Central Park.

"All right," she said, "you talked to them. Did it help?"

"They're both good lawyers." A nonanswer.

She walked with her head down, studying the path.

"What are you telling me? That I'm wrong? That I should do what they say?"

Her voice was level, but he had the impression, as he'd had in their previous conversations, that she was on the edge, maintaining a precarious control.

"I'm telling you that they're good lawyers," he said.

"They want me to plead guilty."

Ryan had put himself in an impossible position. His motive talking to Rosen had been to sidetrack the idea of a plea bargain or, failing that, to make himself more comfortable with it. He had achieved neither, but in a sense he had made himself part of the team, however temporarily. He could not now, in all conscience, advise her to ignore Rosen's advice. But the alternative amounted to urging her to plead guilty, and he was not willing to do that either. For his own peace of mind he wanted a trial, and if she was guilty he wanted her to pay the maximum penalty, not some artificially arrived at minimum.

She stopped to watch two ducks make a tentative entrance into a scummy pond.

"I still want you to defend me."

"And I still don't see why." Except to manipulate the jury.

"I told you. These other lawyers don't seem to get it that I'm innocent. All they want is to get this over with the easiest way they can."

"They're trying to represent you—the best way they can. It's no service to a client to go along with her wishes without a fight when you think she's wrong."

That made her look at him. "Why not? Who's working for who?"

"It's your decision in the end. I'm sure they've both told you that."

"Then why don't they listen to me?"

"They have to be sure you understand that a courtroom is a lousy place for a defendant to gamble on winning. People plead guilty to get a lesser charge or an agreed-on sentence because it's better than losing in court and getting put away for the maximum term."

"But that's for people who are *guilty*."

Theoretically she was right. What happened in practice was something else. Ryan came to it from a prosecutor's point of view. Every aspect of the trial process was a tool, if not a weapon, from subpoena through final sentence and even parole. The overtaxed judicial system had transformed the promise of a fair trial into a threat: if you turned down a plea bargain and were convicted on trial, the longer sentence you would certainly end up with was the fee you paid for putting the state to the trouble of trying you. Rent for the use of the courtroom.

He said none of that. He had already given the theory of plea bargains enough time to satisfy his conscience. He wanted her to want to stand trial, and he wanted her to leave him alone.

He tried to make her see that if she was not going to plead then she should have a lawyer who would play the case like a chess master, with no personal stake, with no motivation but the contest itself. He could not tell if he was making any impression on her.

Instead of responding she led them off the path toward a hump of gray rock and a tree with branches bowed under the weight of dark August leaves. She found a place to sit in the shade of the tree and patted the rock beside her. The gesture was so innocent, her expression so earnest as she looked up at him, sitting with her ankles crossed like a schoolgirl at afternoon tea, that Ryan could not resist sitting down next to her.

"There's one other thing, Michael." Her voice was soft. "I haven't wanted to say anything about it because it's not part of what we're talking about." Her eyes scanned his face, their color deepened by the shadow of the tree or by some emotion he could not read. "But it's why I so desperately need to have a lawyer I believe in. A lawyer I know I can trust." She looked down at her hands clasped in her lap. "And it's why that lawyer has to be you."

Her head rose. She brushed a wing of dark hair clear of her face and looked into his eyes. "I'm pregnant."

He heard the words without at first absorbing their full meaning. Then he saw.

"When?" It was hard to breathe.

She was looking at her hands again. "A few days before . . ." She did not finish.

"Who knows about it?"

"My father. Jeff Rosen."

Ryan stood up and paced a small circle that brought him quickly back to face her. He was having trouble thinking.

"When are you due?"

"I don't know exactly. Some time in late March or April."

"Rosen didn't say anything."

"I asked him not to. I didn't want it to influence how you thought about me." She looked up at him. "Not until you had a chance to find out everything else you wanted to know."

He could not help thinking that somewhere the gods were laughing at him. A father deprived of his son, now he would be the grandfather of a child deprived of a father.

How right she was to think that the prospect would affect his judgment.

"When did you find out?"

"I wasn't sure until long after I was arrested. Weeks."

"What took so long?"

"I . . . Do you really want the details?" And when he did not answer: "I'm irregular. I thought the grief and the anxiety were changing my cycle. I thought I was sick to my stomach because of Ned, and the police . . . all of that."

"So when Ned was . . . killed, you didn't have any idea."

"No."

"Too bad," he said without thinking. "It would have helped with the jury."

9

___

WHEN HE LEFT JENNIFER, RYAN WANDERED THROUGH Central Park, intending to think about what she had told him. He found that the very fact of it made all thought impossible.

He walked across town to the Hudson, not ready to be hemmed in by walls. Riverside Park was alive with West Siders enjoying the tag-end of the day: dog walkers, joggers, couples and single mothers and fathers with strollers, kids playing park baseball. Everyone, everything, seemed exaggeratedly normal and placid, a subject for a latter-day, urban Norman Rockwell, a world apart from the agonies of family discord, betrayal, and violent death.

He stopped where a stone wall gave an unobstructed view of the river and watched the sun go down behind New Jersey. The sky was streaked with color, the sun a blood red balloon that hovered over the jagged edge of the cliffs until it was pierced by the silhouette tip of a smokestack and sank quickly from sight.

It was a consummation Ryan had briefly wished for in the aftermath of Ned's murder—to sink quickly from sight. His world had been void. No family, no hope of reconciliation, nothing to work for. Odd that his son's death had not made his own brief contemplation of suicide seem any the less sensible.

Now everything was different. Life, it seemed, was a territory of unexpected new babies. A territory where unforeseen renewal walked hand in hand with grim irony—because odds were, the seed of Ned's earthly immortality was being nurtured by the very person who had extinguished his life.

For a long time, Ryan did not move, watching the colors leach from the sky and the lights twinkle on in the skyscraper apartment houses across the river.

He realized that the background noises of happy people and dogs had disappeared. The sky was deep purple, pierced by the first stars. He looked around. The park lights were on, no one in sight. He hurried up a flight of stone steps and came out in a small plaza ringed by cannon, at the base of Soldiers and Sailors Monument, memorial to sons killed for reasons their fathers could understand.

When he woke up in the morning, daylight bringing him to foggy consciousness long before the alarm clock was ready to, the dream image in his mind was of himself and Jennifer. He was kneeling beside her, one arm outstretched. Straddling his palm, the way Ned had in that long-ago picnic, was Jennifer's baby.

In the shower, his mind cleared abruptly. Who would be brining up that baby?

If Jennifer went to jail it would be Kneeland who raised the child. Ryan could fight for custody, but he didn't have a chance. Mothers got the benefit of the doubt in Family Court, and even if Jennifer was convicted of killing Michael, she had not harmed any children.

What kind of life would that be for a kid, going up to the prison every week with Grandpa Kneeland to visit Mommy, waiting for her to get out of jail? Hearing the stories at home of how she had been falsely accused, and at school being taunted as the child of a murderess. Worse—the child of a mother who had killed your father, over sex.

It was not a life Ryan was willing to imagine for his grandchild. For Ned's son, or daughter.

Not just that—if he denied Jennifer now he could expect her to close him out of her child's life forever. Whether Jennifer was guilty or innocent, convicted or not.

If there was anything he could do to prevent that, he had to do it. Even if it meant getting an acquittal for Ned's killer.

Still, he could not say for sure that she was guilty. He did not believe she wasn't, and he might never, but one route to the truth lay in untangling the grimy skein of Ned's dealings—a job that would be much easier with the power of the court behind him as Jennifer's defense counsel.

And always there was the baby to remember. Protecting it and protecting his connection to it.

A new chance, a new beginning.

He decided to call Griglia to get his version of the plea bargaining. Carefully. If Michael Ryan showed up as Jennifer's defense lawyer, the D.A. would remember this conversation.

"Nobody's brought a deal in for approval so far," Griglia told him, "but if she wants to plead I can't say my people won't listen."

"I don't get it. Are you worried about getting a conviction?"

"You know better, Michael. If we can get a decent plea we'd always rather have that than a trial. That doesn't mean we're going to give it away. Assuming the question of a plea comes up at all."

They said their good-byes. Ryan wondered if the D.A. was giving him a line or if he was out of touch with what was happening. As Griglia himself had said, with four hundred lawyers on his staff he could hardly keep track of every case.

At Pane, Parish the architects' final plans for the new offices were in, two sets, as Ryan had requested in another lifetime. He rolled one set up and slid it into the mailing tube they had been delivered in so he could carry it home.

"Mr. Ryan, call on five-one," the paging system informed him. He picked up the conference room phone.

"I had a call from Becker at the D.A.'s office," Jeff Rosen said. "He gave me a week to take the deal. If Jennifer doesn't plead by then he's withdrawing it. Can you talk to Jennifer? She won't listen to me."

"She won't listen to me either, not on that one." *Even if I were willing to suggest it.*

Ryan hung up worrying that his call to the D.A. had somehow precipitated this.

Bob Legler's secretary told Ryan her boss was in a client conference. Ryan went back to the construction plans but he could not take his mind off Jennifer.

As soon as Legler was free Ryan walked down the corridor to his office, went in and closed the door behind him.

"What's up?" his friend asked.

"I've decided to defend Jennifer." *Just like that.*

"Well." Legler did not hide his surprise. "Well." And then, "I seem to remember something about a lawyer not taking a case if his ability to provide effective representation would be impaired by the intensity of his personal feelings."

"Is that what you think?"

"Don't you?" Legler shook his head—exasperation or bewilderment, Ryan could not tell. "You're also not supposed to take on a matter you're not competent to handle."

"Not unless I associate myself with a lawyer who is," Ryan countered. "Granted, I've never practiced in the state courts, but all that means is I have to hire a damn good second-seat lawyer."

"You're *serious* about this?"

"Yes."

"I'm not sure what to say, Michael. Maybe you should wait, think it over. Go someplace where you can look at the stars at night and breathe decent air."

"Don't patronize me. We've been through too much together."

"Am I patronizing you? I guess I am. Sit down and I'll start again."

Warily, Ryan sat down.

"Have you thought about the firm in all this?" Legler asked him.

He hadn't.

"There's a certain irony, your deciding to take on a murder defense after campaigning against our building a criminal practice. I remember you're the guy who used to stand up and say he couldn't understand how people went from prosecuting the bad guys to defending them."

"What are you saying? You want my resignation?"

"This is me, remember? Partner and friend, with the accent on friend."

"Not if you're more worried about the firm than you are about me."

"If that's how you see it."

"Tell me how else."

"I'm worried about you. I think this is a wrong decision, a terrible decision, bad for you in every way. I also think it's remarkably misguided professionally. How can you even think of being involved in this? I'm relieved you have the sense to see you'll need help, but even then . . . Michael, it's crazy. The victim's father defending the accused murderer! It's the worst kind of . . . I don't even know what to call it. I mean, look, you're too close to the client to be objective, *and* you're too close to the victim. I thought it would be good for you to get a look at Ned's life, as his executor. But this means having to analyze every detail of his murder over and over, having to hear the story of his last hours from dozens of people. And all this only a few months after his death. How can you possibly have any objectivity? How can you keep a clear head dealing with the case?"

Ryan had no answer.

Legler looked hard at Ryan, head inclined at the familiar angle. "I don't want you to take this wrong, but I couldn't live with myself if I didn't remind you that after Alison's death you insisted on trying a lawsuit against the advice of your friends. And you weren't ready for it. Your concentration was shot, your judgment was off and your person-to-person skills were on hold. And your client—our client—

suffered for it. If you really want to help your daughter-in-law the last thing you should be doing is acting as her defense counsel.''

Against all reason, Legler's words drove the doubt from Ryan's mind. "I'm glad to know where you stand. Here's where I stand— I'm going to do this. If it means leaving the firm, I'll do it."

"I can't dissuade you?"

"No."

"Then I suppose we have to get the executive committee together and talk about what it means to the firm."

Ryan stood up again. "Just one thing. I don't want the D.A.'s office to know about this until I'm ready." When Legler did not respond, Ryan added, "Unless you want to make it harder for me."

"No, Michael, I don't want to make it harder for you." Legler sounded tired. "I won't raise the issue until you're ready, and we'll keep our conversations about it confidential."

"I appreciate it," Ryan said on his way out. He felt as if he were jumping on a roller coaster as it crested its highest rise. He was in for a wild ride, and once he was on there was not likely to be any way to get off before the very end.

Jennifer was silent when he told her he would represent her. Then, quietly, she said, "Thank you."

"There's a condition."

"What kind of condition?" Immediately, she was wary.

"Secrecy."

"What do you mean?"

"My being your lawyer is going to cause a lot of comment."

"Because you're Ned's father."

"Exactly. It may cause legal difficulties, too. So we have to keep it secret until we're sure I can do it. Secret from *everybody*, including your father, for now. If it gets out too soon I'll have much more trouble with the legal part of it. It's not going to be easy getting myself approved by the court as your lawyer."

She was clearly unhappy about it. "If you're sure it's important."

"It's very important."

He went home and sat by the window. Like old Grandpa Yosef— his father George's father. Brooding on past battles.

Legler could be right. That the Gibson case was the kind of history that repeated itself, that his emotions would lay him low this time, as they had then. And there was something else: the Michael Ryan who had controlled the courtroom from the minute he stepped into the well might be too long dead to be resurrected now.

The executive committee at Pane, Parish came within two votes of recommending that Ryan take an indefinite leave of absence from the firm if he was going to defend Jennifer. Before the secret ballot Bob Legler voiced a worry that Ryan himself had not been able to wish away.

"We have to bear in mind that this may all be for nothing. We have to assume that the prosecutor is going to file a motion to disqualify Michael as soon as his name appears on a single piece of paper because of the way it would prejudice the case if the victim's father appears as counsel for the defense. It means there's no doing this halfway. Once Michael announces his intention to represent Jennifer Kneeland Ryan this firm becomes known as one that will participate in high-profile murder trials, even if Michael is disqualified as counsel before he files his first motion."

After that, even Ryan's support among the younger partners almost failed to win the day.

Ryan was relieved to have his narrow victory, more than he had expected to be. He would have gone on, on his own, if he'd had to, but Pane, Parish was his home. He had not realized how he felt about it until he'd contemplated seriously the idea of being without it. "I don't believe these guys," was the reaction of Rick Briggs, leader of the group that had campaigned to add criminal defense work to the firm's repertoire. "If you win you'll be a hero. If you lose you dragged the firm into your personal mess with you."

There was truth in it. Ryan's partners had carried him for the three years since Alison's death and the Gibson case because of who he had once been and because they felt sorry for him. Now he had forced them to face a divisive choice, a choice most unwelcome to the very partners who had championed him these past years. If this worked out badly, easing him out of the firm would be the most natural thing in the world.

10

HAVING COMMITTED HIMSELF TO DEFENDING JENNI-
fer, Ryan had to find a co-counsel who could get him past his
unfamiliarity with the state courts, and he had to do it without
alerting anyone at the D.A.'s office.

In essence he was looking for a smart, experienced assistant.
The defense lawyers he had worked against as prosecutor ten years
ago and more were by now too well established for the job to
interest them. If they weren't too big for this, they weren't good
enough. He needed somebody relatively young, somebody with
talent, experience and a burning desire to make the leap to promi-
nence.

He turned for help to Rick Briggs, who in his battles to add
hotshot criminal lawyers to the firm had amassed a formidable array
of résumés and recommendations. Ryan studied them and then got
Briggs and his allies to tell him what they could about the ones he
picked for his short list.

On his way to meet Kassia Miller, the most promising of his
candidates, Ryan debated with himself the pros and cons of having
a woman associate for Jennifer's trial. On the pro side, a woman
might be an asset with the jury. On the con side, he had no idea
how he would feel working so closely with a woman. There were
women at Pane, Parish, and there had been women in the U.S.
Attorney's office when he was there: not that many at first, more
by the time he left. Some of them were first-rate lawyers. But if he
was honest with himself, he had to admit they made him uneasy.
He did not know why, but they did.

The glass-walled midtown bar was crowded with after-work
professionals. He stood inside the door, sweat evaporating from his
clammy suit in the refrigerated air, and scanned the crowd.

He was looking for a shorter-than-average woman in a tan summer suit, which eliminated only about half of the women he could see, depending on what you called shorter than average. Her voice on the phone had not been much of a clue to what she looked like. Professional, maybe even a little hard. From the résumé he supposed she was in her mid thirties, information that was not much help here, where everyone seemed to be somewhere between twenty-eight and forty-two. He checked his watch. Their appointment had been for fifteen minutes ago. He had been at least five minutes late himself. Could he have missed her?

"Mr. Ryan?"

"Yes."

She had just come in. "I'm Kassia Miller." She held out her hand, strong and certain.

She was definitely shorter than average, no more than five-two in medium heels. She had shoulder-length dark hair and brown eyes. The promised suit was set off by a peach-colored blouse. His first impression was: neat, tailored, professional. Then, on no evidence he could name: wary and distant.

"Sorry I'm late. I got stuck on the phone."

"No problem." He indicated the swirl of noise and motion around them. "Is this the best place, do you think?"

"Well, at this hour . . . I figured there was no place really quiet and the noise was good camouflage. If we put our heads together, nobody's going to be able to hear us."

"Not even us." He meant it as a joke, but it came out awkward.

They worked their way to the bar; miraculously, a space opened up big enough for two elbows.

"Beer," Ryan ordered. "Anything but light. For you?"

"Club soda."

She put her briefcase on the floor between them.

"Some weather," he said.

"I thought it was supposed to stop after Labor Day."

The bartender brought their drinks. Ryan held up his glass in a silent toast and downed half his beer. Very thirsty or very nervous, or both.

"You have a case you want help with."

Right to the point. "More or less."

"Murder, you said."

"That's how the indictment reads."

"This is the Ryan case, right? Your daughter-in-law is accused of killing your son."

"You do your homework."

"I try to. How do you come to be involved?"

"The defendant has asked me to represent her."

"And you're going to do it."

"Not alone."

"That's smart."

He turned to the bar for his glass and swallowed his reaction with some beer.

"Is it something that would interest you?" he asked.

"Probably." Her brow furrowed for a moment. "Let me amend that. It *might* interest me. I'd have to talk to the defendant and talk to you some more. This is not your everyday situation, and I want to be sure I understand it. And we'd have to work out a method of working together. The first question is, do I interest you?"

"I read your résumé . . ."

"And you have some questions."

"Yes."

"I don't have many answers. It's all there. After college I worked at women's magazines for two years. It turned out that fashion and beauty and exercise and celebrities were not my destiny, and while I was waiting to figure out what was, I parlayed a college research thesis on criminal prosecution into a job as a paralegal with Andy Andreg. I loved it right from the beginning. Pretty soon he was saying, 'Go to law school,' but I didn't want to stop doing what I was doing. I'd been there about two years when he finally bludgeoned me into going to law school at night while I continued to work full time for him. It meant shortchanging some subjects, but having a perfect grasp of fee simple and secured transactions wasn't why I was there. I started doing the real thing as soon as I got out of law school and passed the bar. I like the work. I like everything about it except the hours."

"Do you spend much time in court, or is most of your work inside?"

"I do it all. I probably got into court sooner than most, because by the time I passed the bar I'd been doing inside work, and everything I could do in court without being admitted, for almost six years."

"Tell me about Centre Street. I've never worked there but I'm told it takes a scorecard and a road map to get anything done right."

"Well . . ." She stirred the ice cubes in her club soda with a manicured finger, then looked Ryan in the eye and smiled. The smile lasted only a moment, but Ryan was struck by it. Used to advantage with a jury, it could be a powerful weapon.

She said, "Very good, counselor. I have to decide whether to tell you it's a labyrinthine sinkhole of favoritism and corruption, or a crystal palace of true justice. And I can see how either way it's the wrong answer.''

''You could try the truth.''

''What truth? Whose truth? Every situation is different. No. Maybe there is one truth. If you go there a total stranger, you start out way behind. You can get respect if you're good, and you can get help if you're sympathetic, but too often you're likely not to know what questions to ask. Or who to ask. So you miss some things out of pure ignorance.''

''That's what I want to avoid.''

''So you're looking for more than a co-counsel who knows the Penal Law and criminal procedure.''

''I assumed that was a given.''

''There's some value in spelling these things out. For both of us. I won't say I know everybody. I've been at it long enough to know my way around the courthouse, and I know who to ask for help when there's something I don't know how to handle.''

''Fair enough. Now, if we go ahead with this, it'll keep you busy, for months certainly, and it could be a year or more before we're done. How does that fit with your current obligations?''

''I don't have any matters pending that I can't give to somebody else in the office.''

''What about your personal life?''

''Everybody I know is either a lawyer or a defendant. At the moment I have no major personal life to speak of, but that's not a permanent disability.'' She gave him a look. ''If that's relevant.''

''You won't be able to take time off from the case for a wedding and honeymoon, if you have one planned.''

''That's obvious, wouldn't you say?''

''Spelling things out, I thought you called it . . . I have some other questions, but this will hold me for now. You must have some for me.''

''As I said, I want to talk to the defendant, assuming we get past this stage. Then we can talk again. I'm sure we'll both have plenty of questions at that point.''

Ryan waited. He was sure she had more to say.

She finished her club soda and picked up her briefcase as if she was ready to leave. Put it down again.

''About working methods. If you decide I'm who you want, we have to agree that when it comes to courtroom decisions you'll listen to what I say. I don't want this to turn into a power struggle. And I certainly don't want it to turn into a power struggle in front of the judge and the jury. I have respect for your work as a prosecutor. A *federal* prosecutor. I also know you left the government ten years ago, and after that you were a plaintiff's lawyer in federal civil cases. And the word I get is you haven't been in a courtroom in three years, and when you last tried it you fucked it up royally. If you'll pardon my French.

"As you said, I do my homework. So my point is, you're talking to me because you need me, or somebody like me, and you know it. Okay. So far so good. And a lot of the case is going to be preparation and strategy, and I'm content to let you run most of that, except when it comes to special knowledge. But there's only one boss in the courtroom, and I don't think it can be you. And I'm not even talking about your emotional stake in the case, whatever it is, and how that's likely to complicate life."

"You're very frank."

"Life is short."

She seemed oblivious of the double meaning. She sucked the dregs of her club soda through the straw, making a loud bubbling sound at the bottom of the glass.

"So?" she asked.

Ryan put money on the bar.

"So . . . You come highly recommended. You're obviously intelligent, and I have no doubt you're a competent attorney."

"Thank you. Or do I detect a 'but' at the end of that sentence?"

"Yes, you do. The 'but' is this: I don't much like your style. Honesty is fine. Gratuitous abrasiveness isn't. I think we might have trouble working together."

"We might."

"And I am certainly not going to make any advance promises about deferring to your judgment in the courtroom."

She picked up her briefcase, for real this time. "I shouldn't take up more of your time."

"One more thing, before you go."

"Oh?"

"Given what we've said, I'm willing to suspend judgment long enough for you to meet with the client, if that still interests you."

She looked at him for what seemed like a long time before she said, "All right. Let's try it."

11

RYAN DID NOT WANT TO RISK HAVING ANYONE SEE
Jennifer coming to his office. The press would go crazy once they
got wind of the possibility that he was going to defend her. The
time was coming when he would welcome publicity, but not before
he had met the challenge he expected from Becker. He arrived at
Kassia Miller's office a half hour before Jennifer was due and did
his best to be unobtrusive on his way in.

"The way I've been taught to work," Miller said while they were
waiting, "you start prepping the client from word one. That's not
something you had to worry about as a prosecutor, seeing as you
didn't have any clients."

"I've been in private practice for ten years." It came out sharper
than he intended.

"Representing plaintiffs in corporate lawsuits. Not the same.
Believe me, this is something you have to let me do."

Ryan went along with it. Letting her start with Jennifer would
give him a chance to see her in action, and he did not think it could
do any harm.

Jennifer was ten minutes late, looking fresh despite the continuing September heat wave. A secretary brought her back to the narrow office with a window looking out at the gray towers of
Rockefeller Center.

"I'm Kassia Miller," the lawyer said, extending her hand the
way she had when she met Ryan. "Mr. Ryan and I have been
talking about my working on your case."

"Yes, he told me he was going to hire someone to help out."

Miller shot a glance at Ryan. "That's one way to put it."

Ryan said, "I think you two ought to learn about each other, so
I'll just sit here and keep quiet for now."

55

"Good." Miller offered Jennifer a seat on the small couch and perched on its arm, facing her.

Watching the two women, Ryan had to remind himself that they were virtually the same age—about thirty-five. They did not look like contemporaries: the petite, precisely tailored lawyer, all competence and control; and the sometime actress and rich-girl charity volunteer, elegantly casual, subdued but still with a long-limbed youthful ease. He saw no sign that she was pregnant. Her clothes, a white silk blouse worn over pale gray trousers, were loose but only in a way Ryan took to be fashionable.

"You don't know anything about me yet," Miller began, "except that I'm a criminal defense lawyer, but in the next few minutes you have to make a crucial decision. Either you're going to tell me the truth, or you're going to lie to me—lie a little or a lot. And you'll have to live with the consequences of that choice for the rest of your life."

Jennifer glanced uneasily at Ryan.

Miller went on. "In court you swear to tell the whole truth and nothing but the truth, and the penalty if you don't tell the truth is they can put you in jail for perjury."

"Yes . . ."

"Well, with me you don't swear anything, but the penalty if you don't tell the truth is they could put you in jail for murder."

Jennifer's eyes widened and she sat up straight. Ryan was no longer sure this could do no harm. He was about to interrupt when Miller shifted to a milder tone.

"Remember, whatever you tell me, no matter what it is, stays between you and me. I can't tell anyone about it unless you give me permission."

"I understand that." Jennifer's voice was as stiff as her posture.

"Michael tells me you want your lawyers to believe you're innocent. I suppose it's okay if you want *him* to believe you're innocent. Me, you'd better not care what I think, because if you do you're going to destroy any chance that we can give you a decent defense. You can't be honest with me if you're worrying what I'm going to think about you. You have to believe I'm going to protect you no matter what I think."

Jennifer looked at Ryan again.

Enough is enough, Ryan thought, as Miller was saying to Jennifer, "This is the only relationship like it in the world—lawyer and client in a murder case. And I'm beginning to see that this case is unusual that way. You and I need to have a relationship all our own, just the two of us, separate from the relationship you have with Michael. Because I'm going to ask you to tell me about every little wart in your life. And you have to trust me to use it only to defend you and not to reveal it to anybody at all, not even Michael if you don't want me to.''

Ryan could not believe what he was hearing.

Miller stood up without giving either him or Jennifer a chance to speak. ''Michael and I are going to go outside now, and we're going to give you time to consider what I've been saying. I keep my confidential files locked up, so you can browse around the office if you think it will help you get a better sense of who I am.''

She left the office and walked down the corridor without pausing to see if Ryan was following her. She stopped at the door to an empty office barely big enough for a first-year associate. ''We can wait in here.''

Ryan closed the door firmly behind him. ''A separate relationship! What the hell do you think this is?''

She sat down in the chair behind the narrow desk. ''Look, I'm sorry I popped that on you like that, but it seemed necessary.''

''What seemed necessary? Making policy without talking to me about it first? In front of the client?''

''Somebody has to get the information from her that you can't.''

''Just exactly what does that mean?''

She shook her head once, a sharp motion that tossed her soft dark hair emphatically. ''Do you suppose for a minute she's going to be honest with you about your son? I'm not talking about some general history with a few affairs and a nasty business deal thrown in for flavor. I'm talking about gut-level honesty, all the little details that we won't know if we need or not until this is all over.''

She let the angry question hang in the air, then continued more calmly. ''I couldn't say that to her—not in so many words, because it would scare her off for sure. Right now she doesn't know enough to think about things like that. But unless she hired you as an act of pure manipulation we have to assume she cares about your opinion. In ways none of us understands, least of all her. If we're going to try this case we need information that I don't for a minute believe she's going to tell you, not freely and not fully.''

Ryan thought, the things this woman wants to keep from me are the very things I need to know. No, he corrected himself, not what I need to know, what I want to know. For the first time he saw the danger he was in, trying to serve two masters: protecting his grandchild with the best defense for its mother, and satisfying his own desire to know more about Ned.

Miller was studying him. ''If you took on her defense because you want to be some kind of voyeur in your dead son's life, I guess this won't work for you. But if that's why you took this case, I don't want any part of it. Nobody ever won a murder trial by trying to do something else."

Jennifer was standing by the door, ready to leave, when the two lawyers returned.

"I thought I made it clear to Michael how I feel about lawyers who tell me I have to do this and I have to do that. I have to plead guilty. That's what the others said." She was talking rapidly, her voice tense with restrained anger. "Now *you* want me to confess. That's what you meant, isn't it: I should trust you enough to tell you I did it. But I didn't. And I don't want any lawyer who thinks I did."

This last was to Ryan, who said, "I think you may be misunderstanding."

"If you *are* misunderstanding, it's my fault," Miller offered. "All I'm saying is that I want you to believe that I'm on your side whether you're guilty or not. And telling the truth doesn't stop at guilty or not guilty. That's the least of it. I need to know everything about you. And Ned. Your whole life."

Jennifer made no move to sit down. "I can understand that you need to know a lot about me. But I want Michael to hear it, too. He's my lawyer, not you."

"That's right, I'm not your lawyer." A touch of anger. "And I won't be, unless I'm convinced you'll tell us the truth."

"I didn't mean to offend you," Jennifer said.

"Why don't we all sit down and see if we can make this work," Ryan said.

Jennifer hesitated, then sat stiffly on the edge of the couch. This time Miller sat on a chair facing her.

"The first step is for you to tell us your story. Start wherever you're comfortable. Assume I know nothing about you, because it's true."

Jennifer took another moment before she settled back. She began with the night of the murder. The story she told was not much different from the one Ryan had already heard from her. She and Ned had gone to a roof-garden party thrown by gallery owner Hugo Hill to introduce three of his artists, all of them women. Ned had been behaving well until he was introduced to one of the guests of honor—the sculptor, Tina Claire. He had carried on with her outrageously and Jennifer had reacted with an angry outburst, building to the point where she smashed a serving bowl. Ned had walked out on her then, and she followed him. They had a second argument in the study and gallery in Hugo Hill's apartment below. This time she was the one who walked out. Ned did not follow her. That was the last time she'd seen him.

"I'm going to need more than that," Miller told her.

"I don't know what more there is."

"There's plenty more. All about you and Ned, about the people at this party, about what there might have been in Ned's life that could have got him killed."

"A burglar."

"I beg your pardon?"

"A burglar. Isn't that possible? Somebody was there to rob Hugo, and Ned saw him . . ."

"Maybe it's possible," Miller said. "But at this point thinking about it that way doesn't help." She paused, and Ryan had the feeling she was shifting gears.

"In a case like this I have to be able to get inside your skin, and Ned's too, as far as possible," she told Jennifer, with a softness Ryan had not heard in her voice before. "You're the only one who can help me do that."

Jennifer shifted in her chair, glanced at Ryan. "I'm not much good at this kind of thing."

Miller gave her a smile of encouragement. "Why don't you start right from the beginning of your time with Ned?"

"Okay, I'll try." She turned toward her questioner. Ryan felt left out.

"Ned and I first met about four years ago. He was working with my father. I was married then. It had gone bad but I guess I was still trying to make it work." She shook her head at the memory. "Anyway, I ran into Ned now and then. At parties with my father, mostly. Sometimes he was being very serious and businesslike, trying to impress somebody, but every so often I'd catch him trying to connect with some woman. I remember thinking how it might be to have him after me like that, but when we were together, talking, he was pretty restrained, even after my divorce. That was when things started to change, though."

She stood up. Paced. Stopped by the bookshelf, staring at the small figurine of an elephant in a space between treatises on the rules of evidence. She touched it with a tentative finger, traced a line along its back and trunk.

"Souvenir of Kenya," Miller said.

"Do you have something to drink?" Jennifer asked.

Not alcohol, Ryan thought, his mind going instantly to the baby she was carrying.

"Coffee?" Miller suggested.

"Club soda, if you have it."

"Michael?"

"Coffee."

"Back in a minute."

"This makes me nervous," Jennifer said to Ryan when they were alone. "I mean, I'm talking about your son."

"You can't let that bother you. You have to think of me only as your lawyer."

"I guess you're right—I have to get over it. The most important thing is, I trust you."

Ryan drew a slow breath. Life made no sense; people made less. "Then this shouldn't be a problem."

Miller came in with a cup of coffee in one hand and two cans of club soda balanced in the other. "I couldn't manage glasses."

Jennifer popped the top of her can and drank eagerly. For a moment she looked like a college girl: dark hair loose around her shoulders, head thrown back to drink deeply, cheeks flushed as if with some secret excitement.

"There I was," she resumed, "feeling like I was beginning life all over again at thirty-one. I started to notice Ned, really notice him, for the first time. And all of a sudden I found myself looking forward to the next time I saw him. He was putting some deals together with my father then, so he was at Fifth Avenue a lot, and I was staying there, too, looking for a new place to live."

Ryan wanted to hear more about those deals, but he caught a tiny motion of Miller's head he thought was a signal not to interrupt.

"You know what I really liked about Ned? He was smart, and he knew what he wanted. Not like me. I don't think I ever did. I think that's what attracted me to him the most. I mean, it didn't hurt that he was young and sexy. And the fact that he didn't hit on me the way men always do, you know? I bet you get that, too."

Miller's response was a brief smile. Ryan was glad she had kept him from talking. He had the feeling that for the moment Jennifer had forgotten he was there.

"People used to make comments about how Ned must have been looking for a mother when he married me. Not just that I'm seven years older, but his mother had just died when we got engaged. People said how could you? It bothered me, too, getting married at a time like that."

She seemed suddenly to remember Ryan. She looked at him uncertainly. He nodded at her to go ahead. Miller had been right, sooner or later he would have to leave them alone with each other. He wanted it to be later.

"I thought we should wait to get married," Jennifer resumed. "But he wouldn't listen. He said mourning for his mother and loving me were separate, he could do both at once. He was right, too. I mean he really did mourn for his mother. Sometimes it was very bad. He wouldn't cry, but he would lie there hugging himself, rocking on the bed. It helped if I got into bed with him and held him. Like a baby almost."

The things we never know, Ryan thought.

"But you know what's strange? I always felt like he was older than me. I've always felt like a kid, inside. When I was married the first time, my husband was older and successful and very conservative, so I pretended to be grown up. It was like having a role to play. Be a character who is married to a successful man on Wall Street, who goes to fancy parties. I used to go to parties with my father, from when I was twelve, whenever he didn't have a date, until he got married again, and sometimes after that. So when I was with Peter, my first husband, I played that same role. And when I was in acting class or someplace with just my friends I was myself again, a kid. One of the things that made me sure I couldn't stay with Peter was that I had less and less chance to be the real me instead of this pretend grown-up, and Peter was getting stiffer and more boring every minute.

"With Ned, the wonderful thing was that I found somebody my own age. I mean, he wasn't, not really, he was seven years younger, but he liked a lot of the same things and even though he was very intense and driven some of the time and I can be sort of . . . undirected, I guess is the charitable way to put it . . . we were very comfortable with each other. In a way, I looked up to him. For that sense of certainty he had. And he was never dull, like Peter. He had this fire, this terrific energy. It was very sexy, and he could do the most wonderful, unpredictable things.

"I knew he had an active past. There was a time when he seemed to be always looking for someone to screw"—she looked quickly, uncertainly, at Ryan—"and I think it had both meanings . . . Sometimes it was even the wife of somebody he had a deal with. Like it was part of getting the better of the other guy."

The flow of narrative stopped abruptly, dammed behind a twist of pain. She drank from the can that had been forgotten on the table by her chair.

Kassia Miller said, "Around the time he died, how was your marriage?"

Jennifer was silent, struggling with the question. "I don't know what to say. We had our ups and downs. The last couple of days . . ." She fought back tears. "The last couple of days were good. But before that . . ." She took a breath. "It was terrible. I mean, I could tell you it wasn't, but it was." Her voice was a low monotone. "Now I keep thinking, I can't make it better anymore . . ."

She stopped and reached out toward Ryan as if she could touch him from across the room. "I guess you must feel something like that, too. It's weird—he didn't think you cared about him."

Could that be? Could he have been that far off the mark, expressing his feelings for his son?

"So it wasn't all that great between Ned and me," Jennifer went on. "What made it worse was that he got so distant and moody the last few weeks. It didn't take a genius to see he had something on his mind."

"Do you know what was bothering him?" Miller asked before Ryan could.

"No. He never talked about it."

"Did you ask him?"

"Once. It was making me crazy. We were out somewhere, the two of us. We didn't do that a lot, there was always somebody to entertain for business, or Jim Morris with some kind of crisis about the things they were involved in together. It was an occasion if the two of us ever went someplace just to be together. There's a place we liked uptown, sort of Art Deco with French bistro food, I think that's where we were, and I asked him. He said not to worry about it."

"Do you remember exactly what you asked him?" Ryan had to strain to keep from sounding like an interrogator.

"No. Not exactly . . . Something like is there anything I can do, you look like you're carrying the whole world on your back."

"And what did he say?"

"He just said not to worry about it."

"Anything else?" Ryan was sitting forward in his chair.

"No. Yes. He said it wasn't going to last much longer."

"How did he sound?" Miller asked. "Angry? Relieved?"

"When I first asked him it seemed to make him angry, like what are you talking about? But then he got quiet and said don't worry. And there was something about the way he said it . . . like things were going to get better. I don't know, maybe I'm imagining it."

"Do you have any idea what it was about?"

"No. We didn't talk much about his business. In the early days we did, more. But not for the past year or so. He was working all the time, late most nights, and things were going very fast for him. Those medical clinics he set up with Jim Morris—they only really took hold in the last few months. Before that it was an enormous amount of work and not much return. It all fell into place at the end of last year, and there was a lot of following up to make sure it was going right. I don't know, that's what Ned told me, anyway."

"Do you think whatever was bothering him was about the clinics?" Ryan asked.

"I don't see how. From everything he said, that was going fine."

"Was there anyone he worried about or complained about? Any business deal that seemed to trouble him?"

Jennifer paused to consider the question. Waiting, Miller crumpled the soft-drink can in her hand and lofted it across the room into a wastebasket, a bank shot off the spines of some law books. Ryan could not help a glance toward the door to see if anyone outside had noticed. It was closed, of course.

"There was one deal he used to swear about," Jennifer said. "It had something to do with a mortgage he arranged on a piece of property in New Jersey. I think it was for a shopping center. Something about Ned having to change the terms of the deal at the last minute and the guy got very upset and made threats."

"Threats?" Ryan said.

Jennifer seemed startled to have the word jumped on. "I don't think it was about doing anything violent. More like he was going to hurt him legally or financially somehow."

"Do you know the man's name?" Miller asked.

"I don't remember it."

"If we went over a list of Ned's business dealings, the mortgages especially, do you think you would recognize the name?" Ryan asked.

"I don't know how much of his name Ned ever told me."

"We ought to try it, anyway," he said.

12

"WHAT DO YOU THINK?" RYAN ASKED AFTER JENNI-
fer left the office.

"I think at this stage we'd see suspects at a convention of bish-
ops," Miller said. "Who knows, maybe we'd be right. How about
we get the hell out of here?"

"We're not done."

"You bet we're not. Let's go for a walk, or sit in a bar, or both.
We can explore the questions raised by our chat with your client."

"What do you think of her?"

"Sad."

"The question is, do you think she killed Ned?"

"Not for me, it's not the question."

"It's what matters to her." Ryan's words slipped out angrily.
Why was he jumping to take Jennifer's side? Not smart, he told
himself. She's a client. She may have killed your son. Forget for
now that she's going to be the mother of your grandchild.

"Could be it matters to her." Miller was surveying him coolly.
"Or it could be a way to manipulate the situation. All she has to
do is claim our belief in her is slipping, and we all get uptight about
pleasing her. And she's going to be tough to deal with even without
that. She's smart enough and insecure enough to pick up on a million things to worry about, and she's likely to make a fuss over
every one of them."

"Then you're not interested?"

"I didn't say that. I was answering your question about what I
thought of her."

"Yes or no will do. Are you interested?"

"You're going to have to stop picking fights with me, Ryan, or
we're not going to get anything done."

"That's a yes?"

She glared at him. "It's a provisional yes. And it's on my terms, as already enunciated. That puts the ball in your court. You had some doubts about being able to work with me."

"Do you think *you* can work with *me*?"

She did not answer.

"If it's any help," he said, "I'll admit you're right about you and Jennifer having a separate relationship."

"Telling her story just now she was beginning to see it herself, how hard it is to tell you some things."

"That's what turned me around. Now, about your so-called 'terms.' I'm lead counsel. You're second seat."

"No. I told you . . ."

"It has to be that way to keep me on the case. My argument to the court is going to be that she's entitled to the lawyer of her choice, and I'm it. As far as who actually calls the shots, I expect us both to be sensible about that."

"That depends on what you mean by sensible."

"Look, lady, you're the one who said 'stop picking fights.' "

"All right. Truce. But don't call me 'lady.' "

She was like a terrier, he thought. She wouldn't let go. It made him laugh. Her face went momentarily dark, and then she saw the joke and laughed with him.

"Let's get that drink," he said.

They found a place called the Blarney Bar, cheap meat and potatoes in a steam table by the door, and a long dark bar. Not a place that turned into a madhouse during the after-work rush hour. They got a draft beer and a club soda at the bar and carried them to a booth.

"You're satisfied about her reasons for wanting you?" she asked.

He sidestepped that one. "Becker is going to think her real reason is to make improper use of the fact that I'm Ned's father. To get sympathy from the jury. That's why I'm so sure he's going to want me disqualified. Not because I'm Clarence Darrow."

There was something odd in her expression.

"I say something wrong?"

"Not relevant. I'll tell you someday, maybe. So you're not Clarence Darrow."

"Right. But Jennifer believes she has real reasons to want me to represent her."

"And you choose not to look past that."

"I suppose I don't." He had to let that stand, for now. It was risky not telling her the whole truth, but if she didn't end up on the team he didn't want her to know Jennifer was pregnant. The best he could do was temporize. ''I choose to accept her at face value, because I have my own reasons for wanting to represent her.''

''There's a question I have to ask.'' Her brown eyes steadied on him. ''Could one of your reasons be that you think she's guilty and you want to screw up her defense?'' She saw the anger in his face and added quickly, ''I had to ask that.''

''No you didn't. Not if you really did your homework about me. As I was saying, I have my reasons. The same as you have your reasons.''

''Me?''

''Don't play innocent. It doesn't become you.''

''Look, Lee Bailey was, what, twenty-six, when he defended Sam Sheppard. I was barely out of the magazine business when I was twenty-six. I have a lot of lost time to make up for.''

''I guess that explains your zeal.'' It was a cheap shot. He had chosen her partly for that hunger.

''Recognize my good instincts and my skill, that'll be plenty. As for my *zeal*, appreciate it for the good work it produces. Aside from that, it's my problem.''

They finished their drinks in silence. Neither of them was inclined to make small talk. On their way out Ryan said, ''Before I make up my mind I'd like to see you in court.'' Knowing already he was nearly certain to hire her.

Her client was accused of armed robbery. He had been arrested on a streetcorner immediately after the alleged robbery by a pair of Housing Authority cops who testified that they had seen the crime committed. Her cross-examination was limited to getting each of them to describe with great specificity the location of the arrest and how they had seen the crime from their patrol car as they cruised their housing-project beat. Ryan had expected her to take a tough, no-nonsense approach with the cops. Instead, she was mild, not quite flirtatious, and seemingly befuddled by the details she asked the cops to go over carefully and repeatedly.

After the lunch break she presented her case. Her sole witness was a neighborhood barber who told a story of having watched the arrest happen directly in front of his shop window. She got the same level of detail from him as she had from the cops. With her own witness she was visibly more in control, but not so different from her style in the morning that she risked confusing or alienating the jury. The substance of her defense was that the barbershop was three blocks north of the corner where the cops had testified they made the arrest. The barber had seen no crime, only an arrest.

If the cops had lied so often and in such detail about the location of the arrest, she asked the jury in her summation, wasn't it likely they also lied about its substance? The jury brought in an acquittal in less than an hour.

"That was some performance," Ryan said later. "And I do mean performance."

"I choose to take that as a compliment."

"Why do you think the cops lied?"

"Do they need a reason?"

"You don't believe that."

She shrugged. "The only reason I can think of is that they were outside their territory when they made the arrest. That's major trouble for housing cops."

"How did you find the barber?"

"Hard work and luck. I sent out an investigator to canvass the neighborhood. He kept asking until he found somebody who saw something."

"And the luck was that the barber didn't look out the window a minute earlier."

She laughed.

"So, are we doing this?" she asked as they walked down the courthouse steps onto Centre Street.

"It looks that way, doesn't it?"

13

THE TOP ITEM ON RYAN'S AGENDA WAS PREPARING HIS argument against the motion to disqualify him that he was sure Becker would file. He picked one of the firm's brighter second-year associates, the best he had been allowed by the executive board, and put him to work researching the question of a defendant's right to be represented by the lawyer of his choice. As camouflage, the client number Ryan was using for billing time spent on the case had the three-number prefix the firm used for *pro bono* work.

Ryan had an uncomfortable meeting with Jennifer and her father to discuss fee arrangements and to swear Kneeland to secrecy about Ryan's involvement in the case. Kneeland was proper and polite, but Ryan was under no illusion that the developer was happy about his daughter's choice of lawyer. For everyone's sake, dealing with him would be Kassia Miller's job.

Ryan wanted to have a separate office where they could assemble all their files and begin preparing the case without attracting the attention that was inevitable if he and Miller spent much time in each other's law firm.

Kneeland says put the money where it counts, Miller reported: If you need an office near the courthouse at trial time, that's something else.

They solved the problem temporarily by working separately. Ryan arranged for Jake Kaplan to give Miller a series of briefings on Ned's business and financial manipulations, complete with excerpts from Ned's checkbooks, ledgers and other records.

Within days of deciding to proceed, Ryan went back to walking the two and a half miles home from the office. He had stopped taking the walks when Ned was killed: while Ali's death had produced a period of frantic activity before the slide into despair, with Ned's there had been only numbness.

He was glad to be out walking again. This was his favorite time of year in New York, the crisp clear days of late September: the leaves beginning to turn red and gold, the air seemingly clean, alive with the hum of the city reenergized after summer's lethargy. Until now, he had noticed none of it. It was as if making the first real commitment to representing Jennifer had brought with it, along with a new anxiety, new energy. He did not know how long it would last. Life had taught him not to waste it.

Ryan arrived at Miller's office, as scheduled, late on the day of her first one-to-one client conference with Jennifer. He used the temporary I.D. Miller had arranged for him so he did not have to be announced every time he visited her.

He found her at her desk, poring over the papers from Jake Kaplan. She looked up when he came in but did not greet him. Something was clearly wrong. Ryan hung up his raincoat on the back of the door and sat down to wait for the storm to break.

She stacked the papers and put them aside. For a moment she regarded Ryan in silence.

"Jennifer is pregnant," she said finally.

"Yes."

"Why didn't you tell me?" Her voice was level but her anger was clear.

"I couldn't, not until we were sure you were going to have the job."

"That was more than a week ago."

"After that, I thought it would be better if you heard it from her, the way you did. Help establish your special rapport."

"That really bothers you, doesn't it?"

He let it go by.

"Now we just have to decide how to use it," she said.

"That she's pregnant? It's not relevant."

"The hell it's not."

"She didn't know about it when Ned was killed."

"Not officially. Not by some test."

"What then? By instinct?"

"You think women don't know these things? Her body knew. Who can say how that affected her emotions?"

"I thought it was supposed to make you kinder and gentler. Maternal."

"Yes, and maternal means protective, too. Maybe she was having a maternal instinct toward the bitch who was going after the father of her child."

"And where do we go with that? She says she wasn't there when he was killed. She says she didn't do it. We can't put in a maternal-hormones defense, not any more than we can put in a Twinkies defense or any other kind of diminished capacity. Not if she didn't do it. And if you think I'm going to argue in the alternative—she didn't do it, but if she had done it, it would have been her hormones that made her do it . . ."

"Not explicitly, of course not."

"Then we'll never get it into evidence. The jury will never know."

"They'll know if she's still pregnant during the trial."

"And what chance is there of that?" Major trials in Manhattan rarely started less than a year after the crime. Even an ex-federal prosecutor knew that.

"She's not due until the end of March. We could start in the middle of February and still have a six-week trial."

"Sure. If we can promise the judge the kid won't be premature.

And assuming we could be ready for trial. We're talking about four months, max.''

"We can do it. We have to do it. Think about the effect it would have on the jury, seeing her sitting there day after day, ready to give birth any moment to Ned's child.''

He thought about it. There was no denying its appeal.

"It means not wasting a minute," she said. "We need to get a judge assigned right away so we can get the pretrial motions going.''

"I'll have to get my brief ready.''

"As soon as you can.''

"It worries me, going too fast. We don't have any idea what our case is going to be.''

"There'll be time for that.''

"There'd better be. Pregnant will help us, but it isn't enough.''

"Now, there's a man speaking.'' She swiveled her chair so she could look out at the rain. "Is that why you took the case?'' She turned to face him. "Because she was going to be the mother of your grandchild?''

He did not answer at once, and she did not rush him.

"Would you be happier if I was doing it for money?'' he asked her. "Or glory?''

"I'm happy with anything that brings out the good lawyer in you.''

Ryan called Craig Lawrence. The two of them had worked together in what Lawrence called "the bad old days"—Lawrence as an F.B.I. special agent and Ryan in the U.S. Attorney's office. They were fundamentally different, Lawrence as offhand as Ryan had been focused and direct in those days, but each had come quickly to see past the other's surface, and they recognized the same failing in each other. Neither was interested in advancement or office politics, in building a reputation or a following, or even in praise. All either cared about was the *work*: getting it done and getting it done the best way possible. It was a trait that had not always served Ryan well. In retrospect he saw that it had contributed to the destruction of his family. Its effect on Lawrence had been more obvious. It got him fired.

For Lawrence that had been, as he later put it, "a blessing in no disguise.'' He quickly built a thriving detective bureau employing other former special agents, ex-police detectives, and for surveillance a flock of part-timers, mostly would-be or ex-actresses. An expert at the pleasures of bachelorhood since his days as a college fullback, he took a certain amount of ribbing about the fringe benefits of his choice of staff. Ryan thought there could be few better investigators in the business.

"I know what you want," Lawrence said when Ryan reported he might be getting back into trial work. "You want me to drop everything else and work on this one personally."

"I know you're busy," Ryan said, not contradicting him.

"Yeah, but you want me to drop everything anyway. Well, it's your lucky day, my friend. I'm winding up a couple of jobs this week and next. Most of the new stuff that's coming in I can lay off on my overworked employees. If you need me in the next two weeks you get me part time. After that I'm all yours."

Miller called Ryan at home the next morning. "I just had a call from Jeff Rosen. He says Becker's willing to get the case assigned at their next court appearance. That means we go in for our regular court date next week and the assignment judge says, well, let's get this assigned and get on with it, and if everybody's there and nobody has a good reason not to, the judge spins the wheel and we get assigned a trial judge. Only for us, we'll have our choice of two wheels. The regular wheel and the P-wheel."

"P-wheel?"

"P for prolonged, I think, but mostly it means big press cases. It's supposed to be more-experienced judges who can handle long, complicated cases, only it's almost as full of jerks and incompetents as the regular wheel."

"Sounds great."

"These wheels aren't like the federal wheel; the judges are only listed once each. When a judge gets assigned, his name gets pulled out of the wheel. They start with six names in the wheel, then you have five, then four, until the wheel is empty. Then they fill it up again."

"So you can get a wheel with only one or two judges in it."

"Depends on the timing."

"And if there are two judges left and you hate them both?"

"If you find out in time, maybe you get sick or get called away on an emergency."

"And come back when the wheel is full again."

"That's the theory. It doesn't always work."

"I take it this is one of the places where it helps to know somebody."

"It doesn't hurt. Especially if there are two judges left in the wheel and you like them both and you're third on the calendar."

"Only one thing matters right now," Ryan said. "A judge who won't kick me off this case."

14

KASSIA MILLER ACCOMPANIED JEFF ROSEN AND JEN-nifer Ryan to the New York State Supreme Court assignment part the following Wednesday. Michael Ryan waited by the phone in his office.

Miller's call came just before eleven. "As of this moment we're thirteenth on the calendar call, and there are three judges in the P-wheel. One terrible, one okay, one pretty good."

"Maybe you and Rosen ought to get sick."

"That's what I'd do if we weren't in such a hurry. But I got talking to a friendly calendar clerk and he says there's only one case ahead of us that could remotely go to the P-wheel, so I thought maybe it was worth hanging out to see who they draw. It could save us a couple of weeks."

"I'm not there," Ryan said. "Play it the way you see it."

She called again at one.

"The good news is the other case drew the bad guy, so we got on the wheel with two judges, both more or less okay for our side."

"What's the bad news?"

"The bad news is, of the two, we didn't get the better one."

"Who did we get?"

"Anthony R. Corino. They call him Tony Boy. I don't know why. I'll tell you about him when I see you. I've got to start clearing the decks at my office. I'll be done around eight, say eight-thirty to be safe. And I'll be hungry."

They agreed on a restaurant. Ryan held the receiver button down only long enough to break the connection, then dialed Craig Law-rence.

"Supreme Court Justice Anthony R. Corino," he told the investigator.

"That our man? I'm on it, right away."

Lawrence called him back a few minutes after seven.

"You still there?"

"We never close," Ryan said. "What have you got?"

"Anthony R. Corino, a/k/a Tony Boy, a/k/a Hang 'Em High Corino."

"Hang 'Em High? You're kidding."

"Not for a minute."

"Tell me about it."

"It's what it sounds like. A no-nonsense guy, they tell me. Some people say he's a closet racist, doesn't care much what the minority types do to other minority types. He'll do what he can to force a plea so he can keep cases like that out of his courtroom. He's a major believer in deterrence and retribution, thinks rehabilitation is a crock."

Ryan was no believer in rehabilitation himself, but that did not mean he was eager to be in Corino's courtroom as a defense attorney.

"He also likes to set examples," Lawrence said. "He's already said he's looking forward to this case."

"Just what we need. What kind of examples?"

"Like putting upper-class types away for long stretches."

"Are you sure? Miller told me he was somebody we could live with." What the hell could she have been thinking of?

"I only know what I hear. Want me to keep asking?"

"You'd better."

Ryan was not in much of a mood for the upbeat atmosphere at the restaurant he had suggested. He took a chance on catching Miller at the office.

"I was about to leave. Anything wrong?"

"I need to stay here and do some work I hadn't counted on. Come over here and we can order in."

Waiting for her, he reread the excerpts his associate had found in federal and state court decisions about the defendant's right to choose counsel. The research job had not been a simple one, even with the aid of a computer data base service. One of the young lawyer's requests had returned the message "Your search has been interrupted because it probably will retrieve more than five hundred documents." Others had turned up nothing. Going through the

material now, Ryan concentrated on the cases in which the court
had restricted the defendant's right to have the counsel of his choice.
Ryan's argument needed to be strongest showing how those cases
did not apply.

He had intended to be civil when she arrived, to have sandwiches
and talk about other aspects of the case before he got to Anthony
Corino. Instead, the judge was the first subject out of his mouth.

"I thought you checked up on these judges. I thought you were
supposed to know what was going on down there at Centre Street."

"Spare me the sarcasm. What's on your mind?"

"Anthony Corino."

"That much I figured out myself."

"How did you check him out?"

"Same as the others. I asked around about him and I checked
the file at the firm where people put notes about judges. After every
case you're supposed to write one up. Not everybody does, but it's
still helpful. I started there. I went through all the judges on the
P-wheel list and made notes on index cards, with ratings, plus and
minus."

She stopped abruptly. "Why am I telling you all this? I did the
research to my own satisfaction and I used the results to make a
decision. Period."

"And you decided that Tony Boy Corino was an okay judge for
us to have."

"It looks that way, doesn't it."

"What about 'Hang 'Em High' Corino? Is he in your files, too?"

"Yes, I saw that, too."

"But you didn't mention it."

"No."

"You didn't think it was important."

"Not very."

"My God! Not very?"

"The man gives tough sentences. I admit that could make a
difference down the line. I told you after we drew him that we would
have been better off with the other one."

"How could you think he was acceptable at all?"

"Sentencing only matters if the verdict is *guilty.*"

"At which point it matters very much. And if a judge is a hardass, guilty is that much more likely."

"*If* he's a hardass. I don't think Corino is."

"What do you think he is?"

"A judge who doesn't fit an easy category. A human being."

"I'm not talking about easy categories. I'm talking about what's on the record. What the man has done over time. You want to know what I've heard about him? That he's big on retribution. That he's a blue-collar racist who also likes to make examples of wayward upper-class whites. Does that sound like our kind of judge?"

"It's obviously not going to do me any good trying to convince you I wasn't wrong. Let's drop it for now, okay? We're stuck with the man. Let's make the best of it."

Make the best of it! Ryan thought. He had hoped he was wrong about having trouble working with a woman; it didn't look that way. A judge's alleged humanity had never been number one on his list of things to count on.

When he got home he parked himself in front of the television. He'd had enough reality for the day.

The phone rang. It was Jennifer.

"I heard we have a hanging judge."

"Where did you hear that?"

"A reporter called to ask my reaction."

"We agreed you wouldn't talk to reporters."

"Don't change the subject."

Ryan did not like her tone, but he understood the reason for it. "It's true the judge's nickname is 'Hang 'Em High.' That's not the same as a hanging judge."

"It sounds the same to me. How did we get this judge?"

"It's a random process. They spin a wheel, like roulette."

"I thought Kassia had experience operating in this court. I thought that was the idea."

"Yes. She does."

"Then why do we have a hanging judge?"

Ryan closed his eyes and counted silently to three to keep from snapping back at her—her anger about this was not that different from his. He was about to tell her that Miller had researched the judges, not him, but he stopped himself. It would not help to show Jennifer a crack between her lawyers into which she could later hammer a wedge. The fact that he was already thinking of firing Miller was separate from this.

"We went over the judges' records carefully. Corino is all right for us." Not an easy lie to tell, but it would get easier. "He's not the best, but he's not the worst, either."

"I don't like that nickname."

"He has another nickname, if that helps."

"What is it?"

"Tony Boy. That's not so threatening."

She was silent.

"What did you tell the reporter?" he asked her.

"I said I was innocent and I was looking forward to proving it in court."

"All right. That's all right. But don't do it again."

"I'm not a four-year-old, Michael. You don't have to talk to me that way."

No winning that one. "What else did he ask you?"

"It was a she. She asked me about Kassia. Was she my lawyer?"

"What did you say?"

"I said I'd met Kassia and I thought she was very smart, and that she was working with Mr. Rosen."

He let out his breath. "Jennifer, in words of one syllable: *Don't talk to the press*. If any reporters call, say no comment. You shouldn't answer the phone yourself. What happened to the guy with the brown suit?"

"Brown suit? Oh. You mean Bo. He was only for a few weeks, when the reporters were all over the place."

"Then let the maid answer the phone, or get a machine and screen your calls. For the next week or two, especially."

"Why? Is something happening?"

"Yes. But we've got to be extremely careful about not letting word get out in advance. I mean it. It's not a joke."

"None of this is a joke. You don't have to tell me that. What's going to happen?"

"I'm going to make my debut as your lawyer."

15

THE FIRST STEP WAS A CONVERSATION WITH JOE Becker.

"I need to see you," Ryan told him.

The A.D.A. suggested lunch in Chinatown. "Dutch treat," he said.

On the way down, Ryan went over his strategy. If Corino disqualified him, the least it meant was losing any chance of getting Jennifer into court before the baby came. The best way to avoid that was to convince Becker not to challenge him in the first place.

I have the Sixth Amendment on my side, he would tell Becker: the accused is entitled to representation by counsel. The courts all say the right to counsel is meaningless unless you can have the counsel of your choice. I'm her choice. The judge is going to see it my way and if he doesn't I'm going to appeal all the way to the Supreme Court. It's a guaranteed major delay in the trial. You're going to lose witnesses, and the ones you keep are going to lose their memory. You're going to suffer months of the worst publicity you ever saw. And when it's all over, assuming you can still find a jury anywhere in the country that will listen to you, you're going to be no better off than if you hadn't bothered, because I'm going to win on appeal. And if all that isn't enough to convince you not to challenge me, maybe I'm talking to the wrong man. Maybe I should go tell this same story to my old friend the D.A. and see what policy he wants to follow on this.

It was a bluff, mostly. Delay meant losing the advantage of Jennifer's pregnancy, so if Becker got Ryan disqualified, the decision to appeal the ruling would not be automatic. But Becker didn't know that.

Becker was waiting at the restaurant when Ryan arrived.

"My materials on the case are in the office, so I can't do much show-and-tell for you here," Becker said after the waiter brought their drinks. "I did bring one or two things along I thought you might want to have a look at. We're doing pretty well. We got a good judge . . ."

"Whoa. Wait a minute." Ryan did not want to hear any more.

Becker, cut off in mid word, was obviously bewildered. He poured some of his Chinese beer into a glass, but he did not drink it. "Something wrong?"

"No, nothing's wrong. Sorry if I startled you."

"It's okay." The A.D.A. took a sip of his beer. "You have something you want to talk to me about."

"I've decided to get back into trial work."

Becker was about of offer congratulations, but something he saw in Ryan's face killed the impulse.

Ryan said, "I've found a case I believe in, one I think I can do a good job on. Most important, it's a client who really needs me."

"They're the best kind," Becker said carefully.

"That's the heart of it for me," Ryan went on. "It's somebody who has trouble trusting lawyers and communicating with them. It's a tough case. I don't for a minute think I can guarantee an acquittal, but the important thing is I can make sure she has a defense she believes in, which she hasn't had so far."

Becker's eyes narrowed when Ryan said "she."

"Maybe you should tell me who this is."

"Jennifer Kneeland Ryan," her father-in-law said evenly, holding the prosecutor's eyes with his own.

Becker said nothing. He looked fixedly at his beer glass, looked at Ryan, picked up the beer glass and drained it. He turned in his chair and waved across the restaurant for a waiter. "Check, please."

"We have a lot to talk about." Ryan did not want him to leave.

"We don't have fuck-all to talk about, Mr. Ryan. I told you about my case. I had you in my office and I told you about my case! What kind of shit do you think you're pulling?"

"I'm not pulling anything. When I came to your office I had no idea . . ."

"Bull. Shit." Becker made it two distinct words.

Ryan said, "If you think about it, you didn't tell me anything." For once he was grateful for a waiter's sluggishness delivering a check.

"Save your breath." Becker waved for the waiter again.

"I'm sorry you feel this way," Ryan said, fighting contradictory impulses to sound soothing and to respond to Becker's anger. "I wanted to tell you this in person, before I made it formal. I didn't want to take you by surprise any more than I had to."

The waiter arrived. "Want order?"

Becker stood up, almost colliding with the waiter, and threw a ten dollar bill on the table. "See you in court, counselor." He picked up his briefcase and strode toward the door.

The waiter watched him go. "Want order?" he asked Ryan.

"Sorry." Ryan left Becker's ten on the table and added one of his own. Dutch treat.

Ryan hurried west from the corner of Bowery and Canal, threading his way through the Chinatown lunchtime crowd, looking for a public phone that worked. Neighborhood people thronged at the foodstalls, eager for fresh fish and fruit, sold side by side. The crisp air of early autumn was full of overlapping conversations in excited Chinese.

Spotting a row of phones on the next corner, he stopped at the head of the subway stairs. Two squat women with plastic shopping bags almost knocked him down from behind. He grabbed the handrail as they shouted at him in Spanish and maneuvered their way past for the descent into the maelstrom of people below.

Unaccountably, one of the phones on the corner was not broken. He called the D.A.'s office.

"He's on his way to lunch, Mr. Ryan," Griglia's secretary told him. "Can I take a message?"

"Can you catch him?"

"Hang on," the secretary said, responding to the urgency in Ryan's voice.

"What is it, Michael?" the D.A. asked without preamble.

"I need to talk to you. It's important."

"I've got a lunch date and then a meeting with the mayor at two-thirty."

"We could ride up there together."

"Not Gracie Mansion. City Hall."

"You must have fifteen minutes you can spare."

"Is it really that important?"

"Absolutely."

"Okay. You can buy me lunch. But I want you to know I'm giving up a chance to do important office business—with the sexiest A.D.A. in living memory."

Francesco Carlo Griglia was a first generation Italian-American, son of a cobbler, who had fought his way up from the Lower East Side. Straight A's at City College had led to an honors scholarship at law school, where he and Michael Ryan had been rivals and allies. They had entered the school's moot-court competition as partners and handily made the semifinal round, where disagreement over what law applied to their hypothetical case led to a schizophrenic brief and two oral arguments so disparate they might have been given by opposing sides. They did not reach the finals. Francesco, by then mostly called Franky, did not deign to participate in the consolation round. It was not to be the last time he would refuse to blink in a dispute with Ryan.

They were both a lot older now, Ryan reflected as he waited for the D.A. to join him. Maybe this time they could find the road to a middle ground.

Ryan had picked a four-star restaurant west of the courthouse, in the old meat-packing district by the Hudson River. It was the one place nearby he was sure they would get a table, be left in peace, and not run into anyone from the D.A.'s office. Not at fifty dollars and up per person per lunch.

"The first thing is," Ryan said when the D.A. was seated, "this lunch isn't a bribe."

"Lucky thing we go back twenty-five years so I can justify it if somebody asks. What's on your mind? No—I know what's on your mind."

Could it be? Could Becker have told him already?

"It's got to be about Joe Becker, right? What's the matter, he's not cooperating?"

"No, that's not it. Tell you what, let's eat some lunch and catch up a little. We'll have time at the end for the good stuff."

"I don't have all afternoon."

"They serve small portions."

Griglia laughed. "Okay."

They both ordered the three-course fixed-price lunch. Griglia had red wine, Ryan drank water.

"I didn't realize how long it's been," Griglia said.

"Eleven and a half years."

"Cristo! That long?"

"Who's counting? You look good. Better than you did then."

The D.A. was meticulously barbered and manicured, his shark-skin suit hand tailored. He had put on twenty pounds or more in the years right after law school; now he looked as if he had taken it all back off.

"I was a dumb greaseball in those days. I was forty before I figured out all that oily energy wouldn't get me where I wanted to be."

"You there now?"

"Temporarily."

"You're going to run."

"It's no secret."

"After that?"

"Who knows? I'll be happy to serve the people as D.A."

Ryan laughed. "I bet you will. Going to shake things up a little?"

"We'll see. I have big shoes to fill. Dewey. Hogan."

"That's all?"

"I have great admiration for all my illustrious predecessors. What about you? You don't look so hot. Been through a lot, the past few years, huh?"

"I'm glad I suggested this lunch—I needed some compliments."

When they were finishing their main course Griglia said, "Okay, Michael, why are we here?"

"This is my second lunch today. My first one was with Joe Becker. He walked out on me."

"I thought you said he wasn't the problem."

"Not the way you meant. I had something to tell him. He got upset. I wanted you to hear about it from me first."

"Okay. I'm listening."

Ryan speared a piece of baby carrot and moved it around his plate. Looked up at Griglia. "Jennifer Ryan has a new lawyer."

"So? We can handle it. How bad can it be? Edward Bennet Williams is dead."

Ryan focused on the carrot. "It's me."

"What? What are you talking about, it's you?"

"I'm defending Jennifer Ryan."

"What! For killing your son?"

"For *not* killing my son." There was no other way to play it.

"O madonna sifilitica! What do you think, we indict people for the hell of it? I'm surprised at you."

"She says she didn't do it." This was no place for Ryan's true opinion. "I believe her."

The D.A. chewed on that with the last bite of his duck breast.

"So what do you want? You want me to drop the charges because you think she's innocent? This is craziness, Michael. There are a thousand lawyers in this town who could defend the woman."

"She doesn't think so."

"What the hell does she know?"

"Defendants get their choice of counsel."

"Come on, Michael, this is bullshit. We know better. You wanted to talk to me, that isn't what you wanted to say."

"I'm going to do this, Franky. I'm going to defend her. I thought it was crazy, too, at first. But not anymore."

"I'll tell you something, Michael. I have a duty to the people of this community, and don't laugh, because I take it seriously. The cops say this woman is guilty. Becker says she's guilty. The grand jury says she's guilty. My job is to see she gets put away. The way I see it, having you in court prejudices the people's case, and I don't see how I can let that happen."

"That's why I wanted to talk to you. This is important to me, and I'm going to push it as far as I have to. Bear in mind, the federal appeals process doesn't exactly intimidate me."

"Sure, and I have a whole appeals bureau that lives to make law at that level. This isn't about how big anybody's dick is, arguing appeals.''

"All I want is to try this case.''

"I don't see what I can do for you.''

A waiter exchanged their empty main course plates for dessert plates arranged like tiny sweet sculptures. Neither man picked up a fork.

"I don't know what to say, Michael.''

Ryan knew what to say; he did not know whether to say it. He sat there with the name in his mouth unspoken, a bitter morsel of history.

"What?" the D.A. demanded. "What else? I can see it in your face. Joey Baldasaro, right? That's what you're going to say to me, huh, Michael? You still hold it against me, all these years later because I went after a lot of slimeball drug dealers and your pal Joey got a shiv in the belly.''

"He was helping me make a case.''

"That's a long time ago, Michael.''

"Fifteen defendants walked when Joey B. got gutted on Fifty-fourth Street because you couldn't wait the way I asked you to. Between my people and the Bureau we lost eighteen, twenty man-years of work on that case because Joey wasn't there to testify for us. So if I hold it against you thirteen years later, I figure I've got a few more years coming.''

The D.A. did not reply.

"You owe me, Franky. I never thought I'd say it. I never thought I'd collect.''

"I owe you. You think I owe *you* for that?''

"I think you owe a lot of people, starting with every single person those fifteen dirt buckets victimized until they finally got put away or whacked out. But yeah, I think you owe me, too.''

"And for that you expect me to go against my own people, tell them how to run their cases? Go against everything that makes sense to me about this?''

"No. I expect you to decide that your office doesn't need to spend the time and money it's going to cost pursuing this to the Supreme Court. Or the bad publicity. Think about what the papers will say: The D.A.'s office is trying to deprive the defendant of the lawyer she wants and at the same time they're keeping the father of the poor murdered young man from vindicating the daughter-in-law he believes in. Why are they being so pointlessly cruel? What are they afraid of?''

Ryan could see Griglia getting ready to erupt.

"Understand me, Franky, that's not what I want, and I won't do anything to create it. I don't have to: it's inevitable once Becker tries to get me disqualified. If he does. But there's no reason why he should. And if he doesn't, then I'm okay and you're okay. That's all there is to it. Joey Baldasaro is to remind you that your first idea about how a thing *has* to be done isn't always right."

"And how the hell am I going to convince Becker it makes any sense for him to go up against you without fighting it first?"

"It's in his interest not to fight it. The case will get a ton of attention. Why should he start out being the villain?"

"I don't think he'll see it that way."

"You could always take him off it. Try the case yourself."

"You're kidding, right?"

He was, but he didn't see any reason to admit it.

The D.A. pushed his untouched dessert plate away. "Look, Michael, I see it means a lot to you. I confess I don't get it but, hell, we stopped seeing the world the same way a lot of years ago. I'd like to help. I don't see how I can. If it was anything else, you know? Joey Baldasaro, well, I'm sorry about that. I should have waited to make those arrests. You were right, I was wrong. It happens."

"I was hoping you wouldn't let it happen this time."

When they parted Ryan had no idea if he had done himself and his client any good. Or any harm.

Late that afternoon he got his first sign, in the form of a phone call from Justice Anthony R. Corino.

While he did not want to interfere with anyone's First Amendment rights, the judge said, he'd heard from the D.A.'s office that Ryan was thinking of filing papers as counsel of record for Jennifer Ryan. Considering the inflammatory nature of such a filing and the probability that the D.A.'s office would oppose Ryan's qualification, they had asked Corino to seal any such papers and put a gag order on the related proceedings. Corino, sensitive to the press circus already generated by the case, was inclined to grant such an order. The judge hoped that in the meantime Ryan would choose to conduct himself in a manner that would not compromise his later adherence to the order, if one were issued.

Miller had been right. Tony Boy Corino was not a judge who played exactly by the book.

* * *

Ryan filed his papers as Jennifer Kneeland Ryan's defense counsel the next day. Two days later Joe Becker filed his motion to disqualify.

16

AS SOON AS IT WAS READY, RYAN WENT OVER HIS AS-sociate's draft of the brief for Judge Corino on right to counsel. It wasn't terrible, but it badly needed restructuring and rewriting. Ryan thanked Shible, god of justice, for the New York court decision that was the keystone of his argument, a case where the defense lawyer was disqualified, appealed immediately, and won on the grounds that his client had the right to be represented by the lawyer of her choice.

Most rulings could not be appealed until after the trial was over, especially in criminal cases. There was a long line of federal cases allowing immediate appeals when a lawyer was disqualified, but it had recently been overturned, and this was the only recent state case. Not being able to appeal immediately meant sitting out the trial on the sidelines and then having to start all over again from the beginning if the appeal succeeded. Not an acceptable alternative.

When he was done rewriting the brief he faxed it to Miller for comment. Until he was sure he was going to replace her she was the lawyer he had to work with.

He was ready to quit for the day when his secretary told him Kassia Miller was on the line.

"I read your brief," she said. "I checked the cases, too."

"Very thorough."

"Do you remember a New York case called 'Matter of Abrams, John Anonymous, et al, appellants'?"

"Sure." The very case he had just been thanking Shible for. "It's my best case on the defendant's right to have counsel of her choice. Some very strong, clear language."

"That's all?" she said.

"No, it's also a nice example of a pretrial appeal from a disqualification order in a criminal case."

There was a silence, and then she said, "Do you have a copy of it handy?"

"It was here before lunch. My desk is about a foot deep in papers."

"Dig it out. I'll wait."

"Why don't you just tell me what's on your mind."

"It's better if you read it. Everything before the right-to-counsel language."

He found the case, still folded back the way the associate had given it to him—to the court's discussion of the defendant's right to choose a lawyer, with the important passages highlighted in yellow.

"Got it," he said, and turned to the front of the opinion, which dealt with the defendant's right to appeal his lawyer's disqualification before the trial started. Ryan had not looked at this part of it before, just checked in the headnote summary to be sure that the decision went the way he wanted.

Reading the opinion itself, he saw that the court was carving out a very narrow distinction and that what he needed to know was in the areas being pared away. He was not sure he got it all, so he read it again.

"How the hell did we miss this?" he said when he was sure he understood what he had read.

"What do you mean, we, paleface?" she asked—the punchline of an old joke, delivered without humor.

She's right, he thought. I missed it, she didn't.

"The language is ambiguous," he ventured.

"Only if English isn't your mother tongue."

It wasn't that open and shut. He could see how the associate might have misread it. But the language was clear if you read it carefully enough. Basically, the highest court in the state had said that if a defense lawyer in a criminal matter was disqualified, the decision to disqualify him could *not* be appealed until the trial was over. The case Ryan was relying on, which went against the rule, was an exception. Jennifer's case was not: it would follow the rule.

Which meant that they were completely at the mercy of Hang 'Em High Corino. If Corino said Ryan was out, he had no recourse. The trial would proceed without him.

"This makes Corino even more important," he could not resist saying.

She ignored the provocation. "There's no reason it can't still be a good precedent for us. On the right to counsel issue."

"I suppose."

He had to be careful. Reversals like this made it easy to forget what was important. Right to counsel was the main issue. If he won, he wouldn't need to appeal. And if he lost he would want to delay the appeal anyway. It was more important to get the trial under way while Jennifer was still pregnant.

Still, he had missed something crucial. It was no excuse that the language he wanted to quote started on the eighth page and his associate had given him the opinion folded open to that page.

"Thanks," he said. "It's a good thing you caught this. I'd better get back to my brief."

He hung up and told his secretary to find the associate for him. He scribbled notes for the tongue lashing the young lawyer had earned. This will hurt me more than it hurts you, Ryan thought bitterly. How many times had he come down harder on Ned than he had meant to, with the mistaken conviction that he was performing his fatherly duty, doing the boy some good. Paying attention. Avoiding his own father's mistakes. So much of his life had been about avoiding George's mistakes.

Waiting for the associate, he thought about Kassia Miller. Hearing her say "us" and "we," he had thought maybe I should say something. Now he felt he had been right to let it go by. Maybe he was being hasty, thinking about firing her. Her catching the bad language in his big case did not make up for Corino, but it was a factor to consider, and so was his own lapse in missing it.

Meanwhile he had to talk to Jennifer about this. If Corino disqualified him it would have major implications for her now. They would need to decide on a strategy to follow.

She was in when he called.

"There's something we have to talk about."

"About my trial."

"Yes. It's technical but it's important. I just found a court decision that says if the judge disqualifies me we can't appeal until the trial is over. It means you might have to go to trial with somebody else as your lawyer. If you get convicted we could appeal my disqualification then, and if we won you'd get a new trial with me as your lawyer."

"Two trials? Can they do that? Isn't that double jeopardy or something?"

"Well, no. Double jeopardy is something else."

"You're saying I have to be convicted before they'll let you be my lawyer."

He could not help smiling. She was wrong on the details, but she had the essence of it.

"It could work out that way."

"No," she said emphatically.

"It's not a matter of choice."

"Yes it is. I won't hire another lawyer. I trust you. I want you as my lawyer now. For this trial."

"And that's what I want, believe me. I'm working as hard as I can to be sure that I am."

"Then why do we have to talk about losing before it happens?"

"I want you to have time to think about it. Because if we *don't* win on this we have to decide what we're going to do next, and we won't have much time to make up our minds."

17

NOT ENOUGH DAYS LATER, RYAN STRUGGLED OUT OF bed with the knowledge that he was hours from the oral arguments on Joe Becker's motion to disqualify him as Jennifer's defense lawyer. It would be his first appearance in court in more than three years. He had tried, the whole sleepless night, to reassure himself with the fact that this was nothing like a trial: no jury to convince, no witnesses to deal with, no line of proof to keep track of. Just an argument in front of a judge, like a debate or an argument in moot court, the kind he had been so good at in law school.

Food was out of the question; he made himself a pot of strong coffee. Rehearsing his argument in front of the bathroom mirror, he nicked himself shaving for the first time in years. He stood over the basin, tissue stuck to the cut on his chin, and watched his hands shake.

* * *

Justice Anthony R. Corino of the New York State Supreme Court met with Michael Ryan and Joseph Becker in a borrowed conference room. A court officer lounged outside the room to insure their privacy.

The man who was going to decide Ryan's fate in this case, and possibly Jennifer's as well, was average height, round faced and mostly bald. He was not fat, but his well-cut suit did not fully conceal a slight paunch. Hang 'Em High Corino's most striking feature was thick black eyebrows; from the way he held his head, he was aware of their dramatic value. Beneath them his brown eyes were small but intense.

"Now, I think I understand the basic issues that we're here to talk about. I read the papers you both submitted. Not everybody would, but I wanted to get full enjoyment out of our show this morning. And I must say, Mr. Ryan, without in any way implying any resolution of the matter or any prejudice to either side, that I am grateful to you for providing me with some entertainment in an otherwise dismal week."

Ryan thought it would be a good idea to smile. Becker did not look amused.

"You're welcome, your honor," Ryan croaked. He tilted the pitcher of water in front of him to pour a glass. He did not want to lift it.

"I don't want you to think, because I said that, that I don't take this seriously," the judge said. "We are addressing substantial rights here and I intend to give this question serious consideration. Before we start I want to remind you this is not a debating society. The purpose of this argument is to help me understand the issues. I don't want to be lectured or badgered. Most of all I don't want to be dazzled by your rhetoric. I want to be educated. Clarity counts. Understood?"

Both lawyers said, "Yes, your honor." Ryan felt as if he were in grade school.

He was glad Becker was starting. Courtroom stage fright was good for you, the conventional wisdom went. It made you sharp. This was something else: a hammer beating against the inside of his head, a vacuum pump sucking air from his chest, and a fist squeezing his guts. He had been away too long.

"Mr. Becker."

The A.D.A. stood up at his end of the table. Someone had put a small lectern in front of him; Ryan had none. Becker put a stack of pages from a yellow legal pad on the lectern and squared their edges. He cleared his throat, leaned down to take drink of water.

The court stenographer sat at her machine next to the judge, in the middle of the long table, fingers poised. Ryan saw it all with greater clarity than he would have thought possible.

"Your honor. Mr. Ryan," Becker said, "I'm going to start out by conceding that under ordinary circumstances a defendant is entitled to be represented by the counsel of his or her choice. But—and this is why we are here today—the courts have said repeatedly that in the interest of the orderly administration of justice the defendant may have to give up what the defendant *claims* is her first choice. The question to be asked is: Does the defendant's choice harm the people's ability to present their case? It's difficult to imagine how that could be more true than it is here."

He looked straight at Ryan, then at the judge. "This is not an easy thing to do. I am going to say things now that make me uncomfortable. Uncomfortable saying them in the presence of this man. He's a bereaved father. I don't want to remind him of that, and I don't want to turn that into a weapon against him. And I take my own unease to be a measure of the effect this man is going to have on the whole proceeding if he is permitted to appear as defense counsel."

This is going to be about me, Ryan thought. He had been so busy focusing on the law he had lost sight of how inevitable that was.

"It's unfair to the people of the State of New York," Becker went on, "and to me as prosecutor on their behalf to be put in the position of having to overcome this man's relationship to the decedent. Our system recognizes the strength of the sympathy that attaches to the bereaved. And it is careful to prevent misuse of that sympathy—so careful that the courts have said a prosecutor can't, during his summation, point even once to the crying parents of the deceased victim sitting in the gallery.

"Does it make sense then for us to permit in the courtroom a defense counsel who with his every word and gesture demonstrates to the jury the emotions of a bereaved father, and with those same words and gestures expresses support for the defendant, not only during his summation but throughout the trial?

"We all know that a lawyer is not allowed to speak of his own personal opinion of the guilt or innocence of a defendant. But by merely sitting next to the defendant in the courtroom Mr. Ryan suggests that he doesn't believe she's guilty. After all, Michael Ryan is the person now alive who is closest to the victim. We have to ask ourselves, 'What is he doing here?' He's like a character witness, an unsworn character witness. If he came to court and testified as a character witness I could cross-examine him. If he testified as a character witness he would open up the whole area of the defendant's character for me to examine. But there he sits, vouching for her by his very presence, and I am not allowed to offer a single witness to contradict that impression. Your honor, I ask you, is this fair to the people of the State of New York?''

Becker paused expectantly and Ryan was sure that Corino was going to say "no it's not fair" and end the whole thing right there.

"And what is it about this man that makes him so special as a lawyer?" Becker asked. "How many good—no, excellent—criminal defense lawyers are there in this city? This is not an indigent defendant. She can afford the best. And who does she want? A man who has never defended a criminal case in the courts of this state. I ask you, your honor, is this credible? Is there not likely to be some other motive at work here? Might it not be that there is an attempt here to unduly influence the jury?''

Becker turned and glared at Ryan: I accuse. So much for the prosecutor's sensitivity to the bereaved father.

"And think of this man's emotional involvement in this case. What are we going to do, six, eight months down the line, after the defendant has been convicted, when this defendant appeals her conviction as a murderer and bases her appeal on the theory that she did not have effective assistance of counsel, that this man—because of who he is, because of his relationship to the victim—was too wrapped up emotionally in this case to do a decent job representing her? Does the court want to put itself in that position, of inviting that kind of appeal?''

Ryan was shaken in a way he remembered from his earliest days as a federal prosecutor. You filed your papers and you thought they were okay, and then you got answering papers and you thought: They shot me full of holes and I'll never recover. It was worse with argument. You heard the other side and you thought: It's all over, they're going to win. Even if they misquoted precedent and misstated facts and law, you were sure no one would see through it.

"Mr. Ryan will no doubt make a speech today full of references to the Constitution," Becker went on. "But however much he wraps himself in the flag, his attempt to obscure the simple facts must fail.

"The truth is that this man came to me as the bereaved father and got me to disclose elements of my case. And now he turns around and he is going to use that information on behalf of the defense. Is this a person whose claim of upholding the system is worthy of belief?

"The truth is that this man, who the defendant claims is the only person she is willing to have represent her, is not a criminal defense lawyer of great or even ordinary reputation. His uniqueness rests only in one thing—he is the father of the man for whose murder this defendant has been indicted. And there is no plausible reason for her to choose this lawyer except to make improper use of that fact."

Becker ended on the accusation, skipping the usual request for a favorable ruling. He stood at his portable lectern as if he were waiting for applause.

"Very good, Mr. Becker," Corino said. "A little heavy on the rhetoric, but all in all a decent job."

Ryan heard the judge praising his adversary and tried to pretend it was a meaningless courtesy. He had a sense of floating over a scene he was not part of. He focused on a single goal: his emotional ability to try this case was an issue; what mattered here was staying in control of himself. If he missed a point in his argument, that was all right, the judge could read it in the brief. But if he appeared anything but cool and professional it would be fatal.

"Mr. Ryan, I presume you have something to say about all that."

"I do your honor." The words came out automatically.

He stood slowly. He looked at Becker. Not to be polite, to buy time.

"Well," he said, and cleared his throat. "I must say, your honor, I'm impressed with the range of Mr. Becker's emotions, but I submit that what is at issue here is the law, not emotions." His voice was strong. Hearing it made him feel steadier. "And the law is settled. Time and again the federal courts, and the courts of the State of New York, have repeated that nothing is more vital to a person accused of a crime than the right to be represented by counsel at all stages of a criminal proceeding, most especially at trial. And the courts have been virtually unanimous in pointing out that the right to counsel is empty unless the defendant has the right to be represented by a lawyer of his or her own choosing.

"Why? Because the relationship between a lawyer and client is a uniquely close and trusting one, nowhere more so than in a criminal trial, and among criminal trials nowhere more so than in the trial of serious felonies. To have an effective defense, a defendant must have complete confidence in her advocate, and the two of them must work together under extraordinary pressure. The state's highest court has said clearly that an individual's right to an attorney of his choice is too important to be disregarded simply because the prosecutor's task may be made easier if he is allowed to divide and conquer his opposition.

"The Court of Appeals made that statement in a case involving ticket scalping. Ticket scalping! Consider how much more important it is for the defendant in a *murder trial* to have a lawyer she believes in and wants to work with. This is a question of the defendant's most fundamental rights."

Ryan paused, for effect and because his mouth was so dry he was having trouble forming the words. He drank some water.

"It's true that the courts have said this right is not absolute. But in the rare cases where a court has limited the defendant's right to choose any counsel she wants, it has done so reluctantly."

As Ryan spoke he had been searching Corino's face for some sign of a reaction. He saw nothing but a round bald face and black eyebrows and a sardonic smile, as if Hang 'Em High was doing just that to Ryan: hanging him up to twist in the wind.

Corino cocked his head curiously and Ryan realized with a chill of panic that he was standing there in silence.

"Why does Mr. Becker ask you to disqualify me?" he asked more ringingly than he had intended. "Is my entry into the case calculated to cause delay? Exactly the opposite. In fact, it is Mr. Becker who would cause delay, endangering my client's vital right to a speedy trial, by forcing her to search for another lawyer acceptable to her, a search that would be long and difficult and not likely to succeed.

"If it is not delay that concerns Mr. Becker, it is certainly not that I have a conflict of interest. My contact with the prosecution was minimal. Mr. Becker told me nothing of importance, nothing he had not already told the lawyer then representing Mrs. Ryan.

"As for his charge that I somehow fooled him into giving me information, at the time I saw him Mrs. Ryan had not yet approached me to represent her. I spoke to Mr. Becker in all honesty as the father of the victim. I held nothing back from him. I did not misrepresent myself in any way.

"When it comes to misrepresenting, it is Mr. Becker who takes the prize. He knows my record in the ten years I was a prosecutor in the federal court down the block in Foley Square. His chief concern in the meeting he and I had was that my greater experience in criminal trials might lead me to interfere with his handling of the case. And to try this case I have associated with me a talented lawyer, one with almost a decade's experience in criminal defense in Manhattan."

Ryan took a breath, then plunged ahead. "I said earlier, your honor, that this was a question of law, not emotion. I particularly want to keep this question out of the realm of emotion because Mr. Becker is so eager to base his argument on unsupportable allegations about *my* emotions.

"I submit, your honor, that the dangers Mr. Becker has waved before the court like so many red flags are in reality that many red herrings.

"Am I supposed to turn this client away because I believe passionately in her cause? Because I care deeply about the outcome of her case? Do we debar a lawyer because he believes passionately in his client's innocence? No more than we say to a lawyer in a personal-injury case, do not be moved by the harm done to your client. Or to a civil-rights lawyer, do not take this case if your compassion for the outcast and oppressed burns too bright. We do not question them, we applaud their zeal.

"Turn it around . . . What about a prosecutor disgusted by the horrible deeds of the defendant? A prosecutor who sees himself as an avenging, protecting angel. Do we disqualify him for *his* passion? Of course not.

"There is ample evidence that lawyers do best who believe passionately in the cause of their clients."

Ryan paused to drink more water and let that last sink in. He was still floating but no longer felt out of control.

"It's an old maxim that if you can't beat the other side's case you attack the other side's lawyer. That is what is happening here, and with that ancient and none-too-admirable tactic, Mr. Becker threatens the most fundamental right of a woman who is about to stand trial for the most serious crime there is, a crime of which she maintains her complete innocence.

"If the judicial system of this state and this nation offers her no other comfort, it must at least respect her right to undergo this ordeal with the support of the lawyer who inspires her faith and trust."

Ryan sat down. He was numb.

Corino looked appraisingly from one of them to the other. "Well, gentlemen, I thank you for your time. I don't have any questions at the moment. If I do, I know where to reach you. You'll be hearing from me when I make up my mind on this." He stood to leave. Becker shot to attention. Ryan was still sitting. "Don't forget that gag order," Corino said in parting. "It's still in effect."

Ryan spent the afternoon in a fog and ended up at the Shamrock.

"Michael, it's not Friday and it's before dinner," Kelly said. "You okay?"

"Ask me next week. You serve dinner at the bar?"

"To you? Sure. You hungry?"

"No, but I didn't eat all day. They say you're supposed to."

Ryan was hungrier than he thought. The food was good. After he ate he closed himself off against the hubbub of Kelly's after-work crowd and alternated draft beer and Irish whiskey until Kelly decided it was time to pour him into a taxi for the short ride home.

18

THE MORNING BROUGHT RYAN THE SURE KNOWLEDGE that he could not afford self-indulgent binges. Whether Corino disqualified him or not, he had to press ahead preparing Jennifer's defense. Miller was right—there was too much value in getting Jennifer into court while she was pregnant for them to lose any time along the way.

He called Craig Lawrence.

"Are you making any progress on the party?"

"I got the guest list from Rosen and I checked it through with his investigator. They hadn't got very far when Jennifer pulled the plug on them. So far we talked to a few people and added some names. Gate-crashers, people brought by people on the list. We're working on profiles. I didn't know how much you wanted to push before you got your go-ahead from the court."

"We're going full speed ahead. If I can't use it, my replacement will."

Jake Kaplan's list of names of the people Ned had arranged to lend mortgage money to rang no bells for Jennifer.

"Do you remember anything else about the man who threatened him?" Ryan asked her. "Or about the deal?"

"It was for a shopping center."

"How big?"

"The shopping center? I don't know. Big."

"The loan."

"Oh. I don't really remember. I think he said five million dollars."

"You said it was in New Jersey. Do you remember where?"

"Not near New York. Southern Jersey, I think."

Ryan rechecked the list of properties and loans Kaplan had included. No shopping centers in New Jersey. Nothing at all south of New Brunswick, which at most qualified as central Jersey. The closest he could find to Jennifer's description was an industrial park near Rahway. Three and a half million dollars. Not five, three point five.

"Could this be it?" He showed her the listing.

"I don't know. I suppose. I thought it was a shopping center."

Ryan took a chance on it. He called the company listed as mortgagor and asked for the man whose name was on the mortgage. He was expecting a runaround and he got one. But if persistence did not get him the man he was asking for, it got him the one he wanted.

"Harry's name is on the papers but he don't talk to nobody about it. Doctor's orders. You want to talk about the mortgage, you talk to me. If it's problems, I don't want to hear it. We had enough headaches with that damn mortgage."

The next afternoon, Ryan drove a rented car past a blue-on-white metal sign welcoming him to the Garden State Productivity Park. A blacktop drive ran between low dun-colored buildings, blankly windowless. The management office was in a small building at the far end of the road. A mock-Colonial portico did nothing to make it impressive. A smaller version of the WELCOME sign at the entrance was nailed over the door.

Karl Dorner, the man Ryan had spoken to on the phone, did not behave like a man who had read his own signs.

"I don't get why you're here. About the mortgage, you said. We pay on time. We don't like it, but we pay."

"Why don't you like it?" Ryan asked.

"Look, Mr. . . . ."

"Ryan."

"*Ryan?* You related to the bastard who got us the mortgage?"

"He's dead. I'm his father."

"I got nothing to say. You want to talk to my lawyer, that's okay with me. I'm a construction and building maintenance contractor. Harry was the deal man. It ended him up with a heart condition and high blood pressure."

"Not because of me. My son and I didn't talk much the past few years." Ryan felt dirty, using his life and Ned's this way. "I just came into managing this bunch of mortgages a couple of months ago, being executor. I'm trying to follow up, find out if there are any problems, see if maybe you want to prepay or make any other modifications."

Saying this, Ryan tried to create with his tone and the slump of his shoulders and the timing of his smile the idea that this burden was as oppressive to him as the mortgage terms were to Karl and Harry. Ryan had been good at this, once. An unspoken "we're in this together" had been one of his trump cards with juries. He could feel himself having to reach for it now, not always sure if he was making contact or not.

"Prepay? You mean pay it off now?" Karl was incredulous. "Where would we get the money? We're sucked dry paying the interest on the damn mortgage. If you want to make an adjustment, try this—adjust the interest to what it was supposed to be when Harry first made the deal."

"What do you mean?"

"Don't give me that shit—*What do you mean?* I mean the man came in here and quoted a decent interest rate with a two million dollar balloon at the end we could refinance, and by the time we were done the interest was up by three percent and it was pay every penny, down to zero in ten years, equal payments, no balloon. His principal changed his mind, he said. As if you didn't know."

"I *didn't* know. Didn't you have a commitment from him on the original terms?"

"Sure. Verbal. We asked for papers. He kept saying, they're on the way." Karl's mouth twisted as if he was going to spit. "Sure, the papers are on the way. Like, your check is in the mail, and I won't come in your mouth."

"Why didn't you tell him to go to hell? Why didn't you go to somebody else?"

"I don't get it. Whose side are you on?"

"I'm trying to understand what happened."

"What happened was the morning of the closing we get the news that the money isn't there unless we go along with the new terms and make these payments that eat up a hundred percent of our profit margin and put us in the red if our occupancy drops by more than one tenant. We had eight hundred thousand cash down on this deal that we were going to lose if we didn't close by a certain day, and that meant we lost our whole business we built up over the years, plus both houses, Harry's and mine. You tell me where else we were supposed to go."

Ryan thanked him for his trouble and got back into the rental for the trip to New York. He drove up the Turnpike through the stink of the refineries and tried not to think too much about the kind of young man who could have starred in Karl Dorner's unhappy drama.

Jennifer was not sure if either Karl or Harry could be the man Ned had told her was making threats. Despite the vagueness of her memory it seemed to Ryan too likely not to follow up. He had Craig Lawrence send someone down to check out the two men.

Lawrence called in a report after a couple of days.

"My guy was at a Rotary meeting last night in scenic Rahway, New Jersey. Met all kinds of friends of Karl's and Harry's. Karl Dorner doesn't have much good to say about Ned, or anybody else, either. Harry Bundesman, that's the other one, he took it hardest when they made the deal with Ned. They tell jokes about how he turned red and his heart popped. Shortly after which he moved away. Far away. For his heart condition."

"How far?"

"Arizona. You want me to send somebody out there?"

"How long ago did he leave?"

"About a year before Ned was killed."

"What about his partner?"

"Dorner? Didn't I say? He belongs to some serious religious denomination that doesn't believe in violence. Very devout—church deacon and all."

"Harry, too?"

"Yeah, but apparently he's a backslider. And there's no congregation in Arizona. He's become a Lutheran or something."

A stab of disappointment told Ryan how much he had been hoping this lead would pay off. He knew better—nothing was ever that easy. "Let's put it in the file. Maybe we'll find a way to use it."

19

ON THE DAY CORINO HAD SCHEDULED FOR HIS DECIsion Ryan got to the courthouse a half hour early, as planned. A wire-service reporter on his way from the cafeteria to the press room spotted him going through the metal detectors and strolled over.

"Hi. Been a long time."

"Hey, Zeke. How goes?" The two men had known each other in Ryan's days at the federal courthouse. "They have you over here now?"

"Here, there, wherever there's action. Today looked slow both places until you showed up. What's happening?"

"Remember what you used to call me?"

Zeke thought about it. "Refused Comment Ryan?"

"It was a bum rap then, but not today. Maybe later."

"Is that a promise?"

Something caught Zeke's eye behind Ryan.

"Well, look who's here."

It was too early for it to be Jennifer. Ryan turned.

"Joe Becker!" Zeke called, moving to intercept the prosecutor. "You have a minute? I was just talking to Mike Ryan."

Becker barely slowed down. "No comment, Zeke." He glared at Ryan as he said it. His voice was icy.

"Jesus, what's eating him?"

"I guess you'll have to wait and see," Ryan said.

He waited for the public elevator with a growing crowd of secretaries, lawyers and probable defendants. Meeting Zeke like that meant the press-room crowd would be thoroughly stirred up by the time Jennifer arrived. The closed courtroom upstairs would provoke them even more. By the time Corino announced his decision the courthouse reporters would have called out the troops for a full-bore press event.

Becker was sitting alone at the prosecution table when the court officer let Ryan into the courtroom. Ryan took his seat at the defense table and said, "Good morning."

Becker glanced over at him and said nothing.

Ryan took a fresh yellow legal pad from his briefcase and put it on the oak table in front of him; next to it he arranged four sharpened pencils—the beginnings of a ritual for the case. He needed familiar objects he could keep in order, keep control over, as an antidote to the poisonous desire to control everything in a process that was beyond controlling.

He looked around, getting his bearings. The courtroom was wood paneled but it seemed cold and alien to Ryan. The veneer had no depth or patina; there was none of the warmth or richness of the federal courtrooms he remembered.

The main courtroom door opened and Jeff Rosen, still Jennifer's attorney of record, ushered her along the center aisle and up to the rail. Kassia Miller was behind them. Ryan opened the gate for Jennifer and took her arm. She was pale under her makeup, but she seemed steady. He walked her to a chair at the defense table. She sat down stiffly and stared straight ahead. She did not look at Becker.

"You all right?" Ryan asked her.

She looked around. "It's bigger than I thought. High ceilings."

"They were big on grandeur in the thirties."

"It's awful. Cold. Is that where the jury sits?"

She was looking past Becker at the two long rows of seats behind a rail of their own along the courtroom's left wall.

"That's it."

"It gives me the creeps."

"You'll get used to it." He had no idea if she would. Her chatter was anxiety talking; he guessed that was usual for a first-time defendant.

"You get here all right?" Hoping to distract her.

"Manuel drove us, Daddy's chauffeur. I'm glad we have Bo again, the lobby downstairs was full of reporters. How did they know I was coming?"

"It's their job. You'll have to get used to it. It'll be a madhouse out there when we leave."

"I hate them."

"We all do, sometimes. You have to remember, though, they

have their uses. You don't want to antagonize them, talk down to them, anything like that.''

"I don't,'' she said defensively.

A door in the corner of the courtroom opened and Anthony Corino strode in wearing his black robes of office, followed by a law secretary.

"All rise,'' the court clerk said.

Here come the judge, Ryan remembered from an ancient comedy show. It did not make him smile.

Corino settled into his high-back leather chair on the bench. The law secretary put some papers in front of him. He ignored them. He began to speak, his delivery flat and uninflected.

"The question before the court is whether the offered representation of the defendant in this case will interfere with the orderly administration of justice or in some way work an unacceptable hardship on the prosecution. Mr. Becker makes a persuasive case that the answer is yes in both instances.

"Though I must say, Mr. Becker, I think you could have said more about the press. The pool of jurors in this case is likely to be seriously polluted by the flood of waste this unusual representation would certainly bring pouring out of the press. This case has already generated more than its share of press attention, and we haven't started yet.''

Ryan's stomach churned. Corino was making Becker's arguments for him.

Jennifer leaned close. A panicky whisper: "Why is he helping him like that?''

Corino's eyes flicked in their direction. "But this is a substantial right of the defendant's we are dealing with here, and Mr. Ryan makes that case adequately.''

Adequately!

"Now, Mr. Becker, these points that you make so persuasively, they all have to do with what takes place in my courtroom. What you describe does not strike me as the kind of thing I'm eager to see here, and it wouldn't have taken half the argument you employed to convince me of that. That is not the kind of courtroom I run.''

Ryan glanced at Becker. He had to give the prosecutor credit: he was not bursting his buttons with pride, not yet. He seemed to be taking his victory calmly.

"Here is what I have decided. I'm going to exclude the things Mr. Becker deplores from this courtroom. That's why I sit up here, to keep that kind of thing from happening.''

Corino's words made Ryan listen closer.

"Mr. Becker, on a provisional basis I have decided to deny your motion."

"What?" Becker could not keep the word from slipping out. "Sorry your honor."

Corino did not acknowledge the outburst or the apology.

"I'm going to deny the motion only on the condition that Mr. Ryan and his client accept certain stipulations that I'm going to suggest to them, and also on the condition that I'm going to make some rulings by which they will have to abide. You, too, Mr. Becker.

"In line with what I was saying about the pool of jurors, I intend to look very favorably on jury challenges for cause by the prosecution when the cause has to do with the juror's feelings about who Mr. Ryan is and why he is representing the defendant. I'm going to question the jurors myself, and I may well excuse some of them. Mr. Ryan, I'm not going to expect any difficulty from you on that score."

Ryan, not yet recovered from the impact of the judge's ruling, was not ready to think about the conditions. Jennifer grabbed his arm, wanting to know what was happening.

"We won," Ryan wrote on the yellow pad. This round, he added to himself.

"With regard to the press, I'm going to lift the seal on these proceedings, unless either of you has an objection."

Becker stood immediately. "I do, your honor."

"You do?"

"Yes, Judge."

"You want them sealed?"

"If the court please."

"For how long?"

"As long as we can. After sentencing."

"You mean after the *trial*, don't you, Mr. Becker? We may not need any sentencing."

"Yes, Judge, excuse me."

Ryan rose. "Your honor, I want to move that the seal be lifted immediately. It serves no further legitimate purpose." Let the world know Becker had tried to keep him out of the courtroom.

"Well, gents," Corino said, sitting back in his chair, his hands steepled in front of his face, "I begin to see how this is likely to go and I must say I don't like it. I'll make a decision about the seal on your motion papers by and by. One way or the other, everything else about this trial will be subject to the following order: no one connected with this trial is permitted to comment in any way on Mr. Ryan's relationship to the victim. The only thing anybody can say is that Mr. Ryan is a lawyer, and his representation in this case is professional and for a fee. You *are* getting a fee, Mr. Ryan? You'd better be and it better be substantial, or we can stop right now and I'll grant Mr. Becker's motion to disqualify you.''

''Yes, your honor, I'm being paid the going rate for trials of this kind.''

''Bravo. Now if anybody, reporter or anybody else, explicitly raises the question of Mr. Ryan's relationship to anyone living or dead, you are instructed to reply in the vein I just described, with the addition that no inference should be drawn from any other relationship besides lawyer and client.

''I'm not asking anybody to be dumb about this. We're not going to deny the truth, and I'm not going to make Mr. Ryan change his name. I *am* going to require him to omit references to his relationship to the victim or the defendant from his questions to witnesses and his other comments in front of the jury. You, too, Mr. Becker, though I can't see why you would want to mention it.

''I am also going to ask Mr. Ryan and his client to stipulate in writing that Mr. Ryan is the counsel of the defendant's choice and that she makes this choice with full information as to Mr. Ryan's lack of experience in the courts of this state and the facts of his record as a defense attorney. Also that the defendant makes this choice with full information as to the possibility that Mr. Ryan's emotional involvement in this case may impair his performance as an advocate on her behalf. And that with full awareness of these factors and all other relevant facts, the defendant waives all right to appeal the result in this case because of any alleged inadequacy of the representation provided by Mr. Ryan. Is that understood?''

Ryan rose slightly. ''It is, your honor.''

''Mr. Becker?''

''Yes, Judge.''

''That's it. I have copies of the necessary papers to make all this official. Mr. Ryan, you'll want to confer with your client to make sure she is willing to have you continue under these conditions. Can you have an answer for me by the morning?''

''We'll do our best, your honor.''

''One other item. The way my calendar looks, I'd like to set this down for trial on the first Monday in February and allow no more than six weeks for trial, including jury selection. If you have a problem with this, put it in writing and get it to me and your adversary by the end of next week.''

Corino stood up. "Adjourned." He was off the bench before the others were on their feet.

As soon as Corino cleared the courtroom door Becker was up the aisle and out.

Jennifer stood motionless, her eyes on the empty bench.

Kassia Miller let out a small whoop of joy. She was glowing with the double victory—Ryan's and the trial date that would assure them of having a pregnant client in the courtroom.

Ryan's own elation was weighed down by a general foreboding. Like a dog chasing a car, now that he'd caught it he had to face the question of what to do with it.

"We won?" Jennifer asked.

"Yes. But there are conditions we'll have to talk about."

"Is that the judge we'll have for the trial?"

"Yes."

"He didn't seem so bad."

I hope you're right, Ryan did not say.

Bo was waiting for them outside the courtroom, ready to form the point of a flying wedge to the elevator. The press was even denser and more agitated than Ryan had expected, all yammering for attention at once. Bright lights mounted atop television cameras or held by technicians turned the dismal green hallway into an instant TV studio.

Ryan stepped in front of Jennifer to shield her and held up a hand for silence. He did not get it, but the throng quieted slightly.

"I have a statement to make."

Microphones poked toward him from every side.

"I don't know what Mr. Becker told you, but we're under a partial gag order from the court. I can say only that I have accepted Mrs. Ryan's request to act as her defense counsel. I've been retained by Mrs. Ryan in a professional capacity, and my representing her shouldn't be construed in any other way. I think we have a good case here. I also think the prosecution has *no* case. In our system, we assume that people are innocent until a prosecutor proves they're guilty. That's not going to happen here. It's a travesty that these charges were ever brought. I think, as time passes, you and, more important, the jury will come to see how true that is. I know some of you from my days in the U.S. Attorney's office, and I know you're all eager to have your questions answered. For now, this is all we can say, and I hope you'll respect that and not trample us on our way out."

He nodded to Bo before the scattered laughter died down, and they powered their way to the elevators. A few reporters followed but faded away when their questions were not acknowledged. The five of them squeezed into an already crowded elevator for the ride to the lobby.

20

THE PRESS DESCENDED IN EARNEST THE NEXT MORN-ing. The phone began ringing in Ryan's apartment at seven in the morning. He answered the first call.

"Mr. Ryan, this is Allen Crown from the . . ."

Ryan slammed the receiver down. Allen Crown was the perpetrator of SON SAYS DAD KILLED MOM.

The phone kept ringing until Ryan left the apartment. It might have been Crown every time, it might have been others. He had to assume reporters would be waiting for him in the lobby. He took the fire stairs to the basement and went out the side entrance, timing his departure so he was concealed from the lobby doors by the building handyman dragging black plastic garbage bags out onto the street.

Ryan had briefed Craig Lawrence and Kassia Miller on each other before they all met at her office. They got straight to business.

"The first thing I have to know is how deep you want to go into this," the ex-F.B.I. man said. "You want all potential prosecution witnesses, all the people we can find out about with any kind of grudge against Ned, all the people who have it in for your client?"

"Absolutely," Ryan said. "Anything that would get us a suspect, or a reason to think this is a frame-up. Any way we can sow some doubt."

"How about the father? Maybe this has something to do with Kneeland, somebody looking to get at him through Ned. It could be revenge, it could be a warning. Or it could be directed at somebody else Ned was in business with. I could cover it all for you, if we had world enough and time. Otherwise we have to set some limits.''

''We don't have world enough *or* time,'' Ryan told him. ''But I don't want to start restricting us yet. We should think of everybody we can.'' To Miller he said, ''Between football seasons, Craig was a lit major. He's never recovered.''

''Everyone's entitled to his little foibles,'' the investigator said with a straight face, and then, ''I haven't heard anything about a mother so far.''

''She ran off when Jennifer was little,'' Miller said. ''That's from an old magazine piece on Kneeland around the time he married wife number two, since divorced. Wife number one departed in the late sixties, on the back of some dude's motorcycle.''

''Where is she now?''

''Address unknown.'' She handed Lawrence a sheet of paper. ''I made a list of all the cops whose names appeared in any of the press coverage of the murder. While we're waiting for the official list from Becker, we ought to check them out.''

''More work for Craig,'' Lawrence said. ''Don't you guys do anything?''

''We ought to talk about where all this is headed,'' she proposed.

''It's too soon for strategy,'' Ryan countered. ''Let's cast as wide a net as we can and talk strategy when we have something to work with.''

Miller was not going to be put off. ''I don't mean nail down the specifics. I'm talking about the broad strokes, so we don't miss stuff that turns out to be important later.''

Ryan stifled an angry response. Remember the Gibson case, he told himself. Don't hold on so tight. Give her a little air.

When nobody objected, she went on. ''I go by the principle that a good offense is the best defense. That ought to be perfect for an ex-prosecutor. Prosecutors always have something to prove, and I think the defense should, too.'' She paused for effect. ''Okay—we can't prove Jennifer is innocent, because we start with that as a given. And anyway, that's the absence of something—*not* guilty. We need to prove something specific.''

''For instance . . .''

''In the murder cases I've worked on we were proving justification, or some degree of mental disturbance. Either one makes a nice, clear goal. We don't have that luxury with this one, because our client says she didn't do it. We need to prove . . . I don't know . . . something. Then there's the other question: Becker's going to put Jennifer on trial—what about us? We have to put somebody on trial, too. The cops? The cops screw up enough so on a good day you can turn the whole trial into a demonstration of how inconsistent their statements are—on small things usually, but it makes the point. Or we could go after the medical examiner's office. Now and then you can stick it to them real good. Some of the other witnesses, maybe.'' She looked down at her desk. ''The natural person for us to trash I'm almost afraid to mention.''

''Ned.'' Ryan supplied.

''There may be other ways to do it.''

He heard her trying to go easy on him, did not know whether to be grateful or offended.

He said, ''I assumed from the beginning we'd be making him the villain.''

''Good. I was worried you'd have trouble with it.''

''I will, but I'll do what has to be done.'' He hoped he could match his words with action. ''My only question is how much good it's going to do us to trash Ned if we don't have something else, too.''

''What do you think?'' Ryan asked Lawrence when they were alone.

''She seems smart enough. Only I kept getting the feeling she has some kind of chip on her shoulder.''

''Everyone's entitled to his little foibles,'' Ryan quoted, then said, ''I have something else for you.''

''Shoot.''

''Ned did a lot of financing. He was a conduit for money looking for a home. He placed sixty million dollars in under two years, mostly as mortgages.''

Lawrence whistled. ''That's a lot of bread for an apprentice baker.''

''Jake Kaplan may have something about where the mortgage payments are going.''

''You want me to trace them back, find the original lenders.''

''Every single one. I don't think it's going to be easy.''

Especially if it's drug money, he did not say.

The next day the three of them got together at Ryan's office to work on a formal request for information about Becker's case. Information was the fuel of trial preparation, and the highest octane was likely to be the material they could get from the prosecution.

Miller had already begun to modify her office's standard letter, a demand on the prosecution to produce the evidence the defense was entitled to see, combined with a request for a bill of particulars about the crime. They went over the letter together, to make sure they did not leave anything out.

"Funny, being on this side of it," Ryan said. "I always used to be the guy people served these things on."

In the afternoon the two lawyers met with their client.

"I have to warn you," Jennifer said, "I don't remember a lot of what happened that night."

"Maybe it would help if I asked you some questions," Ryan suggested.

"All right."

She was sitting back in her chair, hands gripping its arms. Waiting to take off in a plane she doesn't trust, Ryan thought.

"When did you get to the party?" he asked mildly.

"About six-thirty."

"Where were you coming from?"

"Home."

"Had you and Ned been arguing?"

"No. We were all right with each other, except he had been acting so withdrawn for a couple of weeks. I told you about that."

"Were you together at the party?"

"We circulated. We thought it was dumb for couples to hang on each other's arms at parties like that."

"Were you aware of what Ned was doing, who he was talking to?"

"Every so often we caught each other's eye. Actually I was feeling sort of close to him that night. Maybe that's what did it."

"What do you mean?"

"Well, if I was already angry with him, what he did wouldn't have hurt so much. You have to understand, after three years I was good at defending myself when I had to. That night my guard was down. And then to see him with that . . . sculptor. I was mortified. And people were there who mattered to me. I had to say something to him then and there or I could never hold my head up in public again."

"What did you say to him?" Miller asked.

"I don't really remember."

"You can do better than that," Ryan said.

"I can't."

"Did you curse him?"

"I suppose."

"Threaten him?"

"I don't know. I was so upset and then the police came and told me he was dead and that didn't help my memory. I really don't remember."

Ryan remembered. Ryan would never forget that night. The phone message at Kelly's, the trip to the morgue. Standing there breathing the stench of decay and waiting to see if it was Ned under the sheet.

Miller was prompting Jennifer. "You went over to him and said: You asshole. Or: Enjoying yourself? Or maybe: I'm leaving this party and if you ever want to see me again you'll leave with me. Or maybe you said: You slut, leave my husband alone."

"No. I didn't talk to her. To him. And it was more like, I'm not letting you get away with this."

"Did you say what you meant by that?"

"He knew what I meant."

"What *did* you mean?"

"I meant I was calling him on it, in public. I wasn't pretending not to see."

"That was all, that you were calling him on it in public?"

"If he was going to humiliate me in public I wasn't going to play the good little wife. I was going to humiliate him, too, even if it meant embarrassing myself."

"Did you say all that?"

"I didn't have to, he knew what I meant. All I said was he couldn't humiliate me in public and expect me to take it lying down."

"You said that?" Ryan asked. "You wouldn't take it lying down."

"Yes, I guess I did."

"What else?" Miller asked.

"That's all I remember."

"What about breaking the bowl?"

Jennifer stood up and paced.

"It was a bowl of finger food. Little pastries, I don't remember exactly. I was talking to him and he was eating! I picked it up and smashed it. I guess that's how I cut my hand."

"When did you do this?" Miller's voice was subdued.

"At the end. Like punctuation."

"Very dramatic," Ryan said.

"Do you know what you said then?" Miller asked.

"What I told you, that I wasn't letting him get away with it and if he thought so I'd show him different."

"Then he left?" Ryan asked.

"Yes. He just walked out. I wasn't going to let him leave like that. He went down the stairs from the roof. When he heard me behind him he kept going past the gallery to the floor where the gallery owner had his private space."

"Then what happened?"

"He said we should talk."

"Right there?"

"No. He took me into that room, the one they found him in. It was like an office and a private gallery."

"What happened then?"

"Nothing."

"Nothing?" Miller echoed. "That's not what you told me."

"I didn't really mean nothing. Only nothing important. We talked. Ned was angry with me for yelling and breaking the bowl, but he was sorry for what he'd done, too. I was still angry. I said the same things again, how I couldn't let him humiliate me in public, and then I said what would my father think if he knew. When I said that, Ned went all cold. He said don't threaten me with your father. I said I wasn't threatening him but my father was bound to hear. People talk. And he said maybe you're right and he got calmer and tried to kiss me but I pulled away. I said I was going home and he could come or not, it was up to him, and I left."

She was standing by the wall where Ryan's diplomas and awards were hung. One of his Attorney General's Awards was askew. She straightened it.

"That was the last time I saw him. I didn't even let him kiss me." She said it simply, without emphasis. The loss and regret were all the more evident.

Either this woman is a wonder of self-deception or she's a remarkable actress, Ryan thought. Or she's innocent.

"How did your blood get on the sculpture?" he asked.

She seemed to retreat into herself, remembering. "When I pulled away from him I bumped into the stand it was on and I knocked it over. I picked it up and put it back before I left. I guess I had some blood on my hand from breaking the bowl, and it got on the sculpture. That's all I can think of."

"What happened then?"

"Nothing. I went home."

She walked the few steps back to her chair and sat down.

Miller gave her a decent interval before returning to the concerns of the present. "We need to have the clothes you were wearing at the party."

"Didn't Jeff Rosen tell you? He asked that right away. I don't have them. I gave them away."

"You what! When? Why?"

"I didn't want them around. I had this fight with Ned while I was wearing them and the next thing I knew he was dead. How could I ever wear them again? Why would I keep them? I had a box all ready for the Feed the Children Thrift Shop, so I threw them in and brought it over there."

"Were there any bloodstains on them?" Ryan asked.

"Bloodstains!" That brought her to her feet. "Why would there be bloodstains? Whose bloodstains?"

"I didn't mean to imply anything."

"Oh yes you did. What else could you mean?"

"The point is," Miller interrupted, "that if we had the clothes you wore that night and they didn't show any sign of bloodstains it would have helped our case."

"Well, I don't have them."

Ryan walked Jennifer down the corridor to the elevators. "I'm sorry if I seemed hard on you. I'm concerned about you and the baby, and getting this right. I get carried away."

"It's a strange way to be concerned, asking if there were bloodstains on my clothes."

The elevator bell rang. He squeezed her hand reassuringly. "Just try to remember, I'm trying to do the best job I can for you. I'm on your side."

He watched the elevator doors close and knew that he had lied to her. He was on the baby's side, not hers.

Back in his office, he settled into the chair behind his desk. "I keep seeing Becker and his parade of witnesses all with different versions of 'You can't get away with this!' Smash!"

"I won't take it lying down," Miller quoted.

"At least she didn't say I'll kill you for this."

"We hope." Miller drained her can of diet soda and arced it into the wastebasket.

"You're good at that." It was as much a challenge as a compliment. To his way of looking at it, throwing cans across the office was not exactly professional conduct, must less feminine. For Ryan, things like that were matters of character, not cosmetics.

She said, "We ought to call Craig and see if he has anyone else's version of the fight."

"He'd have told us if he did."

They sat in contemplative silence.

"Do you think she's telling the truth?" Ryan asked.

"Most of the time, I do."

"I thought you two were going to be soul mates. Wasn't that the idea, so she'd tell you everything?"

"Don't get down on me, Ryan."

"Why not?" He meant it lightly.

"I've got things on my mind." She stared out the window, as if her preoccupations might be out there.

"About the case?"

"About the case and not about the case."

"If it's getting in the way of your work . . ."

"It's not getting in the way of my work!" She turned back to him. "Sorry. I'm edgier than usual today. I hate to admit it, but once a month I get edgy."

"Don't worry about it," he said. Then, eager to change the subject, "With luck, Craig can track down some of her clothes if she can't find them at the Thrift Shop."

"Even if we find them, they're not much use. Imagine proving they're the same ones she wore."

"Becker is going to make a big point of the cops searching her house for them and not finding them. One more link in the circumstantial chain."

"Becker can't show bloodstains on clothes the jury will never see," she countered.

"They'll be happy to imagine. And unless we put her on the stand, nobody's there to explain it away."

"Speaking of bloodstains, which after a fashion we are," she said, "we need a bloodstain pattern expert."

"We need a what?"

"A bloodstain pattern expert. Someone who can analyze the patterns of blood at the crime scene as a way to tell what happened there."

"Ned got his head beat in. The medical examiner will be happy to count the blows for us. What more is there?"

"Lots."

"How much is this going to cost?"

"What do you care?"

She had a point. His reluctance about analyzing bloodstains did not come from concern about Robertson Kneeland's budget. "Tell you what—I'm going to let you handle the medical examiner and the other forensic experts. I think I'd do better to keep away from the blood and the broken bones."

21

BECKER'S REPLY TO THE REQUEST FOR A BILL OF PAR-ticulars and the demand to produce evidence was served on the fifteenth day after the request and demand, the last moment within the statutory deadline. The reply was not generous.

Ryan faxed it to Kassia Miller and they talked about it on the phone.

"Is this how they do things over there?" Ryan asked. "Letter of the law?" He quoted: "to the extent required they will be provided to the defense at trial pursuant to the Criminal Procedure Law."

"Usually it's just the opposite. The rule is they give early whatever they'll have to give eventually, unless they can think of a compelling reason not to. But this looks like we can count on getting absolutely nothing until the exact time the CPL says he has to give it to us."

"I must have pissed him off more than I thought."

"You may have to become a trash-and-burn litigator in spite of yourself. This doesn't exactly encourage cooperation."

"We'll survive," he said sourly. "Give Becker a call and set something up to check out the M.E.'s evidence."

When he hung up he realized that they'd had a whole conversation without arguing.

Ryan ordered a limousine for their field trip to Hugo Hill's loft. He did not want the four of them hanging out on streetcorners waving for a taxi. The press had backed off for the moment, but a joint visit to the scene of the crime by the accused and her father-in-law attorney was a sure thing for the tabloid front pages.

The gallery owner was a short man with a carrot-red toupee and skin stretched tight by multiple face-lifts. He was wearing a black

112

tunic that left bare a long vee of chest adorned with gray hair, heavy gold chains and a large multicolor medallion. He offered a polite if chilly hello to Jennifer, ignoring the others.

He ushered them all to the private stairs at the back of his ninth-floor gallery.

"That the roof garden?" Lawrence asked, pointing up.

"Yes but it's so raw out."

"I don't mind."

"Come down here first, before you get your feet dirty up there." Hill led them down the stairs and into a hallway.

"In here. I hope you won't be disappointed."

Ryan led the others into the room, not sure what Hill meant about being disappointed.

The room where Ned had died was about twenty feet by fifteen. The floors were closely fitted blocks of polished dark slate; the walls were the color of eggplant, with black trim. The ceiling was a purplish rose color. Drapes the same color hung over a pair of oversize windows. The sparse furniture was a mix of antiques and severe contemporary pieces, set off by the art on the walls and a few pieces of sculpture far too big and heavy to be lifted by one person.

Behind him, as she came into the room, Jennifer gasped.

"What is it?"

"This . . . this isn't . . ." She was pointing. Ryan couldn't tell at what.

In the doorway Hugo Hill said, "It's all different, you know. I had it redone. You can't imagine. It was simply awful. Grisly beyond belief. Who could live here like that? As soon as the police said it was all right I had Alfred in here to gut it down to the structure. I mean I couldn't move out so I had to do *something*."

"Are there any pictures of how it was before?" Ryan asked him.

"Well *I* don't have any, I'm sure."

"Do you know anyone who might?"

Hill made a show of being at a loss for an answer. "You'll have to talk to the police, I suppose."

"You don't mind if we take pictures today?"

"Only if you promise not to publish them."

"We promise."

"I'm serious," Hill pouted. "I've given an exclusive to a very good magazine."

"Don't worry about it," Lawrence said. "Nobody would publish my pictures in a million years."

"Well, I have to go about my business. You can have fifteen minutes. Twenty at most. Then please come upstairs."

They did not take the full time. Lawrence took useless pictures and Jennifer went through the empty exercise of pointing out the approximate places where the sculpture's pedestal had been, where she and Ned had continued their argument, and where he had been standing when she left. But for all the relationship Hill's study now bore to the murder room, it could have been on another planet. They trudged upstairs to the roof garden, where a cold, damp wind was blowing under a sky as dark as Hugo Hill's slate floor.

Ryan had scheduled the trip to Hill's so they could also use the limousine for their visit to the medical examiner's evidence room. Ryan had not been sure about going back to the building where he had identified Ned's body. He told himself it was a test of his readiness to live the next half year in the constant presence of Ned's death.

As soon as the limousine pulled up at the ugly blue-green and gray building, Ryan was catapulted back to the June night when he had arrived here in an unmarked police car accompanied by a pair of detectives. He took shallow breaths, as inadequate a defense against the morgue's foul and pervasive perfume as it had been when they had led him to the curtain partition behind which Ned's body lay on a gurney, covered by a sheet.

Not ready to see Ned's bloody clothes, Ryan read items from the defense checklist while the property clerk set them out for Craig Lawrence and Kassia Miller to examine under the baleful eye of Detective Garrity, one of Ryan's escorts on his earlier trip and the interrogation that had followed it. Garrity did not speak to him now and avoided looking at him.

Here's another one who thinks I'm some lower form of life, Ryan thought. Since the public announcement that he was defending Jennifer he had noticed increasingly that people avoided him or were visibly uncomfortable in his presence. Logically it made no sense. If he believed in Jennifer's innocence—which the outside world had no reason to doubt—defending her was the most natural thing for him to do. But people's reactions did not seem to owe much to logic.

"We finished the neighborhood survey," Lawrence said, back at Ryan's office. "No parking tickets on the block in the relevant hours. The precinct got a couple of complaints: noise, limos obstructing the street. No unusual-occurrence reports. None of the neighbors heard anything but party noises, or saw anything except fancy people coming and going from the party. No one we talked to recognized Jennifer's picture."

"How's your end of things coming?" Ryan asked Miller.

"Good," she said. "I have my experts lined up: fingerprints, serology, bloodstain patterns."

"Bloodstain patterns?" Lawrence was incredulous.

"Go on, laugh. Ignorance is bliss. You two guys must have lived in the same cave the last ten years."

"Anything new on whose money went into the mortgages?" Ryan asked the investigator.

"One fact of interest. None of the companies on that list has a real office at any of the addresses on that list. Every single address is a mail drop or a rented desk in an office suite. Nobody is giving out the names or addresses at the next level, the people who rented the desks or pay for the mail drops. I can dig for them, but it'll take time and it'll cost money."

"We have more money than time," Ryan reminded him.

"What about Kneeland? He must have been part of some of those deals."

"I'll call him when we're done."

Ryan paced the office, went down the hall to the toilet, checked his mail, building himself up to call Kneeland. When he did, just before lunch, Kneeland was not in.

Kneeland returned the call a few minutes after five.

"I called to ask you about the mortgages Ned arranged," Ryan told him. "And I think we ought to get together so we can go over some things about Ned and Jennifer that I need to know for her defense."

"I'm on my way to Europe on business."

"When you come back, then."

"Jennifer's been anxious about that," Miller said when Ryan told her about the appointment with Kneeland.

"Oh?"

"She's funny about her father. She worries what he'll say about her."

"The longer I live," Ryan said, "the less I understand where we get this myth about family happiness. All the fathers and children I know about are alien species to each other."

"Maybe you travel in the wrong circles."

Ryan's secretary buzzed to let him know that Robertson Kneeland had arrived. Ryan went out to the reception area to greet him and lead him through the maze that Pane, Parish was becoming as the firm continued to outgrow its quarters, waiting to move. Ryan offered Kneeland one of the chairs facing the desk. With anyone else he would have used the sitting area.

"I'm interested in anything you can tell me about Ned," Ryan began. "I'm especially interested in anything that might have made him enemies and also his activities, his attitude, his emotional state in the days and weeks before his death."

"What about Jennifer? Are you going to ask me to testify for her?"

"Possibly. We won't make that decision until we're much closer to trial."

"Nobody knows her better than her father."

Don't be so sure, Ryan was tempted to say. I was Ned's father and what did I know?

"If I'm going to be a witness, I understand that means I can't be in court for the trial. Is that right?"

"We can worry about that when it's time. Right now we need to talk about Ned and Jennifer."

Kneeland shifted in the black captain's chair.

"You don't mind if I'm frank?"

"Of course not."

"I mean, your being Ned's father, I don't know how you'll feel about some of what I might tell you."

"I'm Jennifer's lawyer. That's what's important." Hoping to convince himself as well as Kneeland.

"All right," Kneeland said, "I'm willing if you are . . . Ned was an expert at promising things to people, taking favors in return and then not delivering what he promised." He examined his manicured fingernails as he spoke. "He used to joke about it. Before he and Jennifer got together, he did it for sex as well as business. He once told me about promising a woman he'd fix some tax problem she had with the city, so he could get her into bed. Except he had no connections in the city tax bureau. One day they attached her bank account and put a lien on her business. She called Ned—all upset, as you can imagine—and he said I don't understand, the guy told me it was all fixed. He liked to tell that story. It made him laugh."

My son, Ryan thought.

"He used to promise he'd get people jobs, too. Sons and daughters of people he needed to bend the rules for him. The jobs never materialized. Ned was always very apologetic, and he always had a plausible reason."

"How did people react?"

"Ned charmed his way out of trouble more often than anyone would believe. When he didn't, his tricks made his victims very angry."

"Did anybody ever do anything about it?"

"Not that I know of."

"Tell me about Ned's state of mind the last few weeks . . . Was he happy, sad, anxious? As far as you could tell."

"I didn't notice anything particularly different."

"Nothing preying on him, weighing on his mind?"

"Not that I was aware of."

Ryan considered mentioning Jennifer's contrary opinion on the subject, decided against it.

"Did he have any disagreements, any business difficulties, pull any of his special tricks on anybody, at any time around his death?"

"Not that he told me. How is this helpful?"

"I don't want to tell you too much, because I don't want you to tailor your answers. I'm leading you too much as it is." And you're doing a great job of not following.

Ryan kept at it until he was sure there was nothing there, then switched subjects.

"I understand you put up some of the money for the mortgages Ned arranged."

"Yes. A few."

"Were there any you weren't a part of?"

"How would I know that?" A touch of annoyance.

Ryan stifled the impulse to snap back. "I'm trying to find out who provided the financing for the loans Ned arranged."

"What does that have to do with Jennifer?"

"It has to do with Ned."

A pause. "Oh. Yes, I see. I'm afraid there's not much I can do to help. There were only one or two deals that I was part of, and I don't know who the other players were. As far as the other deals, I assumed Ned went to people on the basis that I was involved with him. There are a lot of coattail riders out there. Under normal circumstances I don't let people use my name that way, but Ned was different. He was my son-in-law and sometimes my partner. If he connected with anybody on that basis I don't know about it. I wouldn't have minded if he did. There was no reason for him to tell me."

Kneeland paused again. "I'm sorry I can't tell you more. I hope I've been helpful." He looked at his watch. "Much as I'd like to stay, I'm afraid I have another appointment."

* * *

That night Ryan had dinner with Kassia Miller and Craig Lawrence at the Shamrock.

"I checked out our friend Joe Becker," Miller said. "He's no intellectual giant, but we knew that already. Not a record breaker, either. His won-lost record is right about average, maybe a touch better. To be fair, he's had some of the world's worst cases. Witnesses changing their stories or disappearing, a couple of cases where he wanted to drop them but his boss said prosecute."

She picked a tomato slice from her salad with two fingers and munched on it. "There's another side to the Joe Becker story. I've talked to some people who say he's flattened them like a steamroller. Not quick, but thorough. He makes his points and he doesn't leave a lot of holes to sneak out through. I gather he's the type who writes out his questions in advance and follows the list the way he wrote it."

"Something wrong with that?" Ryan barked, louder than it deserved.

"Oh, no," she moaned. "You don't do that, Ryan, do you? Tell me you don't."

"I write down my questions, yes. What do you do, make them up as you go along?"

"Mostly."

"Not working for me, you don't. This is a murder trial, not Saturday Night at the Improv."

"Maybe you're smart enough to know everything you want to ask a witness before you even hear him say his name. I'm not."

"Time!" Lawrence held up his hands in a T. "I hate to lose my front row seat and all, but all this shouting spoils my dinner."

"I yield to your appetite," Miller said. For Ryan she had no smile. "We'll have to talk about this."

"At your convenience."

"Good. So the bottom line on Becker for now is that he isn't the smartest guy in the world but he isn't the dumbest either. No obvious weak spots, except maybe inflexibility, which I'm hoping we won't match ourselves."

"Hey! I said time out from that crap."

"Sorry, Craig. Okay, then. I'll keep asking around for Joe Becker stories, and I'm getting copies of a couple of briefs he wrote, which might be helpful when we file our motions."

"Any progress on Corino?" Ryan asked her.

"I have a whole file full of appeals-court opinions on his cases.

Very few reversals. I also have a photocopy of my office's file on him. Eyes only, burn before reading."

"Craig? Anything new?"

"A couple of things. We still interested in Daddy?"

"That depends on how interesting he is."

"You be the judge." The investigator speared a slender french fry and scrutinized it like a suspect. "You want to know who Kneeland is, really? He's James Gatz. What was it Gertrude Stein said about Oakland, or maybe it was Cleveland? 'There's no there, there.' That's Robertson Kneeland. An Ivy Leaguer, they say. Before that, Army Air Corps in World War Two. Before that, who knows? No back trail at all. So he invented himself during the war, and after on the GI Bill. He shows up in New York in the early fifties, partners with a guy named Van Den Berg who's the third son in a big food-processing family. Money, but not that much money, and his brothers are already in line to run the packing plants. So he's the money and Kneeland is the front man. They were in a good place at a good time, and they had modest success. Some of this comes from Kneeland's own official biographies. They weren't high-profile guys and they didn't have any one area they stayed in. Kneeland liked variety. Real estate, textiles, a small plastics company—I don't know, maybe he saw 'The Graduate.' This was in the go-go sixties. The next thing I could find out about, Kneeland and Van Den Berg had gone their separate ways. Kneeland was in real estate at that point, I think, and apparently he was also in the securities markets more and more. he got caught in 1970 when the bottom fell out of the stock market, but not as bad as some. What really caught him was the end of that cycle. He was all in bonds when the oil shock hit. He had all this long-term stuff and interest rates started going up to triple, quadruple what he was getting. He hung on as much as he could but he had to liquidate a lot at big losses.

"He used to be a big contributor to political campaigns, in tight with people back as far as the Tammany Hall days, but the file doesn't have anything about bribes. I don't think he's ever been a target of a corruption investigation. His name still comes up connected to politicians but mostly on the sidelines. Like a groupie.

"The thing about Robertson Kneeland is, he doesn't add up. He put up one of those buildings on Park Avenue that insults the Seagram building. That was his high point. By the mid sixties he was expanding in every direction he could think of. Except show business, as far as the file shows. There are probably a hundred guys like him in the city. No, these days there are probably a thousand.

He's worth twenty, thirty million, according to the numbers in the file.''

''What's he doing now?''

''Moving money, mostly. He shows up in the files associated with three or four businesses that bring him into contact with people the Bureau's interested in. One reason for that is he still does some development, as a minor partner, so he gets into the building-trades area that way.''

''He's been on the fringes like that for years.'' When Ned had first gone to work for Kneeland, his name had been a constant tickle in the back of Ryan's mind until he finally connected it with the old office. A friend who was still there had run it through the computer and located the transcript references: Kneeland's name had come up in an organized-crime wiretap not long before Ryan left. Ryan had read the transcripts: there was nothing specific, not even a clear indication of a connection. Kneeland was probably someone the crime bosses had done business with on a one-shot, legitimate basis. Still, it had been another reason not to be happy that Ned and Kneeland were so closely connected.

''Could he be running a money laundry?'' Ryan asked the investigator.

''I doubt anybody's given it a minute's thought. He doesn't show up often enough or conspicuously enough in contact with the real money people.''

''Let me pin it down closer,'' Ryan proposed. ''I'm interested in the possibility that Ned ran into somebody who was a harder case than he was ready for.''

''That's a different question. And it's not a question about Robertson Kneeland. It's a question about Ned.''

''So it is. I guess I was trying to get there sideways.''

''I figured you might be.''

''What else do you have?''

''We're plugging away at the guest list. These are people with an extremely elevated opinion of their own importance and the value of their time. Murder is a novelty for some of them, so we have that going for us. Except that when the novelty wears off these same people may become impossible to reach.''

''How many have you talked to?''

''It wasn't that big a party, unless you're the poor bastard assigned to track down all the guests. Sixty-some people. We've interviewed maybe two dozen so far. Nobody's been willing to swear to anything, and the D.A.'s office has been in touch with everyone we've talked to. Only a few say they won't cooperate with them. Nineteen don't want to talk to us.''

"Keep after it. Any progress on the mortgages?''

"Slow. I'm reduced to my least favorite method.''

"What's that?'' Miller asked.

"Garbageology.''

She laughed. "I can see it now.''

"Not me, thank you. My employees . . . And I got a call from Kaplan. He says some of the mortgage loans went to buildings that rented space to clinics on Shible's customer list.''

Miller raised her wine glass. "Here's to a guy who knew how to cover his bases.''

"I guess I'll have to talk with Dr. Morris,'' Ryan said.

22

DR. JAMES MORRIS ASKED RYAN TO MEET HIM AT HIS health club in a building near the East River. A constant stream of sleek women and muscle-pumped men in skin-tight multicolor costumes flowed through the lobby. Ryan owned baggy sweatpants, faded black gym shorts and a couple of graying T-shirts; his health club membership had probably expired by now, unused; walking home from work had only lasted a few weeks. He knew he should stop ignoring his resolutions to get some exercise. For preparing and trying a major case, it was smart to be in shape.

A muscular man in his mid thirties dressed in electric blue and yellow came down the black metal stairs into the lobby with a casual bounce, looked around, and spotted Ryan. "I'm Jim Morris. There's a juice bar downstairs. We can talk there.''

"I'd rather find a quiet place in the neighborhood.''

Ryan picked a coffee shop like a thousand others. They sat in the back of the smoking section, where they were least likely to be disturbed or overheard.

"Do you know anything about Ned's mortgage brokering?" Ryan asked.

"Only that he did it. Our main business with each other was Shible, the pharmaceuticals distributor. That and the clinics."

"It looks as if some of Ned's loans went to finance the buildings your clinics were in."

"Really?" Morris sounded genuinely surprised. "I didn't know anything about that."

"Even though it had to do with your business together?"

"We sold complete packages to doctors and pharmacists so they could open clinics that would be customers for Shible. Nothing to do with real estate."

"Let's talk about the clinics," Ryan said. "It was pretty clear at the one I went to see that something was going on besides doctors practicing medicine. Since then I've been getting reports from the accountant working on Ned's estate, and the cash flow from some of those places is remarkable."

"We do pretty good business."

"I gather that a couple of the big private hospital companies tried to set up small clinics around the country and lost a fortune."

"We knew about that. They were out in the suburbs, small buildings with a parking lot, like a fast-food restaurant. They called them doc-in-a-box. They did lousy business."

"Then you knew that these places you were helping to set up couldn't make it legitimately."

"We had a different concept. High-density inner-city population, a place with not many alternative health-care providers. The big problem for our clinics was that the patients aren't people who can get third-party insurance like Blue Cross. It was going to be all Medicare and Medicaid.

"We assumed that there would be some fraud. We didn't like it, but we didn't think it was our place to police the clinics once they were open. We helped set them up to get ourselves customers. They couldn't exist if they couldn't find ways to pick up some extra income here and there. And without them big portions of the population would have insufficient medical care, or none at all."

"Assuming your clinics actually provide any medical services."

"Our clinics are real places, not empty lots, and our doctors and pharmacists are licensed practitioners. Nobody is making up bills out of thin air. Sure people stand in line to get pills they can turn around and sell on the street and use the money to buy heroin or crack. And some of them hear they can get sneakers from Medicaid, and when they get their sneakers Medicaid is going to get billed for orthopedic shoes at two hundred dollars a clip. A little of that buys something these people would never have without it.''

''A little of that also puts people in jail. I spent a large part of my career making sure of it.''

''So Ned told me.'' Morris was not impressed.

''Right now my only interest is in Ned.''

''The time to be interested in Ned was when he was alive.''

Ryan did not dispute it.

Morris said, ''Look, Mr. Ryan, I don't want to break your balls. I don't want you to break mine either. You want cooperation and I've been trying to give it to you. I don't think what Ned and I did was so bad, and Ned didn't either.''

''I'm not here to pass judgment. I have some more questions.''

''Ask them.''

''Do you, did you and Ned, get any part of the money these clinics collect from Medicaid?''

''As far as I know we bill the clinics as suppliers, that's all.''

''Kickbacks, profit overrides, under-the-table money?''

''Nothing like that.''

''You send them pharmaceuticals, health and beauty aids, clinic supplies, that's all.''

''Yes.''

''And you give them a hundred twenty days to pay? That's four months.''

''I don't know anything about that. That was Ned's part of it. I'm the doctor.''

''Considering the interest rates, those are very generous credit terms.''

''If you say so.''

''Ned needed to have cash coming in from somewhere to let the clinics have so long to pay.''

''I assumed we paid our bills with the money people paid us when they paid their bills.''

''Not from what I know so far. That's why I'm looking for information.''

''I left all that to Ned. He gave me a check every month. I assumed it was right. Maybe I was foolish. I trusted Ned.''

The doctor stood up to leave.

''You know . . . if you're interested in how Ned kept the money straight, you might get some help from the notebook he carried.''

''What notebook?''

''Ned had a little notebook—leather, dark brown with gold tooling, about the size of a three-by-five index card. He was always jotting things in it and referring to it. I think it was some kind of diary he used for his business deals.''

Ryan called Jennifer.

"Did Ned have a diary where he kept notes about his business?''

"If he did, I don't know about it.''

"A leather notebook, about the size of a three-by-five index card. Brown with gold tooling.''

"Oh. That.''

"You remember it.''

"I thought it was an address book.''

"Have you seen it anywhere since he died?''

"No. I don't think so. I think I would have remembered. Didn't you find it when you looked through the apartment?''

"I didn't know to look for it.''

"Maybe you should look again.''

"Can you meet me there tonight?''

"If you really need me. I still don't like to be there. I tried staying there for a while and it was pretty upsetting.''

"Without you I'm flying blind. You'll know better where to look.''

"All right. But I can't make it until after seven.''

"I'll see you there at nine. I still have the keys.''

He had not planned to arrive at the apartment until eight-thirty. He was there at ten of seven.

He sat in a chair in the dark living room with a single floodlight on in the garden. He looked out at the naked trees; he did not search for Ned's notebook. He had no idea why he had come so early. Sometime after eight he turned off the garden floodlight and sat gazing in the moonlit night.

Jennifer came in at a quarter to nine, moving briskly. She snapped on the living room light, looked around the room. Jumped.

"You scared me!''

"Sorry.'' Ryan blinked at the dazzle of sudden light.

"How long have you been here?''

"Awhile.''

"Why?''

He shrugged.

"You were checking up on me.''

"What do you mean?'' He knew what she meant.

"You came here early because you thought I might do something before you got here. Plant something or take something. Hide the notebook. I don't know. It's your paranoia.''

Partly mine, he thought, partly yours.

''And I don't like it,'' she said.

''Would it help if I told you that you were wrong?''

''No. But it beats *not* telling me.''

''Well . . . you're wrong.''

''I don't mean to be difficult, Michael. I'm nervous. I'm wound up all the time. It's the baby, and it's this trial hanging over me . . .''

''Doing something helps. Let's get started.''

They looked but they did not find. Not the notebook. But in a pile of magazines on a shelf in the study, Ryan came across something else that made him stop.

''What is it?''

He handed it to her.

It was a colorfully printed folder about the size of a magazine. CAMPUS CUTIES, it said in red letters on a golden background, ''a LOVE-ly calendar for the academic year.'' Scattered on the cover were head-and-shoulder color portraits of twelve fresh-faced college girls, like yearbook pictures.

''Why do you think he kept it?'' Jennifer asked.

''It was his favorite business venture at college. He was editor and publisher, I guess you'd say.''

''No kidding.'' She turned to the first page, Miss September.

Ryan knew what she was going to find. The calendar pictures were of the same fresh-faced college girls as the ones on the cover, but on the inside pages the focus was not on faces.

He had not thought about the calendar in years. But he remembered all too well the day Ned had brought it home and showed it proudly to his father.

It had been the end of Ned's first year at college. Alison had driven out to Iowa and come back with Ned and a car full of college stuff. Ryan had meant to go out there with her, to make it a family occasion, but things had heated up unexpectedly at Pane, Parish and there was no way he could leave. Ned's first night home they had all eaten together; Ryan had managed to get away that long. Conversation was spotty, with Ned's brief answers to his father's questions about courses and sports failing to fill deep holes of silence.

After dinner, while Ali was loading the dishes into the washer, Ned had said to his father, ''Come on up to my room.'' Ali had been happy to see them go off together. The rest was vivid, too vivid, in Ryan's mind.

Ned had something to show him, and Ryan knew now that the boy's excitement and pride would have been obvious to any but the densest of fathers. Not to Michael Ryan. Ned had handed him a nine-by-twelve envelope, not explaining, not saying what was inside. Ryan could see him as if it were happening now: a robust nineteen-year-old not quite six feet tall—a healthy inch taller than his father—vibrant with youth, grinning with expectation. In the envelope had been a copy of this calendar. For all Ryan knew it was the very same one.

The rest had been outwardly simple. He had looked at the cover page, as Jennifer had just now, had been perplexed but interested. Had looked at Ned, whose I've-got-a-secret grin must have made his jaw ache, and who had said, "Go on, open it." Ryan had opened it. Seen the first picture, a kneeling girl, smiling back over her shoulder, her only clothing a pair of gossamer panties.

The calendar did not begin to compare to what he'd seen in the U.S. Attorney's office during their intermittent crusades against pornography. But he had remembered the snickering and carrying on those pictures had prompted among some of the Southern District's lawyers, and that had contributed to the sharpness of his reaction. "What is this?" he snapped at Ned in a voice loud with righteous indignation. "Did you have something to do with this?"

Ned had snatched the calendar from his hands. "Not something. Everything." Defiant through the pain. "Every bit of it is mine. My idea, my money. I did it. Hired the photographers, got the girls, everything. And I'm making a fucking fortune on it." He was brandishing the calendar like a manifesto. "Get out of my room."

If he'd given me a clue, if he'd explained in advance, Ryan had thought the times he had gone over the incident in his mind. Trying to make a small excuse for himself. It was nonsense. The evidence had been there for anyone who cared to see it. The boy had invited his father to his room and with all the signs of pride had given him something to look at. How much clearer could Ned have made it that this was something important to him? How hard would it have been for his father to ask even a single question aimed at better understanding the situation before blundering into a reaction? He could have complimented Ned's initiative without approving the way he'd expressed it.

It had been months after that before Ned had made the slightest overture, and then he had been wary, approaching his father more for Ali's sake than in any real attempt at reconciliation.

"Michael, I don't believe this." Jennifer was paging through the calendar.

"Something, isn't it? He was very proud of it. I'm surprised he didn't show it to you."

Or maybe I'm not surprised. Maybe he'd had enough rejection showing it to someone whose approval he badly needed and wanted.

"It was Ned's creation, beginning to end," Ryan said, holding back the pain. "It caused a commotion on campus, and it made him a fair amount of money, I think."

Suddenly Jennifer was crying. She groped for the desk to put the calendar down and then she was huddled against Ryan's chest and his arms went around her.

"It's all right," he said. "It's all right."

But he knew that for him it wasn't all right; knew that his new-found understanding that love should have moderated his response, not exacerbated it, had come too late to do anyone any good.

Somewhere along the line Ned had turned into the man who inhabited stories like the ones Kneeland had told about him, and there was no way to know if having a father he could talk to would have helped to prevent it.

Without warning Ryan too was crying, his first tears since Ned's death, all the bottled-up grief coming out at once. He was shaken by sobs pulled from the deepest part of his body. When they finally began to subside he became aware that he was sitting on the couch and Jennifer was holding him, repeating his name. He took deep shuddering breaths.

"Well," he said, "I guess I needed that."

"Is it the first time you cried?"

He nodded yes.

"I cry every night," she said.

After a long silent moment he asked, "How's the baby?"

"Not much trouble so far, if you don't count feeling seasick all the time."

"You hardly show."

"It's only four months. You want to feel it?"

She took his hand. Tentatively, Ryan let her press it to her middle.

"You don't mind keeping it a secret?"

"Not so far."

"You'll have plenty of time to enjoy him after he's born." Even if you do as badly as I did. "Do you know if it's a boy or a girl?"

"Not yet. I'll let you know."

They went back to searching for Ned's notebook. They did not find it.

"It's strange," she said. "I could have sworn I saw it around here someplace."

"Do you remember when?"

She thought about it. "No. Time is such a jumble now. I can't remember what happened before and what happened after."

They stood in silence for a moment.

"You going uptown?" Ryan asked.

"No. I think I'll stay here tonight."

"Good night, then. I'll let myself out." Unthinking, he bent to kiss her cheek.

23

IN THE MORNING RYAN CALLED CRAIG LAWRENCE TO tell him about the notebook. Then he called Kassia Miller.

"Ned had a big trunk full of personal mementos. Football letter, pennants, that kind of thing," Ryan told her. "It's in Jake Kaplan's file room. Can you go over there and look through it? I doubt you'll find the notebook but we ought to check."

He was in a meeting about the construction of Pane, Parish's new offices when Jennifer called.

"I remembered something. There was somebody Ned used to fight with on the phone."

"When?"

"Off and on, a month or two before he was killed."

"Did you hear the conversations?"

"I just used to hear him. Shouting. Laughing, too. It was very strange."

"You didn't ask him about it."

"It wasn't the kind of thing we talked about."

"Do you remember anything else? The name?"

"I think Ned called him Willy."

"Do you know anybody called Willy?"

"Some Williams and Bills, but no Willy that I can think of. It was about money, though."

Ryan thanked her and called Lawrence.

"Check Ned's business connections for somebody named Willy whose home or business is a long-distance call from Manhattan."

"You have something?"

"You just heard it all."

"That's it, Willy at long distance?"

"That's it. They were fighting about money, on the phone, from Ned's. A couple of months before Ned was killed, maybe less."

"You don't have anything on the last name?"

"I have an idea, but it's a long shot and I don't want to send you off in the wrong direction."

Willy. It went back a long time, and it wouldn't be a long-distance call unless he had moved, but most people moved between high school and age twenty-eight or so. Willy. Ned's best friend in high school, football teammate, fraternity brother. Ryan had seen him at Ned's funeral, but Willy had acted as if Ryan weren't there. Thom Willard. The pallbearer who had not said hello.

Miller called to report on her search through Ned's trunk. "No notebook. I gave it a good look-through. Nothing related to what we're doing as far as I can tell. A lot of sports mementos, like you said. Letter sweaters, pennants, a deflated football with a lot of signatures. Framed pictures of teams he was on, a couple of year-books, some music tapes, old love letters. I made an inventory. You can look at it and see if I missed any connections. You'll know better where some of the things fit in his life."

Unlikely, Ryan thought. "Put it on the fax. I'll get to it as soon as I can." As soon as I can face it.

He worked the rest of the afternoon and into the night on the papers for the last of their pretrial motions. The only motion to exclude prosecution evidence they had any hope for was the one aimed at the new method of DNA blood-typing Becker was proposing to use. The New York courts had not been completely receptive to other tests like it, and Miller had lined up an impressive list of experts to testify about why.

They did not expect much from their other motions. There was no statement of Jennifer's to suppress; there was no evidence seized illegally; there was no prior criminal record to exclude. Identification evidence would come from people who had known Jennifer for years and had seen her that night repeatedly and at close range, so there were no lineups or other questionable identification procedures to challenge. They were going to file exclusionary motions on some of the forensic evidence besides the DNA testing, and a few other motions they had thought of that were not so farfetched they would annoy the judge.

All of the defense motions were duly reported. Even a standard demand for updated discovery of prosecution evidence produced a day's worth of overstatement: "The defense in the Edward Ryan 'art murder' trial today alleged that the prosecution was unfairly withholding information the defense was entitled to. According to papers filed in New York State Supreme Court, the prosecution action 'hinders preparation of the defense case.' "

A common feature of the press coverage was the phrase "defense lawyer Michael Ryan, father of the murder victim." Ryan began to worry that instead of creating a public impression of Jennifer's innocence, the constant drumbeat might numb people to the implications of his representing her.

The Monday after Thanksgiving Ryan called a planning session in the small conference room at Pane, Parish so they would all be up to date on each other's progress and clear about where they were headed. He had learned long ago the importance of being organized before an annual onset of the December silly season.

Before he started the meeting he gave Miller and Lawrence time to settle in and complain about their holidays. His own Thanksgiving had been unpleasant beyond description. He had made the mistake of accepting an invitation from Bob Legler and had spent the day surrounded by all the components of the kind of happy family that was now beyond his reach—parents, grandparents, children, grandchildren—at the table of an old friend in whose loyalty he no longer really believed.

"All right," Ryan said, "let's start off with a strategy update. I can see two main lines opening up for us. To put it in Kassia's terms, something to prove and someone to put on trial. I think we want to focus on the time gap. Jennifer and Ned left the party at eight o'clock or so. The M.E. says Ned died not long before the body was found . . ."

"The autopsy report says probably not much before nine. I'm checking to see if that's from the original autopsy tape or if it's an estimate they made afterward."

"We're looking for the latest time of death anybody estimated. The longer there was between when Ned and Jennifer left the party and when Ned was killed, the more chance someone unknown to us got in there.''

"So that's what we prove," Lawrence supplied. "There was plenty of time for other people to get in there and kill him.''

"If we can. As for the second line of attack, we're still putting Ned on trial. The point is, he made plenty of enemies. But we need specifics. Our best bet there seems to be the mortgage money. If it's as . . . as dirty as it feels, we should be in good shape. And we probably ought to poke around the medical supply company, too.'' He looked at them for comments.

"Basically it sounds good," Miller said. Grudgingly, he thought.

"Okay, with that in mind and two months to go, where do we stand? Kassia?''

"I've got all my people on board and working. The serologist has the prosecution reports and a sample of Jennifer's blood. Becker is sending Ned's clothes and the crime-scene photos to the blood-stain expert, and the fingerprint guy says he'll be done with his report soon. I have two pathologists I'm working with. They're already reviewing the autopsy report. They'll look at time of death, number and order of blows, force of blows, matching the wound to the alleged weapon, so on. Only one potential problem. The M.E. didn't keep any gross specimens, and one of my pathologists wanted to do an exhumation to get a look at the skull. I know it's grisly and upsetting to think about, Michael, but it might be very helpful. We'd want to do it as soon as we can.''

"He was cremated." Ryan's voice was flat.

"No! You're kidding.''

Lawrence shook his head. "Ain't life wonderful.''

"On to the next," she said. "I've put together a file on the assistant M.E. who did the autopsy. Name of Carmen Guevara. She's relatively new, which could be helpful, but it means there isn't that much in the way of prior testimony to look at.''

"Judge Corino?'' Ryan asked.

"Right. I added some more of his cases to the file, and a couple of law review articles he wrote in law school. We're planning to talk to his former law partners, but frankly I expect to hit a stone wall there.''

"I think there's one who'll talk to me," Lawrence said.

"Good," Ryan said. "That's it for me for now.''

"We'll have plenty of holiday reading," Lawrence said. "I'm providing I-don't-know-how-many pages of interview notes of artsy-fartsy types and investment bankers with poles up their tails.''

"Anything we should pay special attention to?''

"There's a couple of good ones. I talked to an actress who works part time for the caterers who did the party. She was tending bar that night."

Ryan sat forward. "Did she hear the fight?"

"Not really. She was surrounded by a horde of thirsty partyers. The reason I bring her up is she said that the cops made no attempt to interfere with the caterers, or to check them out at all. Tippy—that's her name, Tippy Ward—she and the others went about their business pretty as you please and when they were done they dragged these huge garbage bags out to the elevator and left them in the street for the sanitation guys to haul away. Then they crated up their plates and glasses and silver and took them to be boiled clean or however they do it."

"And presumably they swept up the pieces of the bowl Jennifer smashed," Miller said. "So there's no way anybody can check for traces of Jennifer's blood to verify that she cut her hand before she left the party."

"Give the little lady a kewpie doll."

"Craig!"

"Sorry." He grinned. "How about from now on, I call you 'guy,' okay?"

"I answer to Kassia."

"I've been meaning to ask since I met you—what kind of name is that?"

"A made-up kind of name. My folks like to be original. They always told me Kassia was another form of Cassie, which is short for Catherine."

"I was expecting maybe Cassandra, or Cassiopeia."

"I forgot, you're the lit major. You were telling us that the cops trashed our evidence."

"Yep."

"Good," she said.

"Beg pardon?"

"With no fragments of the bowl anywhere to be found, we have a perfect right to get every cop who was at the scene to describe in embarrassing detail how he made no attempt to preserve this valuable evidence. It's the flip side of our problem with Jennifer's clothes. The bowl looms a lot larger from its absence than if big chunks of it were right there in front of the jury with no blood on them. Reasonable doubt, right?"

"Pretty good," Lawrence bantered. "Now maybe you can make good news out of the rest of my report."

She grinned. "Always happy to oblige."

Ryan felt like he was locked out of the bakery looking in. His two colleagues were developing an ease with each other that he seemed to have no place in, for all his years of working with Lawrence.

"Are you making any progress on Tina Claire?" he snapped, sounding more irritated than he intended.

Lawrence gave him a look: what's eating you? "Ms. Tina Claire does not return calls. She does not respond to letters or to telegrams with prepaid replies. In short, she's avoiding us."

"Do you have somebody on her?"

"My people are asking around. This is nobody's coy mistress. She is very sexy, a well-known tease, and she has a boyfriend with a hot temper."

"Bull's-eye!" Miller said.

"Who will probably turn out to have a perfect alibi."

She wadded up a piece of paper and threw it at him. "You're a shit, Lawrence."

"Children!" he said, hoping it sounded like a joke. He wanted to be able to join in, but all he saw was an ex-F.B.I. man and a lady lawyer carrying on like kids. It wasn't his style.

"I had a strange letter from my bloodstain expert," Miller told Ryan on the phone the next day. "She says she needs to keep the crime-scene pictures and Ned's clothes awhile longer. She has an emergency capital murder case in Texas that's going to keep her busy a few weeks. In the meantime she wants us to be absolutely sure we sent her all the crime-scene pictures."

"I thought we asked for everything the prosecution had."

"We did."

"Could Becker have held some back?"

"It would be awfully dumb. He could screw up his whole case."

"Maybe your expert isn't counting right."

"I doubt it."

"Then you'd better draft something for Tony Boy and Mr. Becker that will get us the rest of those pictures."

"Assuming they exist."

Lawrence called to report that he'd found no Willys in Ned's phone records.

"I called 'em all and asked for Willy. Not a one."

"Is there a Thom Willard?"

"I don't remember one."

"Check it out."

* * *

Lawrence was tracking down and interviewing the people on Hugo
Hill's guest list, but Ryan wanted to talk to the three guests of honor
himself. The first one he talked to, a painter who called herself only
Karen, gave him a tour of her Soho loft, where art students under
her lackadaisical supervision were making paintings to be sold as
"Karen originals." Aside from that window on New York art, Ryan
got little from the visit. He was hoping for more from Susan Spada
but started with a question about her work to break the ice.

"I don't work in a single fixed style," she told him. "I like to
have an *idea* I'm working out, that's why Hugo decided to call me
a photoconceptualist. People ask me what it means but I don't
know. I didn't make it up, Hugo did."

She faced him across a round oak table in a room decorated
entirely in shades of ivory and cream. Susan Spada was short, only
an inch or two taller than Kassia Miller. Large dark eyes looked
out of an oval face framed by black hair that cascaded past her
shoulders. Her pale skin was so smooth it seemed not to have pores;
her precise bud of a mouth was red without lipstick. To Ryan she
looked impossibly young and exotic.

"I didn't know your son very well. We met, of course, but the
suggestions in the press about some sort of intimacy are pure fantasy. I can only speak for myself. He seemed very warm, and I
imagine many women would find him attractive."

"You were a guest of honor at the party where he was killed."

"Yes. I was standing quite close to him when his wife was so
upset."

"Can you describe what you saw and heard?"

"It was very disturbing." Ryan thought he saw a flicker of emotion behind the dark eyes, but her expression did not change. "Hugo
brought your son over to meet Tina Claire. Tina likes to have fun
and she likes to tease. She can be so original in how she behaves,
it's sad that her sculpture is so derivative—sort of warmed-over
Giacometti. She really should be a performance artist. When I saw
that she and your son were starting to get involved I wanted to see
what would happen. And then his wife came over and it was like
the old Jackie Gleason show." Her mouth curved into the briefest
hint of a smile. "Pow! right in the kisser."

Ryan winced, imagining a jury hearing that. "Do you remember
what she said?"

"Some of it. She said, 'You bastard, how can you do this to me?
You think you can get away with this? I'm not going to take it
anymore.' " The quotes came out flat, without emphasis or inflec-

tion. " 'I'm going to get you. I swear I'm going to make you sorry.' "

"Did he say anything?"

"Not at first."

"What about Tina Claire?"

"As I remember it, she sort of hid behind him. I think she had one hand in his pocket, and I believe she was pushing her body against him."

"Did she say anything?"

"No, but she seemed to be enjoying herself."

"Did Mrs. Ryan say anything else? Or do anything?"

"She said, 'You think you can humiliate me like this? You think I'm going to take it lying down? You've had it.' "

" 'You've had it'?"

"Yes. 'You've had it.' "

"Do you know what she meant by that?" Not a question he would ask in court, but he wanted to hear her answer.

"I suppose . . . *you've had it* . . . that's pretty final."

"Do you remember anything else?"

"She threw a serving bowl. It broke into a million pieces with Mexican meat pastries all over. It seemed very symbolic."

Ryan winced again. But the symbolism—shattered bowl, shattered marriage, shattered skull, or whatever else she saw in it—could be kept out of court.

"Anything else?"

"When the bowl went, everything stopped. The decisive moment, I thought. And he said . . . her name. That's all. Once. The way you'd talk to a bad dog, or a child. And she said, 'Watch out, you bastard, or next time it won't be a bowl.' "

It kept getting worse. How many people had heard that one?

"And then?" he made himself ask.

"He walked out. She stood there a few seconds and then she went after him."

"How did he seem at that point? Angry? Upset? Why did he walk out?"

"I'm sorry, I don't read minds."

Serves you right, Ryan, he told himself, asking a sloppy multiple question like that, and a question that starts with "why?"

"Let me try that again. Did he seem angry to you?"

"Not especially."

"Apologetic?"

"How would I know?"

"His tone of voice? His demeanor?"

"All I know is he said her name. And then when she kept on at him he took off. What he had in mind I can't tell you."

Ryan thanked her and said he might be back in touch. On his way out he asked if she had spoken to anyone from the police or the D.A.'s office. She had. Had they asked her to testify? Yes. Was she going to? She hadn't decided. Had they said anything to her about talking to him? They hoped she wouldn't but it was up to her.

The pale winter daylight had vanished while he was interviewing Susan Spada. He decided not to go back to work. Instead he stopped in at the Shamrock for a beer and an Irish and a few words with Kelly.

"Landlord served notice," Kelly said glumly. "Double rent next lease, with escalators. I told him I can't make it. He says bring in a fancy chef, redecorate and triple my prices. The neighborhood's changing, he says, or haven't I noticed."

"I don't know what's wrong with everybody," Ryan said. "What happens when all that's left is stores selling mint-green tennis sweaters and Italian shoes? How long can that last?"

"That's what I told him. He's shooting himself in the foot."

"You think he'll listen to reason?"

"What makes him different from everybody else?"

24

"I FOUND THOM WILLARD," CRAIG LAWRENCE TOLD Ryan. "I think he's our Willy. Jake Kaplan says there's a file of correspondence with him in Ned's papers. Young Mr. Willard appears to be the banker who handled Ned's mortgage transactions for him. A bank in Philadelphia."

"Nice work."

Thom Willard came to the door of his office to greet Ryan. His bank was medium size but its executive offices were designed like a sanctum of finance, and Willy dressed and carried himself in a way calculated to bolster that impression. For Ryan, who remembered him as a bloody-kneed pre-teen, the pinstripe suit and pompous stride were testimony only to Willy's self-importance.

He invited Ryan in, seated him on the couch at the opposite end of the office from a shiny reproduction period-piece desk, and made the ritual offer of coffee. Not having spoken to Ryan at Ned's funeral, he had the sense not to offer condolences.

"I'm Ned's executor, as maybe you know," Ryan said after Willy's secretary had served them coffee. "I noticed you handled some of his business."

"All of his mortgage placements, as far as I know."

"How did you get into business together?"

"I ran interference for him in high school. Why not now?"

"Had you been keeping up with each other?"

"Except for a year or so right after college when he dropped out of sight. I think he was off somewhere with his grandfather. Some character," Willy added, not without respect. "I only met him once, but Ned talked about him a lot. You were saying . . ."

"That as Ned's executor I'm looking for details of Ned's mortgage business. I'm also here on a personal mission. Ned and I didn't see much of each other the last couple of years—I guess you probably know about that. I was hoping you could help me get an idea of what his life was like."

"You wouldn't be on a fishing expedition, looking for ways to get Ned's murderer off the hook?"

"Whoa!" Ryan's reaction was instinctive. "Innocent until proven guilty."

"That's fine in court, Mr. Ryan, if you can make it stick. From what I've read she looks pretty guilty."

"I'm surprised, Willy, a smart fellow like you, being fooled by the press. Those people are selling newspapers, not truth."

"That *is* what you came to talk about, then?"

"I came to talk about Ned's businesses. I hoped you could help me put a value on them for federal estate taxes. And I came because I wanted to ask you about your impressions of Ned. And yes, there's the hope I'll come across something that will lead me to the person who really killed him."

"I gather you don't believe Jennifer did it."

"That's right, I don't. I can't say that to a jury, but I can say it to you. I don't believe she's guilty." It came out with a ring of conviction that belied its distance from the truth.

"I don't think I can be much help," Willy told him. "But if you feel so strongly about it I suppose I can at least talk to you. Why don't I get you settled with the mortgage documents and you can ask my assistant any questions you have about that. Then you and I can talk over lunch."

Watching Willy walk out of the office to talk to his assistant, Ryan thought: He's pear shaped already, at less than thirty, with that complacent roll of fat on the back of his neck and a drinker's face. Ten, eleven years ago he was a high-school football hero.

They ate at Willy's club, another appurtenance of his premature middle age, a place where it was forbidden to carry a briefcase beyond the lobby checkroom, as if that kept anybody from doing business.

"Okay," Willy said, "ask your questions."

"Let's start with the mortgages. Where did the money come from?"

"For the mortgages? I don't have any idea. That was all Ned's. We talked about it a few times, but it was only the usual bitching about people who said they were going to invest and didn't pay up in time. Otherwise, he deposited the money and left it with me until the mortgages closed. I helped him find developers a couple of times, and I handled the title searches and insurance and the liaison with banks in other states, and whatever else he needed."

"How did the deposits come in? All at once or in small installments?"

"Why? Is something wrong?"

"No. I'm trying to get a feel for how it went."

"Offhand I don't know. I thought we gave you whatever papers like that there were. I was the guy who held the money for him and made sure it was there when he needed it. I didn't personally perform the day-to-day operations, depositing the checks and so on."

"How long did you keep the money?"

"That should have been in the papers you saw, too. Rarely more than a few days, if I remember correctly."

A waiter stood by the table. Willy inquired what Ryan wanted and checked the items off on a printed list for the waiter.

"I did think of an anecdote that might help you," Willy said, pausing for a sip of his second martini. "Ned had a way of changing the terms on people. I learned this from one or two folks I put Ned together with, and it didn't make me happy, but the deals closed and if it meant some people had a slimmer profit margin than they expected, well it wasn't my business. There was one that bothered me, though. It was a hard parcel to put together, and the zoning variances were a bitch. A major foreign investor ducked out at the last minute. Ned was always interested in placing money, so I put him together with these people. The deal we worked out was that he would finance a fifth of the parcel. And at the last minute, literally the last minute, the morning of the closing, Ned made a major change in the mortgage terms. He didn't present it as a change, you understand; it's not done that way. You wring your hands and talk about an unfortunate misunderstanding, but nobody's really fooled. The developer couldn't live with it and Ned wouldn't back down. I suppose he figured that the deal was big enough that the others would bend a little to accommodate his terms.''

Willy finished his drink and waved to the waiter for another.

"What happened?"

"Ned misjudged it. The developer really couldn't handle it, and the other money people wouldn't, and the deal fell apart. The variances were dependent on going forward promptly, so the whole deal was down the drain forever. A shame. It would have been a beautiful project, made a ton of money.''

"I'd like to talk to the people who were in that deal," Ryan said. And thought: under oath in front of a jury.

"I'll have to check and see if I have the papers on that anymore. Or maybe I can remember some of the names for you. It's almost two years ago and I see so many of these deals come and go . . .''

"I'd appreciate it," Ryan said. For now he was more interested in getting as much as he could from Willy than in pumping him about his arguments with Ned. There would be time for that.

In the morning Ryan told Lawrence about the meeting with Willy.

"That's a pisser," Lawrence said. "Changing the mortgage terms like that.''

"That it is. But I'd trade one guy with blood in his eye and a threat on his lips for a dozen stories about deals where Ned allegedly screwed people.''

"We're doing our best.''

The hearing on whether to admit as evidence new methods of analyzing the genetic material found in human blood and tissues took four days, but for practical purposes it ended on the second day, when Corino ruled irrelevant any testimony about DNA tests other than the specific method used by the prosecution's experts. It meant that most of the defense witnesses would have nothing to testify about. As the hearing progressed Ryan had the feeling Corino had made up his mind based on the briefs and was only paying perfunctory attention. Besides, his crucial decisions so far had favored the defense. Balance, a factor most judges considered, demanded a big one now for the prosecution.

On the day Corino had scheduled to rule on the defense motions Jennifer appeared in court in a gray wool skirt with a bulky, over-sized sweater in a darker shade of charcoal. The sweater came to her hips, concealing her slight bulge of baby-to-be as long as she kept her movements slow and did not stretch or reach.

True to Ryan's expectation, Corino ruled that he would admit the new tests in evidence. "I will instruct the jury, however, that they may decide from the testimony how much weight to give this new technology in their deliberations."

Except for their discovery demands, which produced a few minor items but no additional pictures of the crime-scene bloodstains, the defense had made no pretrial motions they had any real hope would succeed. Of course there was always the possibility that the judge might surprise them and give them one they didn't expect to get. He didn't.

He did say that he was counting on both sides to adhere to the trial schedule he had set up.

"Is the defense going to be ready?"

"Yes, Judge, we are." Ryan kept his tone matter of fact, without eagerness.

Becker grumbled about needing more time to locate witnesses.

Having granted Becker his wish for an exotic new kind of evidence, Corino was not inclined to give him any other leeway this time out. "You've got two months left, Mr. Becker, and you've already had five. Seems like enough to me. It's rare enough to have a defendant ready for trial that I don't want to miss my chance to get this under way on schedule. That means you'll be in here ready to pick a jury on the first Monday in February, unless you've got a very good reason not to be."

Reporters trailed the defendant and her lawyers down the court-house corridor, asking questions about Corino's rulings denying their motions.

"No comment," Ryan said, grateful for the grand sweep of sable that concealed Jennifer as she walked alongside him.

They piled into the waiting car, Ryan in front, the two women in the back. As they pulled away from the curb, Miller let out a whoop.

"Did something good happen?" Jennifer wanted to know. "The

judge let them use that test, and he denied our motions. I was sure today was all bad news.''

Ryan twisted in his seat to face her. ''We're happy because the judge confirmed the trial date.''

''The sooner the better,'' Jennifer said, not for the same reason.

Ryan's secretary and Miller's had been looking for an office they could use through the trial. The few they had found were too small or inconveniently located or required a long lease. The breakthrough came from Kneeland—an empty storefront on the southeastern fringe of Soho, only a few blocks north of the courthouse. All they needed was to hang curtains over the expansive front windows, put up partitions, and install furniture and equipment. Kneeland had it ready for them in less than a week. Ryan could not help being impressed.

When Jennifer came down to see the new office they showed her the desk they had set aside for her.

''There's a lot for you to do,'' Miller told her. ''We want you to go over our notes about the people who were at the party and tell us everything you can about these people, good or bad. And there are parts of our strategy we have to discuss with you.''

''When do you want me to start?''

''Right now,'' Ryan said. ''We'd like you to be here as much as you can until you've gone through all the files.''

''Every day?''

''We'll be here seven days a week,'' Miller said. ''Organizing our case, preparing exhibits, talking to witnesses.''

Ryan gave Jennifer a list of party guests and a stack of interview notes. ''Yell if you have any questions.''

They ordered lunch from one of the nearby restaurants whose delivery menus they had collected. Over lunch the two lawyers talked with their client about what lay ahead.

''There's one thing you have to understand,'' Ryan told her. ''In some ways we're badly handicapped because you say you didn't hit Ned.''

When she started to protest he held up a hand. ''Hear me out. Right now the prosecution's strongest evidence is that blood was found on the sculpture that killed Ned and they have this fancy test to show it has the same genetic markers as yours. No matter how much we deny you did it, the blood ties you to the place and to the murder weapon. If you say you hit Ned, that evidence becomes worthless to them.''

She was leaning forward, eager to deny it. Ryan kept talking, determined to make sure she understood.

"There's a whole barrelful of justifications for a murderous act. Self-defense, fear of future abuse, even sexual pleasure. People get a slap on the wrist for killing their sex partners by claiming it was part of a pleasure ritual. It's a kind of accident. Accident is a good one. But if you say you didn't hit him, then we can't say it was an accident that you did. And we can't talk about emotional disturbance or diminished capacity of any kind. If you hit him, we can examine what happened and try to find acceptable reasons for it."

Ryan saw he wasn't making much headway so he wrapped it up. "Otherwise it's all or nothing. If you say you didn't do it and the jury believes you did, you get the full penalty."

"*I didn't hit him.*"

"As long as you understand the consequences."

"Not a bad day working with the client," Miller said as they were closing up for the night.

"She seems to be in good shape. And she certainly knows her own mind."

"It's still not real to her. Wait until we get closer."

Ryan got his overcoat from the old clothes tree someone had salvaged. "I've been thinking about whether she should testify. I agree we have to start right away preparing her to take the stand, just in case. But I don't think there's a reason in the world to let her get up there."

Miller disagreed. "The jury is going to want to hear her deny she did it. Deny she was even there at the time when the medical examiner says Ned died. If she doesn't, they're going to wonder why."

"Right now, given how little we have, it looks to me like we'll be playing this for reasonable doubt. If we do—if we tell the jury the prosecutor hasn't proved his case—then Jennifer's testimony isn't necessary. Because if Becker didn't prove anything, there's nothing for her to deny."

She started to protest but Ryan continued. "Besides, from what I've seen I don't expect her to be wonderful on the stand."

"She's an actress."

"I'm going to pretend you didn't say that."

"Michael, can I interrupt you?" Jennifer called across the office the next day.

He looked up from the report of their preliminary public-opinion poll.

"I don't see anything here for Ellis and Skippy Turner."

Ryan walked over. "Who are they?"

"Friends of mine from Feed the Children. I invited them to the party because they're interested in contemporary artists, and Ned had been saying for a while that he wanted to meet them. They were talking to Ned right before Hugo Hill came and took him to meet that sculptor."

"Do you think they saw what happened?"

"I know they did. I was standing with them when I first saw it myself."

"I'm glad you told me. Do you think they'll cooperate?"

Jennifer worked at balancing a pen upright on her desk. "I used to think I knew who my friends were. I'm not so sure anymore. I *think* they'll cooperate, but I can't promise."

The Turners had a duplex high above Central Park West with a glass living room like a greenhouse and a terrace puffy with new-fallen snow. There was no child in evidence, but someone had built a snowman, complete with a carrot nose and what looked like coal eyes and buttons. Its ice-crystal surface glittered with reflected light against the coolly brilliant backdrop of the skyline.

"Mostly we talked about Feed the Children," Skippy Turner told him. She was a tall blonde, plain as a board, outfitted from an outdoor-togs catalog. "He seemed very interested. Frankly, I was surprised." She looked to her husband for confirmation.

Ellis Turner had a small, meticulously trimmed beard and he was dressed in the same Maine-woods style as his wife.

"I was surprised, too. Jennifer had always come to meetings and activities alone. I had the impression Feed the Children didn't interest her husband."

"Maybe he was being polite at the party," Skippy suggested.

"Exactly what did you talk about?"

"Our area is the Horn of Africa," Ellis explained. "We talked about that. About the Sudan and Ethiopia and Somalia. It wasn't in the news then, the way it has been lately, all this scandal about aid shipments being diverted or sold. But we already knew there were going to be shortages of food and medicine this year."

"Heavy talk for an art party."

"It didn't last that long," Skippy said. "Jennifer came over, and then the host came, I think it was the host. A silly man with a red toupee."

"That sounds like the host," Ryan confirmed. "Hugo Hill."

"Right," Ellis said. "He came and excused himself for taking Ned away and led him off to talk to that blonde sculptor person."

"Did you watch what happened then?"

"Not really. We talked to Jennifer for a few minutes."

"Right," Skippy said. "But only a few minutes because I remember that something attracted our attention to Ned and that woman."

"Do you remember what it was?"

"No . . . I don't. Do you, honey?"

"No," Ellis said, "but whatever it was, by the time we turned that way they were . . . well, it was hard to see, exactly, but they were doing something more than talking."

"When you say it was hard to see . . ."

"It wasn't that hard for me to see," Skippy said. "It seemed to me they were playing some kind of sex game. I looked at Jennifer to see if she saw it, too, and I guess she did, because she was staring at them."

"Did she say anything?"

"Do you remember?" Skippy asked her husband.

He put his hands behind his head and stared up at the ceiling as if he were watching the scene projected there. "I honestly don't." He smiled apologetically at Ryan. "I was so embarrassed I didn't want to know."

Ryan looked to Skippy.

"Me, too. I felt awful for poor Jennifer. I started to say let's go get a drink or something but she wasn't paying any attention to me, so I said, well we have to be going, please say good-bye to Ned for us."

"And then what?"

"We left."

"Did you see Jennifer go up to Ned, or hear what she said?"

"No," Ellis said. "We were gone by then."

At the office the next day Ryan asked Jennifer to go over again what had happened at the party. He took her through it slowly, pressing for details, going back over some parts two and three times, asking about portions of the story out of sequence. Jennifer kept up with him for more than an hour before she began to show signs of irritation.

"Is this a test?" she snapped after he asked for the third time exactly what she had said before she smashed the bowl. "Are you trying to see how I'd do on the witness stand?"

''More like practice than a test,'' he said. ''We can't decide about your testifying until the last minute, so you have to be ready, in case. But right now I'm just trying to get the clearest picture I can of what happened.''

She received that skeptically. ''Then why are you badgering me?''

''Am I badgering you?''

''Is it because you don't believe me? Maybe you think, she took acting classes, she knows about pretending emotions, so how can I trust anything she says or does?''

The question struck home.

''I'm right, aren't I? Well, the answer is, maybe you can't. I'm not as good an actor as some people. I can't reach inside for emotions that don't come out of the situation I'm in. All I can do is heighten emotions that are already there for me. I can, and I do. I've done it all my life. The training I liked best as an actor was the kind that said, you're full of conflicting emotions all the time and your job as an actor is to find the one you need and bring it out and amplify it. That's what I do best. You want to see happy, I can show you ecstatic, delirious, hysterical. You want to see angry, I can show you towering rage, burning fury, bubbling venom.''

Ryan believed her.

She stopped for breath; her torrent of words had been an effort. When she resumed, she was reflective. ''It's funny, sad, I don't know what to call it . . . That's really what I was doing that night, at the party. I had an audience, I had some real motivation. I was putting on a show. That's all it was—a show. After all, Ned wasn't doing anything that was reason to kill, or even to get killing mad over. I wasn't. Just the opposite. To push my emotions, the way I was, takes a certain detachment. You have to stand outside yourself at least a little.''

She paused again, smiled. A joke at her own expense.

''It looks like all that training finally paid off. I put on a truly convincing performance. A total improvisation, at that. And that's the only thing I'm guilty of.''

25

LAWRENCE CALLED. "I'VE GOT SOME HOT STUFF. I'LL be there in half an hour."

He was ten minutes early, his leather bomber jacket glistening with water, snowflakes melting into its fur collar. He dropped himself into a chair. "Pure hell out there. Joy to the world."

They sat and drank coffee together. Miller turned off her computer and stretched.

Lawrence put his coffee cup on the floor. "I talked to a guy who says the motto of Hugo Hill's party should have been Just Say Yes."

"Cocaine?" Ryan asked.

"Mostly, the way he tells it."

Ryan turned to his co-counsel, the resident expert on local criminal matters. "If the cops confiscated cocaine at that party, would you expect to know about it?"

"The way Becker is playing this, I'm not sure."

"Maybe we ought to ask him."

She disagreed. "If we ask now, we alert him that we know about it, and we give him a chance to bring it out himself in a way that doesn't hurt him. That way we lose any chance to surprise him."

"If we go on rumor and get it wrong, we'll be the ones who'll be surprised."

"Guns," Lawrence interjected.

"What?"

"I was thinking, when the cops come into a place and people dump what they're carrying, what do they dump? And the answer is, drugs and guns."

"And if they confiscated guns it means there were potentially violent people at that party." Ryan was getting revved up. "The drugs say that, too, for that matter."

Miller was not convinced. "I still think we shouldn't ask about

146

it right away. We ought to wait and see if we can verify it without tipping him off.''

They argued it back and forth long enough to drive Lawrence from the office.

''Don't you guys ever stop? It's like a Punch and Judy show around here.''

After checking fruitlessly through their notes on interviews with Hugo Hill's party guests and talking to Jennifer, who claimed she could never tell if anybody was high, Miller conceded that they should ask the prosecution about drugs and weapons.

Becker's response to their request claimed that such materials, if they existed, were irrelevant to the case, or if not irrelevant then not the proper subject of discovery.

Miller drafted a brief for them to submit to Judge Corino. She made a case that reports of any drugs or weapons found on the premises were potentially exculpatory and so had to be disclosed to the defense, and that the same was true of fingerprint reports and any other information relating to drugs or weapons found at Hugo Hill's the night of the murder. In fact, the brief argued, the drugs and weapons themselves were relevant physical evidence.

From the speed of the press reaction, the court papers were read by the reporters covering the case before they got to the judge. ART MURDER MYSTERY, read one headline; COPS FOUND GUNS AND DRUGS.

Ryan spent Christmas week hiding out in a carrel at the back of the law library his firm had co-ventured with two other law firms in the building. He read and reread reports from Jake Kaplan and Craig Lawrence, and notes of all the interviews he and Lawrence and Miller had done with prospective witnesses and people who knew Ned and his businesses.

Ryan had not so immersed himself in this kind of preparation since his first years at Pane, Parish. As time had passed there he had become more and more a strategist, a coordinator, an idea man. He had kept in touch by going into court a few times a year to sit in on trials he had helped prepare, all civil cases; he had always been on the plaintiff's side, never the defendant's.

Until the Gibson case. He could have prepared the Gibson case at this level of intensity. He should have. At the time he had been convinced he was, but actually he had been making himself frantic with meaningless details, micromanaging his associates past the point of endurance, and in general mistaking activity for accomplishment. Without recognizing what he was doing he had almost turned the case into a disaster. When his co-counsel and then his partners had called him on it he had accused them of incompetence and laziness. They had responded by threatening to resign from the case en masse if he was not removed. Since then he had not gone near a court or trial preparation. Not until this case.

Now he sat hour after hour bent over endless pages of notes, absorbing details, looking for patterns. The sides of the carrel made a cocoon of isolation from which he hoped to emerge more nearly like the Michael Ryan who had once been a crack federal prosecutor.

At night, he went straight home, even on Friday. He could not face the Shamrock; it was too full of holiday cheer.

The only holiday-season obligation Ryan could not avoid was Robertson Kneeland's New Year's Eve party. He had wanted nothing more than to ignore the invitation, but Miller had argued the importance of their making an appearance, and finally he stopped resisting just to keep the peace.

"I think we should arrive together," he told her. "If your date doesn't mind."

"I don't have a date. I did, but it got canceled."

"Sorry to hear it."

"Don't be. The jerk."

"You want me to pick you up?"

"If *your* date doesn't mind."

"I don't have dates."

"You have one now."

On New Year's Eve it took Ryan even longer than he expected to get a taxi, and he was fifteen minutes late arriving at Miller's. He told the cabbie to wait while he went to get her.

"Make it quick," snarled the cabbie.

No sooner had Ryan got the cab door open and a foot on the pavement than Miller was on her way out of the apartment building, followed by a tall man in dinner clothes under a rich-looking black Chesterfield. He had wavy dark hair and a moustache and he looked to Ryan like a TV private detective.

Miller ducked her head into the cab and kissed Ryan's cheek. "Not a word," she whispered. She was wearing a simple black dress, her white wool coat draped over her shoulders; Ryan thought the dress and her softer-than-usual hairdo made her look surprisingly feminine.

"This is Daniel. Daniel Sonya, Michael Ryan."

Ryan slid across the seat to make room for them. True to instructions he said not a word.

By the time they arrived the party had spread through the first floor of Kneeland's apartment. Out-of-work actors of both genders in red satin tunics and black knickers carried drinks and hors d'oeuvres. The decorating theme was prerevolutionary Russia. The stairway to the bedrooms was cordoned off with a blue velvet rope. A red-and-black clad man brawnier than the waiters stood behind it to discourage anyone who might have been tempted to ignore the symbolic barrier.

"Who are all these people?" Miller wondered.

"Freeloaders," Ryan said.

She laughed. Her date looked at him as if he had cursed in church.

Jennifer glided over in a cloud of silver. Layers of gauzy fabric hung straight from her shoulders to the floor. Somewhere underneath was a glittering dress that left the tops of her breasts bare and was belted high beneath them, obscuring any sign of her pregnancy. Her dark hair was coiled and twisted atop her head and dusted with tiny diamonds.

"I'm so glad you came. Isn't this awful?"

"Your father has a lot of friends."

"My father does a lot of business. And throws a good party." She stopped, smiled at Daniel. "Hello, I'm Jennifer."

"This is Daniel," Miller said.

"Are you a lawyer, too?"

"Daniel is a tennis player."

Lordy, Ryan thought. And: does he get to speak for himself?

"Michael, my father wants you to meet some people. You go find him and I'll take Kassia and Daniel around and show them who to avoid."

Ryan was in no hurry to find Kneeland. He took a glass of champagne from a passing Cossack or Kulak, he didn't know which. Not a Chirkess, he thought, remembering ancient faded pictures of his grandmother's father.

It was good champagne. He navigated past the piano, where a woman in African dress was playing swing-era standards accompanied on the bass by a man in white tie and tails.

He stood by the window, gazing out over holiday-night New York. The other time he had been here, on a rainy summer evening, he had been too preoccupied to notice the view. Now, on a clear winter night, it was glorious: shimmering crystal towers alight from within. It was like looking at the future, or Oz.

"Michael Ryan." It was Kneeland. "I'm glad you came."

Ryan turned. Behind Kneeland was a roomful of men in dinner clothes, women in designer gowns. Jewels caught the light on every side. The party guests looked as still and artificial as the costumed waiters. He thought: I was right about this, about Ned. If this was what he wanted he was making a mistake.

He said polite hellos to Kneeland's friends but made no attempt to return the conversational volleys they lobbed his way. He gathered that most of them were in deals with Kneeland, or about to be.

The piano player banged out a fortissimo fanfare. The crowd began to quiet down.

"Friends," Robertson Kneeland said. He was standing by the piano with Jennifer at his side. "Friends!" He waited for the tag ends of conversation to die down. "My daughter and I have an announcement to make."

There was only one announcement that Kneeland could be making. Ryan was furious. This would put Becker on notice that he was going to face a pregnant defendant, and it would give him a good month to think of reasons to delay the trial until after Jennifer gave birth.

Kneeland was talking again. "It may not look that way, but we're going to have a blessed event in this family. I'm expecting to be a grandfather in the new year. So I want you all to drink a special toast to the health of my wonderful daughter Jennifer and to the baby growing inside her."

Jennifer looked mortified, though she did her best to smile.

"Doesn't he get it that we were keeping it a secret?" MIller asked Ryan.

"I thought he did."

Jennifer was surrounded by well-wishers. Ryan thought of pushing through to warn her not to say too much about when she was due, but there was nothing to be gained.

A little later Jennifer broke free and found Ryan.

"I'm so embarrassed," she said. "He just sprung it on me. Is it going to hurt us?"

"We'll try not to let it. The important thing is just to say no comment. People may be making nasty noises about when you conceived. You'll just have to ride it out."

Her eyes filled. "Why can't they leave me alone?"

He had no answer. She rested her head on his shoulder and

sniffled. He put an arm awkwardly around her. He could feel the life inside her and feeling it he could almost make himself think it didn't matter what she had done. Life was important. Life had meaning.

Ned's life, too, he could not help thinking.

Jennifer leaned away from him so she could see him. Her hands were on his shoulders and she did not seem to want to disengage from him. He could still sense the baby.

"Let's hope the next year is better than the last one." The corners of her mouth turned up, but the smile did not brighten her eyes.

"If I have anything to do with it."

Her father came over. "Can't neglect your guests."

"Michael is a guest."

Kneeland smiled indulgently. "The Goddards are asking for you." He led her away. "See you later," he said to Ryan.

Ryan checked his watch: eleven forty-five. He did not want to be around for "Auld Lang Syne."

He found Miller. "I'm leaving. Give my best to our host and hostess."

She put a hand on his arm. "Are you okay?"

"I'll be fine. I can't take any more of this."

"You're sure you'll be all right?" He imagined he heard honest concern in her voice.

"Sure. There's a race in Central Park, and fireworks. I'm not going to Forty-second Street."

"Be careful." She reached up to kiss him on the corner of the mouth. "Happy New Year."

He surprised himself by putting his arms around her and holding her tight. "Happy New Year," he said into her hair, and then he fled.

26

TAKING PART OF NEW YEAR'S DAY OFF WAS A LUXURY
Ryan had not been sure they could afford. Ryan himself was back
at the office at eight in the morning.

Kassia Miller came in after lunch with the morning papers.
NED'S BABY FOR JENNY? asked one front-page headline. Inside were pictures of Jennifer taken in the months since her arrest,
with body silhouettes drawn in to show an obstetrician's idea of
how pregnant she might be. There was the inevitable counting on
fingers to determine the latest she could be due, based on the date
of her husband's death. The rest was left to the readers' imagina-
tions.

There was nothing Ryan could do about it: the reports all stayed
on the safe side of libel. For the first time the press coverage of the
case left him feeling soiled and dirty in a way he hadn't since SON
SAYS DAD KILLED MOM.

The new year's work started in earnest with another session with
Jennifer.

"Right now we have two main lines of attack," Ryan told her.
"You were last seen with Ned a few minutes after eight, and the
earliest the medical examiner thinks Ned was killed is at nine
o'clock or close to it. A lot could have happened in that hour. We
want to hammer that home every chance we get. It's too bad you
didn't talk to anybody after you left the party."

He gave her time to think about it, hoping she would remember
something they could use. She got up and paced, stopping to stroke
Miller's elephant, brought here from her office.

"Well," he said, about to go on.

"Michael," Jennifer interrupted.

"You think of something?"

152

She ran a finger along the elephant's trunk. "I went back."

"You went back?"

"I was walking home. I kept thinking about Ned and what a scene I'd made. I was still angry about what he did, but I could see that I had handled it wrong, gone too far. I stopped someplace and had a cup of coffee and thought about it more and decided I ought to try to talk to him again before it had a chance to fester."

"And . . ."

"I went back to Hugo Hill's." Looking at Ryan like: There, I said it.

Ryan closed his eyes and shook his head. A better man would keep his reaction out of his face, he thought. He didn't even try.

He looked at his co-counsel. "Did you know about this?"

"No."

"When was this?" he asked their client.

"I don't know exactly. A half hour after I left, maybe more."

"Quarter to nine," Miller supplied.

"And you went upstairs?" Don't lead her, Ryan scolded himself, let her tell it.

"No," she said, "I . . ." She seemed to be having trouble with it. "I was waiting for the elevator and I thought, I don't want to face those people. I didn't know what I wanted to do. There was a door to the stairs. I tried it and it was open so I went in and started to walk up, but then I decided not to and I sat in the stairway and thought some more."

She sat down at her desk.

"How long were you there?" Ryan asked her.

"I don't know. I wasn't wearing a watch." Staring at her hands on the desk.

"About how long?" Miller asked in a gentler tone than Ryan's.

Jennifer shrugged. "Fifteen minutes."

"That makes it right around nine." The M.E.'s time of death. Ryan could see the center of their case collapsing. "What did you do then?"

"I left."

"Did anyone see you?"

"I don't know."

He caught himself about to snap at her, spoke with control instead. "We have to know if you saw anyone, or if there's any way someone might have seen you. If there are witnesses the prosecution can use to place you at the scene at the time Ned died, we need to know who they are and exactly where they saw you."

"I understand." Subdued.

"Good." He decided not to let the moment go by. "While we're filling in the blanks, what else is there? Bear in mind that New York's finest have been digging around in your past for months and if we put you on the stand, or if we try to use character witnesses, the prosecutor will get it all out there for the jury."

Silence. Ryan waited.

Jennifer turned to Kassia Miller. "Should I tell him?"

"Absolutely."

He looked from one to the other. What the hell had they been keeping from him?

"I don't know where to start," Jennifer said.

"Just tell him what you told me."

Jennifer picked up a felt-tip pen and concentrated on balancing it on end on her desk while she spoke. "I was in trouble before. I mean, nothing like this. School problems and things, years ago. I don't know if it's important, but I guess . . ." She looked at him.

Dreading what was coming, he gave her a thin smile of encouragement. She went back to balancing her pen.

"I was suspended from boarding school once for breaking something. A vase. And then in college a couple of times, I broke things." The pen refused to stand on end. "Once I ran into somebody's car and they made a huge fuss about it. I don't know why— I always paid for the damage, or my father did."

"You broke things? What did you break?"

Ryan waited for her to answer. When she didn't he said, "I have to know."

The pen stood on end for a moment, then toppled. She hurled it across the room. "I can't do this. It's why I talk to Kassia. Can't she tell you? Then if you have questions I'll answer them."

"All right," Ryan said. "Why don't you take a break. Come back after lunch."

Jennifer got her coat.

"Try to remember who might have seen you," Ryan told her as she left. "And anything else the prosecutor might spring on us at the trial."

He went to the refrigerator and got a can of diet soda. Miller had up a hand and he flipped one to her. The toss was short but she snagged it an inch above the carpet.

"She was giving you the abridged version," she told him. "She has a history of violent outbursts."

"Violent outbursts! I should have been an accountant. What kind of violent outbursts?"

"Breaking things with other things."

"Give me an example."

"Well, the way she told it, she'd pick up a . . . well, the time she told me about, it was a candlestick. And she went around smashing things with it."

"Went around?"

"Around the house."

Ryan had been standing by the refrigerator. He sat down.

"What did she break?"

"She battered a table pretty badly, she said. Broke some vases and bowls. A bunch of pictures on a piano top, and the piano top."

He didn't believe he was hearing this. "Why?"

"It was a friend's house. She was a little hard to pin down, but it seems the friend had been sleeping with a guy Jennifer thought was her personal property."

"Sleeping with a guy she thought was her personal property. It's not the same, but it sure as hell is close."

"If it was the same she would have beat up the sculptor, not Ned."

"Bite your tongue," he said.

"That was just for the sake of argument."

"Right."

But there it was, the way the world would see it. The way he could not help seeing it. A jealous Jennifer trashing a friend's house. A candlestick wasn't that far from a statue.

"How old was she?" he asked wearily.

"College. Twenty, twenty-one."

"Becker is going to be in heaven if his people dig this up. Assuming they haven't already. Assuming we don't have an obligation to tell him ourselves."

"It's not relevant. She was a kid, ten years before she met Ned . . ."

"You're suggesting we object when Becker brings it in?" He struck a judicial pose. "The jury will disregard all mention of Mrs. Ryan's tendency to smash things when she's jealous."

"I'm suggesting we file a motion *in limine* and keep the whole business out."

"If we can do it without a delay." He was skeptical.

"It's just a straight application of the rules of evidence," she argued. "We file motion papers, Becker replies, Corino decides in our favor. There's no reason for a delay."

"Except it's not that open and shut, and we've got a prosecutor looking for any excuse to get the trial put off now that he knows his defendant is pregnant . . . And you knew about this.'' He was building up a head of steam.

''Yes.''

''And you didn't tell me!''

''Don't shout, Michael, my hearing is fine.''

''Your judgment isn't.''

She popped the top on her diet soda. It shot a stream of liquid across the room. Ryan ducked but it caught him on the shoulder.

''Shit.'' He grabbed some paper towels in the bathroom and dried his jacket.

''Cold water,'' Miller recommended.

He ignored her and sat down at his desk. ''Why didn't you tell me?'' Controlling his anger now.

''I was going to, when I had more to tell. You've got enough on your mind.''

''When I agreed that you should have a special relationship with Jennifer, this is not what I had in mind.'' He heard his voice getting louder. He stopped and started again. ''What else do I need to know?''

''After the business with the car and the one I told you about she had short stays at a . . . spa, I guess you could call it . . . for emotionally confused rich folks.''

''A spa? A nut house, right?''

''No, not a nut house. A rest home, maybe. Sort of like the Golden Door with a lot of staff shrinks. Folks drying out, some recovering from depression, all very discreet. Massage, aerobics, facials, gourmet diet food and a couple of consultations a day with head doctors.''

''Lovely. And you didn't tell me.''

''She only told me a week ago. I've been working on it. Craig is checking on the place she stayed to make sure they're maintaining confidentiality. I didn't see the point in shouting fire until I knew how much danger there was.''

''More than enough. You'd better start drafting that motion to limit this stuff. I don't know if we'll file it, maybe we won't need to. But we'd better have it ready.''

27

AT THE YEAR'S FIRST SCHEDULED APPEARANCE BEfore Corino to report on their progress, Becker demanded an adjournment until after Jennifer's baby was born.

"How long has the defense known about this and not said a word? It's the worst kind of sandbagging, your honor. We can't go in there with this defendant seven or eight months pregnant—about to give birth, radiant with motherhood—and tell the jury she killed her husband with vicious blows to the head and they ought to send her to the penitentiary."

"Your honor, this defendant, like every other defendant, has a right to a speedy trial," Ryan countered. "If we don't have this trial now, when will it be? Are we going to wait two or three months until she gives birth, and then more months until she can reasonably be separated from her newborn child all day?" He turned to Becker. "Unless you want her to bring the infant into court."

Corino made no secret of his impatience. "Mr. Ryan, if you're going to make a career of defending people based on improper appeals to the jury's sympathy I hope you'll stay out of my courtroom in the future." He shook his head, wearing an exaggerated expression of disgust.

"Mr. Becker. I must remind you that there are nurseries in jail these days. Mrs. Ryan isn't the first pregnant defendant to bedevil a prosecutor, or even the first pregnant defendant accused of killing her husband or lover. I know you're not happy to be trying your case against the dead man's father and his unborn child, but take heart—next time you may get a seven-foot-tall Hell's Angel with KILL tattooed on both arms."

Ryan could only hope the jury would respond to a pregnant defendant as favorably as everyone was assuming they would, because if they didn't the defense team was going to have plenty of time to regret the rush. There was already too much to be done in the month they had left before the trial started, and more was being added every day.

A package arrived from the D.A.'s office. Following Corino's order, Becker had sent the defense copies of all reports relating to anything seized or confiscated at Hugo Hill's. The covering letter affirmed that Becker was preserving the physical evidence until the judge's later decision about whether it was relevant.

According to the reports, the police had found—in potted plants, behind sofa cushions and tucked behind the frames of paintings at Hugo Hill's—five vials or other containers holding between a half gram and three grams of cocaine each, and two loaded handguns. All had been wiped clean of fingerprints.

The defense team had an evening meeting with Jake Kaplan.

"Anything on the mortgagees?" Ryan asked him.

"I sent out letters saying we were closing the estate and was there anything to prevent our hiring a bank or a real-estate management company to do Ned's job of collecting their money. Worded exactly the way you told me. I finally got responses from all of them. Fourteen letters, and they all say the same thing."

He handed Ryan a thin file folder.

"The words are different," he pointed out, "but the idea is the same. They all say they would prefer to have someone of their choosing do the collecting, and they're all offering the estate a settlement that amounts to a hundred percent of what Ned would have earned if he'd lived and done the work for the life of the mortgages. Basically it's an offer we can't refuse. We get the whole fee and do none of the work."

Ryan had been skimming through the letters. "Fourteen minds with but a single thought."

"You think maybe they know each other?" Lawrence cracked.

"I'd love to know who they are," Ryan said. "This has organized crime written all over it and there's not a thing we can do with it. Not without more. We wouldn't get near the courtroom with it."

He stared at the letter in his hand, seeing in it layers of deceit. "We have to push this harder. Follow the money, we always used to say . . . Okay, let's assume Ned was laundering money and find a way to get at it from the other end." He turned to Miller. "Your office must have some clients who deal drugs."

She stiffened. "It's a matter of public record who we stand up for in court."

"That's not what I'm talking about."

"I know what you're talking about, and what Andy Andreg's clients do is none of our business—even if it could help us get Jennifer off."

"Not every kind of information is privileged or confidential."

"I'm not getting into this."

"Okay," he said, and moved on to a less prickly subject. "I'm going to take a good look at Shible, with Jake's help, and see what we can learn from how they handle their money. And what about front companies? There have to be plenty of lists of legitimate businesses suspected of being fronts for drug dealers."

"Sure," Lawrence said. "There are probably a hundred lists like that, maybe a thousand by the time you get done with all the federal agencies and local and state law enforcement and legislative committees all over . . ."

"We don't need the whole country, just around here. In the old days we used to develop that kind of information on a case-by-case basis. There must be something broader now."

"I can maybe get us something if I use up more favors and we're lucky. We could be talking about an awful long list of names."

"All we have to do is get it into Kassia's computer and then our brilliant colleague pushes a few buttons and the little gremlins inside match it up with our lists of companies Ned ran or did business with. Isn't that how it works?"

She made a face but she didn't say no.

"Okay, I'll get to work on it," Lawrence said. "Meantime, I solved one of our other problems. I found Tina Claire."

"The way things have been going," Ryan said, "I'm afraid to ask where."

Lawrence laughed. "Not the morgue. Not even close." He took his time. "Virginia. Some kind of artists' colony."

"Have you talked to her?"

"As elusive as she's been I thought we should just drop in and say hello."

"Done."

"Soon," Miller advised. "Next week we've got our experts coming in every day to brief us."

"And I want t set up some opinion surveys for right before jury selection. We ought to interview some of the people who do that."

They went over the rest of the schedule in as much detail as they could. Too many of the items brought others to mind. Four weeks was looking like a shorter and shorter time, especially in a world made of blank walls and blind alleys.

Again, Ryan found himself in a car service sedan in Brooklyn, watching the Shible loading dock. This time there was only one truck, being loaded with cartons from the warehouse. Ryan was too far away to read the legends printed on the boxes but from the way the warehousemen were handling them they were heavy and fragile.

Ryan checked his watch. Time for his appointment with Shible's chief operating officer—grand title in a company with a single executive, a sales force of two and three clerical employees.

Srini Ramanujan was short, with shiny black hair and matte-brown skin and a round pot belly. His small, windowless office smelled of spices Ryan had little occasion to eat. Ramanujan claimed to know nothing about Shible's using artificially low interest rates and long payment terms to keep its customers, or about how the credit was financed.

"We do not operate in that way to hold our customers with this sort of bribes you talk about." He had a thick East Indian accent and he seemed to be in a perpetual state of agitation. "To say such a thing is a great insult. We have no need. Our business is excellent-quality goods at the best prices. Yes, it is true we have gray-market goods. We purchase only health and beauty aids in this manner. These are perfectly good products, toothpastes and mouthwashes manufactured in the Third World. In this way we supply to our customers the same products as are manufactured here at a price greatly lower than they could obtain otherwise. Our prescription goods are only of the highest purity and they are manufactured in this country or imported in the normal way. Our customers are quite satisfied with our prices and our service."

"I guess I didn't make myself clear," Ryan said. "I'm not interested in making trouble for you. I'm trying to find out who murdered my son."

"What does this have to do with my credit terms?"

"That's what I'm trying to figure out."

"There is no mystery to solve. Mr. Ryan was murdered by his wife. Please leave now. I have business to do."

"I should remind you of something, Mr. Ramanujan. I'm the executor of your boss's estate. That makes me your boss, for now."

"Perhaps so—with Dr. Morris." He was not giving an inch.

"Ned's estate owns fifty-one percent of Shible. I'm the boss. Just me."

"If you are threatening me I resign right now."

"I'm not threatening you. I'm reminding you of my status in the company. Because I need to review all your computer records on finance, sales and inventory."

"I gave your accountant long ago the printouts he asked for."

"Now he needs the raw data."

Ramanujan stood up abruptly. He was too short and soft to be menacing, but there was nothing laughable about him.

"If you are the owner you may have what you wish. For now, I have asked you politely please to leave my office."

Ryan left, not sure if Ramanujan was hiding something or just defending his turf.

Ryan and Lawrence flew to Virginia the next afternoon. It was dark by the time they drove up a winding hill road past a field full of grazing cows. The art colony office was closed, and they had to search to find anyone.

Following the sound of a piano and the light from a window, they opened a door into a wide, high-ceilinged room with white-washed walls. A man in his thirties with long, dark hair and intense eyes was banging out chords on a baby grand piano, singing of a failed latenight pickup attempt. Singing with him was a tall blond man with a reedy voice. Their audience was six men and eight women, all white except for one Oriental, all at least in their thirties except for a petite woman with a cap of shining golden hair sitting with her legs curled under her on a studio bed.

The rapt listeners paid scant attention to the two newcomers, who stayed just beyond the fringe during the wine and chips party that followed the performance. A few people came over and introduced themselves by their first names, asking Ryan and Lawrence how long they were in residence. "We're just visiting," Ryan said.

Lawrence nudged him. The tiny blonde was on her way out a door opposite the one they had come in. They pushed their way past a knot of people around the singers and followed the blonde down a narrow whitewashed hallway lined with artwork.

"Tina!" Lawrence called as she disappeared around a corner. The two men broke into a run and almost collided with her, waiting in ambush just around the corner.

"What do you guys want? I come here to get away from city bullshit."

"I'm Michael Ryan."

"I might've known. I'm not gonna talk to you."

"You were happy enough to talk to my son."

"Don't guilt me, Pop."

"You talked to the district attorney," Lawrence said.

"So what? I don't owe you squat." She looked from one to the other. "All right, let's get this bullshit over with."

Her studio was another high-ceilinged whitewashed room, this one more than twice as big as the room where they had heard the songs. In one corner was a pile of metal scraps. A welding mask and torch lay on a table in the middle of the room along with what appeared to be a partly finished sculpture. It looked like a metal bowling pin flattened and twisted in some surrealist nightmare.

"Make yourself at home." Her tone was acid. She leaned against the table in the center of the room, arms crossed over her chest.

Seeing her in angry repose, Ryan had a sense of what made her so compelling. It was more than her perfectly proportioned body, evident despite jeans and leg warmers and a loose sweater, or her precision-chiseled features. She radiated sex the way a branding iron radiates heat. Only the cheap, tough language didn't fit.

She studied Ryan for a long moment, then turned to the partially finished sculpture on the table next to her.

"See that? It's almost done. It's part of a series with the one that killed your son." Her voice was different now. It was softer, with the breathy quality that had been Marilyn Monroe's vocal trademark. "I was done with all that. I wanted to move on. But Hugo says no, do more of them, we're raising the price, there's all this demand because of the murder. People are crazy. Sick. Don't you think so?"

Ryan did not acknowledge the question.

"I thought your son was a joke, and not a very good one, either. It was a goof what I was doing, playing with him the way I was, stroking him through his pants. I was jerking him off, right there in front of everybody. Is that what you want to hear about?"

Ryan felt Lawrence's hand grip his arm. The strong fingers dug into his bicep, a message that overrode his anger.

Tina Claire smiled. "Having a good time? There's more." She paused, not expecting a response. "I was jerking him off and I was talking dirty in his ear, sort of panting." Her voice was breathier, lower, lubricious enough to cause an orgasm at long distance. "His mind was somewhere else when Hugo brought him over, but I got his attention real quick. If you asked him his name he couldn't have told you. That's how we were when his wife came over. She was mad. I don't think I ever saw anybody that mad. And yelling. I moved around so he was between me and her, but I put my hand in his pocket. He didn't try to stop me, not right away. He didn't really know which end was up."

The roar of a motorcycle interrupted her. "Company." She smiled.

Ryan was a mass of knotted muscle. He tried to relax.

The door opened and a man in a motorcycle jacket sauntered into the room. He was as big and burly as Lawrence, and a good fifteen years younger. His stringy hair was tied back in a ponytail.

"These guys bothering you?"

"No sweetie, I'm bothering them. This is Mr. Ryan."

"Ryan?"

"Little Ned's father."

"That fuck."

"That's enough," Lawrence said.

The biker turned to face him. "Talk nice or I'll ventilate your skull."

He picked up the unfinished sculpture and hefted it.

"Kenny . . . "

"Don't worry about me, worry about them."

"Shall we continue?" she asked Ryan.

"No, that's plenty for now," Ryan said.

"See you in court," she said to their retreating backs.

"Did you see that?" Lawrence asked as soon as they were in the car. "*I'll ventilate your skull.* Be nice to have a videotape of that, wouldn't it?"

"That's what you're here for. A living permanent record."

"I am a camera." Lawrence took out a microcassette recorder and began dictating a description of their encounter with Tina Claire.

"What I ought to do is check if the bastard's got an alibi."

"No," Ryan said. "Don't do that." If it came to putting him on the stand about Kenny's threatening outburst, Lawrence had to be able to say honestly that he knew nothing about the man's whereabouts on the murder night, or about any investigation into that question.

On the plane back to New York Ryan asked Lawrence if he had an investigator Ryan could borrow.

"I need somebody experienced—either sex—who can make some discreet inquiries. Someone I can trust not to tell you what it's about or what the results are."

Lawrence did not have to ask why. "I'll find you somebody."

* * *

Ryan stopped at the Shamrock on the way home from the airport. Kelly was not there.

"He's over in Brooklyn at a racket for his nephew," explained Kathryn, his backup bartender. "Just got promoted to lieutenant."

"No kidding. What kind of lieutenant?"

Ryan's bond with Kelly, built up over the years, was not based on personal revelations. Ryan had the impression there were myriad Kelly sisters and brothers and a tribe of nieces and nephews, but he knew no specifics.

"A cop." Kathryn was smiling. "He's kind of a black sheep. All the other nieces or nephews are accountants or brokers or sell insurance. No cops, no fire, no politicians. You'd hardly know they were Irish."

Kathryn gave him a double shot of whiskey that he poured down in a couple of hearty slugs. He tapped his glass on the bar for another one, but when Kathryn came over with the bottle he changed his mind and covered his glass with his hand. He needed to stay well below his limit from now on. He dropped a ten on the bar and said good night.

The phone woke him. The room was pitch dark, and his head was full of fog. After a while the phone stopped and he fell instantly asleep. The phone woke him again, and this time it did not quit.

"Okay, okay," Ryan protested. "I'll be right there." He did not usually talk to his telephone. Blearily, he looked at the clock. Three thirty-four in the morning.

"Hello."

"Mr. Ryan?"

Not a familiar voice. "Who is this?"

"A friend. I want to do you a favor, Mr. Ryan."

He forced himself to a semblance of alertness, looked around for a pen and paper.

"What favor?" In the drawer, dummy. He fished it out.

"I have some advice for you," said the voice. "Stop poking around where you don't belong. That's how people get hurt. Hurt real bad."

"What?"

"You heard me. Get smart before it's too late."

28

IN THE MORNING RYAN REGRETTED NOT HAVING HAD
the presence of mind to press a button on his answering machine
and record the call.

He called an emergency meeting with Miller and Lawrence.

"If somebody out there wants to be left alone that badly, we
have to figure Ned was up to something that's a good motive for
murder. The question is, what are we doing that's got them worried?"

"Jake's letters to the mortgage-money people?" Miller did not
sound convinced.

"Or my visit to Shible," Ryan offered.

"I got hold of some lists of drug-money fronts." Lawrence dug
a thick sheaf of papers out of his briefcase. "Mostly unsubstantiated
rumors and tips, but some of it is based on solid evidence. Still,
asking around about drug dealers seems like a long shot as a reason
to get threatened."

"We must be doing something right."

"Right or wrong, you ought to consider stopping," Lawrence
said. "Poking a stick into a hornet's nest is a well-known way to
get stung."

"Assuming this isn't scare tactics."

"You willing to take that chance?"

"One thing for sure—I don't want anybody getting hurt."

"How serious are we going to get about preventing it?" Lawrence asked. "Round-the-clock bodyguards is minimum four full-
time people and one overtime shift. Each. Say nine full-time for
the two of you."

"What about you?"

"My bodyguard is built in, thank you."

"You're talking about someone following me around twenty-four hours a day?'' Miller did not sound happy about it. "Can't I just look both ways when I cross? People make threats all the time.''

"I'll leave it at that for now," Ryan said. "But I don't want to let up about either the mortgage money or Shible, so we have to be careful. The best way to protect ourselves is get to the bottom of this thing as fast as we can.''

"I'm not sure about that," Lawrence said. "It's nice to think this threat means we're on the track of Ned's real killer, but we shouldn't fool ourselves.''

"What do you mean?'' Miller asked.

"I mean it's possible we're poking around in places where we could upset applecarts that turn out to have nothing to do with the murder.''

"Like?''

"Some scam at Shible, for instance. Fraud or embezzlement, say. Daylight in the wrong places could threaten somebody's idea of lifetime annuity. They could get real vicious about protecting it.''

"That could be a motive for murder, too.''

"Sure, but so far there's no sign that Ned was making himself that kind of nuisance. Drug kings, on the other hand, kill as matter of policy, and if they killed Ned they wouldn't give a damn if we exposed it as long as we can't convict them. Hell, if they killed him to set an example they'd welcome the publicity.''

"You're saying the killer and the people threatening us could be completely unrelated.''

"Could be.''

They sent Lawrence's lists to a computer service that ran a scanner over it, converting the thousands of names to useable computer data. They had it back by early afternoon and not long after that Miller interrupted Ryan to say, "I think we've got something.''

Ryan went to stand behind her, reading the screen over her shoulder.

"What this means," she told him, "is that Hunter Capital shows up on two lists—our list of companies providing mortgage financing and the F.B.I. list of companies thought, but not known, to be financed by a man named Olivera, who is suspected of being a major wholesaler of controlled substances.''

A few minutes later she said, "Bingo!''

Ryan looked up.

She said, "Match number two. Olivera again.''

She kept at it the rest of the day but there were no more matches.

"That's it. Two matches between our mortgage financiers and presumed drug dealer Felipe Olivera."

"Great. Now all we need is to find a way to verify it. Get somebody credible who can testify to it."

She made a face. "Go ahead, Ryan, rain on my parade."

The phone rang. She jumped.

It was Lawrence with the name of an investigator. Ryan told him about Olivera. "Get the wheels turning on it right away."

"You got it. And I want to get somebody in there tomorrow to sweep for bugs. Should have done it long ago."

"Okay, but I don't want to get carried away with it."

"I can think of worse ways to get carried away. We're talking about serious drug dealers here."

The elevator man had an envelope for Ryan when he got home that night. It had no return address.

"A messenger brought it."

"Did he leave a slip?"

"Nothing."

Upstairs, Ryan opened it, hoping it wasn't a letter bomb.

It was, but not the kind he was worried about. "This is going to be in the Sunday Magazine," said the unsigned covering note from someone at Allen Crown's paper.

Allen Crown's Sunday feature was a study of Jennifer Kneeland Ryan and her circle. From Ryan's point of view it was dynamite, and it was going to explode too close to jury selection for comfort.

Crown had interviewed a wide selection of Jennifer's friends. He used them to paint a portrait of people in their late twenties and thirties playing at being actors, dancers, artists and writers, insulated by family money from the harsh realities of waiting tables or driving cabs or entering computer data on the graveyard shift.

The acting teachers he quoted damned Jennifer by their faint praise. Crown had a field day using her as the archetype of a New York subculture whose popular image he could stand on its head. The way Crown reported it, this was a world of self-deluding and selfish dilettantes, fooling no one but themselves. Even Jennifer's charity work was grist for his mill.

Ryan told himself that anyone who would be offended by that part of Crown's profile was already a Jennifer-hater. He had no such consolation for the section that dealt with Jennifer's private life, and that the other papers and the TV stations were sure to pick up and run with.

Jennifer Kneeland had a history of violent behavior, reported

Crown. She had been suspended from boarding school for breaking an antique vase in a fit of pique at the headmistress. Somehow he had missed the story of the candlestick but he had dug up other incidents from college. A store window smashed, a car driven into the side of a rival's parked convertible. The damage had always been paid for by Daddy, with a sweetener to compensate for the emotional upset. With the exception of the boarding school suspension, Jennifer had suffered no consequences. None, that is, if you didn't count one lengthy stay and one short one in a rest home for the wealthy.

It was substantially what Ryan had already heard, but Crown had given it all a wicked spin. Ryan couldn't help wondering if Crown's version was closer to the truth than Jennifer's.

He called Miller.

"A secret admirer just sent me an advance printout of Allen Crown's newest piece about Jennifer."

"What's he come up with now?"

"Jennifer's record as a mental patient."

"Damn. How did he get hold of that? She told me no one knew."

"Somebody always knows. You'd better file your motion to limit testimony on it first thing in the morning, whether it causes a delay or not. And tell Jennifer we need to talk to her."

In the morning Ryan met with the investigator Lawrence had recommended. He told her he wanted everything she could find on a man he could identify only as Kenny Peters, boyfriend of artist Tina Claire, currently resident at an artists' retreat in Virginia. Under no circumstances was the investigator to communicate any of this—either the assignment or the results—to Craig Lawrence. Ryan was particularly interested in any record of violence Kenny might have, especially violence related to jealousy. He was interested, too, in Kenny's whereabouts on the June evening when Tina Claire was a guest of honor at a party thrown by her gallery owner.

"If you can place him at Hugo Hill's, or if you can find a clear hole in his schedule any time between eight and nine-thirty so he could have been there, put it in your report. Otherwise just say no progress."

Kenny might be the murderer. If he wasn't, he might be a good source of reasonable doubt for the jury—a suspect by inference from Lawrence's testimony and possibly the testimony of others.

For that to be a safe strategy Ryan needed to be sure Kenny had no alibi. At the same time, if he had one Ryan didn't want to know about it—he didn't need the ethical problems the knowledge could cause. It was a tough line to walk.

Lawrence came by the office after lunch with a short African-American carrying a pair of aluminum suitcases full of electronic gear. Nassir Hakim nodded at his introduction to Ryan and offered a powerful handshake. In the two hours he spent in the office he spoke not a word. When he was done he nodded and smiled at Lawrence and packed up his gear. He favored Ryan with another strong handshake and a broad grin and then he was gone.

"I take it that means we're clean," Ryan ventured.

"For now. For the kinds of bugs he can find. He'll be back in about ten days." Lawrence looked around the office. "When you're talking about anything important be sure to keep those window curtains drawn."

"Okay."

"Now we can talk. I got word on that name you gave me. Felipe Olivera. He's a new player. Took over the operation that started with Irish Viera."

"The once-but-not-future prince of cocaine?"

"The same."

At the tail end of Ryan's days as a prosecutor, Dennis Viera had been a nobody, just starting out. Ryan, the phony Irishman, had been intrigued by the ambitious Ecuadoran who was really half Irish. Ryan had followed Viera's career: skyrocketing into the New York drug firmament only to collide with a tough New York City detective over a pair of dramatic and grisly murders.

"Some small-timers moved in on Viera's territory when the cops blew him away," Lawrence elaborated, "but El Grande de Coca down in Colombia didn't like them so Olivera came in a couple of years ago. He cut the small-timers out and when they made trouble about it he cut them *up* . . . This is one nasty *cabrón*. I'm all of a sudden a lot more worried about that threat."

Ryan did not want to hear about the threat. "We need everything we can get on Olivera. This is potentially the best news we've had for Jennifer so far."

Follow the money. Maybe it was paying off. *Cui bono?* the Romans had asked. *Who benefits?*

If only he could be sure that the crime still had to be solved—that Jennifer had not killed Ned in one of her fits of rage.

"Keep after it," he told Lawrence.

"Like porcupines making love. You be careful, too, my friend."

* * *

By the time Jennifer arrived at the office the world outside the windows was already dark. When she took off her coat Ryan noticed for the first time that she was looking unmistakably pregnant.

He gave her a copy of Allen Crown's article about her. She was not far into it before she began to shake her head and make noises of outrage. She looked up when she was done.

"It's all so distorted. Those teachers he talked to hated me, and he left out my best roles . . ."

"Forget about the acting and the charities. It's the part about the way you break things and the people you've given trouble to that bothers me."

"I told you. It's all distorted."

"All of it?"

"Maybe not all. A lot of it."

"If we had known all this earlier, we would have had more time to defend against it. That's why we ask you to tell us everything. The police are interviewing all your friends and all Ned's friends. Your enemies, too. You'd be amazed at how much a good cop can learn from very little, piecing together what he hears from one with what he hears from another. Imagine how you'll feel having something damaging come out in open court when we haven't had a chance to prepare for it or counteract it."

There was something about the way she suddenly turned inward that prompted him to ask, "Is there something else?"

She did not respond. He was about to repeat the question when she said, "Yes."

"What?" Relieved she was being forthcoming but apprehensive about what she would say.

"After we left the party. Ned and I. Downstairs . . ."

"Yes?"

"We argued some more. I picked up the sculpture. I was so furious with him I just wanted to smash something."

She stopped.

Ryan was dimly aware that Miller, too, was waiting for what came next. Frozen, as he was.

"What happened?" Ryan said into the silence.

"I don't remember, really. I never do when I get that way."

"Try."

"Maybe if I do it as an exercise."

Ryan was perplexed.

"Acting," Miller mouthed silently.

Jennifer closed her eyes, visualizing. "I picked it up. It was rough and it dug into my hand. It felt heavy and good. Good for smashing things with.''

Ryan dared to look at her: her arm was bent at the elbow, her fist lightly closed as if grasping something. Her forearm moved up and down slightly, hefting.

It was eerie to watch. Ryan could almost see the sculpture in her hand.

Jennifer moved her arm again, readying a blow. Her face wore the spurious tranquility of someone imagining herself in a past experience. Her arm drew back, about to strike, tensed as if bearing the actual weight.

Ryan had a flash of memory: Ned in the morgue, his head split by the sculpture Jennifer was conjuring in her memory. He was not breathing. No part of his body moved.

At the top of its travel, Jennifer's arm stopped. Her whole body relaxed. Her eyes opened.

"I was going to hit something. There was a clock, I remember. I was going to smash it. But Ned grabbed me. He grabbed the sculpture and he pulled it away from me. I didn't want to let him."

She stopped.

"That's all?" His voice was harsh now.

She nodded.

"He took it away from you?"

"Yes. I said that."

"And that's how you got the blood on it, when he was trying to pull it away from you."

"Yes. I was afraid to tell you."

"You didn't hit him?"

"I'm telling the truth! Why don't you believe me?" She began to cry.

Miller took Jennifer's hands and led her to a chair. Jennifer followed her, half a head taller but looking like a lost little girl following her mother. When Jennifer had calmed down, Miller called their driver to take her home.

Ryan got her coat and held it for her. Good-cop bad-cop had its drawbacks for the bad cop, and he did not want to lose his connection with her baby, whatever she had actually done with the sculpture that night.

"I know I ask you tough questions sometimes. But I'm on your side. You have to remember that."

"Sometimes it's hard for me to tell."

"I know." And sometimes it's hard for me to do, he did not add.

The car had arrived.

"I'll ride home with you," he said when the car arrived.

"I'm all right."

"We could use a few minutes as Michael and Jennifer instead of lawyer and client."

She tried to smile. "Okay."

"How are you feeling?" he asked on the way across town.

"You want to know the truth? Fat and clumsy and ugly."

"It's all in your mind."

"In my hormones, too. My emotions are all out of control. I think about the baby all the time. I have these images of being in jail when he comes. And then sometimes all I can think of is I want it to be over, the pregnancy, so I can walk like a normal person and eat like a normal person, and drink coffee and alcohol, and not fart all the time. Excuse me."

"You're excused." When she was like this it was hard for him to think of her as Ned's killer.

"The only good thing is, now that everyone knows I'm pregnant I can wear comfortable clothes and I don't have to keep sneaking around at the doctor's."

"What does the doctor say?"

"She thinks I'm doing real well. I wish it felt like that. She says the baby's in the right place. Kind of on the small side—nothing to be worried about, but that's one reason why I didn't show until so late. I'm hoping that'll make it easier to get him out into the world."

"It's not much longer."

"Yes it is. It's a whole lifetime. It's after my trial."

There was no answer to that. Instead, he asked a question. "You said *him*. Does that mean . . ."

She did not respond but he thought he saw a smile in her eyes.

"Do you know?"

"Yes. I would have told you but everything today was so unpleasant."

"It's a boy?"

"Yes. It's a boy."

Ryan felt the rightness of it. It had to be a boy. A boy meant starting over with a chance to do it right this time.

"A boy. That's terrific."

Before he could think of anything else to say the car had pulled up at her address.

He helped her to the sidewalk between parked cars. A man was sitting hunched over on the ground, his back supported by the side of one of the cars. A cold night to be homeless, Ryan thought.

Jennifer thanked Ryan for the help. "I feel so clumsy all the time now."

He walked her to the steps of her brownstone.

"I'll help you up the stairs."

"I can make it on my own."

"No, really, I insist." This was no time for her to fall down stairs. He thought of suggesting that she go and live with her father for a while instead of staying here by herself.

He took her elbow, vaguely aware that the homeless man had stood up and was headed past them.

"Hey!" A rough voice.

Ryan turned, his hand going into his pocket, ready to bribe the man to go on his way.

"Freeze, sucka," the man said sharply, and then Ryan saw the gun. And looking closer saw that it was a boy, a teenager.

Ryan reminded himself that the most important thing was to stay cool. All the kid wanted was money, probably for his crack habit, and money was replaceable.

The kid pointed his gun at Ryan's hand. "Best that be money."

Ryan clutched bills where he had been going for change and slowly drew his hand from his pocket.

A car came fast around the corner. It did not have its lights on. Ryan heard a screech of brakes and then sharp overlapping firecracker thunderclaps. He threw himself toward Jennifer, his only instinct to get her out of the way.

The next thing he knew he was on the ground and the car was driving away in a roar of exhaust and a scream of rubber that Ryan heard only through the ringing in his ears left by the gunshots. Pushing himself up he discovered that his right hand and arm were not working.

On his knees, he looked around.

The kid lay spread-eagled on the sidewalk, dead or dying. Jennifer was crumpled on the two bottom steps of her stoop. Ryan prayed that she was all right.

Not trusting himself to stand, he crawled the few feet to her. She was alive, and she seemed for a moment to know he was there. She groaned lightly and her eyes closed.

He struggled out of his coat and draped it over her. Awkwardly, trying not to move her or put any weight on her, he moved his body as close as he could to shelter her against the January cold.

Her and her precious baby.

29

THE EMERGENCY MEDICAL SERVICE DRIVER WOULD
not let Ryan ride with Jennifer. "No room, man. She's hurt, we
have to help her in here. We called an ambulance for you."

Ryan pulled free and headed for Hudson Street.

"Hey man, take it easy, you hear what I'm saying. You're in
shock."

With his good arm, Ryan hailed a cab. "What's the hospital near
here?" He knew, but he didn't remember. His mind was not working. "Follow the ambulance."

"Huh? Where you go?"

The driver's name card swam in Ryan's eyes. Cabbies didn't
speak English anymore. Vladimir. Ryan tried to remember some
of the Russian he had learned in college. What came out of his
mouth was "St. Vincent's."

"Okay. Hospital St. Vincent."

To make up for the slow start, Vladimir drove the few blocks
like an Unser at Indianapolis. He pulled up at St. Vincent's emergency entrance just as the EMS crew was taking Jennifer out of
their ambulance.

Shivering, Ryan reached for his money but it was gone, dropped
in the street, long since in someone else's pocket. He gave Vladimir
his change. "It's all I have—I was robbed."

Vladimir snarled a Russian curse, leaning over the back of his
seat. His anger evaporated when he saw Ryan's arm. The jacket
sleeve was dark and shiny wet. Blood.

"Go, go," the driver urged him.

He lurched out of the cab and grabbed for a corner of the gurney
they were using to wheel Jennifer into the hospital.

He heard shouts, felt people pushing him away. He struggled
weakly against them, calling Jennifer's name.

A blur of noise and motion. He was in a room with bright over-head lights, his teeth chattering uncontrollably. People on molded wooden bucket chairs bolted to a metal rail. Jennifer wasn't there. Everything went black, then he was on his feet being pushed and pulled.

Another room with bright lights. Activity everywhere. Someone pushing at his arm. He struggled to get away. He wanted to see Jennifer, wanted to know she was all right. The baby. How was the baby?

He woke up in a hospital bed. The other bed in the room was empty. He found the call button and pushed it. When no one came he pushed it again, holding his finger on the button until the door opened and a nurse came in.

"Something wrong in here?"

"Jennifer. I want to see Jennifer Ryan."

"Well now, you can't get out of bed until the doctor says so. Does she know you're here?"

"She came here last night. She's hurt, she's shot, I don't know how badly. I have to find out. She's pregnant."

"All right, Mr. Ryan, calm down now. I'll see what I can find out."

She left and Ryan drifted back to sleep. He woke up to see a young doctor standing by his bed. The doctor checked him over quickly and appeared to be satisfied.

"It seems you're a celebrity, Mr. Ryan. There's a whole press corps downstairs. We've also got a woman who says she's your law partner and she needs to know what to tell the judge."

"First I need to know about Jennifer. Jennifer Ryan." He was feeling stronger.

"Yes. She went straight to emergency surgery when she came in, and she's still in the recovery room. That's all I know."

"She's going to be all right?"

"The surgeon will be able to tell you more. He'll be back later. Meantime, you ought to get some rest."

"When can I get out?"

"Tomorrow morning. You've got a bullet wound in your right shoulder, no major damage. You'll be stiff and sore, you'll need some physical therapy, but that's all. Your real problem was shock and exposure."

"What about Jennifer? What about the *baby*?"

"Talk to her doctor."

* * *

He had visitors in the afternoon—Kassia Miller and Craig Lawrence, then Jimmy Kelly. Ryan was weaker than he realized, glad when they were gone. He and Miller had decided to do nothing about changing the trial schedule until they knew more about Jennifer. Her condition was listed only as "stable." Her surgeon was in the operating room again.

The police said the shooting was part of a turf war between crack gangs. The boy with the gun, dead now, had been a lieutenant of a gang prone to trespassing on the territory of other gangs. Once too often, according to the cops.

A nurse came to take Ryan off his I.V. when the shifts changed at four. Dinner came an hour later. The food was as bad as he expected, but he was too hungry to care. He cleaned his tray.

When he went for an after-dinner walk along the hospital corridors the doctor who had operated on Jennifer was doing emergency surgery. Ryan waited for him.

"I'm Michael Ryan." He walked down the corridor with the surgeon. "I came in last night with a gunshot wound. Jennifer Ryan came in with me. You operated on her."

The surgeon focused weary eyes on him. "Oh, yes . . . multiple gunshot wounds." He rubbed his forehead, as if to wake up his memory. "Your wife's a real fighter, Mr. Ryan. It's going to help her recover."

Ryan barely registered the mistake.

"She's all right, then?"

"She should be a hundred percent, barring any unforeseen complications."

"How about the baby?"

The doctor stopped walking. His shoulders slumped.

"I'm sorry, Mr. Ryan, I assumed you knew. The fetus was dead before I started."

Ryan was suddenly dizzy. He grabbed the doctor's arm to keep his balance.

"Here, let's get you sitting down." He helped Ryan to a chair in the nurses' station.

"The baby's dead?"

"I really am sorry to drop it on you like that. Mrs. Ryan was shot three times, once in the upper chest, once in the leg and once in the abdomen. It's a miracle, really, that none of her major organs were hit. But the bullet that penetrated her abdomen killed the fetus outright, I'm afraid."

Ryan sat with his head in his hands, not believing.

"One consolation," the surgeon offered. "The wounds were

clean, and we did everything as carefully as we could. I'd say the total trauma—I'm talking about the physical trauma now—I'd say it wasn't much worse than a Caesarean section. It's quite possible that you'll be able to try again in no time at all.''

H. Robertson Kneeland moved his daughter to New York University Hospital as soon as the doctors at St. Vincent's agreed she could make the trip. Her new doctors' opinion was that she needed a month or more to recuperate and regain her strength. Ryan suspected that they were being conservative, but it didn't matter. Jennifer was not pregnant anymore. There was no reason to hurry.

Joe Becker, operating on a different schedule, was pressing for the earliest trial date. His case was ready. Delay would only hurt him.

Corino did not want to set a definite trial date until he found out how many of his current cases could be moved into the time slot he had cleared for *People v. Ryan*. Some time in March, he told Becker. When Miller protested that Jennifer needed more time than that to recuperate Corino got mad.

"I am full of sympathy, counselor, but your client's doctor says four to six weeks' recuperation. March is a good six weeks away, and you were supposed to be ready for a trial in less than three weeks."

She had a response, but Corino cut her off. "You've been pressing for a speedy trial. You had a client whose pregnancy you neglected to mention when we set the first trial date. Don't let me see you drag your feet now that she's lost the baby."

Ryan went to visit Jennifer at the hospital during the day, hoping to avoid Kneeland. He sat by her bedside and held her hand. Neither of them spoke.

For whole stretches of time he had been losing himself in the identity of advocate building a case. Very abstract. Not father of the victim, not father-in-law of the defendant. Now, tragedy had forced him back into a more human role. He had thought once that he and Jennifer might share the grief of Ned's death. This more recent grief was one they could genuinely share. For both of them the baby had been the last best hope to recapture what had been lost.

He felt her hand stir in his. She was crying silently. He squeezed her hand and let her withdraw it. He did not know how to console her . . . He did not know how to console himself.

Ryan wished his own tears would come. Anything was better

than lying awake at night staring up at the ceiling the way he had been since the shooting.

"Poor Michael," Jennifer said when her tears had subsided. "It makes me so sad to see you hurt like this."

"Not just me. You're the one . . ."

Someone knocked on the door.

Jennifer glared at it. Another knock.

"Come in," she said grudgingly.

Jennifer's private duty nurse, waiting outside while Jennifer and her father-in-law visited, poked her head in. "Meal time."

"I'm not hungry."

"You have to get your strength up," Ryan said.

She smiled at him. "All right. For you."

She picked at the food, nibbled a few bites. Put the fork down.

"I wonder where Grandpa George is. Do you think he knows about any of this?"

"I don't have a clue. He's a mystery to me." And the last person he'd have expected Jennifer to be thinking about.

"Ned used to talk about him. He came to visit us once, after the wedding. I never met anybody like him."

Just like George. Show up when you're least expected so you'll make the biggest impression.

"What makes you think of him now?"

"The baby would have been his great-grandson. Someone to carry on the family tradition. Now we're the last Ryans left in the world."

He did not know what to say.

"Special Ryans I mean." She managed another smile. "Russian Ryans."

"Not Russian." He tried to get into the spirit of it. "Circassian. Georgian. Not Russian."

"You're right. Ned would never have forgiven me if I didn't get that right." She took Ryan's hand. "We ought to swear some ancient Circassian vow of family solidarity."

Ryan was becoming increasingly uncomfortable, trying not to show it. He was almost relieved when Jennifer started to cry again.

She let his hand go to get a tissue. Blew her nose and wiped her eyes. "I'm sorry, Michael. I don't seem to have much control over my emotions right now. I'm not very good company."

Ryan stood up. "You probably need to be alone awhile. I'll come back and see you soon."

"You'd better," she said, and smiled weakly before she turned away to look out the window.

* * *

Again, Ryan could not sleep. His shoulder throbbed and his soul ached. He tried to think of other things.

An idea formed, dim at first, then clearer. He had been threatened, and not long after that he had been shot. A crack-war shoot-out was an elaborate disguise for an assassination attempt, but it could probably be arranged, especially if you ran a drug empire.

But how had they set it up so quickly? Riding with Jennifer had been a spur-of-the-moment decision. Could they have been watching the office and followed him? Possibly, but then how did they get that first kid to Jennifer's place in time to waylay them?

There were ways. All it would take was good communications and somebody smart running the operation. Once the two of them got into the car, how many destinations were there? Jennifer's was the best bet.

And if the shooting had been provoked by their nosing around in Felipe Olivera's affairs, then Michael Ryan was primarily responsible for the death of his own unborn grandson. The idea did not make sleep any easier.

In the morning he went to the police. They had him talk to Detective Garrity, who was not exactly receptive to Ryan's theories.

"Why didn't you say something before?"

"I got shot. My grandson was killed. I wasn't feeling very analytical."

"It's damn unlikely."

"I don't see why. I was threatened and I didn't change what I was doing and not long after that I was shot. You have to assume it had something to do with the threat."

Garrity took a report form from a drawer and fed it to the typewriter on his desk. "Okay, let's write it up." Without enthusiasm.

He took care of the preliminaries, then asked, "Do you have any evidence of the threat?"

"What kind of evidence could I have?"

"Written note, witness, recording. You're the lawyer."

"No evidence. Just my word."

Garrity's face told Ryan what the detective thought of that.

The newspapers and television were more receptive. They had already featured the shooting, focusing in the death of the baby-to-be and on the upcoming trial. The story of Ryan's alleged threat let them squeeze more out of the gory shooting.

Only Allen Crown departed from a matter-of-fact reporting of

Ryan's allegations, calling the whole idea "megalomaniac paranoia." Unless, he said in his column, there was another motive. "What could be more self-serving? Could Mr. Ryan be trying to create a phantom murderer out there desperate to keep the defense away from the awful truth? I'm taking this latest Ryan whopper with a big dose of salt."

Jake Kaplan called with a report on Shible Medical Suppliers. Ryan put him on the speaker. The healing shoulder made a painful problem of holding the phone to his ear.

"I hate to do this to you," Kaplan said. "I know you've had enough bad news lately."

"I might as well get it all over with at once."

"Shible's computer had a head crash. It destroyed the disk that stores their computer data."

"Destroyed? . . ."

"Think of it as a bad fire in the files, or a really efficient shredder."

"Isn't there supposed to be second copy? Backup?"

"Supposed to be. They claim they don't have any."

"And we believe them?"

"Do we have a choice?"

"I'd like you to go down there and see what you can find in their printouts and whatever else they still have. If they give you trouble, we'll go to court."

Destroying records was getting to be a national pastime. In this case, as always, it was an excellent sign that somebody had something to hide. And in this case destroying the records had probably hidden it—whatever it was—beyond any use or value for Jennifer's defense.

30

JENNIFER RECUPERATED AT HER FATHER'S. VISITING her became a daily ritual for Ryan. Kneeland was rarely there. When he was, he greeted Ryan and went about his business. He seemed no more eager for Ryan's company than Ryan was for his.

Ryan could only marvel at the strangeness of it. Kneeland had been business partner, mentor and friend to Ryan's son; Ryan was defending Kneeland's daughter against a murder charge. On top of that, they had both just lost their hope for a first grandson, barely two months before he was due to be born. Yet they had no use for each other.

"I think about revenge a lot," Jennifer said one afternoon. "Not just for me. I feel I owe it to Ned. He used to say it played a big role in his heritage."

"Did he talk about that a lot?"

"Oh, yes. I encouraged him. It's all so fascinating. Tribes of brave Circassian warriors in the mountains, Ned's great-grandfather fighting Stalin . . ."

"Well . . ."

"Not personally, I suppose."

"Not personally."

"The revenge part worried me, I have to admit. I was afraid when they accused me that revenge would be all you would think of . . . And then, I didn't say this exactly, but it was another reason I was sure you knew I was innocent. Otherwise you'd have been out for blood. Mine."

"Did it ever occur to you that some people are not as hung up on their so-called heritage as others?"

It gave her pause. "No, I . . . Ned was so proud of what he was. All the old stories and traditions."

"Did he tell you about how the greatest glory of a Chirkess warrior was in how much he could steal, and his greatest shame was being made to give any of it back?"

"Really? Is that true?"

"A noble tradition of the old country."

Ryan's venom on the subject was ripe with age. He had heard the stories as a child, always a major theme when his father was in the house, that rarest of events. Memories of brave Circassian warriors! A joke. George Ryan, christened Gyorgei Rianishvili, had not seen the Caucasus since he was a baby. As for old Grandpa Yosef, Ryan remembered only a remote old man sitting by a window saying not a word. Besides, Grandpa Yosef was a Georgian through and through, dark and intense. Devious, too, no doubt, a survival trait among the Georgians, a trait little Gyorgei had certainly inherited. Old Yosef's wife was the Circassian, Chirkess, whatever you called it. Straight and strong even in old age, fruit of the once-fierce old mountain people long ago turned flatland wheat farmers. Customs honored only in stories from the past, memories already generations old long before canny Yosef Rianishvili, self-proclaimed hero of an ephemeral Georgian republic, had charmed a barely nubile peasant girl into leaving home and family and then, in the shadow of Stalin's descending boot, swept her and their young son away to a better life in the West. America, where little Gyorgei could grow up into a charming fraud who regularly abandoned wife and son for months, returning as unpredictably as he had left. The Ryan heritage.

Ryan took his daughter-in-law's hand. "Don't torture yourself about revenge just because you think Ned's heritage demands it. Whatever tradition of vengeance they had in the old country, it's long ago and far away."

Kaplan called with more news about Shible.

"I had my rendezvous with Rama-whatever. I got him to see that cooperation might be the lesser evil and we dug up a couple of floppies with data on bank transactions. No details about payables and receivables, so it's hard to make any sense out of it. I did notice one thing—a lot of payments around nine thousand dollars. There's no way to tell if they're normal payments or not. If they were cash then it could be money laundering."

"Because of the ten-thousand-dollar reporting rule."

"Then again, it could be that Shible sells deodorant in nine-thousand-dollar lots."

The conversation stuck with Ryan. Suppose the deposits Kaplan had found *were* cash being laundered. How? By being loaned out at relatively low interest rates as Ryan had thought at first? That was one way. There was another way, too, he saw now. Ramanujan had talked about buying gray-market health and beauty products overseas and importing prescription medicine. With a regular flow of money into foreign banks, and goods actually shipped in return, it would be easy to rig the invoices so you were paying for a lot more than you actually bought. The extra money could be diverted for your own use once it was out of the country.

If that was how they were working it, Shible's credit terms could even be relatively innocent, actually a way of holding customers so that a substantial volume of overseas business could be maintained.

Either way, this latest information strengthened the idea of Shible as a possible source of motives for murder.

For the first time in days Ryan's shoulder kept him awake. Instead of taking a painkiller he stayed up drinking and brooding.

He set himself the problem of getting past the physical difficulty of anyone but Jennifer's having killed Ned. It was well and good to lean on that empty hour or two with the jury, but what opportunity did it really provide?

The defense strategy was to imply that the killer was somebody from the party. But who? None of the guests seemed to be a candidate. The reports on Tina Claire's boyfriend made it virtually certain he had an alibi.

If it was Olivera's people—and why them?—how had they known Ned was at Hugo Hill's, and why pick that place and that method when they could have had him shot down in the street any time they wanted to? The way perhaps they had later arranged for the shooting of Ned's father and widow and unborn son.

Ryan knew that if he tried to make Olivera part of his case in court—assuming there was evidence enough to do it—Becker would argue that a person with a violent reach as long as Olivera's would never have chosen such an unlikely murder site and method. And yet . . .

And yet. Something was bothering Ryan. Something was out of place. He hoped he was not imagining it. The whiskey was softening his brain, leaving him only enough clarity to sense his need, now, to believe that Jennifer was innocent. The alternative was more than he could bear—too many Ryans either killer or victim.

Surprisingly he woke up clear eyed. He stopped by to see Jennifer in the morning. The maid let him in.

Jennifer was on a daybed in the living room. A splash of sunlight brightened a silk gown the color of pewter.

She smiled, brief but warm. "I'm glad you're here, Michael. I feel so alone this morning."

"Where's your father?"

She pulled the robe tight around her. "He left. Yesterday. He had business."

"And he left you alone?"

"There's the maid. And I can call a driver to take me to the doctor."

"Not much company."

She reached for his hand and pulled him over to sit next to her. "How's your shoulder?"

"Getting better. You?"

"I'm weak and I hurt and I cry a lot. Otherwise I'm great."

"I don't understand your father leaving you like this."

She picked at imaginary lint on her robe. "That's how he is. I've had a long time to get used to it. He gets caught up in things. It's not that he doesn't love me, he's just got his own way of showing it. He used to go off on business or a vacation and then he'd try to make up for it by doing too much for me, not money so much as *doing* things, like getting my car fixed. As if I couldn't do it myself. Sometimes I felt like I didn't exist except as this person in his mind . . .

"I always have to remind myself that he has this war inside him about the women in his life. When I was a kid I was a cross he bore, as publicly as he could, so he could show the world how wonderful he was to this little girl whose no-good mother had run off on him. Mom was about thirty when she left, and I guess Dad was thirty-five or so. And Roger—his name was Roger—was twenty-three. Boy did Daddy hate her for that. Imagine that, leaving the great Robertson Kneeland for some guy on a motorcycle who lived with a million other dirty people in some rundown farmhouse." She smiled, a combination of irony and rue. "When we talk about my father, we're not talking about a man who feels safe and trusting with women."

At the office Ryan got a call from Craig Lawrence. "I've got some news," Lawrence informed him. "Something unexpected."

"Craig'll be by later," Ryan told Miller when he got off. "In the meantime I want to start on sample summations."

"Okay. Which side do you want?"

"I want each of us to do one for each side. I'll start with the prosecution."

He pulled out his file on the prosecution case and sat down to study it. He did not expect it to be encouraging, but at least it would give him a coherent argument to work on. The defense side, right now, was too much like hunting elephants with a fly swatter.

Lawrence came in batting his arms against the cold. "Am I the only one ready for spring?" He poured himself coffee and pulled up a chair.

Ryan waited until the investigator was on his second cup before getting to business. "You said there was something new."

"Something new is Mr. Donald Garfield, a guest at Hugo Hill's party who is in New York and wants to talk to you. He says he has some information that may be of use."

"Who is he?"

"A real-estate developer from Chicago. Ned and he were talking a business deal, and Ned invited him to Hill's party. He says he'd already decided not to do the deal. He went to the party out of politeness and curiosity. That's from the interview I did with him on the phone last month. I always leave people my number in case they think of anything later. It looks like this one did."

Don Garfield was a big man in every dimension who moved as if he were constantly afraid of breaking something. He spoke with a matching tentativeness in an accent acquired considerably to the south and west of Chicago.

"I didn't really know Ned Ryan, and I didn't want to say anything against him. I still don't. Except there was all that business in the papers a while back about the D.A. holding out on you, and it weighed on my mind. Then I saw about the shooting and how Mrs. Ryan lost her baby and all. I figured there was a chance I could give her a boost, and that if I could I ought to."

"We appreciate it," Ryan said. "What can you tell us?"

"It's like I said, I don't want to say anything against the man, but the reason I didn't get in business with him was I heard some . . . things about him."

"Where?"

"Here and there. I don't remember exactly who. The thing is, why I wanted to talk to you, there was a guy at the party who did some business with him and wasn't happy about it. I didn't ask him for chapter and verse—I was more interested in this lady I was talking to. But I'd say he was real unhappy with Mr. Edward Ryan."

"What did he say? Do you remember any of the words?"

"It was something about Ryan acted like the people he did business with weren't human. One funny thing he said—that if you saw Ryan in your kitchen you'd call the exterminator."

"When did you talk to him?" Ryan asked, keeping the eagerness out of his voice.

"I'd say it was about half an hour before that fight he had with his wife."

"Do you remember anything at all about why the man was so unhappy?" Ryan willed himself to ignore what this might reveal about Ned.

"Something about a deal he was in that got killed because Ryan played games with the terms. Enormous changes at the last minute, the guy said."

"What kind of deal?"

Garfield thought hard, shook his head. "Maybe it'll come back."

"Do you remember his name?" Too much to hope for.

"You go to a party like that, you remember anybody's name? I didn't remember it then, I sure don't remember it now. Something foreign, I think."

"What did he look like?"

"Medium size, skinny, curly hair—brown, I think—and a moustache. Kind of a big moustache, like a bandito, you know?" Garfield mimicked twirling the ends of a moustache beside his cheeks.

"How old?"

"I'd say forty. I do remember he was with this fine-looking woman. Tall, taller than him, nice body." To Miller, "Sorry, ma'am." Then: "Kind of on the thin side."

"Eyes? Hair?"

"Black hair. Short, maybe, or tied back. I don't know what color her eyes were. Dark, I'd say."

"Do you remember her name, or what she did?"

"Name, no. What she did . . . maybe an artist. A lot of them were artists. A model, maybe. He was her date, I'm pretty sure. He said he didn't know Ryan was going to be there. He was hopping mad about it, too—kept looking over at him."

"We've got a list of people at the party. You think it might help if you looked it over?"

"No sir, I sure don't. But I'm happy to do it for you anyhow."

He did not find the name. He promised to think about the incident, especially the man's specific words and who he might have been, and get back to them if he remembered anything more.

Garfield paused on his way out. "Part of the reason why I called was, the guy from the D.A.'s office asked me to testify for them. I don't want to be taking sides in this."

"Do you know why the prosecutor wants you to testify?"

"I'd say it's because I'm a businessman instead of an artist. More reliable, you know."

"I'm sure that's part of it."

"There's one thing he was interested in that I don't know if anybody else saw."

"What's that?"

"I saw Mrs. Ryan leaving the building. I was coming out of the elevator by myself and I saw her walking across that little lobby there, like she was coming from the stairs. She looked kind of upset, too."

"Did she see you?"

"I don't think so."

"When was this?"

"About nine, maybe. Give or take."

"You're sure?"

"Not to the minute."

"But you expect to testify about it."

"I don't know about flying in special for the trial. I suppose I'll do it, but I sure wish they'd find somebody else." He turned again to go.

"We're grateful for your help," Ryan told him. "We'll be in touch with you again soon. In the meantime, if you can think of anything more we'd really appreciate it."

"I'll tell you, I was damn pissed about all this—a man I'm pretty sure I don't want to do business with invites me to a party, and I end up involved in a murder trial. I guess he got even worse out of it, but still . . . Hell, I didn't even score with that lady."

"Maybe you should be glad," Miller said to him as he was leaving. "You can never tell what you might catch."

"So she wasn't invisible when she went back there at nine o'clock," Miller observed.

"Hey, let's look at the bright side," Lawrence said. "This bandito sounds promising."

"If his name really isn't on the guest list he may not be easy to find," Ryan put in.

"That's good," Miller countered, "because we don't want to find him."

"I beg your pardon," Lawrence said.

"There are two possibilities. Either this bandito killed Ned or he didn't. If he didn't kill him, he was doing something else at the time, so he's got an alibi. If he did kill Ned, chances are he's got an alibi he cooked up. A guy who hates Ned and said so at the party and has an alibi is no use to us. What we need is a guy who hates Ned and said so at the party . . . and *can't be found*.''

Ryan didn't argue. Strategically she was right, and his own surge of hope was hardly reason to conclude that Garfield's bandito was actually the killer.

''We also need to find other people at the party who this bandito talked to about how much he hated Ned, so it's not only Garfield we're relying on,'' she said. ''And we have to keep Becker from knowing we're doing it, so he doesn't go looking for him.''

''Garfield is already in Becker's camp,'' Lawrence pointed out. ''So that may be a lost cause.''

''I don't think so. I believed him about not taking sides.''

Ryan listened, poker faced. Or so he thought until Miller said, ''Don't sulk, Ryan. If we play this right it's a big piece of our case. And there will be plenty of time to pin the crime on whoever it is . . . after we get Jennifer acquitted.''

That night Ryan's mind danced with images of men with curly hair and luxuriant moustaches. He tried to channel his thoughts to ideas about how to find the man. But Miller was right—they had to be careful not to alert Becker if they could help it. And not to alert their quarry, either.

31

JENNIFER WAS EAGER TO GO OUT THE NEXT TIME RYAN visited her. They walked to the zoo.

As they went, Ryan told her a heavily edited version of Garfield's story. One of them too excited about the bandito was enough.

"I don't remember anybody with a moustache like that," she said.

"It's worth spending some time on. Sit down when you have a chance to and try to picture the party, like a movie in your mind." He saw that she was smiling. "Aren't there acting exercises like that?"

"Yes. I'll try some."

"Good." He bought them a pair of admission tickets and they went in behind a bubbling stream of grade-school kids.

"Did Ned ever say anything about people who sell drugs?" he asked.

She looked at him. "Everybody talks about that. You can't live in the city and not. We have friends who do a line of coke and then complain about the crack pushers."

"What about knowing them, or having any dealings with them?"

"Drug pushers? Do you think they had something to do with it?"

"I'm not sure."

They stopped to watch the polar bears clamber over their rocks.

"It looks real," Jennifer said, "but they're all cooped up in there."

"No bars."

"It's still a jail."

Time to change the subject. "Can you think of any reason someone would want to shoot you?"

"Me? I thought they were having a gang war."

"Yes, well . . . we don't want to take anything for granted."

Ryan was energized by having a concrete lead to follow. He would start with what he knew. Ned might have changed terms or reneged any number of times, but the deal breaker that stuck in Ryan's mind was the one Thom Willard had told him about. So far Willy had not come up with any names from that deal. He called the Philadelphian to press him harder.

"Didn't you say there were foreigners involved?"

"Yes, but they got uninvolved before the deal was put together. And fell apart."

"I need more information about it. I can send an accountant down, or an investigator, to check through any records you think might help."

"The dead didn't close, so I don't know what they'll find."

"Somebody's got to remember something."

Willy sighed. "I'll try to find your man a place to start. If I do, I'll let you know."

* * *

As the week passed, Ryan became increasingly uneasy about not hearing from Willy. Late Friday, with Ryan at the edge of his patience, the banker called. He had found some papers and some names, if Ryan was still interested. Ryan assured him that he was.

Lawrence took a late train to Philadelphia on Sunday so he would be there and ready to start first thing Monday morning. He called Ryan with his first report at lunchtime.

"Nothing much. Willy has some old loan applications, a title search, a few other things. I wish Garfield had been clearer about what the hell he meant by a foreign name. I mean, Ryan is a foreign name to some people."

You'd be surprised, Ryan did not say.

Monday night Ryan tried to bury his impatience in the oblivion of television. He was not aware of the specifics of what he was watching, only the flow of greed and violence and insinuations of sex. His mind ticked over in the background, anticipating what action he would take if Lawrence found the bandito. His shoulder ached.

The lead story on the late news was a shootout between crack gangs in the West Village. It got Ryan's attention—it involved the same gangs whose bullets, according to the police, had ended up in him and Jennifer. And the baby. The news reader speculated that this latest incident was in revenge for the earlier one.

Tuesday afternoon Ryan got a call from Detective Garrity.

"Did you hear about the shooting last night?"

"Yes."

"We found some guns with the bodies. Ballistics ran a check."

"What did they find?" Playing the game.

"One of the guns is a match for the one that shot you and your client."

"How certain is that?"

"As good as Ballistics can make it."

"I take it that means you're going to stop looking for the people behind shooting us."

"Don't have to look any farther than the morgue. The case is cleared, as far as we're concerned."

But if Felipe Olivera could have arranged the first shooting, Ryan thought, he could have arranged the second one, too. Right down to planting the incriminating gun.

You're being paranoid, he told himself.

* * *

Ryan's physical therapist was based at the same health club where Jim Morris worked out. Ryan arranged to meet him late one afternoon.

"How's the defense coming?" Morris asked.

"We never found that notebook. Are you sure about it?"

"That Ned had it, yes. What was in it, no."

"Are you sure he still had it at around the time he was killed?"

"No. Not completely."

"What can you tell me about Srini Ramanujan?"

"Not much. Ned found him, I don't know how. He's a real character. Temper hotter than that rat stew he calls curry. He seems to do a good job, and I guess it makes sense having an Indian in that job. A lot of Shible's customers are, too."

"Do you think he could be skimming or working some kind of deal on the side?"

"Srini? I never thought of him as dishonest. I get my check every couple of months and it seems big enough. I have enough to think about without worrying if Srini is skimming a little."

"Do you think Ned would have been that relaxed about it?"

"He never had suspicions about Srini that I knew about."

"What about people with business grudges against Ned? Did he ever talk about that?"

There were some stories, Morris said, but never anything explicit and never anything that sounded too serious.

Ryan told him Kneeland's story about the woman with tax problems.

"Ned never told me that one, or anything like it. That's not the Ned I knew."

"People show different faces for different reasons."

Morris's eyes narrowed. "Tell me something, Mr. Ryan. Do you believe all the stories you hear?"

"If you've got some evidence to the contrary I'd love to hear it."

"Only that I liked Ned and trusted him and never had any reason to regret it."

Lawrence's daily reports from Philadelphia were not encouraging. The people who had lost money in the deal all recognized Ned Ryan's name, but none had been directly involved with him. If any bore a grudge, it seemed too abstract for violence. And no one remembered a thin, medium-size man with curly hair and moustache and a foreign-sounding name.

* * *

Ryan wanted to buy time to find the bandito. Given Kassia Miller's opinion on that subject he could not tell her why he had decided they should slow the process down, but she was more than ready to delay purely as a matter of strategy. The problem was finding a reason, in the face of Corino's clear lack of sympathy for changing the schedule. The best approach seemed to be a slow recovery by Jennifer.

She had moved out of her father's apartment into a brownstone town house owned by some friends who were out of the country.

Seeing her for the first time in several days, Ryan was alarmed. Her clothes fit her loosely and her skin was pallid against her dark hair. Purplish circles smudged the area beneath her glazed blue-gray eyes. A slow recovery did not seem such a fiction.

When he suggested to her that delay was always helpful to the defense the color came back into her face.

Delay might be good because prosecution witnesses left town or forgot what they saw, she raged, but it did not help your sanity if your every waking moment and all your dreams were haunted by the accusations hanging over you and the awful possibility that you might end up in jail for years.

Ryan had never seen her so worked up before. Was this what she had been like at the party?

"I can't stand much more, Michael," she said finally. "I lost my husband. I lost my baby. I hurt all the time. I'm accused of a crime I didn't commit. Let's just get it over with."

Ryan could remember the pleasure he had taken using his prosecutorial power as a lever. He had applied pressure to move stubborn people, and move them he had. He had not thought too deeply about how that pressure might feel on the receiving end. Now he was learning.

He called Jake Kaplan and explained the problem of finding the bandito.

"You want me to look for deals that didn't happen? I've heard a lot of strange ones in my time but this takes the cake. I can talk to some people he did deals with, see what they remember."

"Fine. Only, be vague about it. Just the general question. If anybody asks why, you're concerned about suits against the estate."

Kaplan called back two days later. "Nothing so far."

* * *

Ryan called Lawrence in Philadelphia.

"What the hell is taking so long down there?" It came out sharper than he intended.

"You want to come down and do it yourself?"

"It's important."

"I know it's important. It's also not here. I'm coming back." Lawrence hung up.

Great, Ryan thought. Now I'm alienating my allies.

He decided to take a chance on calling the four people on Hugo Hill's guest list who seemed most sympathetic to Jennifer. It seemed unlikely that they would run to Becker with the news that Michael Ryan was looking for a medium-size man with a moustache. None of them remembered talking to anyone fitting the bandito's description, or anyone with a grudge against Ned.

Ryan was staring at the wall, unable to work, convincing himself that it was safe to continue through the guest list to people whose loyalty was more questionable, that finding the bandito was more important than keeping Becker from learning about him, when one of the people he had spoken to called back. She remembered talking to a man who looked like that, she said, but she had no idea what they had talked about.

Better than nothing, he thought when he hung up. Before this, Garfield's word had been their only evidence the man existed.

Ryan met with Craig Lawrence and Jake Kaplan to review their lack of progress locating the bandito.

"Why don't we give it up," Lawrence suggested. "Kassandra said from the beginning we're better off without him, as long as we have Garfield's testimony. And you said one of our witnesses talked to him. So maybe the Kass is right. We've got enough for the jury, and if we think about it too hard Becker's going to get the idea, too."

Badly as Ryan wanted to find the man, he had no good argument for doing it now.

The defense team was working morning to night, eating lunch and dinner in the office. When they had first moved in, the twenty-by-forty space had seemed generous to Ryan under its towering ceilings, sparkling with new gray-white paint. As the days of hard work wore on, he felt increasingly closed in, oppressively aware of every tic and mannerism of his colleagues.

They speculated again about Becker's case, they made new lists of probable prosecution witnesses, debated them, tore them apart

and started again. Ryan and Miller finished their mock summations
and traded sides for a second round. Lawrence made appointments
with the partygoers they might call as defense witnesses. Each had
to be brought in, reinterviewed, and prepared for an appearance on
the witness stand. The initial results were disappointing. As Lawrence had predicted, people were reconsidering their months-old
decisions to testify. Too many of them were out of town, or going
to be out of town, or pretending to be out of town.

Jennifer still looked meager and haunted but she claimed she
was feeling stronger. Ryan continued to visit her, and she began to
spend a few hours each day in the office. She was subdued and
withdrawn, watching and listening but not taking her usual active
role. And sometimes Ryan felt as if she was avoiding him.

Ryan could not get the bandito out of his mind. Miller's admittedly
cogent reasoning that he should be left undiscovered, echoed by
Lawrence, had not muted the desire to find the man.

Alone in the office one afternoon, Ryan indulged himself and
called Hugo Hill to ask if the gallery owner remembered a tall dark
model or artist who had come to the party with a curly-haired,
moustachio'd businessman.

"It doesn't ring any bells," Hill told him.

He pressed it, describing the woman more fully, adding details
about the man. Kassia Miller came in as he was finishing.

"Sorry," Hill said, "it still doesn't ring any bells."

"If you think of anything, call me," Ryan said.

"Who was that?" his co-counsel asked when he hung up.

He told her.

"And you were asking him about the mysterious guest."

"Yes."

"Damn it, Ryan, how can you be so damn *childish*?"

If she'd had an office door to slam she would have. As it was all
she could do was stalk to her desk and sit down hard. She misjudged, connecting only with the front edge of the wheeled chair,
which squirted backward, planting her on the floor.

Laughter burst from him before he could stifle it.

"You bastard! You think this is funny?" She was still on the
floor.

"No . . . Sorry . . ." he managed through his laughter.

"Oh, hell, of course it is." Grinning. "But damn it . . ."

"You're right, I shouldn't have called him."

"We're working too hard," she said.

32

FOR A WEEK THEY MET WITH EXPERTS. RYAN LEARNED more than he wanted to know about skull fractures and digestive processes and blood typing, a science that had made enormous strides since he'd last had anything to do with it. He tuned out completely for the description of contrecoup brain injuries—bruises caused when the brain ricocheted off the inside of the skull like a billiard ball off a rail.

"I had a talk with Kneeland," Miller reported on Friday morning. "He wanted to know if he should stay away from court, in case we wanted him to testify. I said it wasn't likely we would because even if we used character witnesses he wasn't appropriate. He said what about Ned's businesses? I said I'd ask you."

"The jury is going to see him as biased, so if we can use anybody else for a given piece of testimony we will."

"You think there's anything he has special knowledge about?"

"Hard to say . . . It's possible. We'll miss having him in the spectator's gallery. And how will Jennifer feel without him?"

"She's having friends come every day. She says she'd like to have him there but she understands he may have to stay away. He says he wants to do what's best for her."

"How nice that everyone is being so agreeable," he said. "All right, tell him to stay home. Once he's in court, we can't use him at all. This way we can keep our options open." And I won't have him looking over my shoulder every day.

Friday afternoon was reserved for Miller's bloodstain pattern expert. Lawrence, who had been happy to skip the others, insisted on being there for this one.

The description "bloodstain pattern expert" did not call to Ryan's

195

mind a person remotely like the woman who showed up at their office on Friday. Lynne Archbold, Ph.D., was about five four, with an hourglass figure, prematurely iron-gray hair and dark eyes exaggerated by enormous round glasses. She had so much energy she seemed to bounce into the room.

Miller made the introductions and led Archbold through a listing of her training and experience. Her bounciness worried Ryan. It was hardly the best demeanor for an expert witness on subjects like the aerodynamic flight characteristics of human blood. He would have preferred a professorial type, male if possible. Or someone who looked like Sherlock Holmes.

"When you were describing your qualifications I noticed you didn't say what your Ph.D. was in."

"Art history."

Ryan was nonplussed. Lawrence laughed.

"Nice parlay," the investigator laughed.

"Have you done the same thing all your life?" Archbold shot back.

"Pretty much."

"How sad."

"You were concerned about not having all the crime-scene photos," Miller interjected quickly.

"Very. And I'll tell you why. The first rule of analyzing blood-stain patterns is don't even begin to draw conclusions unless you have all the stains. The problem there is—two problems. The first is, the crime-scene unit wasn't too interested in bloodstains. They were focusing on the other aspects of the scene. So some of the images are not as sharp as they should be for proper analysis.

"The best way I work, really, is visit the scene, lift some impressions of the important stains and use the room as a matrix for working back from the stains to the events. The exact texture of the target—that's the object the flying blood hits—and the exact dimensions of the room are very important. But I understand that in this case I don't get any of that. This is doubly unfortunate because my problem doesn't stop with fuzzy pictures. The dear darling police also neglected to photograph parts of the room."

She let the statement sink in.

"You're missing some stains?" Ryan asked.

"You could say that. You could definitely say that. That's why I kept asking for more pictures."

"Can you draw any conclusions?"

"Some. If you've got a projector I'll show you some slides."

Miller set up the projector and the screen. Archbold gave them an hour's worth of slides and patter about the history and science of analyzing bloodstains. Archbold's delivery continued to be as energetic as her entrance to the office, caroming the words past like bumper cars. Ryan found it all surprisingly fascinating, and Lawrence was clearly spellbound. When the slide show was over, she did a demonstration of a bludgeoning, describing the path of all the blood thrown off by the wound and the weapon. Ryan kept seeing Jennifer the time she had mimed raising the sculpture to ''smash something.''

''That's basically all there is to it,'' Archbold said. ''We can use the basic principles I've entertained you with to determine the exact position of the assailant, and sometimes of the victim, too. Because the different blows usually produce different amounts of blood, we can say some things about the movement of the two parties, and often about the handedness of the assailant. It's not magic, but it's damn powerful. The sad part is not every jurisdiction buys it yet. Pathologists play at it, but they get a lot wrong. They're medical people, and this isn't medicine, it's physics—fluid dynamics, mechanics.''

''How much can you give us with what you've got?'' Ryan asked.

''I can say you've got four blows by a right-handed assailant. I can say the victim was moving downward and to his right as the blows were struck. That's probably partly avoiding the blows and partly because he was collapsing.''

''Is that anything the head wound people won't be able to tell us?''

''The part about moving down and to the right. They can maybe tell you the angle of the blow, but not the position of the head relative to floor, walls and ceiling.''

''Does that do us any good?''

''That's for you to know. One thing—because I don't have all the stains, I have to testify about probabilities. Otherwise I can talk about near certainty.''

''I guess we should think about it before we put you through trial preparation.''

''I'm in town a couple of days this trip, so there's no hurry. What makes it sad is I can make a guess there might have been something real useful for you.''

''Can you tell us what?'' Ryan asked.

''I could, but I won't. It's a guess—it could be all wrong and send you on a wild goose chase.''

''Why don't you let us be the judge?''

''If you let *me* be the judge of my own professional standards.''

I keep offending people, he thought.

"The only way I can tell you more is to have the missing stains," Archbold volunteered. "And that, I gather, is not in the cards."

"It doesn't look that way."

"Too bad."

At home he could not sit still, could not abide the idea of another microwave dinner, did not want to go to the Shamrock. He wandered the empty apartment. Living room, dining room, study. The spare room that in his fantasy of years ago was going to be Ali's study and a guest room for Ned.

He found the tug of melancholy's undertow. On an impulse he called Kassia Miller at home. He hung up on the third ring.

He wandered some more. Picked up a whiskey bottle. Put it down unopened.

He sat in his grandmother's chair—the chair where Grandpa Yosef had sat in silence all the days Ryan had known him—and thought about the past and his dead son and his grandson who never was, and wondered if it was possible anymore that he could himself be returned to life.

They started the last week before trial with a strategy session.

"I still think emphasizing that the time of death is uncertain is a plus for us," Miller said. "Even if Garfield places her there at nine, we still want to keep that window of opportunity as wide as we can."

"I'm not disagreeing." Ryan wrote TIME OF DEATH in big letters on the whiteboard they were using to plot their trial strategy. "The question there is, can you push the time of death *past* nine? He wasn't discovered until almost ten."

"The way the M.E. is stalling with the original autopsy notes, my guess is we can. It's the only place we'll get any real mileage out of the medical evidence. They're going to kill us on the blood typing, and four major blows to the head doesn't look like an accident."

"Your bloodstain person isn't going to help us there."

"She'll make it worse, I think. That business about how he was trying to avoid the blows."

"So we've got the hour Ned might have been alone, and maybe more—maybe almost two hours. And we have someone at the party who expressed violent anger toward him. We've got drugs and guns at the party." He wrote BANDITO and, below it, DRUGS AND GUNS.

"We probably ought to challenge Garfield's identification of Jennifer at nine. I know she was there, but Garfield barely knew her, and he could be mistaken."

"We'll have to go easy on him on cross, though, or he'll rebel for sure, and we need him for the bandito."

She smiled. "The woman's touch."

"So far this is all material we develop out of the prosecution witnesses. The closer we get, the more I think we want to get as much as we can out of what Becker puts up there. All of it, if possible."

"Assuming we get Guevara to say what we want."

"That's your job."

"Yes, with help from the questions I get from our medical experts. Assuming Dr. Guevara cooperates."

"You'll get her to cooperate. What else do we have?" It was a rhetorical question. They'd both been over and over the prosecution and defense cases.

"We have Ned got what he deserved, whoever did it."

NASTY NED, wrote Ryan. MANY POSS. KILLERS.

"Can you do that, Ryan?" she asked flatly. "Can you make that case for all the world to see?"

"I'll do what I have to. I just wish we had some better evidence."

"You and me both. Normal marriage is next, I think."

"Beg your pardon?"

"What we're trying to prove. Ned and Jennifer had a stormy but solid relationship. Normal marriage."

He wrote it down. "And the quarrel they had at that party was no different from others they'd had before."

"You think we can include smashing the bowl in that, without bringing up her past?" she asked.

"Sure. Wasn't your generation taught to express its anger? Not to hold back? Let it all hang out?"

"My generation! Is that how you think of me, Grandpa?"

"I'm not Grandpa." And I'm never going to be, he thought.

"My candidate for villain is Tina Claire," Miller said. "Even though it looks like the boyfriend has an alibi."

"I agree. But we have to be careful because the more we make Tina Claire a villain, the more we make her a provocation for Jennifer's murderous rage."

"I sure wish Jennifer was still pregnant."

"So do I," Ryan said. "So do I."

They went over it a couple of times to be sure they were not leaving anything out. They made lists of the places their case needed shoring up, at the same time avoiding overt acknowledgment of how weak it was. Without a confession from Garfield's bandito or a way to get Ned's connection with Felipe Olivera in front of the jury, it was the only case they could make. Laying it out left Ryan shaken.

As a prosecutor he had felt the weight of the burden of proof that was always his. From that perspective, the defense's job had seemed easy: poke holes in the prosecution case, however irresponsibly. The prosecution owed allegiance to the truth, he had thought then; the defense's only constraint was the rules of the game. Now, seeing it from the other side, he was unprepared for the prosecutor's control over the shape of the trial. More than he had expected, he was going to be dancing to Becker's tune.

As the trial date drew closer Ryan felt increasingly at sea. The more he pressed for a feeling of control over the case, the more elusive it became.

He had never got used to the feeling that no matter how much time he had to prepare for a major trial and no matter how hard he worked, the trial date arrived a week too soon. People he had worked with had told him they felt that way sometimes, and sometimes they didn't. For Ryan it was as sure as the sun coming up in the morning.

For this one, any time would have been too soon. There was too much at stake for him ever to feel ready. Legler had probably been right—he should never have taken it on.

He supposed he had done a good job of preparation. He had made sure all the leads were followed and all the potential witnesses were researched. Most of the time he had been the kind of commander his troops needed, resisting the crazed overattention to minor detail and the totalitarian management style that had almost scuttled the Gibson case. And he had kept his emotions from getting in the way too often. All in all, with help from Kassia Miller and Craig Lawrence, he had behaved like a competent lawyer, if not the whiz-kid he once had been.

But he did not fool himself: no matter what people said about trials being won and lost before anyone set foot in a courtroom, preparation was preparation, and trial was trial.

TRIAL

1

ON THE MORNING OF THE FIRST DAY RYAN SHOWERED
and shaved and, wearing an ancient terry robe, ate a breakfast of
two poached eggs, dry toast and two cups of coffee. Then he dressed
in a freshly pressed navy-blue suit, a white shirt and a blue-and-
red-and-white striped regimental tie.

It was all part of an old ritual, one he had not had reason to
perform in years. The familiar motions brought back some of the
old pretrial feelings. Slotting the cufflinks in his sleeves and
straightening his tie, he remembered how in his early days as a trial
lawyer he had felt like a gladiator adjusting his armor. Over the
years he had come to relish the breathless combination of anxiety
and exhilaration. Now, putting on his jacket, he could feel his heart
beating. This time he did not think it was exhilaration.

The press was out in force when Jennifer and her lawyers arrived
at the grim entrance of the courthouse at 100 Centre Street. In the
thirteenth-floor courtroom, Joe Becker was already at the prosecution table. Sitting next to him was a tall woman in a dark blue
pinstripe suit. Her straight brown hair was long enough to touch
the back of her chair.

The defense team arrayed themselves at the long oak table to the
right of the prosecution's. Ryan was nearest the prosecution table.
Beyond it to his left was the vacant jury box. To his right was Kassia
Miller; Jennifer sat next to her.

Corino was in the courtroom and on the bench before Ryan had
a chance to come to his feet.

"We have some small matters to take care of before we bring in
our potential jurors," the judge said. "At the moment, we're waiting for a member of the prosecution, so please bear with us, Mr.
Ryan, ladies."

Ryan glanced at Miller next to him, wondering if she was going to take offense at Corino's "ladies." He saw no sign that she had even noticed, but before he had quite looked away she threw him a quick, savage grin.

While the judge busied himself with papers, Ryan arrayed his yellow pad and pencils on the table, then took his jury-selection notes from his briefcase and reviewed them. So far he was all right. His pulse was fast and his mouth was dry, but his mind seemed to be working.

He tried to minimize the deconditioning power of the years without practice. He told himself that trial work was like riding a bicycle: you never forgot how, it was in your bones.

Yes, and like riding a bicycle there was that same wobbliness when you got back on after years away from it, that same heart-stopping decompression in your chest when you first pedaled out into traffic. All your deftness lost, and all the nuances of balance you had built up by continual practice. Recapturable, perhaps, but only at the price of barked shins and skinned knees. And that was something he could not afford now.

After ten minutes the judge said, "Mr. Becker?"

"Any minute, your honor."

True to Becker's work, there was a small commotion at the back of the courtroom. Ryan turned to see. If this was a surprise he wanted time to adjust.

Francesco Griglia strode deliberately up the aisle to the rail, followed closely by two men not as tall and considerably younger.

Becker left the prosecution table and went to open the gate. The D.A. swept through, leaving his equerries standing beyond the rail.

"Sorry I'm late, your honor."

"Now you're here, I suppose we can begin." Corino did not sound pleased. "Mr. Griglia, I understand you have some words you wish to say at this time."

Griglia nodded. "Your honor, in view of the special nature of this case, and in particular of the unusual representation which appears on the defense side"—he made a gestural turn toward the defense table—"my office has decided that it is in the interest of the people to make a change in counsel who will be presenting this case to the jury. I know this is unusual at this late date, but in light of the latitude the court has allowed the defense in regard to representation I trust that the court will also allow the prosecution some leeway."

"What can I do for you, Mr. District Attorney? Whom do you have in mind?"

"Well, your honor, we'd like to keep Ms. Warneke, as a matter of continuity, and we'd like to keep Mr. Becker, too, on a secondary basis for certain special purposes."

"We don't want to confuse the jury with too many lawyers."

"No, your honor, I am very aware of that."

"Who do you propose as lead counsel?"

The judge's question contained no curiosity; he already knew the answer. Ryan was afraid he did, too.

"That would be me, your honor," Griglia said in an even voice, as if it were the most ordinary thing in the world.

Miller did not fully stifle a groan.

Corino said, "I assume you've made arrangements for carrying out your other duties. I always like to think my trials are going to be short, but I can't say I have high hopes for this one."

"I recognize that emergencies in my office are possible, your honor. I believe I can deal with them when the court isn't in session, but it's in the event I can't that I want to keep Mr. Becker on the team."

"I'll take it under advisement." The judge turned to the court reporter. "Off the record, please." The reporter lifted her hands from her stenotype machine. "Step up, all of you."

With the five lawyers in front of him, Corino leaned forward on the bench.

"I'll tell the bunch of you right now, if you think you're going to turn this courtroom into a circus you'd better think again. I'm giving you all the room I can on this. I suppose at this point if one of you told me you conscientiously believed the case could best be tried by a monkey, I'd at least have to think about it. But don't take that for any promise of latitude in how you conduct yourself. If I'm going to have a monkey in my courtroom, it's damn well going to be a *housebroken* monkey. Do I make myself clear?"

There was silence.

"I asked you a question, gentlemen and ladies. I expect an answer."

"Yes, Judge," the five lawyers chorused.

"Good. Now, I asked for the prosecution's witness list and any questions or comments relating to jury selection. I've looked at what you gave me. I have a question for Mr. Griglia. Are you serious about this witness list?"

"Your honor?"

"We'll be here all year with this many witnesses."

"Your honor, as to some of these people, we don't yet know which of them will be available or how many of them we may need to call. We prefer if we can avoid it not to subpoena people who have important reasons to be out of the jurisdiction, and in the interest of completeness we wanted to list all our potential witnesses.''

''I don't want a long line of people in here reciting the same facts over and over.''

''Neither do the people, your honor.''

''All right, then, is there anything else? Any other motions, anything else we need to take care of before we start? Mr. Ryan, no objection to Mr. Griglia?''

''If your honor please,'' Ryan said. ''We'd like a brief recess to discuss this.''

''Fifteen minutes. If you need more you'll tell me why.''

''Is there a place we can talk?''

''Use my robing room.''

A court officer in blue trousers and white shirt, with a gold badge and a gunbelt, led them to the small room behind the bench.

''What does it mean?'' Jennifer asked.

''It means the District Attorney has decided your case is important enough or interesting enough to come into court and prosecute you himself,'' Ryan told her.

''That's not good, is it?''

Ryan was searching for Griglia's reason for pulling this stunt. Glory, again, Franky's favorite. And maybe a touch of the personal as well. Franky had always had a gunslinger's urge to know if he or Ryan was the real top gun.

''Michael?'' Miller prodded.

''He'll be tougher to beat than Becker,'' Ryan allowed himself to say.

''Didn't the judge said something about objecting?'' Jennifer asked.

''I don't see how.'' He looked to his co-counsel.

''We can make some noise about knowing who our opponent is and not having him come and-go.''

''Better for us if he does,'' Ryan said, ''and Corino knows it. This one's inevitable—let's get back in there and be gracious.''

At Corino's order, court officers led the jury panel in, an overflow crowd of ordinary people, some openly curious, some careful to look somber and responsible, a few clearly annoyed at the inconvenience.

The judge welcomed them to his courtroom, explained the seriousness of their business and the importance of each citizen's obligation to serve on a jury. ''If you were sitting where the defendant is, you'd want a jury made up of people who understood their responsibility and were living up to it with all their attention and care. That's what we expect of you.''

He told them what case this was and read the indictment. There was a considerable stir in the courtroom.

He introduced the court personnel and the attorneys for both sides, and he explained the jury-selection procedure.

''I noticed by your reaction that many of you have heard of this case. How many of you have read something in the newspapers or seen something on TV about it?''

About three-quarters of the panel raised their hands.

''I guess the rest of you live on Mars.''

They all laughed.

''I'm glad you enjoyed that, ladies and gentleman—we don't get to do a lot of laughing here. This is not a game show, and it is not 'The People's Court.' This is real life, and there's a real person on trial here. Now, this trial may take a long time. Every weekday for many weeks. I hope not, but I know how lawyers can be, and I think these two lawyers are going to be very careful that you have all the information you need. And because of all the press attention, there may come a time when you have to go and live in a hotel until you've all reached a verdict. Now if any of you feel that serving on this jury would be a hardship, please raise your hand and we'll see about whether to excuse you or not.''

Almost half of the hundred and twenty potential jurors thought the case would impose too much on their lives.

''Now I'm going to tell you that if you don't have a serious reason you will not be excused. Jury duty is not something you can walk away from on a whim. The court officers are going to pass out a written questionnaire about your hardship and there's an oath to swear at the bottom when you sign it. Leave your hand up if you want one.''

A few of the hands dropped. When the questionnaires were filled out and collected, Corino and the lawyers reviewed them and agreed to dismiss the ones with obviously persuasive claims. The rest Corino questioned closely, then gave the lawyers a chance.

Ryan was careful about how he challenged the hardship claims. If they were not released from the panel he wanted them to think it was because of Griglia. Reluctant jurors tended to identify with the defendant, who was also in court against her will.

It took them two days to get a full pool of jurors.

''I have some general remarks to make,'' Corino told them.

"For the benefit of those who don't know it yet, lawyers in this case are not your everyday lawyers. The lawyer who speaks for the people is the Acting District Attorney for Manhattan, which is major news, as you may have guessed from the way we have been besieged by the press. Even more unusual is the fact that the defense lawyer, Mr. Ryan, is the father of the man whose murder brings us all here." Corino looked pointedly around the courtroom. "Now, hearing that, it might occur to you to think something along these lines: Poor Mr. Ryan lost his son and he must believe in his client and he's suffered enough, so I ought to give him some extra consideration. Well, I'm here to tell you, ladies and gentlemen, that is not a permissible way to think in a courtroom. It goes against the very heart and foundation of our system of justice. Sympathy and kindness are out of place here, every bit as out of place as hatred and revenge. The only things you can consider are the evidence that is properly presented to you and the allowable arguments the lawyers may make."

He sat back in his tall leather chair, surveying the rows of jurors arrayed behind the lawyers.

"Ladies and gentlemen, from time to time in these proceedings, if you become part of them, you are going to be told to disregard things that you hear. This is not easy for anyone, but it is possible. You would do well to forget such matters entirely, but if you remember them you need only remember also that you are to put them to one side in reaching any conclusion. If you think about it that way, you'll see it's not as hard as it sounds."

He gave them a moment to consider it. Ryan wondered what he was reading in their faces.

"Now, the first thing you are to disregard, and the one it's most important to disregard, is who these lawyers are. If you insist on personalizing them, remember this: you know nothing about their motives. The fallible human beings inside those professionals may be searching for the truth or for personal glory, acting out of love or out of hate. Only one thing is certain: if you try to guess their motives you will be wrong.

"For your purposes these men are here only as attorneys. Anything else about them does not matter. All that matters is the *evidence*. I am asking you now to search your consciences and ask yourself if you can truly put these other questions aside and attend only to the evidence that will be put before you properly and in accordance with the law as I instruct you in it. This is not a simple task, and there is no shame in not being up to it. If it's a serious problem for you, you will have a chance to say so."

He paused. "The court officers are going to pass out some questionnaires now. These have some general questions about your life and your background. I'm going to ask you to fill them out fully and honestly, and sign the oath on the last page. If you have any questions, raise your hand."

The questionnaires took the rest of the morning.

Lawrence joined them for lunch. He was not happy with the prosecution's witness list.

"I see why the judge was bitching. There have to be twenty names from the party. He can't be serious about calling them all—the jury would string him up by his thumbs."

"Typical prosecution trick," Miller said. "Confuse the opposition."

"Just what I need—a mountain of extra work."

"And he's happy to make us do it," Ryan said. "But if I know Franky Griglia, he also wants to have everybody and his brother on the list so he can wait and see what the jury looks like and then pick his witnesses to match."

They went over the list together. Jennifer, sulking for no reason Ryan knew about, paid attention only when both lawyers reminded her that her future was at stake. She could not identify any of the names they did not recognize, except to say that one or two of them might be women Ned had "dated."

"Why would they be testifying?" she wanted to know.

"That's a good question. Unless they can say Ned was afraid of you."

"That's ridiculous."

"Or unless you had some contact with them yourself. Did you call any of them, or see them?"

"Why would I do that?"

"Nobody's accusing you of anything. We just want to be prepared for these witnesses."

"I don't remember who I called or didn't call. I'll try." She pushed herself away from the table. "I'll see you at the office," she said, and left.

"Sometimes I wonder," Ryan said.

"Clients get that way," Miller told him. "It's a lot to absorb, a lot of pressure to be under all the time. They withdraw, they get irrational. They also panic, and cling, and get weepy. And yell and second-guess. Jennifer isn't as bad as some. I've said it before, Ryan—welcome to the wonderful world of working with a client."

* * *

Back at the office the results of their latest juror-attitude poll were in. Of three hundred people the pollsters had called, chosen to reflect a rough demographic profile of the jurors in recent major felony cases in Manhattan, more than half had refused to answer the questions.

"Everybody's sick of being bothered by people they don't know," Miller said.

Ryan summarized the pollsters' summary. "Most people know about the case, most of those people know the accused was the victim's wife. Most of the ones who know that also know the defense lawyer is a relative of the victim. Most of *those* think my defending Jennifer is a sign she's innocent. However, most of the whole sample think she's guilty. Sixty-five percent guilty to thirteen innocent to twenty-two no opinion. Followed by a disclaimer about the wide margin of error. No significant change from last time. Mush."

Despite Ryan's annoyance with the poll's vagueness, the numbers sounded more than a little scary. As a prosecutor he had wished in vain for a ready-made hanging jury. Now it looked as if he might get one.

2

WHEN THE DEFENSE TEAM RETURNED TO COURT AF-
ter lunch there was a pile of photocopied questionnaires on the defense table, and a similar pile in front of Griglia.

Ryan settled himself in his chair, slid the tall stack of questionnaires to where Miller could reach them, then realigned his pad and pencils. There was a fourth chair at the defense table, empty for the moment. Miller's jury-selection expert was late.

Just before the judge arrived to start the afternoon session Morton Sisley pulled the fourth chair to the end of the table so that he was facing the jury box. Ryan was glad Sisley would be out of his line of sight. The self-styled sociologist-anthropologist was too prim and dapper by half: "fussy" was the word that came to Ryan's mind.

The jurors were brought in, again filling the spectators' gallery except for the two rows reserved for the press and the front row on the prosecution side, reserved for guests of the court. Ryan closed his eyes and concentrated on images of jury selections past.

Picking a jury was something he had done so many times they blended into a puree, but it had been ten years now since he had done it regularly—in a different kind of courtroom, sitting on the other side of the aisle, under very different rules. And it was four years since he had done it at all.

They had debated how to handle it. In federal court, Ryan had learned to watch jurors answer questions posed by the judge. In state court the lawyers did most of the questioning and used the opportunity to indoctrinate the jurors.

Though Miller was the one with the specific experience, there was good reason for Ryan to do the lion's share of examining the jury panel. It was the best way to acquaint the jury with him and give him a chance to develop a rapport with them. Griglia would be putting on a show up there. If during the defense's turn Ryan sat back and watched—the way he had in federal court—the jurors might think of him as cold and aloof, or afraid, or incompetent.

"You can do your jury watching while Griglia is questioning them," Miller had suggested.

"It's not the same," Ryan told her. "Besides, I'll be watching Franky, trying to figure out how to do this."

Now, about to step into the lions' den, Ryan turned to Miller, who was having a murmured consultation with Sisley.

"Ready?"

"When you are, C.B."

He looked at her.

"Never mind," she said. "Old joke."

The clerk called the proceedings to order. Twelve names were drawn and twelve people wearing blue-and-white "juror" buttons were led into the well of the court to fill seats in the jury box. Ryan kept his eyes on the potential jurors' faces as one at a time they came up and sat down. He did his best to keep his expression neutral, neither judgmental nor ingratiating, not betraying the turmoil within.

Judge Corino began with homilies about the duties of citizens and the importance of serving on a jury, repeating and extending his earlier remarks. He spoke slowly, using the full resonance of his voice, his hands loosely on the pages of an open book as if he were about to turn a page—a prop, surely—his head tilted just enough so that he was looking at the jurors from under the black ridge of eyebrows. The mythic pose of American justice.

He asked the men and women in the jury box if they were related to any of the members of the prosecution or defense teams, or the defendant or the victim, or knew them outside the courtroom. None were. None did. A clerk read aloud the names of potential prosecution witnesses followed by a short list of tentative defense witnesses, mostly medical experts. Corino asked the jurors if they were related to or knew any of them. None were. None did.

Did they have relatives who were police officers or other law-enforcement personnel? A balding man in a business suit had a brother in the F.B.I. Would he be inclined to believe the word of a police officer simply because he was a police officer? The man laughed. "Not hardly."

"Thank you, that will be all."

The man looked at Corino, bewildered.

"You're excused."

More bewildered, the man made his way out of the jury box.

"Ladies and gentlemen, we all like a joke now and then, but I remind you that we are doing serious business here."

When they were sober-faced enough to suit him he asked them if they had ever been the victims of violent crime, or had any close relative who had been a victim. Five hands went up. A stocky woman had been mugged and almost raped. Would that dispose her unfavorably to the defendant? No. A fit-looking man in his thirties had been beaten by a bunch of kids on a March of Dimes walkathon in Central Park. The other three had relatives who had been mugged. None of them thought the experiences would affect their judgment.

Next to Ryan, Miller jotted a few notes on her own yellow legal pad. Sisley was looking through the twelve questionnaires he had pulled from the bigger pile.

"I mentioned before how this case has been catnip for the press," Corino said. "I assume you've all seen some of the newspaper or television reports, or the magazine articles. Is there anyone who hasn't?"

One man hesitantly raised his hand.

"Nothing? You haven't seen anything?"

The man, thin and frail and in his sixties, wearing thick-lensed eyeglasses, said, "Well, I don't see that good. My wife reads the papers and tells me what's important."

There was scattered laughter in the courtroom. Corino contrived not to notice it.

"What about television?"

"Like I said, I don't see so good. All I watch is 'Wheel of Fortune' and the 'Tonight Show.' "

"Do you think you could see the witnesses and evidence all right?"

The man hesitated. "I think so."

"Suppose there were some exhibits to read?"

"I know how."

"All right," the judge said. "The rest of you, have you formed an opinion of the case from the press coverage? If you have, raise your hand."

Ryan watched the jurors decide what to do. They were under oath, but they also guessed that this question could disqualify them. For the ones who wanted to serve—and by their faces, Ryan guessed that included most of these twelve—it was a dilemma. Two women and three men raised their hands.

About forty percent. The defense's attitude polls had found twice that percentage with definite opinions. Somebody was lying or holding back or misreading the data. It confirmed Ryan's feeling that trying to make the art of jury selection into a science was a waste of effort. More important than what the jurors said about their opinions or themselves, more important than their ethnic or economic backgrounds, were the person-to-person dynamics that would never be a matter of rules or numbers on a chart.

Corino asked the jurors who had formed opinions based on the press coverage if they could put those opinions aside. One of the men thought so. Corino turned his attention to the others. Did they think people always told reporters the truth? Did they think most reporters cared more about the truth or meeting deadlines or pleasing their editors?

If you were accused of a crime, Corino asked them, would you want people to judge you based on what appeared in the newspapers and on TV?

He got three of the four jurors to agree that they would put aside their preconceptions. The lone holdout he excused. Names were drawn to fill the two empty seats and Corino quickly ran down the basic questions with the newcomers. Then he called a fifteen-minute recess to give the lawyers time to look over the jurors' questionnaires.

It was not long enough. Corino called the court to order while the defense lawyers were still reading and gave the floor to the District Attorney.

"Thank you, your honor." Tall and imposing, Griglia went to the lectern, which had been set up facing the jury box. He had no notes.

Ryan had forgotten—Franky always knew what he was going to say. It had been his reputation since he was a green young A.D.A.

He began with the standard thanks to the jurors for their time. He explained that he was going to ask hard questions and it wasn't because he doubted anybody or questioned their desire to do the right thing: it was only to learn more about them and be sure they understood what was required here.

Ryan scanned the panel. A nice mixture of faces, old to young, all colors and shades of skin. Lawyers in federal court joked a lot about the inferior quality of state juries, but these people looked all right except for a few stern and forbidding countenances. Ryan made a note to ask them some personal questions to see if their faces relaxed when they were talking about something they liked.

Griglia put both elbows on the lectern and leaned on it. "I'm going to get right to the point and say I wish I could put people on the witness stand for you who saw this crime go down. It's best for everybody that way." His easy delivery matched his relaxed posture; all that was missing was a brass rail to put one foot up on. "But the truth is, nobody saw this crime. Nobody we know of except the victim and the person who did it. Nobody's going to come in here and point at the defendant and say, 'I saw her do it.' "

He turned to look at Jennifer, then back to the jury. "So the question I have to ask each and every one of you is, do you think you can vote to convict a person of the serious crime of murder, when there is no eyewitness testimony?"

He took them one at a time, not rushing them. One after the other—some with hesitation, a few without—the jurors said yes, they thought they could.

"Suppose the judge tells you you can find the defendant guilty if you believe the people have proved her guilty beyond a reasonable doubt? Do you think you'll be able to do that?"

He did not pause for an answer. Looking at each juror in turn as he spoke, he said, "That's a harder question than it sounds like. You have to ask yourself, in searching your heart, are you willing to take evidence with no eyewitness account, which for that very reason may cause you to say 'of course I have a doubt because there was no eyewitness,' and still vote to convict the defendant?"

"How much doubt do I have?" asked Mrs. Diaz in seat number

one—the jury's foreman if she was not challenged. A Hispanic-American housewife from Washington Heights, she was the mother of three, married to a housepainter. Her English was heavily accented but fluent. Ryan had no doubt at all that Griglia had hooked her.

"That's the right question," the D.A. said. "Some of you may be convinced by the people's evidence beyond *any* doubt. But suppose you are sitting in the jury room deliberating on your verdict and you still have some little doubt, a chance in a million that . . . some piece of the ceiling fell down, or some other unlikely thing. Would you be able to follow the court's instruction and say all right, that's a doubt—nobody saw it happen, maybe there's some other possible way it could have happened—and could you look that doubt in the eye and say, yes, it's a doubt but it's not a *reasonable* doubt, and follow the court's instructions and vote to convict this defendant?"

Mrs. Diaz thought about it before she said yes, she could convict the defendant.

"Could you do it, do you think, if that means this woman goes to jail for many years, and you still have this little doubt in the back of your mind?" The question was put to Mrs. Diaz, but Griglia's head turned to cover the whole jury box.

Mrs. Diaz hesitated.

Griglia stepped into the breach. "Because if you can't put that doubt aside and say to yourself my doubt is not *reasonable* and go ahead and vote to convict as the court instructed based on the proof you've seen . . . if you can't do that, and many people couldn't, then I ask you to let us know that, and we'll be grateful to you, all of us, for your honesty."

It had been fifteen years since the last time Ryan had seen Franky Griglia in a courtroom, and the master had not lost his touch. If anything he had mellowed over the years into a greater command of nuance and inflection.

Now he was telling the prospective jurors it was all right, it was no more than human nature, to say, no, I couldn't ignore a doubt if I had one. And by casting it in that light he was making it a challenge—a test of their strength of character—to be able to look that small and very understandable doubt right in the eye. To face the doubt and admit it was not reasonable and then to vote for conviction.

Griglia directed his next questions to Michelle Jackson, an African-American in her thirties who worked for the telephone company.

He asked her if she had ever seen anyone do something and not understand why they did it.

"Yes."

"Something they meant to do?"

"Yes."

"Someone you knew well?"

"Yes."

"So you can accept that people do things, and mean to do them, intend to do them, for reasons that other people may not share or even understand?"

"Yes."

Suppose, he said, the judge gave an instruction that motive is not something the prosecution has to prove. "Could you accept the possibility that the prosecution could prove beyond a reasonable doubt that the defendant intended to do a certain thing, even if there was no proof of *why* she intended to do it?"

She thought longer before saying she could.

"So if the court says you should convict the defendant if you're convinced of her intention to do the criminal act, even if you don't know *why* she did it, even if you don't understand why *anyone* would want to do it, could you vote to convict in spite of that?"

It took her a while but finally she nodded and said, "Yes, I could."

"What about the rest of you? Does anybody have even a little problem voting to convict somebody even if you don't understand why they committed the crime?"

A couple of people nodded.

"You would have trouble convicting a person whose motives you didn't understand?" Griglia asked each of them and moved on quickly when they each said yes, an answer guaranteed to prompt a challenge for cause when the time came.

Griglia switched to questions about the jurors' lives out of court. What did they do for fun, where did they go for vacations? Were most of their friends married or divorced? Life-style questions. Questions to relax them and soften them up. And then he got to the good stuff.

Had anyone ever lost a child? Or had a friend or close relative who did?

Ryan wanted to object but remembered Corino's warning that he'd give Griglia latitude on this subject. It would not be smart to call attention to it with no hope of accomplishing anything.

Mrs. Diaz knew two women who had lost young children. Did she feel sorry for them?

Very sorry. There was nothing worse than losing a child.

Ryan felt the anger like a tangible thing. Griglia was appropriating his grief and twisting it into a weapon to use against him.

He could not let him get away with much more of this, but he had to pick his moment.

Anyone else? Griglia asked. A fiftyish woman artist from the East Village knew people who had lost children to AIDS. And how did they react?

"They were completely devastated at first. By the time the children actually died they were trying to accept it."

Ryan stood slowly. "Your honor?" No aggression in his voice. "May we approach for just a moment?"

"Please."

"I don't see the point," Ryan said at the sidebar, still outwardly calm.

"There's a major issued here of Mr. Ryan's playing on the sympathies of the jury," Griglia countered. "I want to see where those sympathies lie."

"Then do it!" Ryan did not like how his voice sounded.

"I think we can let him pursue this his own way, Mr. Ryan." Corino was matter of fact. "I know it's uncomfortable for you, but I did tell you I'd be giving the prosecution plenty of room on this subject."

As expected. Ryan went back and sat down.

"I'm going to ask you all a hypothetical question," Griglia told the jurors. "Suppose somebody gets murdered. A young adult, say. How do you think his family would feel about finding the murderer? Do you think they would have a special interest in finding out who did it? Yes?" He held up his hand. All the jurors did, too.

"All of you. And suppose the family decided they knew who did it. How many would give their opinion extra weight?"

Everyone again. Was Griglia going to challenge them all?

"Now I want you just to think about this. Don't raise your hands. Suppose the victim's family disagreed with the police. No, don't raise your hands. Would you still give their opinion extra weight? If the police caught someone and the family thought it was the wrong person. I'm going to ask you that one at a time."

He looked a question at Corino and started for the bench. Corino waved Ryan up to join them.

"I'd like to do this one at a time, out of the hearing of the others."

"All of them?" Ryan wanted to know.

"Wouldn't you?"

Griglia was taunting him, not even trying to hide it.

Ryan wanted to wipe the smugness off Griglia's face, the D.A.'s extra three inches and forty pounds of weight-room muscle notwithstanding.

"Can I have a moment, your honor?" he asked, then turned to Miller without waiting for Corino to nod. "You'd better handle this," he said so only she could hear. "It's your territory and, besides, all I can think is I want to deck the bastard."

From his chair Ryan watched the slow parade of jurors, one by one, to the bench. They formed a little huddle, Griglia on one side of the prospective juror, Miller on the other, the circle completed by the court stenographer and Corino on the bench.

When it was over, Miller came back to the defense table. "It wasn't too bad. We'll lose about four. Three of them I'm just as glad to see go." She gave him the list. "Truth is, I think he's doing us a favor."

3

WHEN GRIGLIA WAS DONE, CORINO SAID, "MR. RYAN?"

It's only twelve potential jurors, Ryan pep-talked himself.

He collected his notes and his prepared questions and went to stand at the lectern, gripping its sides to keep his hands steady. There was a hollowness in his chest that no amount of air could fill, but he plunged ahead.

"Ladies and gentlemen, my name is Michael Ryan. I want to thank you in advance for your attention and the honesty you bring to your civic duty as jurors. I'm going to share the pleasure of getting to know you today with my co-counsel, whose name is Kassia Miller. But first I'm going to talk to you myself.

"Mr. Griglia asked you some questions, and I'm going to do the same. You won't be surprised that my questions will be different from his." He smiled. It felt natural, and it calmed him.

"Later on the judge is going to tell you something like this: Throughout this whole trial you have to consider Mrs. Ryan to be innocent—until after you've heard all the evidence and all the argument." He looked from juror to juror. They were paying attention. For now.

"Mrs. Diaz, can you accept the idea that all you know about Mrs. Ryan is what you will hear and see in this courtroom—what the judge rules is proper and admissible evidence?"

She gave his question the same careful thought she had given Griglia's.

"Yes."

Ryan turned to the man next to her, young and muscular, dressed in freshly pressed khakis and a polo shirt.

"Mr. Sarrubbi, what do you think? Is my client innocent? Right now as we sit here."

"Sure." Bright pupil giving the right answer to an easy question. Nothing honest about it.

"Mrs. Diaz, suppose the judge tells you that calling Mrs. Ryan the defendant means nothing at all about her being guilty of any crime."

"I don't understand," said Mrs. Diaz. "The police arrested her. There must be some reason."

Good. Mrs. Diaz would be dismissed for cause unless Griglia found a way to rehabilitate her.

Ryan still felt strange, out of place, but he was warming up. He used his next questions to the individual jurors to talk about how the whole burden of proof was on the prosecution and the defense did not have to prove anything.

"Jennifer Ryan doesn't have to say another word. She's already said she isn't guilty, and those are the words that count. She has no further explanation to make to anyone, because she is innocent, presumed innocent. And we all have to keep on believing in her innocence unless the prosecution proves she is guilty. Proves it *beyond a reasonable doubt*. That is a very high standard of proof, as the judge will tell you. A standard that becomes even higher when the proof rests entirely on circumstantial evidence. Mr. Griglia didn't talk about that much, but I will."

On that note Ryan turned the show over to his co-counsel. She gave him a barely perceptible nod and the hint of a smile as they passed each other.

"Hello, I'm Kassia Miller. I have the honor of working with Mr. Ryan, and I'll be helping him show why you should have doubts about the prosecution case.'' She paused to look at the jurors and let them look at her.

"How many of you have ever watched soap operas?"

After a moment, hands went up, not high. Ten of them.

"What about the nighttime soaps, like 'Dynasty' and 'Falcon Crest'?" Everyone, even the old party who had said he only watched "Wheel of Fortune" and the "Tonight Show."

"And would you say those people live different lives from the people we know around the neighborhood?"

Nods of agreement and a lot of smiles.

"Do you watch those shows regularly?" No response. "Mr. Crawford?" A rotund African-American in a green shirt.

"Sometimes."

"Ms. Johanssen?" A tall, plain-featured blonde, dressed for success.

"No, I don't."

"What do you watch?"

"Channel Thirteen. Public broadcasting."

"Do you watch 'Masterpiece Theater'?"

"It depends on the show."

"Okay . . ." And to the whole panel: "All these shows are about rich people with unusual lives. And they all have nasty villains, because it's fun to boo and hiss at the bad guys." She looked around at the jurors. From where he was Ryan could not see her face; he had to imagine her smile.

"Now, if you serve on this jury, you're going to be hearing a lot about rich people, and you're going to be hearing a lot about nasty people." She picked out a juror. "Ms. Jackson . . ." The telephone company employee. "Who's your favorite villain, the one you really love to hate?"

"Oh, I don't know. I guess I hate Alexis the worst. Alexis on 'Dynasty.' " Hate and admire, Ryan thought, watching her face.

"Okay, good. Do you think she's a realistic character?"

"Yes."

"Suppose you heard about a woman who didn't seem to care if her husband had affairs as long as he kept them secret, but threw a fit if he embarrassed her in public. Could you understand that as a way a person might act?"

"On television?" Several of the other jurors laughed.

"In real life."

"I suppose I could."

"Have you ever been in a place where you yelled at somebody in public?"

A slow grin. "You mean, like my kids?"

"Your kids or your folks or your husband. Anybody."

The grin widened. "I sure have."

"Did it bother you that there were people around?"

"I don't know if I even thought about it."

"You never thought about the other people around when you were yelling?"

"Sometimes."

"But you kept on?"

"One time I stopped, I remember. I was real embarrassed."

"Suppose you heard about a person who made a big scene at a party, yelling and throwing things, because she thought it was more embarrassing to keep quiet about what was going on than it would be to make a scene. Could you accept that a person might act that way?"

"Is this the same woman you were talking about before?" More laughter on the panel and a tap of the gavel from Corino. "Sure I could accept it. Some guys, getting yelled at in front of their friends is the only thing they understand."

Griglia stood up. "Your honor?"

"Ladies and gentlemen," the judge said, "try not to volunteer any more information than you're asked for. Just answer the questions."

It looked certain that Griglia was going to challenge Ms. Jackson. A definite loss for the defense.

Miller moved on to another juror.

"We were talking about television a minute ago. They have courtrooms on television all the time. Part of the fun with a TV trial is to guess who did it. Do you find that?"

"Yes."

"You enjoy it?"

"Yes."

"There's not a lot of time for evidence on the TV shows I've seen."

Heeding Corino's admonition, the juror waited for a specific question.

"Wouldn't you say?"

"I don't know."

"An hour show, with commercials. And time out for the hero and heroine to do some kissing. How much time does that leave?"

"Not much." The juror was smiling.

"So if you're going to guess if the accused person is guilty, you have to do it in a hurry. Based on some small clues here and there. Right?''

"I suppose.''

"Do you expect it to be like that here in court?'' A friendly question, not a challenge.

"I guess not.''

"But if you like to figure out what happens next in a TV trial, will it be difficult for you to keep yourself from reaching a conclusion in this trial until the whole trial is over?''

"I don't know.''

"If the judge gives you that instruction? That you should consciously avoid coming to a conclusion until you and the other jurors are in the jury room deliberating?''

"I'd try.''

Miller moved on again, elaborating on the two themes that were her assignment: If you don't approve of someone's values and habits, that's not the same as thinking they're more likely to commit a crime. And, a juror has to suspend judgment until all the evidence is in. When she had taken those themes as far as they would go with this group, she sat down and Ryan stood up.

He addressed his first question to Sarrubbi, who was continuing to bother him. "Do you think it's possible the police could arrest the wrong person for a murder?''

"People make mistakes all the time.''

"Mrs. Wu''—a young Chinese woman, simply but elegantly dressed—"do you think that because the police and the prosecutor have brought Jennifer Ryan to this courtroom, her lawyers have to show that the police and prosecutor are wrong?''

"I'm not sure.''

"If the judge tells you the defense has no such responsibility, could you accept that? Completely?''

"Yes, I think so.''

"Mr. Sarrubbi, do you think the purpose of a trial is to find the whole truth?''

"I don't know about that.''

"What do you think the purpose is?''

"To see if we believe the evidence. No—maybe more like, to decide what the evidence means. To decide if it adds up to innocent or guilty.''

"So you're saying it's like a balancing act.'' Ryan made his hands into the two trays of a balance scale and weighed them up and down, heavier first on one side, then the other. "More evidence here or more evidence there.''

"Well . . . to see if the evidence proves guilt. Like you were saying, beyond a reasonable doubt."

By the end of the day they were done questioning the first twelve potential jurors. Corino called a short recess to give the lawyers time to assess their impressions.

The defense team ran quickly through the twelve names. With a little discussion they were in agreement on how to handle everyone except Sarrubbi. Kassia Miller and Jennifer thought he was all right, and Sisley thought he would be a help to the defense.

Ryan wanted to challenge him. "He's too smooth and cocky. Know-it-all. And he's too precise. He's an engineer. He's going to love the blood-typing evidence: DNA, genetic structure. High tech."

"He's young and smart, our two main criteria, and he pays attention," Miller argued. "He won't be a me-too. He'll make the others think, or annoy the hell out of them."

"I'm afraid he's going to strong-arm them," Ryan countered. "He's a karate coach at his church in his spare time. How controlling can you get?"

"He's a volunteer at the church, so he'll be sympathetic to Feed the Children."

Ryan was not buying it. "We've got an unconventional, flamboyant upper-crust client here. Excuse me Jennifer, but that's how it looks from out there."

"They should try it from here," she said.

"I wish they could," Ryan said. "But since they can't I don't think we want a self-satisfied potentially pedantic control freak with a first-generation white collar."

"He's definitely heterosexual," was Miller's nonsequitur.

Sisley had been listening in silence. Now he said, "He scores high on eye-contact and engagement with Mr. Ryan and Ms. Miller. With the prosecution he scores middle to low. I noted contextually positive words twice as often as contextually negative ones in his answers to you."

"I guess I'm a dinosaur," Ryan said, unconvinced. "I don't know about contextually positive words. I'm going by my gut. Jennifer, it's up to you."

"Does it matter? They all think I'm guilty anyway."

"You really ought to keep him," Sisley cut in.

"I think so, too," Miller said.

It was Ryan's hunch against their apparent certainty, and he did not know how much of his reaction to Sarrubbi was a remnant of a prosecutor's aversion to domineering jurors.

"Okay, we'll keep him. You owe me one."

He was unhappy with the decision as soon as he announced it.

Corino called the lawyers to the bench. Having given Griglia all the room he wanted during the *voir dire* questioning, the judge made fast work of the challenges. His clerk held up a chart with the jurors' name cards stuck into slots for the seats they were occupying. Four of them were excused by consent, the man with the bad eyes and the three Miller had been content to lose on Griglia's bereaved-father questioning. The D.A. got the fourth of those excused for cause and then challenged Michelle Jackson, the phone-company employee who thought the only thing some guys understood was getting yelled at in front of their friends.

Ryan protested. "Nothing in her answers warrants her being excused for cause." Let Griglia use up a peremptory challenge if he wanted her off.

"She shows a clear pattern of bias in favor of the defense." Not very specific, or very strong.

"I don't see it that way, Mr. Griglia," Corino said. "There's no cause here."

But when it came to peremptory challenges Griglia named only Ms. Johanssen, the one who watched PBS, and not Jackson.

Which meant that challenging Jackson for cause—expecting to fail—had been a way to get Ryan on her side, to keep him from considering her too carefully. Even so, he decided not to challenge her. Whatever it was Griglia liked about her didn't stand out enough to panic Ryan into wasting a peremptory.

Ryan successfully challenged Mrs. Diaz for cause, based on her remark that there had to be a reason if the police arrested somebody. On his peremptories he had to restrain himself from saying Sarrubbi.

The clerk read out the eight names of the jurors being excused and had the others move up into the first four seats in the jury box. The jury foreman would be Mrs. Wu, the elegant computer programmer.

Four jurors was more than Ryan had expected from the first twelve, and prosecution and defense had each only used one peremptory challenge, another surprise.

Corino called a halt for the day. Ryan felt like a marionette with its strings cut.

On his way home Ryan stopped by the Shamrock.

"I spent an hour in court today," Kelly informed him.

"What'd they get you for?"

"Very funny." He served Ryan his beer. "You looked pretty good up there."

"Kind of you to say."

"Some of those jurors . . ." The unexpressed opinion was not a compliment.

"It takes all kinds."

Kelly busied himself rearranging bottles on the back-bar shelves. "Maybe I should keep my mouth shut, but there was one guy I sure as hell didn't like. The one in the front row. Mr. Muscles."

"Sarrubbi?"

"I guess. He got on the jury, right?"

"Right. Why didn't you like him?"

"Looked like a wiseass to me."

"Me, too."

Kelly poured shots of specially aged Irish and brought them over. "Why'd you let him on?"

"Democratic process."

"Yeah? You have that in court?"

"For that one we did."

Kelly raised one of the shot glasses. "Confusion to our enemies."

"Amen, brother," Ryan said. The whiskey was smooth, but it burned going down.

Ryan woke up thinking about the case, worried that he had become too fixated on the search for Garfield's bandito, too involved in the recollections of half a hundred party guests.

Follow the money, he reminded himself.

Willy and the mortgage money. Ramanujan and Morris and the pharmaceutical company. And the clinics. It all had to be tied together somehow.

He and Lawrence and Kaplan had gone over the mortgage transactions carefully enough to convince themselves that Ned's money was coming from Olivera, at least indirectly. But that without more was a dead end.

The clinics and Shible. It seemed likely that Olivera's money was being laundered there, too.

Could Ned have been involved in Medicaid fraud? Ryan didn't believe it. That was the clinic owners, if it was anybody. Another dead end.

Temporary dead end, he told himself.

Showering, a jumble of disconnected thoughts and images came together in his mind. He hurried, dripping, toweling himself as he went, to his study.

He took out the mortgage papers and the other records he had collected at Willy's bank and went through them again.

There it was, clear as day.

Ned had handled sixty million dollars in mortgage money in less than two years. His fee had ranged from three quarters to one percent for each deal he did. It was not a high fee as such things went, but the total was over five hundred thousand dollars, almost twenty-five thousand a month, which bought a lot of art made by attractive young women. All open and aboveboard, if you didn't count the fact that the money Ned was moving around to make those fees probably came from Señor Olivera's crack and cocaine business.

The part that Ryan focused on now was the way the money came in and went out. From what he could see, almost all the money had come in at least six days before Ned put it out for the mortgages. And it had not sat in Willy's bank. Ryan could not be sure from the papers in front of him, but if the money had gone into Treasury bills while it waited, it added up to another hundred thousand dollars in short-term interest. And if the money had been used to buy commercial paper, loans considerably less secure than T-bills, the total could be considerably higher. Somebody had pocketed the money. Ned? Willy? Both of them? A tidy motive for murder, in some circles.

It was a beginning. A new beginning.

That was how these things went. You pushed as far as you could in one direction until it didn't go any farther. Then you looked around for a new place to start.

Still damp, the towel forgotten, he reached for the phone to call Jake Kaplan.

"I have some numbers I want you to check and then I want you to have a talk with Craig Lawrence about tracing where the money went."

He headed for court with a lighter step than he had the day before. Jury selection proceeded much as it had begun, except that the acceptance rate went down. The next sixteen prospects added no one to the jury.

Griglia kept probing how the jurors felt about a relative of the victim representing the defendant, and Corino continued to allow the D.A. wide latitude excusing jurors who seemed likely to be even a little sympathetic to Ryan because he was Ned's father. There was nothing Ryan could do but endure it.

The more he saw of Griglia, the more impressive he seemed. Relaxed and easygoing most of the time, he missed very little. If his questions to the jurors sometimes rambled, it was in a way that kept him from seeming above the process or the people. He was not boring and he did not get visibly stale. He alternated with Saundra Warneke often enough to show his respect for her. He was going to be a formidable adversary at trial.

"Do you believe women are capable of murder?" was Griglia's favorite question after the ones about bereaved parents. He was also inclined to ask, "If the evidence showed the defendant to be guilty, would you have trouble voting to convict because it means sending a woman to jail?"

Most potential jurors said they thought women might be murderers. The first time one admitted some uncertainty on the subject, at the end of a long day, a tired Ryan saw no way to keep the woman, a juror he would have welcomed, from being excused for cause.

Miller got up and asked her, "Suppose the prosecutor brought in three credible eyewitnesses and they all identified the defendant as the person who committed the crime, would you have any trouble voting for a guilty verdict simply because the defendant was a woman?"

"No. Certainly not."

They lost her anyway, but Griglia had to use up one of his peremptory challenges. And he had to back off the subject, to keep from giving the defense too many opportunities to suggest a standard of proof far beyond any he could meet.

Lawrence was at the office after court on Thursday for his regular update on investigating the jurors. And this time he had news about Ned's mortgage financing, too.

"It looks like you were right: Ned was putting the money out short term and skimming the interest."

"Good work." Good for the case. What it said about Ned he could think about later. "I'll call Jake in the morning to see about pinpointing it in the books."

"I didn't say you could pinpoint it. I said it *looks* like he was doing it."

"Can't anybody get anything right!" Ryan exploded. "What good is 'looks like' in court?"

"Hey. We do our best, you know."

"Calm down, guys," Miller said.

"We're on the eve of going to court, here," Ryan said. "So far our whole case is counterpunching. Not a good jab of our own. Much less a knockout punch.''

"We're doing our best," Lawrence repeated. "I could poke around from the other end—Olivera and company, but when it comes to information like some guy who launders money is skimming the float, I'm too out of touch with drug enforcement to know who'd have it.''

"If we knew that Olivera knew Ned was skimming that money, we could make a case that Olivera killed him for it. It could make all the difference.''

"It'd make all the difference if we had a videotape of the murder, too, but it's not going to happen.''

"Is there anybody at the Bureau?''

"You mean anybody who'll still talk to me? You're kidding. I've been eating up favors like popcorn." Lawrence hauled himself to his feet, tired and with a full evening's work ahead of him. "I'll try to get somebody to ask around, but I may come up empty, and if I don't it may take time.''

"We don't have much time.''

"Thanks for sharing that," the investigator said, disgusted.

4

BY THE TIME THERE WERE ELEVEN JURORS SELECTED they had been at it more than a week. Daily observation of Griglia's jury-selection technique had not told Ryan who Griglia's ideal juror was, or exactly what kind of people the D.A. had been trying to avoid. He had only one obvious prejudice: he challenged all the Irish jurors. Ryan relished the irony.

The eighth person they questioned for the twelfth seat was a man of sixty-eight, a former civil engineer named Constable. Tall and spare, he was dressed precisely in white shirt, blue suit and silver-gray tie. Pen tips graced his breast pocket, where Sisley kept a bright square of silk.

Constable answered Griglia's questions politely and economically, and he gave Ryan the same courtesy. There did not seem to be any reason to excuse him for cause, and Ryan guessed that Griglia would want him on the jury. The prosecution was down to one peremptory challenge; the defense still had two. Ryan knew Sisley and Miller would want to use one of them to challenge the engineer. Arguing against Sarrubbi, Ryan himself had relied on the principle that the defense did not want engineers on the jury. And yet he felt there was something about Constable worth hanging on to, if there was only a way to bring it out.

At the end of his ingenuity and about at the end of his strength for the day, Ryan asked, "Do you have any hobbies?"

The engineer narrowed his eyes appraisingly but did not answer.

"Mr. Constable?"

He sighed. "I write poetry."

"Really?" Ryan did not hold back a smile of surprise. "What kind of poetry?"

"The kind nobody reads."

"You don't publish it?"

"I don't. Others do."

"How long have you been doing this?"

"Since I retired."

"Can you tell us some of the titles?"

"I don't know what good they'll do you."

"I don't either, not until I hear them."

Ryan's answer seemed to please him. In his unassuming way he recited, " 'Trouble in Elsinore.' 'The Shadow Knows.' 'Seventh Inning.' 'On the Way to the Mountain.' " Like a grocery list. "Does that help you?"

"I think it may. Thank you."

Sisley was dead set against him. "Rigid, rigid, rigid."

"I like him," Ryan said.

"Do you see how he dresses? We need someone with a tolerance for the unconventional. This man is a civil engineer."

"Retired. He writes poetry."

"And what's that supposed to tell us? Poetry. Can you imagine the poetry of a civil engineer? And you see how he sits. Like he's got a pole up his"—Sisley glanced at the two women—"spine."

"We can afford to challenge him," Miller pointed out. "We'll still have another challenge left in case there's somebody terrible later."

"His *indices* are all wrong," Sisley announced as if that was the last word on the subject.

"I say we keep him." Digging in his heels perhaps more than it called for. "And you owe me one, remember?"

"If Michael feels that way," Jennifer said, "I think we should go with it."

Ryan decided he had to confront Thom Willard directly about Ned's skimming interest on the mortgage money.

Miller volunteered to come along for the train ride to Philadelphia; there was some business she could take care of there, she said. Ryan was not delighted: he saw plenty of her all day long. He brought notes for his opening statement to work on. She brought magazines.

"When was the last time you had any fun?" she asked him as they sat in the train waiting for it to leave Penn Station.

He looked at her.

"Not since your wife died, I'll bet."

Not since the separation, he did not tell her. Not since even before that.

"You need to relax, Ryan, while you still can. I watch you up there with the jurors and I think, This guy is brilliant, only he's strung out so bad and wound up so tight the best parts are in danger of getting lost."

"Is that the complete diagnosis?"

"Most of it."

"I assume you have a prescription."

"I think you should have some fun. Get away from work, even for a few hours. Before opening statements, if you can, because it'll be impossible after."

"I appreciate the advice."

The train lurched into motion. Ryan opened his briefcase and got to work.

Willy met him in the dark empty bank. He was surprisingly forthcoming.

"Yes, Ned was manipulating the float on his mortgage money. I told him it was dangerous and he ought to stop."

"Dangerous?"

"It's somebody's money. Usually you'd put it in a secure, no-interest account. He was buying T-bills and commercial paper with it and selling them when it was time to pay out the money to the mortgagor. Sure it was relatively safe, but he could have got caught if interest rates went up in a hurry. And if there was interest, it belonged to the people whose money it was.''

"So you thought he was going to get himself in trouble.''

"Yes.''

"You and Ned were arguing about it.''

Willy didn't flinch. "You bet we were arguing. We argued a lot. Always, since high school. It was part of what we did. It kept us both honest.''

"But not this time.''

"This time, especially.''

"He stopped?''

"No. He got letters of authorization from the lenders.''

That was the last thing Ryan wanted to hear right now. "Can I see them?''

"If I can find them.''

Willy led him into the outer office and rummaged through one file drawer after another, muttering about his secretary. With an exaggerated "ah" he pulled out a thin folder and handed it to Ryan. There were eleven letters, from as many of the lender companies. As in their correspondence with the estate, they all used nearly identical wording.

"This isn't part of the regular file. It's my own personal record. To cover my ass, I suppose you could say. I didn't want these people coming after me if they found their money missing.''

"Rough customers?''

Willy stiffened. "I assume anybody's rough if you let somebody take their money.''

"Especially drug dealers like the ones Ned got his money from.''

The banker stared at him. "Who told you *that*?''

"I thought you did.''

"Let me put it this way, Mr. Ryan—if Ned was involved in anything like that I certainly did not know about it.''

"Then why did you think it was dangerous?''

"I already said, people don't like to have their money taken. Or put at risk, however small. Even if they're not drug dealers.''

The two lawyers took a late train back.

"No luck, huh?'' Miller guessed.

"Not much. Ned was skimming, pocketing interest he shouldn't have been earning in the first place. Willy warned him not to. So Ned got letters from the lenders saying it's okay, you have our blessing.''

"So we can't claim they were angry enough about it to kill him.''

"Unfortunately. And Willy, no surprise, denies knowing anything about drug money. So it's a dead end there, too."

Ryan opened his briefcase and got to work. He looked up as the train flashed past the Rahway station. "Home of yet another dead end." Karl and Harry, whose mortgage terms Ned had changed at the last minute.

At Newark Miller said, "I heard the weather report for tomorrow. Unseasonably warm and sunny, they say. And I say we go on a picnic."

He did not respond.

"I love your enthusiasm. Look, I know we see a lot of each other. Here's what we do. We go on a picnic, but I wander off somewhere and leave you alone. I just want to be sure you do it. There's a terrific old place a couple of hours outside the city, all by itself by a lake, surrounded by cliffs. They won't have any rooms on short notice, but I think we can go for the day."

Ryan knew the place she meant. He had spent a winter week there with Ali and four-year-old Ned, one of their few real vacations as a family. "How about someplace closer to home."

"You name it."

"There's a park on the Hudson. Formerly the estate of a rich lawyer, as a matter of fact."

"You used to live around there, didn't you?"

"A couple of towns north."

As promised, Sunday was warm and bright. In keeping with Miller's idea that it should be a day off for him, she came by to pick him up in a rented car with a packed picnic basket on the backseat.

The park was virtually empty and the grounds had recently been tended. The stark branches of the trees were softened by a haze of pale yellow-green buds.

"Okay," she said as they started along a path toward the river, "let's synchronize our watches so we can meet to eat, then I'll get lost."

"Only if you want to."

He walked slowly, trying to ignore the jangling impatience in his brain and appreciate the new life on the trees and the warmth of the air. She walked with him. Neither of them spoke.

He found a pavilion he remembered, a minor promontory overlooking the river. He leaned on the stone rail and let himself be consumed by the river and the tiers of soft cloud in a rich blue sky.

After a time he turned to look at his co-counsel, silent beside him, focused on the view. She turned to meet his gaze.

"Nice," she said.

"Very."

Later, he said, "I'm going for a walk."

"Swing by here on your way back and pick me up."

He walked slowly again, letting thoughts and images flow through his mind. Ned. Alison. Jennifer and her baby . . . The trial to come. The months of work just past.

He stopped to admire a tree of pale pink-white blossoms backlit by a slant of light from the afternoon sun. He could not remember the last time he had seen this way, had patience or attention for the world's fierce beauty.

He went back and they fetched Miller's picnic basket and spread a blanket on the ground.

"I didn't know you could go so long without talking," he said as they unpacked china and glasses and a bottle of red wine.

"I'm full of surprises."

The meal was one. Chicken coated with sharp spices, collard greens, tomatoes and okra, garlic bread.

"You didn't cook this?"

"Hell no. This is courtesy of your favorite Upper West Side eatery. Not that I don't know how."

"I'm sure you do."

"The hell you are. You've never seen me so much as make coffee. You probably think I send out for boiled water."

He laughed. "I guess I don't really know much about you."

"Pretty strange, when you consider how much time we spend together."

"You seem to know a lot about me."

"You and your family are part of my job."

"Tell me about you."

"Ah, the Ryan charm. Nothing like a flattering question." She smiled her full-wattage smile. "But I'll answer it anyway. Give me a place to start."

"Clarence Darrow."

"You remember that?"

"Maybe I'm full of surprises, too." In this case, a surprise for both of them.

"Okay. Clarence Darrow. That's my dad's name. It embarrassed him. C.D. Miller is all he ever goes by. He admires Darrow, though, that's the funny part. More for the political trials, defending Debs and Scopes, than for Leopold and Loeb, and all the other murderers."

"And that's how you got to be who you are?"

"Only indirectly. Nobody ever pushed me to be a lawyer, or anything else. I had a very permissive education, the kind where they say we'd rather you were a happy truck driver than a reluctant brain surgeon. That was when people had respect for brain surgeons. Today it'd be investment bankers, I guess."

"Where was all this?"

"Colorado. Boulder, and then Denver. My folks are both college teachers."

"They're alive?"

"So are three of my grandparents, my sister and my brother. Aunts and uncles. I've been lucky that way. No deaths in the family, to speak of. I can't begin to imagine what that's like."

He asked her another question to get off the subject.

By the time they had finished eating, the sun was going down. They watched it set in silence.

He stood up to shake out the tablecloth they had spread on the blanket. Miller was facing the now sunless west, her legs gathered under her. For an instant she reminded him of Ali, in the picture he had found at Ned's, that picnic so long ago. His eyes burned.

She turned to look up at him. Whatever she had been planning to say remained unsaid.

"Ryan? You all right?"

He nodded, the tablecloth forgotten in his hand. She stood up and took its free end. "Let's fold this up and get out of here."

Empaneling four alternates went more quickly than finding the twelve jurors.

Ryan was not unhappy with the result. It was a varied and balanced jury: a mix of ages and races, seven men and five women, not as well educated as many federal juries but better than he had been warned to expect. Older on the average than the defense team's goal, but not in a way that worried him.

In the end it had been a matter of instinct for Ryan, and no doubt for Griglia, too. Griglia might have assumed that the fifty-three-year-old woman with a twenty-six-year-old stepson was good for the prosecution, and Ryan that the attractive forty-year-old art director was good for the defense, but they were both as likely to be wrong as right, and not only because the older woman was a book editor and the art director had never been married and lived with her aging mother.

More important to Ryan than generalizations about each juror had been his sense of how they might interact in the jury room. Given time to analyze his instinct about Constable, the retired engineer, Ryan had decided he would be a stronger voice than his mild manner implied, and the poetry, Ryan thought, indicated a mind that was eager for meanings beneath surface appearances. Ryan's hope was that Constable would counterbalance Sarrubbi, the other engineer, who was half Constable's age. Ryan had come to see leaving Sarrubbi on the jury as his biggest mistake so far.

Judge Corino said a few words of congratulation to the assembled jurors and asked the lawyers if they had anything more before he sent everyone home to prepare for opening arguments the following morning.

"One thing, your honor," Griglia said. "The people have found an additional witness, someone we just learned about. I thought it would be best if we informed the court now, before opening statements, so that we can see if any of the jurors are acquainted with him."

"Why don't you tell us who it is, Mr. Griglia."

"Yes, your honor. The man's name is Nicholas Maclean."

Corino turned to the jury. "Is any of you related to or does any of you know a man named Nicholas Maclean, or have any business with him?"

No one said yes.

"All right then, ladies and gentlemen, as far as I can tell, we're ready to begin. Our court day will start at nine-thirty in the morning, and I do mean nine-thirty. We will work until one, recess for lunch until two and then work until at least five, longer if necessary. I'm told there are judges who are often tardy and who say ten minutes when they mean thirty. I am not one of them. I am prompt and I expect you to be prompt. I am willing to endure a trial that is long because of substance, but not one that's long because of sloppiness.

"I'll see you all at nine-thirty in the morning." He left the bench with his usual speed.

"Okay, team," Ryan said. "Let's get back to the office and make sure we all know what we're doing tomorrow."

Jennifer was still in her chair, her eyes blankly fixed on the witness box.

"It gets a lot realer all of a sudden, doesn't it?" Ryan tried to sound upbeat. "There's no help for it but to put one foot in front of the other. Once it's under way it'll get easier." It felt like the right thing to say. He had no idea if it was true.

In the elevator down to the lobby, he noticed that Miller was watching Jennifer closely. From where he was, he could not see her himself.

Back at the office Ryan said, "Let me call Lawrence with this new name and then we can have a war council."

"Wait, Michael," Jennifer said. Her voice was strained.

He put the receiver down. "What?"

"I can tell you who he is."

"Oh?"

"I know him. Knew him. He's . . ." She sat down at her desk, closed her eyes. She stayed that way, withdrawn, while Ryan and Miller waited.

She opened her eys and fixed Ryan with an almost defiant stare. "He was my lover."

Ryan went blank.

Jennifer said, "Michael, it's really nothing."

He did not answer.

Miller went to him. "Are you all right, Michael?"

"I'm fine. Just leave me alone."

He had no idea how long he sat there. Snatches of conversation penetrated the fog. He got up and went into the bathroom at the back of the office and splashed cold water on his face and head, rubbing his hair dry with paper towels before he went back into the office.

"All right. Can we go over it again, please?"

"I met Nico at Feed the Children," Jennifer said in a flat voice. "We worked together a lot. Sometimes a bunch of us went out for lunch, or a drink, and I could see he was interested. And I thought Ned was having these, I don't know what to call them, flings. Sleeping with other women. So I decided to, well, just to flirt a little, at first. To get back at Ned, I suppose. Nico was nice enough, and he was married, so that made it safe. I didn't think he would ever tell anybody. I never dreamed he would testify in court."

"Why not?"

"I thought he was a gentleman." She was mocking herself.

"Did Ned know?"

"Not at first, but then one night he came home late and I don't know why but I knew he'd been with another woman. Sexually, I mean. I was really sure. So I asked him, and he admitted it. And that was when I told him about Nico."

"What did he say?"

"He didn't love it. I mean, you have to understand, we were having a screaming fight. Then, when we calmed down, he said,

'As long as you say it doesn't mean anything to you I can hardly complain, can I?' ''

"Did you tell this turkey that Ned knew?"

"Yes."

"Were there any others?"

"Any other what?"

"Lovers."

She hesitated.

"Listen to me, Jennifer. I've got to know the truth. Were there any other men in your life besides this Nico?"

"No. None."

"No flirtations? A little necking, maybe?"

Jennifer burst into a rage. "You hate me, don't you? You think I'm lying to you." Quicksilver, she turned the anger against herself. "I'm so stupid. Some things, I just think, if I tell Michael and Kassia about it they'll . . . I don't know exactly what . . . you'll stop believing in me. And you have, anyway."

Ryan waited for her to calm down. Miller brought her a glass of water. She drank it greedily.

"It's not as if he mattered. Ned was important in my life, not Nico. He was—it was a way of proving to myself that you could have lovers and it didn't change anything, the way Ned said."

"How did it end?"

"I broke it up."

"When?"

"Six or seven months before . . . before Ned died."

"Why did you break it up?"

"It didn't matter to me. It served its purpose. It was a nuisance."

"Did you tell him that?"

"Most of it."

"Is there anything else you want to tell me about it? Things you said to him that I should know about? Things you said about Ned?"

Jennifer appeared to think about the question. "No."

"You didn't tell him you wished Ned was dead?"

"I might have. I said that to a lot of people. I told you that already."

"How did you leave it with him?"

"I thought we were on good terms."

"But he didn't tell you he was testifying against you?"

"No." Subdued. "I don't understand why he is."

"We need to talk to him. Is it better if you call him or if I do?"

"Kassia is best."

"Just as well. I don't know if I could handle it."

* * *

"You okay?" Miller asked Ryan after Jennifer left.

"That's a joke, right?" He stood up and paced. "You told me once I never had a client and I didn't know what it was like. Well you sure were right about that. What do you do when your client is a full-time liar?"

"I don't know. I never had one."

"You have now."

"She's scared and confused. I don't think she actually lies. She tells part of the story and doesn't correct us when we draw wrong conclusions."

"Forgive me if I call that lying."

"Don't yell at me, Ryan. I didn't do anything."

"Sorry. You better call the guy. I'll call Lawrence on the other line."

Neither of them got through. They left messages.

Ryan collected papers on his desk and shoved them mechanically into his briefcase.

"Want to go over your opening again?" she asked him.

"Not now. Thanks. I'll practice at home."

"It helps to have an audience."

"I'll be okay."

"You're sure?"

"You're going to make somebody a fine mother someday," he said, not kindly.

"I doubt it. I'll see you here tomorrow. Eight thirty. Don't be late."

He went to the Shamrock. It was more crowded than at his usual hour, full of the young bankers and brokers and, probably, lawyers who lived in the new high-rises on Broadway. He decided he could drink his own booze.

5

RYAN SWAM UP THROUGH A MURKY SEA, DIMLY AWARE
of a pounding noise and a muffled shout—a word that might have
been his name. His head throbbed. He let himself drift down into
darkness.

Something shook him hard by the shoulder. Now he heard his
name sharply, loud. The room was too bright when he opened his
eyes. He closed them.

The hand shook his shoulder again. *"Michael!"*

He forced his eyes open, slits to keep out most of the light.

"Wake up, asshole," the man said, and left him. He heard the
voice again, in the other room, talking. Only one voice. He opened
his eyes all the way. He was at home, in his own bed. He closed
his eyes.

"Goddamn it, Michael!" The man grabbed him under the arms
and hauled him into a sitting position against the headboard. It was
Lawrence; he went back into the living room and made another
phone call.

Ryan, head pounding, sick to his stomach, was not sure what
the fuss was about, only that Lawrence was angrier than a hangover
called for.

The bathroom smelled awful. In the night he had apparently
thrown up, and his aim had not been perfect. He wadded up some
toilet paper, ran water in the sink and bent to wipe up where he
had missed. And was immediately, predictably, sick. This time his
aim was better. He washed his mouth out, brushed his teeth and
stood himself under the shower. After a while Lawrence poked his
head into the bathroom.

"You're clean enough. Put your clothes on and come have some
coffee."

He sat down at the dining room table and stared at a mug of inky coffee and a plate of eggs he did not want to eat.

The doorbell rang. Lawrence went to answer it.

Kassia Miller strode into the room and stopped by the table, glaring at him, a tiny furious dynamo in a trenchcoat, so angry he could feel the intensity of it. Without a word she stalked into the kitchen.

Gradually the world returned to Ryan. Today, if it was still the day after he last remembered getting home, was the first day of the trial of Jennifer Kneeland Ryan. Opening day. He did not want to ask what had happened at court.

Miller and Lawrence came into the dining room with coffee cups of their own and sat down opposite him.

"How full was that bottle in the living room when you started?" Lawrence asked him.

"Full."

"Jesus."

Ryan raised his coffee cup in both hands. The coffee was hot and bitter. "How did you get in?"

"I picked the locks. You ought to put in something better."

"When you two are ready, we have business to do," Miller said.

Ryan bit the bullet. "What happened?"

"When you weren't at the office by nine fifteen and you didn't answer the phone I called Craig and told him to get over here and see what was happening. He had the good sense to send a man with a portable phone to wait on the courthouse steps so the minute he found you his man came up to the courtroom with a message. Corino was all set to hold you in contempt and I don't know what else. String you up, maybe. I told him you were sick and begged for a one-day postponement. The man was livid, but he gave it to us. The press was all over me, and they're all over the place downstairs now. A fine fucking mess."

He didn't think of her as using language that strong; it bothered him.

The doorbell rang. He jumped.

"It's okay," she said. "At least I hope it is."

Lawrence went to answer it.

"The judge had one condition for giving us the day. He wants a doctor's note. Just like a little kid. Mikey can't come to court today because he has the flu." Her tone was rich with disdain. "Luckily, I have a friend who's willing to help."

Lawrence came back into the dining room followed by a man who looked more like a ski instructor than a doctor.

"Is this the patient?" The voice matched the rest of the package.

"Yes. Michael, this is Dr. Kimble."

"Maybe we can go in the bedroom so I can give Mr. Ryan a quick look-see."

"There's nothing wrong with me."

"Sir, I'm going to write you a letter for the judge. I'm going to do it because Kassia asked me to. But I'm damn well going to examine you first. And I'm not going to hang around while you show us all how ungrateful you are."

Ryan submitted to having his blood pressure taken and various tappings and probings.

"You ought to get yourself some exercise. There's a decent body in there, not much extra weight. You're soft, is all. You play any sports?"

"I swim. Used to swim."

"Do it more often. It's a better way to relieve tension and fight depression and anxiety than bending your elbow. I'm going to diagnose stress exhaustion and overwork complicated by an unspecified viral infection. Don't let it happen again. This is a one-time-only offer."

"What happened to the tennis player?" Ryan asked when Kimble was gone.

She did not respond.

"Charming fellow."

"Don't complain, Ryan. He was there when we needed him."

"And I wasn't."

"You said it—I didn't."

Lawrence spent the day with Ryan. The investigator slept in the spare room and in the morning he got Ryan up early so he could spend half an hour in the health-club pool.

He studied his notes for the opening over a light breakfast and coffee in the car that took them to the office.

"How are you this morning?" Miller asked him coolly.

"Bright eyed and bushy tailed."

"Spare me."

Jennifer was at her desk, intent on a book. Ryan did not greet her.

There was the expected crowd of reporters at the courthouse, and the broad steps were thronged with the curious.

Molly O'Hara, star reporter for a network affiliate, had been fresh from journalism school when Ryan was a prosecutor. She smiled a greeting and asked him, for the benefit of her viewers, if he was feeling better and what had been the problem yesterday.

"Bit by a bug."

"A bug, Mr. Ryan?" Allen Crown called out. "I heard it was something you drank."

Ryan pushed ahead and through the courthouse revolving door.

Upstairs, the dim green corridor was divided into halves by a line of police sawhorses. The half along the wall opposite the courtroom door was the province of hopeful spectators lined up for the privilege of hearing the opening statements of the Acting District Attorney and the father of the victim.

Ryan took his seat at the defense table and pulled his few pages of notes from his briefcase. He was aware of Miller and Jennifer to his right, Griglia and Saundra Warneke at the prosecution table to his left. He shut them out of his mind.

He responded to the clerk's All Rise and watched Hang 'Em High Corino walk in and mount the bench. The judge threw Ryan a quick hard look and settled into his chair.

The jury entered, lockstep, eyes front. Two of them, the engineer-poet and the art director, ventured glances at yesterday's truant.

Corino began with a minimum of formalities, including a quick overview of the trial process: Opening statements would be followed by prosecution witnesses, with defense cross-examination. Then defense witnesses, if any, with prosecution cross-examination. Finally, closing statements and the judge's explanation of the law. He reminded the jury that opening statements were not evidence, and turned the courtroom over to the prosecutor.

Griglia moved smoothly to the lectern in front of the jury box. He was wearing a double-breasted dark blue suit that had obviously been tailored for him, its cut more extreme than off-the-rack standard. Incongruously, it was too tight across the upper back, where it revealed the bulge of carefully tended muscles.

The back was all of Griglia that Ryan could see. He was not used to being so far from the jury box. He slid his chair back to the rail and over toward the center of the courtroom so he could have at least a partial view of Griglia's face, the best he would be able to do.

Ryan, the ex-prosecutor, wondered if the D.A. was going to turn and point at Jennifer when he began. Sure enough, he twisted around and extended his arm in the direction of the defense table—straight out of the Golden Oldies album of cheap prosecutorial tricks.

"That woman," he said, damning finger aimed at Jennifer, "that woman stands accused of murdering her husband, Edward Ryan, by repeatedly beating him over the head with a blunt instrument. And the evidence that you will hear in this courtroom will show you that Edward Ryan, known to everyone as Ned, that Ned Ryan was indeed killed by being beaten over the head with a blunt instrument. By a piece of art, a metal sculpture, which you will see. That he was killed by being beaten over the head with a piece of sculpture after that woman, the defendant, his wife, verbally attacked him and threatened him in front of many people, at a party they were both attending.

"The evidence will show that they left the party together, continuing to fight, and that the next time anyone saw Ned Ryan was when his body was found later that night in another room on the same premises, his head bloody from the blows inflicted on it. And the evidence will show that blood was found on the murder weapon. Ned Ryan's blood on one end, the end that he was hit with, and someone else's blood on the other end, the handle end. And the evidence will show that the blood on the end that was held by the person who clubbed Ned Ryan to death matches blood taken from the defendant."

Having caught the jury with the basics, Griglia expanded on the theme. "As the days pass, ladies and gentlemen—and we hope there will not be too many, but you'll understand our need to tell you the whole story—you will hear and see this evidence from the people who witnessed it. You will hear first from the police officers who answered the call to nine-one-one and went to the home of a man named Hugo Hill where they discovered the body of Edward Ryan lying in a pool of blood, with his head beaten in. You will hear from the emergency medical service personnel who answered the call in the hope that they could rescue Ned Ryan but found only a lifeless shell of a twenty-seven-year-old young man.

"You will hear from the detectives who came and questioned the people who'd accepted Hugo Hill's invitation to a cocktail party not expecting to have it end in murder, and the detectives who searched the murder room for clues. And then, ladies and gentlemen, you will hear from the medical examiner who performed the autopsy on Edward Ryan."

He took a moment to survey the jury and then shake his head. Ryan could not see the D.A.'s face but he figured that Franky was probably giving them his troubled-by-the-evils-of-the-world frown.

"You are going to hear this bright and intelligent young woman, a medical doctor trained in the specialty of forensic pathology, describe in gruesome detail—I apologize for that, but it's necessary—the horrible damage done to Ned Ryan's head, and to his brain, by the blows that were struck by his killer. And you will hear, too, that the autopsy results are consistent with a time of death of approximately nine p.m., a time when, as you will also hear, the defendant was on the premises where the murder took place.

"An expert in blood typing will tell you that Ned Ryan's blood and hair were found on a piece of metal sculpture near the body and that on the other end of the same piece of sculpture there was blood that matches the defendant's. And we're going to give you a short course in modern biology, too, because the tests this expert uses are based on the latest technology there is, matching people to their blood by the basic building blocks of heredity. Not matching blood by type A and type B, the way we used to, where there are only four different types of blood for everybody in the world. Today we measure the structure of the genetic material called DNA in the blood sample so precisely that only one person in many million would match.

"But you're not just going to hear from police officers and medical experts. You're going to hear from Hugo Hill, who gave the party, and from some of his guests. They're going to tell you that the defendant had at least one extramarital affair, not long before the murder, and that she did it in anger at her husband. Because the witnesses are also going to tell you that the defendant was a jealous woman and that her husband behaved in a way that inflamed that jealousy."

Griglia broke to take a drink of water. Ryan doubted that he needed it: it was a way to underline what he had just said, give the jurors time to think about it. Ryan might not be able to see the D.A.'s face but he could see the jurors', and so far Griglia had them mesmerized.

"You're also going to hear that Ned Ryan was not the world's nicest guy. He had affairs. He loved his wife but that didn't make him treat her well. Ordinarily we might have sympathy for a wife who was treated the way the defendant was. She had reason to be unhappy. She probably had reason to get a divorce. She did *not* have reason to club her husband to death.

"On the night Ned Ryan was killed he flirted in public with another woman, in the middle of a party where the defendant and other people could see him. You will hear that, too, from several people at the party that night. You'll hear it from the woman he was flirting with, who will also tell you how the defendant came over in a fury to yell at her husband, and how the defendant then picked up a large serving bowl and smashed it, in anger at her husband's behavior.

"You will hear all this and more, and it will all point unvaryingly in the same direction. That the defendant followed her husband from the party in Hugo Hill's roof garden, downstairs into Mr. Hill's private quarters, where, after more arguing, she took a piece of metal sculpture about the size and shape of a bowling pin and beat her husband's head in with it. Hit him not one, not twice, not even three times. Hit him four savage blows to the head, each one sufficient to cause massive injury, until blood streamed from the wounds and damage was done to his brain, and he died."

Griglia acknowledged that the burden of proof lay on the people's shoulders. "I gladly accept that burden on your behalf and on behalf of all the people of the State of New York."

That said, he rested an elbow casually on the lectern and leaned toward the jury.

"You know, there's a lawyer in Texas who talks about Smith & Wesson divorces." He made a gun with his hand. "Someone pulls the trigger and, bang, the marriage is over. In New York, it's harder to get a gun than in Texas, so we have a greater variety of instant divorces. Kitchen knives, sometimes. Baseball bats. In this case, a work of art."

This was material for a summation, not an opening. Ryan decided not to object: the custom was not to interrupt the opening statement short of a major abuse, and he wanted the same leeway from Griglia when his turn came.

"And," Griglia was saying, "let me remind you that no one ever said 'Hell hath no fury like a man scorned.' "

There was laughter in the courtroom and in the jury box.

Griglia drew himself erect again and fixed each juror in turn with his gaze as he spoke.

"I have an obligation, ladies and gentlemen, one I have accepted willingly and with enthusiasm, an obligation to prove that woman"—he turned and pointed again—"guilty of murder beyond a reasonable doubt. And so do you have an obligation. Your obligation is to follow the law as the judge explains it to you, and the evidence as you see and hear it presented in this courtroom. And if you follow that obligation according to the evidence that will be presented here, you will, you must, find the defendant guilty as charged."

Griglia stood there for a moment, immobile, commanding, then he dipped his head almost imperceptibly, midway between a farewell and a bow, and sat down at the prosecution table.

No one applauded, but there was that feeling in the room.

"Mr. Ryan?" the judge said.

Ryan made himself stand up and go to the lectern. He felt stiff, his every movement calculated, like the millipede paralyzed by the question of which foot to put first.

"Ladies and gentlemen," he said, "my name is Michael Ryan, and I represent Jennifer Ryan, who is the defendant in this trial."

And I am the father of Ned Ryan, he did not say, the man whose ugly and painful death has brought us here, and who I am now going to have to make you hate, on behalf of a treacherous woman I was gullible enough to believe in.

"Now," he said, "that man"—and he turned and pointed at Griglia—"that man has told you that he has the burden of proving the charges made against Jennifer Ryan. Proving them *beyond a reasonable doubt*. And indeed he does have that burden. A heavy burden. A burden he will not bear successfully, because his evidence will not support it." He stopped and looked at each of the jurors. "His evidence will not support it.

"The other side of that coin is: the defense does not have to prove anything. We don't even have to put any witnesses on the stand if we don't think it's necessary. This is not like on television where the defense lawyer figures out who really did it before the last commercial. All I'm here to do is to help you see that that man"—he pointed again—"has not met his burden of proof. That he has not proved the things he says he is going to prove. That the evidence does not say the things he says it does."

As he spoke Ryan felt growing in him the old eagerness for the thrust and parry of battle.

"There used to be a car ad on television. A man would come on and say all kinds of things about these cars, how you could buy them for a few dollars and how they came with a chauffeur, and then on the screen underneath him you'd see written what the truth was. For the next little while, I want you to think of that man who just spoke to you as Joe the car salesman, and to think of what I'm going to say as the writing at the bottom of the screen."

"Objection!" shouted Griglia.

Ryan turned to look at the judge.

"Mr. Griglia?" Corino asked.

"Characterizing counsel," Griglia said.

You mean calling you a liar, Ryan thought.

"Be careful, Mr. Ryan. And Mr. Griglia, it's customary to let your opponent conclude his remarks with the same latitude he gave you."

"Thank you, your honor," Ryan said as if the judge had ruled in his favor instead of warning him. He looked at the prospective jurors and he saw that some of them were with him and some of them were against him, and he thought maybe I'm going to be all right after all, because the important thing was not that he had failed to win every one of them over at this point but that he could see which was which.

"So, ladies and gentlemen, here is what the evidence will really show. That Ned Ryan was bludgeoned to death, under circumstances known by no one. That a piece of sculpture was found in the room with him that may have been the murder weapon, and that on that piece of sculpture was blood that may have been Jennifer Ryan's. Blood that may have got on that sculpture in any number of ways, at almost any time before or after Ned Ryan was struck on the head. That's *all* the evidence will show. Oh, and one other thing. Mr. Griglia is going to drag in here all manner of backyard gossip. He's going to show that Ned and Jennifer Ryan had a less than perfect relationship. As you listen to the evidence you might think about what your marriage or *any* marriage would sound like if all you knew about it was what you heard in court. In this case, the prosecutor is going to show, if you can believe this, ladies and gentlemen, he's going to show that these two married people argued with each other. Even in public sometimes. Well, that may be interesting to hear about, but it's not evidence of murder."

Ryan took a deep, slow breath, hoping the pause would appear to be intentional emphasis and not the antidote to anxiety it really was.

"The evidence is also going to show that Ned Ryan had a lot of enemies, that Ned Ryan was not a pleasant man or even always an honest man to deal with in business, and that Ned Ryan was involved in illegal activities with some very dangerous people."

Ryan felt himself getting carried away. These are promises you're making, he reminded himself, and they're going to hold you to them.

"A prominent chief judge of this state once said that a prosecutor could get a grand jury to indict a ham sandwich. I don't think he was exaggerating by much. Jennifer Ryan is not a ham sandwich. She's a human being. Like you, like me, like Mr. Griglia. She yells when she's angry, she cries when she's sad, she laughs when she's happy. As it happens—as you'll hear, thanks to Mr. Griglia's gossip—she was angry with her husband in a public place on the evening he died. You will hear why, and I think you will understand that anyone under the circumstances would have been angry. You will be told that she yelled at her husband. You will be told not only did she yell at him, she broke some crockery.

"Bang!" He slapped the lectern. Jurors jumped. He smiled at them. "For dramatic effect."

He erased the fun from his voice and his expression.

"You will also be told that after yelling at her husband she killed him."

He stopped, this time because he wanted to, because he was in control, and as he looked at the sixteen people in the jury box he knew that for this one moment at least, they were with him.

"The prosecutors will tell you that, but they will not prove it. I submit to you that the prosecutors will not offer you convincing proof of anything but the yelling and the dramatic effects. Yelling is yelling. Yelling is not killing."

He took another pause, looked at them all again.

"Listen to the testimony, ladies and gentlemen. Listen to it all, listen to it carefully and critically. Listen to it with an open mind. Most of all, hold your conclusions until you have heard all the evidence, and all the argument, and until the judge has fully explained the law to you. If you do, you will have no choice but to find Jennifer Ryan *not guilty* of any charge, not guilty of anything except being the widow of a man who inspired enmity and hatred and the desire for revenge in almost everyone he dealt with and with almost everything he did."

6

THE FIRST WITNESS WAS ONE OF THE PATROL COPS who had discovered Ned's body. Griglia established the time the cop had received the call from his dispatcher, his arrival at the loft building and the fact that he had discovered the body.

The D.A. interrupted the cop's testimony to authenticate and enter in evidence diagrams and models of Hugo Hill's roof garden and the two top floors of the loft building occupied by his gallery, offices and living space. At the lunch recess Griglia was still questioning the draftsman who made the diagrams.

The defense team emerged from the courtroom into the glare of a corridor bombarded by television lights, and waded through the reporters to the elevator bank. A court officer was holding an elevator for their trip down. Then it was wade through more reporters and dive into the car to the office for a lunch Ryan had little appetite to eat.

When Miller got up to cross-examine the diagram maker after lunch she was holding one of the police photographs not yet entered in evidence. It was a careless shot of the outside of the building, the kind of picture that got taken because it was called for on a list, not because anyone thought it would have value as evidence in this particular case. Miller asked that it be admitted as defense exhibit A. Griglia did not object.

She asked the witness to refer to his finished diagrams. Did he see any indication of a fire escape on them?

"No." He did not have to look very hard.

She had a court officer hand defense exhibit A to the witness and asked him to look at the picture's right edge and say what he saw.

"I'm not sure."

Miller pressed the policeman to look more carefully. Inevitably he admitted that yes, it looked like a fire escape over there, and yes, the fire escape seemed to have landings on the eighth and ninth floors.

"Thank you," she said. "That's all." Not needing to draw conclusions from it yet. Let the jury think about it, and let the prosecution worry.

She turned to the judge and offered a motion that the prosecution's diagrams and models be modified to include the fire escape.

"Mr. Griglia?"

"No objection, your honor. We'll take care of it by the morning."

Smart, Ryan thought. No excuses, no explanations. Don't call attention to it.

"For efficiency, we would like to use this as is, today," the D.A. added. "We won't be referring to that part of the diagram."

"No objection, your honor."

Griglia put his cop back on the stand and led him through the discovery of Ned Ryan's body and the bloody sculpture. He marked the sculpture and entered it in evidence with proper identification by the cop.

Ryan forced himself to listen, made some notes. Nothing was said about the drugs or guns the police had found. Was this the right cop to ask about that? Or about the broken bowl that had been swept away?

The judge recessed for the afternoon at five fifteen, when Griglia was done with his direct examination. The jury would think overnight about the picture Griglia and the patrol cop had painted of the scene at Hugo Hill's after the body was discovered. In the morning Miller would resume the defense's attack on the police procedure.

Ryan was not much use in their first after-court debriefing and preparation. He posed some possible questions for cross-examination and speculated with Miller about the likely next witnesses: more cops and the medical examiner.

"I'm tired," he said. "Can you manage without me until the morning?"

"No problem. You had a hard day, you can use the extra rest. A hard day and a good day. You did great this morning."

"Considering they say eighty percent of the jury will have made up it's mind by the time I sat down, I hope so."

"You believe that?"

"Actually, I think it's nonsense. I'll see you in the morning."

He stopped at the Shamrock. The early evening crowd he hated was there, but he stayed anyway. He sat at the bar with a mug of beer and watched Molly O'Hara report on the trial's first day and interview him on the courthouse steps. He was struck by how beautiful she looked on the Shamrock's big-screen television, all gleaming red hair and green eyes, and how pale and weary he seemed by contrast. She reported the opening statements as a draw between him and Griglia, though she did give him extra credit for having compared Griglia to the lying car salesman.

He'd done her some favors when she was starting out, treated her better than some others who gave little time to a neophyte. Maybe it was paying off in a way he hadn't figured on. Maybe he still had an ally in the press after all these years. Not only Molly, there was Zeke, too. They almost made up for Allen Crown.

Ryan ordered a shot of Irish and some food. He drank the whiskey, but he did not eat the food.

Kelly came down to his end of the bar when Ryan held up his glass for another shot.

"Michael, my boy. Don't you think you might be careful with that stuff? You've got to be in court early in the morning."

Ryan tugged his wallet from his trousers and slapped some money onto the bar. He went home where he could drink in peace and raised a glass in silent toast to all the people who didn't want you to drink when you needed it most. Jimmy Kelly and Kassia Miller and Miller's sanctimonious boyfriend. How little the doctor knew about what was good for what ailed you.

When the alarm woke him at seven in the morning he got dressed and grabbed a gym bag and went to the health club for a swim. He swam hard for a half hour, soaked in the whirlpool tub, then swam for another half hour. The masseur had some free time, so Ryan signed up for it. When he was done he took a long hot shower and a short cold one. His whole body tingled.

The day was overcast but not particularly cold. He walked over to Central Park and down the length of the Great Lawn, then across, breathing deeply of the damp air.

To hell with them, he thought. Let them do without me.

He spent an hour at the zoo, watching through the underwater window as the penguins swam and dove, then taking in the antics of the black-and-white-faced monkeys dangling from their vines. Corino had had the right idea: Jennifer should have had a monkey defend her. It was what she deserved.

"I saw on television you weren't in court today, Michael," Kelly said when Ryan pulled up a stool at the bar that evening.

"I don't need to go every day. That's why there's two of us."

Kelly looked at him hard. "Live and learn, they say. You ought to tell Molly O'Hara and the others about it, too."

"I'll drink to that, when I have a drink."

"I hate to say no to an old friend, but I like you too much to help you ruin yourself."

"Aren't we self-righteous! No wonder your landlord thinks you're a lousy businessman."

"Michael, I'm going to assume you're under a lot of strain, and I'm not going to take offense. But I am going to give you that drink on the house and ask you politely to leave, in the interest of preserving our friendship."

Ryan's temper flared, but the vestiges of his internal warning system told him to keep his mouth shut and get out. He walked straight into someone coming in the door.

"Hello, Ryan. Going somewhere?" It was Kassia Miller.

"Another bar," he said. "Or home."

"Home," she said. "That sounds better to me."

He stood aside for her. She did not move.

"Not going in?"

"I came to find you."

He walked out. She followed him. He kept going; she walked by his side.

"This isn't the way home," she said.

"I decided on another bar."

"How about your Caribbean place?"

"I'm not hungry."

"I am. I was too busy to have lunch."

"Am I supposed to feel guilty?"

She did not answer.

It was early for the regular crowd. The restaurant was almost empty. They sat in a booth by the window and drank their beer and club soda in silence.

After she had ordered food, Miller said, "All right, Ryan, what's this about?"

"What difference? You're good enough to try this case without me."

"Bullshit. It's a two-man job, as you well know. And I had the feeling for a while there that we made a damn good team."

"We may make a great team, but it's a lousy game. I had the jury in the palm of my hand there for about a minute yesterday. There they sat, fascinated by this man who was standing in front of them bad-mouthing his own son. And why? To defend a woman who's probably his killer. A woman who started lying to me before I took the case and hasn't stopped since."

"You don't believe that."

"Who says?"

"You're saying it now, and I understand it, but I don't think you really believe it."

"Don't put money on it."

"All right, Ryan, however you want it. But even if you think she's guilty right this minute, that doesn't mean you can walk out on defending her."

"Watch me."

"You can't, and you won't. You know why? Because you're a lawyer down to your bones. You have the legal system wired into your circuits. Quitting now—assuming Corino would let you—is an announcement to the jury that you've lost faith in your client. And that's a total betrayal of the way things are supposed to work. You're an officer of the court. You have an obligation to your client and an obligation to the court, and both of them say you have to stay on this case and give it your best."

"We can say I'm sick. Or I'm incompetent because my emotions are getting the better of me. Plenty of reasons that have nothing to do with her. We can say I lost my son and my grandson and this trial causes me so much grief that I can't do my professional duty."

"You were already bereaved and emotionally involved in the case when you made your big plea not to be disqualified."

"I was wrong. And nobody had shot my grandson then."

"Okay. Maybe you could get away with that. But how would you feel about it?"

"Better than I'll feel if I keep going."

"I doubt it. You may have been a prosecutor for ten years, Mr. Ryan, but deep down you know that no lawyer has the right to be judge and jury. Your judgments about guilt and innocence don't count. Right now you think you were wrong before. But you know perfectly well that tomorrow you could decide that you were wrong today. You've devoted your whole life to the idea that the people who determine guilt or innocence are the twelve people in the jury box, and they do it by having both sides of the case presented to them as well as possible. So if you want to sleep at night, you'd better be sure Jennifer has the best defense any human being can give her. Otherwise you'll never really be sure about the verdict."

He did not like hearing it—it was too close to thoughts he'd had himself.

He looked out the window at Broadway. Saw only the night, a street, a drugstore, a streetlamp. Light without meaning.

"It's funny," he said quietly, "the hopes you have at the beginning. Your life, your family. How your son is going to have the kind of love and support you never got. Edward Michael Ryan. Edward was Ali's father's name. I thought it had all been made in heaven. That place we had our picnic, you and me? The three of us went on a picnic there once. It was early spring, like now. Ned wasn't even a year old. Looking back, I guess things were already going wrong then. I was at the office twelve, fourteen hours a day, but then we still thought it was temporary. And that particular day, that picnic we took, everything in the world seemed possible . . .

"Now I sit here and I wonder, how am I supposed to understand that I'll never again see my son who I didn't set eyes on or talk to for three years before he died? He's been dead going on a year and I don't have that straight yet. When he was a kid I'd just be getting to think I had a fix on him and then one day I'd come home and he'd have grown into somebody different. By the time he was killed I didn't even have a clue who he was. It took murder to give me a clear view of him—somebody running headlong away from every-thing I ever tried to teach him.''

The waitress brought another beer for Ryan and a club soda and a plate of food for Miller. She poked a fork at it but did not eat.

"You're good at this, giving yourself a hard time."

"I'm the champ. These days I know more ways to wonder what I did wrong than I ever did exceptions to the Hearsay Rule."

"A little of that goes a long way."

"Tell me about it. I wake up, and there it is. Sometimes it fol-lows me to sleep. It'll pass, I guess. Or it won't."

"Has it ever occurred to you that Ned had two parents?" she said. "Have any of your friends ever said to you, maybe it's not all your fault? Assuming fault is the right word. Aren't you committing the sin of pride, taking it all on yourself? What happened to free will? And what about all the other people in Ned's life? His mother. His famous grandfather. His friends. Didn't they have any influ-ence? I'm not saying you had nothing to do with it, but for heaven's sake give somebody else a little credit, too."

As they emerged onto Broadway from the restaurant stairway she said, "I understand you have a spare room."

He looked at her.

"Yes."

"Good. Starting tonight you have a tenant."

"I won't be baby-sat."

"Ryan, you should be flattered. You have no idea how many men are dying to have me spend the night."

"No, I don't." Harshly.

"You are some piece of work, Ryan, you truly are."

They continued in silence. Passing a late-night drugstore, she stopped.

"I need to duck in here a minute. Toothbrush."

"I have some," he offered.

"Euphemism."

"I have that, too."

She laughed. "What? For all your unexpected lady guests? Is this a side of you I don't know?"

He managed a thin smile. "An unopened package."

She laughed again and put her arm in his. "Come on, Ryan. We have another big day tomorrow."

"What about clothes?"

"There's a dress in the office. After you took your unannounced day off I figured I'd better be prepared. And on the way home tomorrow we can stop by my place and I'll throw some things in a suitcase.''

He slept badly. His shoulder ached for the first time in days.

Sometime during the night he woke up with the thought that this trial was not only about him and Jennifer. Like it or not, he had a commitment to Kassia Miller and to Craig Lawrence, too. They'd put more than half a year of their lives into this, giving their best and relying on him to do the same. He owed them as much.

7

IN THE MORNING MILLER BUSTLED AROUND THE apartment more than seemed necessary. Too often she knocked on his bedroom door to check his progress. He resisted the impulse to yell at her.

On the ride downtown she filled him in on the day he had missed. The car pulled up at the courthouse and he steeled himself to run the gauntlet of reporters.

"How are you today, Mr. Ryan?" Molly O'Hara called.

"Much better thanks." Bless you.

Allen Crown darted forward. "Drunk again, Ryan?"

Miller clamped down on Ryan's arm to keep him from tearing into the reporter, who scurried away without waiting for an answer.

The regular nine-thirty start was delayed for a brief conference with Ryan in the robing room. Ryan was not looking forward to the inevitable dressing down for his absence, but he'd been through it with tougher than Corino.

The judge surprised him. "Mr. Ryan," he said, "I've spent my whole career in state court, but I remember a time when every trial lawyer in New York knew about a federal prosecutor named Michael Ryan. So when you said you could handle the emotional side of this case I believed you.'' He shook his head. Looked at Ryan over steepled hands. "I'm going to give you a chance to withdraw from the case now, in favor of Ms. Miller—if your client agrees and if you inform me before we begin tomorrow."

"There's no need for that, your honor. I'm committed to seeing this through."

Corino's expression did not change, but his voice turned chillier. "If you stay, bear this in mind. I'm not easily fooled, and I'm not reluctant to hold a lawyer in contempt or to recommend disciplinary action, if that's warranted. I'm going to hope and assume that we never have reason for another private chat like this."

Detective Garrity was the prosecution's courtroom detective for the trial. He was in his Sunday best for his turn on the witness stand, his hair slicked down and his manner clipped and efficient as he answered the D.A.'s questions with only a hint of the bullying swagger that was his preferred style.

Griglia took Garrity quickly through a description of his arrival at the crime scene, and of what he found there. The jury had already heard some of it from yesterday's police witnesses.

"The body was partly on its side with one leg drawn up in a fetal position but facing the carpet. The way it was, I couldn't see the head wounds clearly, but the hair was matted with blood and there was blood on the carpet around it."

The body. Ryan tried to visualize a department-store dummy but instead he saw Ned at the morgue, Garrity hovering in the background.

"Did you notice anything else?" Griglia asked.

"There was a large metal cylinder lying on the floor near the body. It was about three feet long and ten inches across."

"Could you tell what it was?"

"From what I'd seen around the place, it was a stand or a pedestal, like you'd put a small statue on."

"Anything else?"

"A rough metal object less than two feet long, something like a twisted bowling pin."

"Where was that?"

Garrity checked his notebook. "About ten feet from the body, between the body and the door."

"I show you people's exhibit eighteen. Do you recognize it?"

"It appears to be the same as what I saw at the crime scene."

"Did you notice anything in particular about it then?"

"It seemed to have a quantity of what appeared to be blood on the thick end."

"Detective, in the course of your investigation did you have occasion to talk to people who were guests at the party?"

"Yes, I did."

"What, if anything, did your questions to them include about their observation of the defendant?"

"We asked for descriptions of her clothing."

"And how did they answer?"

"The descriptions I received were consistent." He opened his notebook again. "Black-and-white checked suit with a gray blouse, possibly silk. Black-and-white checked shoes. The women all said they remembered the shoes really well."

Garrity was playing for a laugh, and he got it. Ryan decided not to object to the hearsay.

"What, if anything, did you do with that information?"

"We obtained a subpoena and a search warrant and we served them on the defendant at her home."

"What, if anything, was the defendant's response?"

"She said she no longer had the clothes she wore that night. We searched and didn't find the suit or the shoes. We found three gray silk blouses, but the defendant said they weren't the one she wore the night of the murder."

"Did you have occasion to look anywhere else for these clothes and shoes?"

"The Feed the Children Thrift Shop."

He again did not find what he was looking for, Garrity said, although the shop had a record of receiving "miscellaneous clothing and footwear" from the defendant on the day after the murder.

Griglia moved on.

"Did you speak to the defendant at any time on the night of the crime?"

"Yes, I did."

"When was that?"

"Late that night. Around midnight."

"And where was she?"

"At her apartment."

"Did you have a reason to visit her at that time?"

"I told her that her husband had been killed."

"Could you describe her demeanor as you observed it the night of the crime?"

"She was calm, I would say. She received the news without becoming visibly upset."

Ryan heard Jennifer's indignant huff of breath.

"Thank you, detective, that's all."

It was Miller's turn. She walked to the lectern and put down some notes, then stood clear.

"Detective, have you since the beginning of your investigation of this matter had occasion to receive books of account and other business records relating to the activities of Edward Ryan?"

"Yes, I have."

"Did you go over those books with a police accountant?"

"Not that I remember."

"Did anyone else?"

"Objection."

"Sustained."

"Did you check those books for irregularities?"

"No."

"Did you use them as a source of leads to people Mr. Ryan might have cheated or had difficulty with?"

"No."

"You didn't?"

"That's what I said." Garrity was trying out his tough-cop act. Keep it up, Ryan thought: Get the jury on her side.

But Griglia saw it, too, and tried to head Garrity off. "Your honor, there's no need for Ms. Miller to badger the witness."

The judge looked at the petite lawyer facing the heavy-set six-two detective. "He doesn't look intimidated to me, Mr. Griglia. Ms. Miller, just ask your questions and move on."

She smiled at Corino. "Thank you, your honor. Detective, did you see in those books or business records accounts of mortgages and similar loans made by Ned Ryan, several for substantially more than a million dollars each?"

"No."

The D.A. stood up. "Your honor, I object to this entire line of questioning, and I'd appreciate a comment from the bench about the evidentiary value of questions."

"Leave something for me to do, will you please, Mr. Griglia?" Corino said. "Ms. Miller, I think we've had enough, unless you can show us you're going somewhere."

"I definitely am, Judge. These questions go to the issue of the thoroughness of the police investigation. If these people just took the first person they thought of and accused her of this crime, the jury has a right to know it."

Her last words were delivered in competition with repeated shouts of "Objection!" from the D.A., and finally Corino's own, "All right, all right."

"Approach the bench," Corino said.

Ryan stayed in the background and let Miller argue it on her own. The conference did not last long, and when it was over Griglia sat down looking unhappy.

Corino leaned across the bench in the direction of the jury. "Ladies and gentlemen, I'm going to let Ms. Miller continue this line of questioning but first let me remind you of something I told you at the beginning of the trial. Questions by the lawyers are not evidence by themselves. Answers by the witnesses, combined with the questions that the answers are responsive to, those are evidence. If Ms. Miller asks Detective Garrity did he see a purple cow outside the police station and he says no, that's evidence that he did not see a purple cow. It is not any kind of evidence at all of whether there are, were, or ever will be any purple cows, outside the police station or anywhere else. The purple cow exists only in the question, and the question itself is evidence of nothing. Is that clear? Go ahead, Ms. Miller."

Ryan could just see Griglia past Saundra Warneke. The D.A. looked less unhappy than he had a moment before.

Miller asked Garrity more questions about Ned's mortgage transactions and about where the money came from. Bolstered by the judge's instruction to the jury, Garrity's professions of ignorance became more definite as the questions continued. Then she asked him whether he had checked to see if Ned's associates were drug dealers, a question that brought an explosive objection from Griglia and an admonition from the bench. She said "Thank you, detective, that's all."

Griglia had questions on redirect.

"Detective, in the course of investigating the murder of Edward Ryan, did you have occasion to follow up on his business relationships?"

"Yes, I did."

"Yourself, or others?"

"Myself and others."

"And what did you find, briefly?"

"That Ned Ryan was a sharp dealer who made the same kind of business friends and enemies as anybody else like that."

"Objection," Ryan said.

"Sustained. The jury will disregard the answer. If you have something specific to ask, Mr. Griglia . . ."

"No, thank you, your honor, I'm done."

* * *

Griglia pursued the question of the missing clothes with his next witness, the shoe-store clerk who had sold Jennifer the black-and-white shoes—for six hundred dollars. A designer-shop clerk described a black-and-white checked suit Jennifer had bought for twelve hundred dollars plus tax.

The Feed the Children Thrift Shop's manager had received a donation from Jennifer Ryan on the day after Ned Ryan's death. It included a suit, a silk blouse and a pair of shoes, among many other items. She could not be more specific because the thrift shop gave a standard tax-deduction valuation for donated garments "of a certain quality," and kept no detailed records of the specific items. Sales records included only a similar general description of items sold: dress, suit, pants.

Miller cross-examined her about the clothing donations the shop received.

"Designer labels, aren't they?" she asked, a lead-in to a series of questions about the richness of the clothes discarded by the charity's benefactors.

"And was Mrs. Ryan a regular contributor?"

"Oh, yes." The manager seemed sad to have lost such a good donor. "She was very generous."

"And what was the condition of the clothes she donated?"

"They were very well kept."

It was not precisely the answer they wanted, but it was close enough. Miller did not press the issue. "Thank you. That's all."

Ryan did his best to follow all the direct testimony as if he was going to do the cross-examination himself. He had lost the habit of courtroom concentration and badly needed to get it back. There were too many times that a word or a gesture would set his mind wandering in another direction and he would come back into focus to discover that he had missed a question and answer. Acceptable for a spectator or even a reporter. Not for one of the lawyers trying the case.

He could not suppress an ex-prosecutor's respect for Griglia's approach. The establishing questions were smooth and condensed in a way that got information across with no impression of hurry and developed a rhythm that led smoothly to the important points. Breaking that rhythm was part of Ryan's job. Griglia did not make it easy.

If Griglia had mellowed into a master builder with his witnesses, he had always been a wrecking crew with opposing counsel. Ryan was expecting the D.A. to run roughshod over Miller or to provoke her into making mistakes. It did not happen, and Griglia began to let up, clearly worried that he would turn the jury in her favor if he didn't.

When it was Ryan's turn to do the cross-examination he was not as shaky as he'd expected to be. It was an odd sensation, cross-examining a cop. When he had been a prosecutor the law enforcement people had always been his witnesses.

The witness was Detective Stein, Garrity's partner. Saundra Warneke questioned him about his observations of the physical layout of Hugo Hill's two loft floors and roof garden, and the accessibility of the room where Ned's body had been found. Warneke's running battle with Miller on the subject of the Crime Scene Unit's thoroughness made the assistant D.A. meticulous about having Stein describe the care he had exercised every step of the way.

Ryan started by asking the detective if there was more than one door to the murder room. Only one, he said. Windows? Yes, but it's the eighth floor. Did he check for signs of forced entry? Yes, and found none. So access to the room was only by the one door and access to the floor was only by the stairway? Yes, because the elevator was rigged not to stop on that floor.

Ryan took a breath, anticipating the next questions he had prepared.

"Is there a fire escape?"

"Not to that room."

"To that floor?"

"I don't know."

"You don't know? Didn't you check?"

"Only in that room. I had other things to do. Maybe one of the other . . ."

Ryan cut the detective off before he could say more.

The prosecution had put most of its cops on the stand the day Ryan had missed: the detectives who had been summoned to Hugo Hill's to conduct preliminary questioning of the twenty-seven people still there when the body was discovered, and some of the cops who had collected and preserved blood samples and other crime-scene evidence. Miller had harried them about their failure to supervise the caterers and the resulting loss of the bowl Jennifer had shattered, and poked at them in general to find the places where they had been sloppy or forgetful or plain dumb.

The D.A.'s final cop had found the cocaine and one of the guns. Griglia had him describe discovering them and then asked, "Detective, considering crime scenes at parties and other gatherings of ten or more people, how many have you investigated in your career?''

"Over a hundred."

"And speaking only of the past five years at what percentage of those, if any, did you find drugs or weapons?"

"I'd say nearly a hundred percent."

"It's not uncommon then, in your professional observation?"

"Oh no, just the opposite."

"And in what percentage of those instances, if any, do you recover fingerprints on the drug containers or weapons?"

The detective grinned. "Almost never."

Griglia finished the day, and the week, with one of the Emergency Medical Service paramedics who had answered the 911 emergency call.

On cross-examination Miller pressed the witness hard with questions about the condition of the body. Had he made any attempt to determine body temperature or to look for signs of morbidity, lividity or anything else that would indicate how long Ned had been dead at the time the paramedic examined him, which was about twenty-five minutes after the body was first discovered? The paramedic admitted he had done nothing in this area beyond noting that there was no sign of rigor mortis.

The testimony reached Ryan through a defensive filter made partly of willful ignorance. The visit to the morgue had already caused him enough nightmares.

Jennifer was clearly uncomfortable being with Ryan. She left the office as soon as she was sure her lawyers did not need her. Ryan was not unhappy to see her go.

He and Miller reviewed the day's testimony over an ordered-in Chinese dinner. She was still surprised that the cops had missed the fire escape.

"It happens," Ryan told her. "Things slip between the cracks or fall between the stools. Everybody thinks it's everybody else's responsibility."

"And nobody says the emperor is naked?'

"If anybody notices except the boss, they usually figure it's because of some decision they don't know about and they'd better keep their mouth shut. With Griglia taking over so late from Becker, that's exactly the kind of thing that gets missed."

They finished before ten, early for them. On the way back to Ryan's apartment they stopped at the Shamrock.

Kelly came to greet them. "Welcome."

"You're in a good mood," Ryan commented.

"Landlord gave me six months' grace to decide what I'm going to do."

"And what are you going to do?" Miller asked him.

"Take six months to decide. What can I get for the most beautiful member of the defense bar?"

"Just the defense bar?" She grinned. "I'll have one of those beers like my friend."

"And one for you," Ryan told him.

Kelly joined them for a toast and then went to work the other end of the bar.

Ryan drank some beer. "I have a question for you."

"Sure."

"No offense, but, here you are in a ruffled dress, it's the end of a long week and you still look good enough to draw a compliment from a jaded bartender . . ."

"Yes?" Keeping her smile from getting too broad.

"And I watch you in court and, smart and tough as you are, sometimes you could be a regular southern belle if you had the accent . . ."

"Why, Michael Ryan, how you do go on." Her drawl was a reasonable facsimile.

"Right. And we've been working together for most of a year, and all I've ever seen was a . . ."

She waited, not helping him.

"Never mind," he said. "I'm out of line."

She put her hand on his arm. "No, you're not. It's a perfectly good question. I shouldn't tease you about it. I even have an answer."

"I'll be glad to hear it."

She put her beer mug on the bar. "It's like this. I saw long ago there's nothing I can do about the hardships that come with being a woman, except endure them. So I decided I was entitled to take whatever advantage I could find. If people's reactions to my being a woman give me a chance to manipulate them in court, I'm happy to do it. Nobody can say they didn't ask for it. But it's not something I do with everybody. Especially not with you. We've had to work together, for a long time, as allies. The only way I can do that is on a basis of equality and honesty. Being a woman isn't something I can turn on and off, but I can do my best to make sure you don't treat me like one." Her eyes were on him, steady and clear. "Because I don't ever want to feel I'm entitled to manipulate you."

Ryan slept well and got up early enough Saturday morning to go for a swim. Miller had coffee and oatmeal waiting for him when he got home. He consumed both with gusto and then they headed for the office.

The defense team began the weekend with a review of the week and look ahead to the next five days in court.

When they were done with the day's preparation, Ryan and Miller took a cab uptown.

"Well, Mr. Ex-prosecutor," she said as they bounced over the potholes in the road, "it looks to me like you're back in the saddle again."

"In a manner of speaking."

"That's good, because it's time for me to sleep in my own bed for a change, catch up on my mail."

He was not prepared for it. "It's up to you."

"You'll be okay?"

"If you mean will I get to court on Monday, the answer is yes. And I'll be at the office first thing tomorrow, boning up on Mr. Hugo Hill and the others we think we'll be facing next week, while you work on the medical examiner."

"Let me make a suggestion. Sleep late tomorrow. Come in at noon."

The phone startled him out of sleep just before eleven. He reached for it but stopped himself, remembering the last call that had pulled him out of sleep. He groped for the call-record switch on the answering machine. He was not going to make that mistake a second time.

He picked up the phone.

"Hello."

"Michael, it's Craig. Did I wake you?"

Relief did not absorb the adrenaline coursing through his veins.

"Michael?"

"What's up?" Catching his breath.

"Good news, I hope, but I didn't want to wait and have to tell you in front of Kassandra. I got a phone message from Donald Garfield."

"What did he say?"

"I'll play it for you."

There was a click, and Ryan heard Garfield's voice.

"Amazing the kind of thing you remember when you put your mind to it. That guy I was telling you about, the one with the moustache, I swear he said something about Ned Ryan giving him a heart attack. Or else it was a heart condition. He looked okay to me, but I'm sure no doctor."

Lawrence got back on the line. "Mean anything to you?"

It took a moment to fall into place. "It might. The problem is, the deal I'm thinking of closed okay. Lousy terms, but it closed. Garfield told us the deal his man did was killed."

"You got anything better?"

"No, I don't. Congratulations. You just won a trip to Arizona."

"Arizona?"

"Where the guy from Rahway moved to."

"What guy from Rahway?"

"The one Ned screwed on the mortgage terms at the last minute. The one he told Jennifer about, who threatened him. Harry Somebody."

"Son of a bitch. I forgot about him."

8

GRIGLIA STARTED THE WEEK WITH A SUCCESSION OF two-foot by three-foot blow-ups of autopsy and crime-scene photos showing Ned's body with a pool of blood around his head like a medieval halo. Corino had the jury removed from the courtroom while Griglia and Miller jousted over whether the photos were too inflammatory to show the jurors. Hang 'Em High compromised by cutting the pile of pictures in half, allowing Griglia to use blow-ups of the milder group on an easel at a distance from the jury, and to pass around among the jurors at the appropriate time eight-by-ten-inch versions of the gorier ones.

Along with the pictures came testimony from Dr. Elissa Guevara, a soft-spoken assistant medical examiner in her early thirties, about what she had found when she had examined Ned Ryan's corpse.

She testified that Ned Ryan had died of multiple fractures of the frontal bone caused by blows to the head, and she described the wounds in detail, laying the groundwork for the expert who was to follow her.

"To what extent if any would such a beating have produced splashing or spattering of blood?" Griglia asked her.

"Not on the first blow, but on the later blows I would say there was at least moderate splattering of blood."

"What do you base that on?"

"On the amount of bleeding I observed and the nature of the injuries, and also on the spattering on the walls and ceiling that was evident from the crime-scene photographs."

"And in your opinion, how likely is it that the assailant would be splashed with some of the victim's blood?"

"Extremely likely. It's virtually certain, I'd say."

She testified that she had determined the approximate time of death based on the contents of Ned's stomach and the degree of rigor mortis and the amount of lividity from pooled stagnant blood in the parts of his body he was lying on, as she had observed it and as it had been reported by the EMS personnel and the assistant medical examiner who had visited the scene of the crime.

On cross-examination Miller established that Guevara had made notes during the autopsy that were not included in the report she filed later.

"And isn't it true that in your original autopsy notes, made before you knew that the body had been discovered at nine forty-five, you indicated a time of death between ten and eleven o'clock?" Step one in widening the window of time when Ned might have been killed.

"Yes, but . . ."

"Thank you, doctor. Now, based only on the medical evidence you personally observed and on your professional experience, can you say with a reasonable degree of medical certainty that Edward Ryan was dead when he was found lying in a pool of blood at nine forty-five p.m.?"

"I can say this—based on the report . . ."

"Please, doctor. Yes or no."

"Well . . . no. But if . . ."

"That's fine doctor. So then, if you cannot say with a reasonable degree of medical certainty that Edward Ryan was dead at nine

forty-five, can you say that the blows which killed him were not
struck at, say, nine-thirty?''

''Well, there was considerable bleeding . . .''

''If you would just answer the question.''

''Well, as to the exact time . . . no, I can't . . .''

''Let me ask you another question. You described using the contents of the stomach as a method of determining the time of death.
Can you elaborate on that?''

''Yes. The canapés had mostly passed from his stomach. So I
would estimate that at the time of death at least an hour had passed
since he ate anything.''

''But it could have been longer.''

''Yes.''

''Shorter?''

''That's more difficult. Possibly. But not a great deal shorter.
These are not precise measures. Some digestion continues after
death, but we try to take that into account.''

''How great a variation would you say there might be?''

''Fifty percent, perhaps more. But there are other factors.''

''So then would you say the blows could have been struck at
eight-thirty, assuming he last ate at no later than eight o'clock?''

''Conceivably.'' Very reluctant.

''Thank you doctor.''

Griglia stood up at the prosecution table.

''I have some questions on redirect, your honor.''

''It's almost time for lunch,'' Corino noted.

''I won't be long.''

The judge did not look happy. ''All right, go ahead.''

''Dr. Guevara, in determining the time of death, you said just
now that there were other factors. Could you elaborate?''

''Well, as I've already said, there was the fact that rigor mortis
had not begun to be noticeable, and the small amount of lividity—
that is, the discoloration due to the pooling of blood—these all point
to a relatively recent death.''

''How recent?''

''Not more than two or three hours.''

''That's two or three hours from when?''

''From the time the medical examiner arrived at the scene of the
crime and made these observations.''

''What time would that be?''

''Midnight.''

''So then the attack occurred sometime between nine and ten
o'clock?''

"I would say so, yes."

"Objection as to the form of the question," Ryan said.

"Sustained. Rephrase it."

"Would you tell us with a reasonable degree of medical certainty based on your examination of the deceased and other relevant medical evidence at what time the death of Edward Ryan occurred."

"Yes. I would say he was killed at some time . . ."

"Objection."

"Mr. Ryan?"

"Your honor, the witness was asked only when death occurred."

"Yes. But I don't see . . . ah, yes. Dr. Guevara, please confine your answer to the terms of the question."

"Could I have the question repeated please? I don't know what I did wrong."

The court reporter read the question back.

"Oh, yes. I can state with a reasonable degree of medical certainty that death occurred between nine and ten p.m. But of course there were . . ."

"Objection. She's answered the question."

"Sustained."

"And how did you come to establish the time of death as being between ten and eleven in your original autopsy notes?"

"Those were very rough notes based on partial information. They never represented a final conclusion."

"Doctor, is there any other factor that narrows the time period?" Griglia asked her.

"Yes. There were people present after nine forty-five."

"Thank you, doctor, that's all."

Miller stood up. "Your honor, I have a few questions on recross."

"Go ahead."

"Doctor, you said just now that there were people present after nine forty-five. But didn't I understand you to testify that Edward Ryan could have been alive when his body was discovered? Based on the evidence you were able to examine, and the report of the EMS paramedics and the medical examiner who was at the crime scene."

"Well . . . It's not very . . ."

"Yes or no, doctor."

"Well . . . I suppose . . ."

"That's yes, then?"

"Yes."

"And is there any way to tell, based on the medical evidence alone, that Edward Ryan was struck on the head at any time before, say, nine-thirty or nine thirty-five?''

The medical examiner said no, though it clearly made her unhappy.

''Thank you, doctor.''

On schedule, Lawrence called from Arizona.

''I checked the guy out. No moustache. Not much hair, either. On the plus side, what he's got is brown and curly.''

''Get a picture,'' Ryan told him. ''We'll draw a moustache in if we have to.''

''Got some already.''

On Tuesday morning Hugo Hill appeared in court in a blue blazer and gray flannel trousers. His white shirt was set off by a wine-colored wool tie.

''Do you believe this?'' Miller whispered to Ryan. ''This is the guy with the bare chest and the gold chains.''

''The rug's the same.'' If anything the carrot toupee seemed more artificial.

Hill's manner was as subdued as his dress. Griglia led him through a quick description of his business as the owner and operator of three art galleries. He had Hill sketch out the ways in which receptions and openings and parties helped him maintain and expand a circle of wealthy art buyers. And then he asked about Ned Ryan, establishing that he had been a regular client for almost three years at the time of his death, that he had purchased about a hundred thousand dollars worth of art in that time. ''That's what he paid. Of course, it's worth more now.''

''And did he have any preferences, among your artists?''

''Yes. He only bought the work of young women. That was one of the reasons he came to me. Most of my artists are young women.''

''Is there any reason for that?''

''I like their work. And they attract rich men.''

Corino did not share the spectators' amusement. He rapped his gavel and glowered at them from under his eyebrows.

Griglia moved quickly to the planning of the party for Karen, Susan Spada and Tina Claire.

''Well, really, I wasn't ready to have another party, but he insisted.''

''Who was that?''

''Ned Ryan.''

"And what did he insist on?"

"He wanted to meet Tina Claire."

"Did he say why?"

"Not in so many words."

Miller poked Ryan.

"What words did he use?"

Ryan stood. "Objection, your honor. Hearsay."

Corino called them to the bench. Ryan was glad to have Miller there: the federal version of the Hearsay Rule—limiting testimony about things said out of court by someone else—was not as strict as the similar rule in New York. Things Ryan was accustomed to seeing admitted as evidence might be excluded in New York and he did not know precisely where the boundaries were.

Despite the defense objections, Griglia and Warneke convinced Corino to apply the rule in a way that allowed Hugo Hill to testify to most of what the prosecution wanted: that he had thrown the party when he did as a way to introduce Ned Ryan to Tina Claire.

Next, Hill finished describing the guest list and answered questions about the layout of his two floors of loft space and the roof garden where the party was held. He described how he used the room in which the body was found: part study, part personal business office and part private gallery for a few choice pieces given to him as gifts by his artists. People's exhibit eighteen, a sculpture called "Wingless Bird," he said, had been a gift from Tina Claire, one he particularly treasured. He said that while he had made no attempt to lock up the eighth floor, where his private apartment was, it never occurred to him that anyone would go down there. The elevator did not stop on that floor, and the door to the private quarters from the building's main stairway was locked.

Hill said, too, in testimony admitted over objections, that he had been concerned about the party because he knew that Tina Claire was a volatile person who liked to play sexual jokes on the unsuspecting. He had, he said, warned Ned Ryan about this.

Griglia asked for clarification of the fire-escape question. There was a fire escape, Hill said, at the other end of the eighth-floor loft space from the study-gallery, and access from the outside was barred by special security gates. He had been robbed before, years ago, and he had installed the gates as a result. Special quick-release handles on the inside allowed rapid exit in fire or other emergency.

Ryan picked up on that in his cross-examination.

"Is there any way to tell if the gates have been opened from the inside?"

"I don't know."

"Are you aware if anybody examined them in the course of the police investigation?"

"No."

"Objection."

"I just asked if he was aware, your honor."

"I'm going to sustain it, Mr. Ryan. I don't see the relevance of his awareness."

On direct examination Griglia had deftly undercut the robbery scenario, establishing that except for the one robbery long ago Hill had not been bothered, and that the successful burglars had taken stereo equipment and cameras, not art.

Even so, Ryan pressed for details about the value of the art in the room where Ned had been found, and in the ninth-floor gallery. Then he returned to the party. How many had been on the guest list? How many had come? Hill didn't know? Had he made any attempt to keep out uninvited guests? Or to monitor the movements of the guests, known and unknown, once they were there? Had he hired any sort of security people? The locked doors he had mentioned, could somebody have unlocked them from the inside? And let in other people who, if they did not attend the party, Hill would never have known were there?

Hill was not happy about answering some of Ryan's questions, a reluctance that inspired Ryan to bear down on him harder, until a glance at the jury warned him to let up.

In the course of questioning the gallery owner on other subjects, Ryan had thrown in an occasional question about the current state of the room, about the renovations that had been done and about their timing. These had come as asides, with not much weight attached, apparent diversions from whatever other line of questioning had been occupying Hill's attention.

Now Ryan drew them all together. "In fact, Mr. Hill, isn't it true that as soon as you could you destroyed the crime scene totally, removing all and any evidence that might have remained of the presence of others in that room, and making further examination of the room, especially by the defense, impossible?"

He walked back to the defense table without waiting for Hill's answer. He was beginning to remember the pleasures of cross-examination. He had been right to think of being in court again as like getting back on a bicycle: he still felt awkward, but now and then there was the smoothness of a well-executed change of gears or the exhilaration of a sweeping turn well and gracefully made.

Griglia did not have any redirect. As Ryan sat down he heard Corino making preadjournment remarks. Somehow the afternoon was gone. They went back to the office to debrief and prepare for another day's testimony.

Lawrence was waiting for Ryan at the Shamrock when he got done at the office. The investigator had a handful of black-and-white telephoto eight-by-tens of a slender, balding man with hollow cheeks and eyes sunk in his skull. On three of the prints Lawrence had sketched in extra hair and different-shape moustaches.

"I faxed these to Garfield. He wasn't sure about the name. 'Could be,' he said."

"What about the face?"

"The moustache was different, but otherwise it looks like what he remembers."

"Not the best I.D. I ever heard."

"Wait till you hear the rest, then make up your mind."

"What rest?"

"Our man Harry Bundesman took a trip last June. Back East where he came from."

"When in June?"

"Mid June."

"Around the fourteenth?" The murder date.

"Seems that way. And get this—within a day or so of getting back he was in the hospital with a heart attack."

"Son of a bitch. Did you get anything else?"

"Not yet. I can send somebody to check his movements in Jersey, and I talked to a P.I. in Scottsdale we can use if we want more from there. I figured it was premature to go for the credit card bills. Assuming you want the guy."

Yes, Ryan wanted to say. I want him. Go get him and read him his rights and bring him back in custody. But this wasn't the old days. Lawrence wasn't F.B.I. any more, and Ryan wasn't an assistant U.S. Attorney.

"Let's put it on hold," he said, hating the fact that he had no choice. "Miller was right, we don't want to spook him, and we sure don't want to tip Griglia off about him. For now we just need to keep track of him so we can get our hands on him when we need to."

9

GRIGLIA'S FIRST WITNESS FROM AMONG THE PARTY
guests was Tina Claire.

It made no sense to Ryan. He had expected Griglia to set the
stage, build up an image of the party for the jury, let them see the
conflict coming in the testimony of other guests, then put Tina
Claire on the stand.

This way, she appeared in a vacuum, with only Hugo Hill's testimony to set up the circumstances. Griglia had to have a reason.
Most likely he was afraid she was going to be a difficult witness
and wanted to get her testimony over with as early as possible, to
give the jury time to forget or distort the details.

Whatever his reasoning, Griglia had caught the defense with their
collective pants down. They had not even made a firm decision on
who would cross-examine Tina Claire.

For the occasion she was wearing a tight black leather skirt and
a white silk blouse that was buttoned high enough to show only a
hint of cleavage. The multicolor metal band around her neck was
likely to be her own work.

Not a bad compromise, Ryan thought. For her to help Griglia,
she had to look sexy enough and even threatening enough to have
inspired a murderous rage, but nice enough to keep the jury from
sympathizing with Jennifer. Still, Griglia had a narrow line to walk.

He started slowly. Where do you live, what do you do? Where
were you educated, how long have you been a sculptor? Tina Claire
had an impressive list of prizes, grants, fellowships and awards.
The artistic credentials would presumably earn her points with the
jury.

From the introduction, Griglia went straight to the heart of the
matter. He established that she had been invited to a party by Hugo
Hill as one of three honored guests to meet patrons, in particular

Ned Ryan, who had just bought several pieces of her work. She had arrived promptly at five-thirty, the hour the party was called for.

"Did you have any particular feelings about Ned Ryan as you went to that party?" Griglia asked.

"Yes, I did."

"What were they?"

"They were not good."

"Why?"

"I'd heard that he tried to screw all the women whose art he bought, like spending the money entitled him to something extra."

Ryan was on his feet in the middle of her answer, objecting strongly.

Griglia had a response ready. "Your honor, I'm offering this testimony only to prove that Ms. Claire heard rumors and they affected her state of mind. And her behavior, as the court will see."

"I'll allow it. Objection overruled. . . . But, one thing, Mr. Griglia . . ."

"Yes, Judge?"

"We don't need the content of the rumors from now on. The fact that they existed is more than enough."

Griglia nodded and turned back to his witness.

"Did a time come when you met Ned Ryan?"

"Yes."

"And what happened then?"

"I was standing in a group of people and Hugo came over with this guy, not a bad looking guy, and he introduced him. This is Ned Ryan, who's your newest fan. Something like that."

"And did Mr. Ryan say anything at that time?"

"No."

"What if anything did you observe about him?"

"He looked sort of spaced, you know? Like his mind was on something else."

"Objection." Ryan was trying to break Griglia's rhythm. The prosecutor was going to get the information in anyway.

"Sustained."

"Can you describe how he looked? His physical appearance or his actions."

"He wasn't focusing on me. He had a kind of blank, distant expression."

"And what if anything did you do then?"

"Well, I turned to the others who were standing there and I said, like, 'You'd better leave us alone.' "

"And did they leave?"

"Yes."

"What if anything did you do then?"

"Well, I'm kind of a mischievous person . . ."

"Objection."

"Mr. Griglia, once again would you try to formulate a question the witness can answer properly?"

"Ms. Claire, without characterizing yourself, what kind of person you are or anything like that, can you tell the jury what you said and did?"

"Like I was saying, I got him alone with me."

"I'm sorry to interrupt, but when you say alone, do you mean you left the party?" Griglia smiled at her.

Lord, Ryan thought, he's being charming.

Her smile in response was not as successful as Griglia's, more like a simper.

"Oh, no. I mean, I took him off a little distance, not far, where nobody else was standing, near a table with some big bowls of finger food. I didn't want to leave. If we left, then nobody could see us."

"Does that mean you wanted to be seen?"

"Objection," Ryan said, standing quickly. "Irrelevant. Process of the mind. Ms. Claire's intentions are not competent testimony."

"Withdrawn."

Griglia was pacing along the rail that separated the well from the rest of the courtroom.

"What if anything did you do then?"

"I made a political statement. An artistic statement."

Ryan stood. "Your honor?"

"The jury will disregard that answer." Corino leaned toward the sculptor. "Just tell us what the statement was."

"It was guerilla theater."

Ryan was momentarily stunned. Could Franky have thought this up by himself? It didn't seem likely to be Tina Claire's idea, but you never knew. Ryan remembered Susan Spada's scathing judgment that Tina Claire ought to be a performance artist.

"Objection," he said, but she was already elaborating.

"To make the statement work you have to do something outrageous." She was warming to the role, shifting in the witness chair. Somehow she had contrived to have the top button of her blouse come undone on its own. It seemed possible to Ryan that the temperature in the courtroom had gone up a couple of degrees.

"Objection!"

"Objection sustained," Corino said. "The jury will disregard those remarks."

"Can you describe what you did?" Griglia asked his witness.

"Well, first I started to talk to him." She had shifted to her breathy voice. "About how glad I was he liked my work and how happy I was to meet him and how I'd heard all about him."

Ryan would have asked for a sidebar conference about proper demeanor on the witness stand, but he was afraid he would only make enemies on the jury. The men were having a great time. Even a couple of the women seemed to be enjoying the show. And there was the chance that if she kept it up she would sabotage herself, and Griglia.

"And I said how we should get to know each other better." She smiled. "Things like that."

"And were you doing anything, any physical activity, at this time?" Griglia's voice sounded thicker than it had on the last question.

"Not right away."

"Later?"

"Yes. As I talked to him I started to move closer, until I was real close."

Her voice had sunk almost to a whisper. Griglia asked her to speak up.

The judge chose that moment to intervene. "Ms. Claire, we appreciate your attempt to give us a feeling for what was happening, but it's not really appropriate for a courtroom. If you could sit very still and speak up in a clear conversational voice, right into the microphone, we might not have as much fun, but I think the interests of justice would be better served." The mild words were belied by the controlled sharpness of his tone.

"I'm sorry, your honor." All innocence. "I'll try to do what you said."

Ryan had to hand it to Griglia. He had shown her at her most inflammatory, and by giving her her head had engineered a scolding from Corino that would keep her from losing the sympathy of at least some of the jurors.

"Now, Ms. Claire, you were telling the jury about how you were talking to Ned Ryan."

"Yes."

"Could you go on, then?"

"Yes. I was very close to him. And I was talking about like how glad I was to meet him, those were the words, but it was not in a conversational tone, you know? I was talking real soft.'' Corino's warning did not keep her from duplicating the tone.

"Objection."

"Sustained. Words and actions, Mr. Griglia."

"Yes, Judge, thank you." And to Tina Claire: "And then what did you do?"

"I put my hand on his penis."

There was a stir in the courtroom and on the jury. The bus driver, usually slumped and seemingly half asleep, sat up and stared.

"Beg pardon?" Griglia asked the witness.

"Objection," Ryan said. "Asked and answered."

"I didn't hear," Griglia protested.

"Overruled," Corino said to Ryan, and to the witness. "You can say it again."

"I put my hand on his penis."

"How did he react?" Griglia asked.

"He liked it."

"Objection."

"Sustained. The jury will disregard the answer."

"What did he do? Just his physical actions."

"Well, he kind of pushed against me."

"Was he aroused?"

"Yes, he was."

Ryan stood up. "Your honor, is this necessary?"

"Approach the bench please, gentlemen. Ladies, too."

A court officer took Tina Claire from the witness stand to the nearest corner of the court, next to the jury box. The bus driver and the machinist followed her slow stroll with particular interest.

Corino studied the D.A. from under his eyebrows. "The tender familial sensibilities of defense counsel aside, he has a point, Mr. Griglia. I'm not sure I see the relevance myself."

"Your honor, I believe the behavior of Ms. Claire and Ned Ryan, the specific behavior, are essential to the jury's understanding of what happened."

"This is ridiculous," Miller burst out. "It's an affront . . ."

Ryan grabbed her arm and she stopped.

He said, "Your honor, the immediate tactile perceptions of this witness as to matters that could not possibly have been perceived by anyone else cannot be relevant here by any stretch of the imagination. This material is being offered merely because of its inflammatory nature."

"I'm inclined to agree with Mr. Ryan."

"Judge, this is behavior that inspired a murder . . ."

"We don't know any such thing," Ryan countered.

"Oh, yes we do." Griglia let himself lose his temper. "And the jury will know it too, unless we blindfold them."

"I'm not saying you should omit the testimony altogether," Corino said testily. "Just leave out the deceased's erection. And whatever else like that."

"Your honor, it's vital to my case. And there's no reason to exclude it. It's perfectly competent testimony."

"I made my ruling, Mr. Griglia. Don't push."

"But, your honor . . ."

"Mr. Griglia. I said something when you first came in here about proper behavior in my courtroom. Do you recall?"

"Yes, Judge." Conceding gracefully, not capitulating.

He went back to the lectern to resume his questioning.

"Were you aware of the fact that his wife was present?"

"Oh, yes. That was the idea. I mean, I didn't mean for him to get *killed*."

"Objection! Move to strike."

"Right you are, Mr. Ryan. Strike the question and answer. The jury will disregard it."

"What happened next?" Griglia resumed coolly.

"This woman came storming over. I didn't know then who it was."

"Is she in the courtroom now?"

"Yes."

"Can you identify her for the jury?"

"That woman." She pointed at Jennifer.

"The defendant?"

"Yes."

"Please let the record indicate that the witness pointed to the defendant," Griglia said. "And what did she do?"

"She was yelling about how he wasn't going to get away with humiliating her in public, and this was the last straw and she wasn't going to take it lying down."

"Those were her words?"

"That's what I remember."

"And what would you say her demeanor was?"

"Well like I said she was yelling. Really. I'd say she was out of her gourd mad."

"Objection."

"Sustained. Can we have a more temperate answer?"

"Ms. Claire, in plainer words, can you describe her demeanor?"

"Give me an example."

Griglia looked to the judge for permission, and got it.

"Was she angry or upset, or was she . . . teasing, or playing a joke?"

"Oh, no. She was dead serious. She had blood in her eye."

"Objection."

"Sustained. Strike the last part of the answer."

Ryan wished he could take solace in the ruling but he had to assume the words were indelibly in the jurors' minds: *She had blood in her eye.*

"Did she do anything besides shout?"

"She picked up this bowl full of food, some kind of Spanish pastries, I think, and she smashed it. It was real scary, the pieces went everywhere."

"Objection."

"Sustained. The jury will disregard it. Try again, Mr. Griglia."

"Without characterizing it, now, scary or anything like that. Tell the jury exactly what she did."

"She picked up this bowl." Her hands raised overhead in apparently unconscious imitation. "And wham! down on the table."

"Was she holding it when she smashed it?"

"No. She let go. She threw it."

"And what did the deceased do?"

"Ned? He didn't do anything. He stood there."

"Did he say anything?"

"Maybe he said her name."

"And can you tell us what his demeanor was?"

"I don't know really. Confused more than anything. He was still, you know, aroused? And there was his wife yelling at him."

"Objection. Move to strike."

"I don't think we need to strike it, but try to control your witness, Mr. Griglia."

"You would say he appeared to be confused, is that right?"

"Yes."

"And then did anything more happen?"

"After she broke the bowl he turned and walked out."

"And what did she do?"

"She followed him."

"Did you see either of them after that?"

"No. They didn't let us look at the body."

"Objection."

"Indeed. Mr. Griglia?"

"Sorry, your honor. I'm done with this witness."

She started to get up.

"Stay where you are, young lady," the judge told her. "I'm sure the defense has some questions for you."

Ryan looked at the clock. It was not yet twelve. No chance of asking for a lunch recess.

"Can we have ten minutes, your honor?"

Corino checked the clock, himself. "No more."

They went down to the end of the hall to caucus.

"God that was awful," Jennifer said.

Ryan saw the tracks of her tears. At the height of it, locked in battle with Griglia, he had forgotten she was there. Now all he could think was how glad he was she had cried. The jury would not have missed it.

"Yes, it was awful," he agreed. "And now we have to decide who's going to go after her."

"Me," Miller said. "We need to see her get mad at a woman."

Ryan stifled his impulse to claim the cross-examination for himself. She was right. "Okay, what do you want to hit her on?"

"Jennifer, did she say anything that was different from what you remember? About anything you did or anything you saw."

"I don't know."

Ryan wanted to yell at her, shock her into usefulness. He held back.

"So we can't challenge her on the facts," he said. "It would be nice to get something on the record that opens the door on her boyfriend." He was still their best illustration of the irate-cuckold theory, alibi or not.

"I don't know how easy it's going to be," Miller said, "but I'll give it a shot."

"All right, let's get back in there early and keep Corino happy."

The judge called the court to order precisely ten minutes after the recess began.

Miller stood up and went to the lectern.

"Good morning, Ms. Claire. I'm Kassia Miller."

"Hello."

"That must have been a strain for you, some of that testimony. Now that you've had a few minutes' rest, I'd like to go back to the beginning for just a minute."

"Okay."

"This party you were talking about, we've heard it described as a pretty large party."

"I don't know. Depends."

"How many people would you say?"

"I don't know."

"Would you say more than ten or twelve?"

"Yes, more than that."

"Would you say more than fifty?"

"I don't know, I didn't count." She smiled—a small victory.

"Were you at the party alone?"

"I was the guest of honor."

"Did you have an escort?"

"I get around fine on my own."

Griglia said, "Your honor, I fail to see the point."

"I'll be glad to tie it in, your honor."

"Go ahead with the questions. Overruled, Mr. Griglia."

"Did you have an escort?" Miller asked again.

"No."

"Did you arrive at the party with anyone?"

"I don't remember."

"Did you leave with anyone?"

"You bet I did. I left with a bunch of cops."

Laughter in the courtroom. Corino exercised his gavel.

"Would it refresh your memory to learn that several people have said you were at the party with a man named Kenny Peters?"

"Your honor, I object. No such testimony is in evidence."

"Sustained."

"Just because sometimes I go places with him . . ."

Griglia was standing. "Will your honor please instruct the witness?"

"You don't have to answer the question if I sustain Mr. Griglia's objection. The jury will disregard any answer."

Ryan could feel Miller's frustration. She tried something different.

"Do you have a boyfriend?"

Tina Claire shifted in her chair. Uncomfortable now, not sexy. "What does that mean?"

"Someone who shares your living space some or all of the time."

"No."

"Or someone with whom you have a regular or an ongoing sexual relationship. Do you have one of those?"

"Objection."

"Mr. Griglia?"

"The witness's private life is not remotely relevant."

"It is," Miller countered, "if it bears directly on the substance of her testimony. We're happy to make an offer of proof."

"Approach, please," Corino told them. Again, the bus driver

and the machinist appreciated the view of Tina Claire being escorted from the witness box.

Griglia was talking even before he reached the bench. "Your honor, the defense is trying to bring in on cross-examination material which, if it belongs in this courtroom at all, is part of the defense's direct case. Unless the defense wants to make Ms. Claire its own witness."

"Your honor, even if we were to concede Mr. Griglia's point, which we certainly don't, Ms. Claire would clearly be a hostile witness from our point of view."

"All right, Ms. Miller, go ahead for now. But if you step more clearly over the line, I'll rule on it on the spot."

She waited for the witness to be seated again and opened an attack on her credibility. "Would it surprise you to learn that quantities of cocaine were confiscated at that party?"

She smiled broadly. "No it wouldn't."

"Before you testified here, did you meet with Mr. Griglia?"

A pause. "Yes."

"To discuss your testimony?"

"Yes."

"Many times?"

"What's many?"

Miller let it go. "On the night of the party, had you taken any drugs?"

She turned to the judge. "Do I have to answer that?"

"Yes."

"I don't remember."

"Cocaine?"

"I don't remember."

"Do you not remember because the drugs affected your memory?"

"I didn't say that!"

"Do you usually remember it when you take drugs?"

"I don't take drugs."

Miller looked at the witness, at the jurors, then back at the witness, taking time to let her incredulity register.

"Not at all? Not socially? Not for your work? Never? Is that true?"

"Well . . ."

"So you take drugs sometimes. Is that right?"

"I'm not some kind of coke head."

"Your honor . . ."

"The jury will disregard that outburst. Just answer the question, Ms. Claire."

"Yes. Sometimes."

"And when you do, do you remember?"

She saw the trap. "Sometimes."

"But the night Ned Ryan was murdered is not one of the times you remembered. Is that right?"

No answer. The sculptor stared at the floor.

"Ms. Claire?" Miller prodded. "Is that right?"

"Objection, your honor," Griglia said. "Asked and answered."

"Sustained."

"Ms. Claire, when Ned Ryan's wife came over to object to what you were doing with her husband, and she was visibly upset, did you stop?"

"Stop what?"

"What you were doing?"

"I, well . . . I . . ."

"*Did you stop?* Yes or no?"

"No." Defiant. The real Tina Claire.

"You didn't even think of stopping, did you?"

"No! Why should I!"

"Your honor, I object!" shouted Griglia over his witness's response.

"I have no more questions of this witness," Miller said in a tone of pure contempt, and sat down.

"Anything else Mr. Griglia?" the judge asked.

Griglia contemplated his witness, obviously considering whether he had a way to make her look better.

"No, your honor, nothing more."

"Then let's break for lunch. We'll resume at two."

10

THAT AFTERNOON AND THE NEXT MORNING GRIGLIA
and Warneke used the testimony of party guests as a way to paint
a picture of a marriage filled with publicly visible hostility. Ryan
and Miller alternated on cross-examination, using the opportunity
to build a case that Ned and Jennifer had always been volatile people and a volatile couple, and that nothing about their behavior on
the night of Ned's party was notably different from how they had
behaved before. Griglia objected repeatedly to Miller's questions
but took care to do it without raising his voice, so the jury would
not think he was bullying her.

When the defense team debriefed at night, Miller said she was
sure Griglia had been trying to push her into a loud, intemperate
response, to remind the jurors how a woman could flare up when
she was provoked. "He almost got me a few times, too, and then
I saw what he was doing."

Griglia's witnesses the next morning were Jennifer's friend from
Feed the Children, Ellis Turner, and a woman who had hurried
over to join Jennifer after the Turners left, as she stood watching
Ned and Tina Claire.

The woman, a sometime journalist in the world of art and entertainment, identified herself under the District Attorney's guidance
as a trained observer of people and events, and her description of
Tina Claire's antics was the clearest the jury had heard. She was
the first witness to say that Ned had appeared to be involved in what
was happening, a collaborator or at least a willing recruit. And she
had seen it from the same vantage point as Jennifer.

"What was the defendant's reaction?" Griglia asked.

"She said, 'That bastard, I'll kill him.' "

"Those were her exact words?"

"Yes."

"Your witness," Griglia said.

After some preliminary questions, Ryan asked, "Have you ever said, in a moment of anger, 'I'll kill him,' or 'I'll kill her'?"

"No."

"Have you ever heard anybody else say it?"

"I don't think so."

"Let me put it another way. Have you ever heard the expression 'Kill the umpire'?"

"Is that baseball?"

Ryan was groping for a way to salvage this when he realized that her denials might be better for him than the more realistic and credible answers he had been looking for.

"Thank you." Quitting while he was ahead. "That's all."

On redirect, Griglia asked her, "Did the defendant say anything else?"

"No—she said, 'That bastard, I'll kill him,' and then she rushed over there and started in on him. I couldn't hear what she was saying. And then she smashed the bowl."

"And when she said 'That bastard, I'll kill him,'" was she smiling?"

"No. She was furious."

Griglia gave it a moment to sink in, then thanked the witness and sat down.

"We aren't doing so well today." Ryan said as they sat down to another office lunch of cold cuts and salads.

"Some days are like that. You get to a point where they're making all their best points and you just have to do what you can and absorb the damage and figure you'll get your turn later."

"I liked it the other way, being prosecutor. You put your case out there and the jury has it all before you have to start taking any real damage."

"Unless the defense torpedoes your witnesses on cross."

"You still have the momentum."

Miller licked mustard from a finger. "And I'll bet the defense didn't torpedo a lot of your witnesses."

"Not if I could help it."

In the afternoon, the jury got the artist who called herself only Karen.

Griglia established who she was and then asked her if she had known Ned Ryan. She had.

"How well did you know him?"

"We were lovers."

"For how long?"

"A few months."

"How often did you see him?"

"Once or twice a week."

That's wrong, Ryan thought. She told me once a month.

"How did it start?"

"Hugo Hill introduced us, because he—Ned, that is—was buying my work and he wanted to meet me."

Corino sustained Ryan's objection to her testifying about what Ned wanted. A careful step at a time, Griglia brought out that Ned had made an obvious pass during their first meeting. And she had been knocked out by him, she said.

Again, Ryan thought he was hearing wrong.

"And did you and he talk about his wife, and his marriage?"

"Often."

That's wrong, too, Ryan thought. All of this is wrong.

The next hour was a question-by-question battle between Ryan and Griglia about how much Karen could say about what Ned had said about his marriage.

Griglia convinced the judge to let in the statement he was most eager to have the jury hear, that Ned had said, not once but several times, that if he wasn't careful his wife "was really going to give it to him."

"And did there come a time when Ned Ryan's wife communicated with you?"

"Yes. She called me on the telephone."

"Can you tell us the substance of the conversation?"

"Yes. She said If Ned knows what's good for him he'll never see you again."

"What did you take her to mean by that?"

Ryan objected, thinking how predictable this was—Jennifer and her exaggerated language. No point even asking her about it . . . just assume it as a given and find a way to counter it.

"Sustained."

"I'll rephrase it. Could you tell us anything about the emotional content of that communication or her demeanor, without commenting on the specific meaning of the words?"

"It was a threat."

"Objection."

"Overruled."

"Who was it directed at?"

"As I understood it, it was directed at Ned. She said I should tell him what she had said, that if he knew what was good for him he would stay away from me.''

''What happened after that?''

''I told him about it, and I told him that I didn't like it. I'm not there to take threatening messages from his wife.''

''Was that the only communication you had from her?''

''No. She did it again about a month later.''

''When was that?''

''A couple of months before Ned was killed.''

''And what did you do?''

''I told him to get lost until he straightened out his private life.''

''And did you see him after that?''

''No. I spoke to him. He called to say he wanted to come over. I asked him if he had fixed things with his wife. He said yes, but he didn't sound too sure.''

Ryan objected.

''Sustained. Just the words please, not your thoughts.''

''He said yes, and I said if you're telling the truth then you're welcome.''

''And what happened?''

''Nothing. I never saw him again.''

''Thank you. Your witness.''

Ryan took a moment to put his notes on his original conversation with her in front of Miller.

''Hello, Ms. Karen,'' he said in what he hoped was a pleasant tone.

''Hello.''

''Ms. Karen, do you remember a time a few months ago when I came to visit you?''

''Yes.''

''And did we have a conversation at that time?''

''Yes.''

''And did we talk about sex?''

''Yes.''

''Sex between what two people?''

''Me and your son.''

''Your honor!'' Griglia shouted.

''Strike that from the record,'' Corino told the court reporter. ''The jury will disregard it. And I remind the witness that Mr. Ryan is the defense counsel here, and that's all. Mr. Griglia, this is your witness. You should exert better control.''

''Yes, Judge.''

Ryan observed a moment of silence.

"Now, Ms. Karen, what did you tell me about how you and Ned started to have sex?"

She allowed a pause for apparent thought. "I don't remember."

"Was it the same as what you told the D.A. just now?"

"I don't remember. I suppose it was the same."

Ryan moved away from the lectern toward the defense table and reached out for the notes Miller handed him.

"Ms. Karen, suppose I told you that you said"—he looked at the notes—"that it was warm and cozy and the chemistry was right and it just happened. Safely, of course."

She stared at the pages in his hand as if to divine what they were.

"Ms. Karen?"

"Maybe."

"That it was warm and cozy and the chemistry was right and it just happened between you."

"I might have told you that."

"And did you also tell me that you and he never talked about his wife?"

"I don't remember."

"But it's possible you said that."

"Yes, it's possible." Her charm was wearing thin along with her patience.

"And it's possible your sexual relationship with Ned Ryan started the way I just described, the way you told me it did. It just happened because it was warm and cozy."

"It's possible! Anything's possible."

"Do you have a lot of affairs?"

"No."

"A lot of sexual encounters with different people?"

She stared at him, angry now.

"I'm sorry, I'll withdraw that question." He smiled at her. "An attractive woman has so many opportunities, so many men pestering her."

"Your honor," Griglia said, rising slightly.

"Is there a question in there somewhere, Mr. Ryan?" the judge asked.

Ryan acknowledged the expected barb with a tilt of his head, then went on. "Ms. Karen, are you bothered a lot? Do men come on to you?"

"Yes . . ." A little wary.

"When you don't want them to?"

"Yes."

"Do you enjoy that?"

"No."

"It's not flattering?"

"No, it's creepy."

"Objection, your honor. Is this remotely relevant?"

"Mr. Ryan?"

"If your honor will give me a few more questions . . ."

"A few more."

"Thank you, your honor. Ms. Karen, would you say you'd learned how to turn a man off?"

"Women have to."

Ryan held his breath expecting Griglia to object but for some reason he missed it and Ryan hurried on.

"Is it fair to say that when you connect it's because you want to?"

"I don't when I don't want to."

"Then is it also fair to say that when you began your relationship with Ned Ryan you wanted to do it? That it was mutual?"

"I guess."

"You had as much to do with it as he did?"

"You mean I seduced the poor lamb?"

Ryan looked surprised. "Did you?"

She took a breath to snap at him but caught herself before she said anything. She looked over at Griglia. Ryan pivoted to catch his response, to make the point with the jury.

The D.A. was staring at his fingertips, trying to seem impassive and uninvolved.

"Oh, hell," Karen said. "Who knows who started it? It was all very innocent. Like going to the movies. I've been more involved with people I never kissed goodnight. One guy, we were in love for months, I mean *in love*, and we never touched each other once. *His* wife should have worried."

"Thank you, Ms. Karen, that's all."

"I have something more, your honor." Griglia stood up at the prosecution table. "Ms. Karen, you called it innocent just now, but did you also testify that you and Ned Ryan were having an affair?"

"Yes."

"And were you?"

"Yes."

"And did he make any attempt to conceal it, to your knowledge?"

"No."

"Not even from his wife?"

"Not that I know of."

"Thank you, that's all."

"I really blew it with Karen," Ryan said after Jennifer left the office that night.

"It was a terriffic cross," Miller told him. "And you didn't even write the questions in advance."

Ryan recognized the teasing as a compliment but he was in no mood to acknowledge it. "She was up there lying about Ned and she made me so angry I couldn't resist hammering the whole truth out of her, long after I'd battered her credibility. Great for the truth, maybe, but no help for our case." Whoever had started it, Ned's affair with Karen was motive for Jennifer's alleged murderous anger. Protracted cross-examination had kept the issue and the person in front of the jury longer than necessary.

"The worst of it is," he went on, "I took away from the image of Ned seducing other men's women, and that weakens the notion of a legion of bloodthirsty cuckolds out to get him."

His co-counsel wadded up a page from a legal pad and bounced it off the top of his head.

"Give yourself a break, Ryan. Tomorrow is another day."

11

RYAN GOT UP EARLY FOR A LONG WORKOUT AT THE pool. He was feeling refreshed when he and Miller and Jennifer arrived at the courthouse.

Allen Crown pushed his way in front of them as they were passing between the rectangular thirty-foot-high granite pillars—supporting nothing—that formed a symbolic gate to the courthouse plaza. The way was narrow here, and Ryan could not go around him.

"Mr. Ryan, I hear the D.A. said that with you for the defense he can't lose."

Ryan turned to go back but there were too many people pressing behind him. Crown kept talking.

"He said if I can't beat Ryan I'll hang up my jock."

For once, Ryan was glad to have his anger leave him speechless. He shoved past.

It was bullshit and it should not have bothered him. He shouldn't have felt a surge of anger when Franky Griglia said hello to him on his way into the courtroom. Shouldn't have but did.

Griglia put Susan Spada on the stand. She looked even more ethereal here than she had in her own home—the courtroom and everything in it seemed cruder by contrast.

Yes, she had been at the party, she testified, and yes she knew Ned Ryan, through Hugo Hill. Ned Ryan had made a sexual approach to her, suggesting acts she was not interested in. He had been very direct about it. She had told him no but had not wanted to offend him because he was an important patron of hers and Hill's.

At the party she had been standing near the food table, not far from Ned and Tina Claire, whom she also knew through Hugo Hill, when the defendant had rushed over, very angry. She had heard clearly what the defendant had said: You bastard, how can you do this to me? You think you can get away with this? I'm not going to take it lying down, not anymore. I'm going to get you. I swear I'm going to make you sorry."

" 'I'm going to get you'?" Griglia asked. "Were those the actual words?"

"That's right."

" 'I swear I'm going to make you sorry'?" Making sure the jury did not miss it.

"Yes."

"Did she say anything else?"

" 'Do you think you can humiliate me like this? You've had it.' "

" 'You've had it'?"

"Yes."

"Was that all?"

"No. He turned away from her and took some pastries, I think they were empanadas, from a bowl that was on the table."

"Did she do anything?"

"She picked up the bowl and she smashed it on the table."

"And was she holding it when she smashed it?"

"No, she threw it."

"When it broke was her hand on it or near it?"

"No."

"And did she say anything then?"

"She said, 'You watch out or next time it won't be a bowl.' "

"Did you take that to be a threat?"

Ryan objected. Corino sustained him.

Griglia tried again: "How would you characterize her behavior?"

"Threatening."

Ryan objected again.

Having accomplished his objective, Griglia said simply, "Thank you, Ms. Spada." And to Ryan, "Your witness."

Ryan, still boiling about Allen Crown, was glad they'd decided that Miller was going to do this cross-examination. They had made the choice on the theory that any question Ryan asked the delicate Ms. Spada would seem overbearing compared to the same question asked by his petite co-counsel.

"Have you ever been married, Ms. Spada?" she asked.

"No."

"Engaged?"

"No."

"Have you ever had a steady boyfriend?"

Before Griglia could object Susan Spada said, "I'm gay."

Miller let it pass without comment. "You said you knew Tina Claire?"

"Yes."

"And you know her work."

"Yes." Disdainful.

"Did you ever have a sexual relationship with her?"

"Objection," Griglia said. "It's irrelevant."

"It goes to credibility, your honor."

"I'll allow it. Overruled."

"Did you ever have a sexual relationship with her?"

"Not on your life."

"What would you say her demeanor was when Mrs. Ryan was showing how upset she was about what Ms. Claire was doing?"

"Whose demeanor?"

"Tina Claire's."

"She didn't seem to care."

"Would you say she was pleased or aroused or turned on?"

"Which one?"

"Any of the above will do."

"No."

"Do you recall having said that she was turned on by Mrs. Ryan's behavior?" A casual question, no great weight on it.

Susan Spada seemed about to deny she had said any such thing, but something made her look more closely at Miller. The lawyer returned her gaze unflinchingly.

"I might have," Spada conceded.

"By turned on, did you mean sexually?"

"I might have."

"Turned on because Mrs. Ryan was upset about what Ms. Claire was doing?"

"Objection."

"Sustained."

"Did you have the impression that Ms. Claire was interested in the general reaction of the others in the room?"

"Objection."

"Sustained."

"Would you be surprised to learn that a quantity of recreational drugs was found on the party premises?"

The photographer took a moment to catch up to the change in subject.

"Surprised? No."

"Was it your observation that some people at the party showed signs of drug use?"

"Some."

"Alcohol?"

"Some."

"People were intoxicated?"

"It was a party."

"Were you?"

"Was I what?"

"Intoxicated?"

"No."

"Were you using drugs or had you used them any time that day or the night before?"

"Isn't that incriminating or something?"

"Judge, can you help the witness?"

"It's no crime to say you were taking drugs some time in the past. Or that anyone else was."

"Thank you, your honor. Well, Ms. Spada, had you used any drugs or controlled substances in the thirty-six hours before the party?"

"No."

"None at all?"

"None at all."

"Did Ned Ryan eat the little empanadas he took from that bowl?"

"Did he . . . ? Oh. Yes, I think he did."

"Is the answer yes, then?"

"Yes, I think so."

"Yes, he ate them."

"Yes."

"You saw him?"

She took a moment to think. "Yes."

"You said a moment ago you observed people who showed signs of using drugs, is that right?"

"If I said so."

"Who?"

"I beg your pardon?"

"Who? Who did you see at the party who behaved in that way?"

"You want me to name names?"

"I want you to answer the question."

"I won't do that."

"Judge?"

Corino leaned across the bench toward the witness. "This isn't a political inquisition, this is a murder trial. You have to answer the question."

"I won't."

"Suppose you think about it just a moment before you decide, because if you don't answer the question now, then I'll hold you in contempt and you'll have to think about it in jail."

Griglia stood up. "I object to the whole line of questioning."

"Your honor," Miller said quickly, "it's important not to discuss this in front of the witness."

"I agree," Corino said.

"I'll answer the question," Susan Spada offered.

"My objection stands."

"Overruled. Go ahead, answer the question."

"I don't remember."

"You don't remember! You just testified that people were high. How could you testify that people were high without knowing who?"

"I had a general impression that some people were high. But there were a lot of people I didn't know at the party, and I didn't take any notice of which people I did know were high or not. Anyway, you can't always tell."

"You can't think of a single person whose behavior struck you

as influenced by drugs or alcohol?'' Now Miller sounded perplexed. "Not one?"

"I don't think so."

"How about Tina Claire?"

Susan Spada smiled brightly. "Maybe. Yes. Maybe Tina Claire."

"Thank you, that's all."

Griglia was on his feet. "Ms. Spada, what makes you say that
Tina Claire . . . ?" He stopped himself almost in mid word.
"Withdrawn," he said and sat down.

Susan Spada sat, waiting.

"That's all," Corino told her. "You can step down now."

"Michael," Jennifer said when they were in the car on the way to
the office. He twisted around in the front seat so he could see her.
"That business about the D.A.—what Allen Crown said this morning about why he took the case . . ."

Oh, Lord, Ryan thought, here we go. "Yes?" he said, and realized even before she spoke that at some point over the past days
he had warmed to her again. Finding Harry the bandito probably
had something to with it, knowing he had been within reach of the
party and that something he had done that day had been enough to
punish his heart.

What he felt for Jennifer wasn't affection, he decided—it was
more like sympathy, empathy, compassion. How hard this had to
be for her.

She said, "I think it's all nonsense. Even if he really said things
like that, it's . . . I don't know, some kind of tactic. I just hope you
won't worry about it."

"Thank you. I appreciate your saying it."

D.A. SEES EASY WIN, RYAN NO OPPONENT, the afternoon
edition headlined the rumors around the D.A.'s office. It was vin-
tage Crown, good research used as foundation for speculation and
innuendo. Crown had found not one but two of Ryan's co-counsel
on the Gibson case to say what a botch he had made of it.

Ryan wanted to shrug it off, but he couldn't. The trouble was
how easy it was to believe. He could hear Griglia saying it. That
was the worst part. Not that Griglia would think it, that he would
say it. Laugh about it, even.

The image of Franky Griglia laughing about what a pushover
Michael Ryan was going to be opened a floodgate. Anger poured
through, anger Ryan had not known was there, anger that went
back to law school, to the pompous and willful way Griglia had

torpedoed their clear shot at the moot-court championship that Ryan had sweated for for a whole year, the best way he could see then to break out of the pack. Anger that had built over the years of rivalry that could have been, should have been, cooperation. Ten years when Griglia would not give an inch any time he was in a situation where federal and local law enforcement required one side's bending to accommodate the other's needs.

Joey Baldasaro only crowned it all: Griglia rushing for the glory of a major drug bust despite Ryan's urgent request that he hold off until Ryan could finish developing a case and pull out his informant.

It had all been a disaster. Half of Griglia's targets had slipped through the cops' hands. Baldasaro, already suspected by his partners in crime but innocent of any connection to Griglia's dragnet, had been split from wishbone to groin on a West Side street, taking the punishment for someone else's treachery. And Ryan's case against fifteen mob captains had ultimately foundered for want of Baldasaro's testimony.

And now, more than a decade later, all of that added up only to Franky Griglia's laughing at Michael Ryan's supposed incompetence.

He knew he would have to fight to keep the need to rub Griglia's face in the dirt from becoming too important to him. He had seen other lawyers get too caught up in that kind of personal battle, and he had watched their judgment go to hell.

12

GRIGLIA'S ATTRACTION FOR THURSDAY MORNING WAS Nicholas Maclean, a tall, wiry blond in his late thirties, wearing a standard Wall Street suit tailored so well it seemed like part of his body.

Griglia offered him to the jury as a person who had worked with the defendant at a charity called Feed the Children. He had become closer to the defendant, Maclean testified, when their conversations began to include the defendant's complaints about her husband.

"And after that, did there come a time when your relationship with the defendant changed?"

"Yes."

"How?"

"We became lovers."

Ryan, knowing what was coming, was watching the jury when Maclean answered. Some of them, too, seemed to have anticipated the revelation, Constable for one. The engineer-turned-poet was proving to be one of the most alert of the jurors. Of the other jurors, it was the men who seemed more surprised by Maclean's news, especially the bus driver and the office equipment salesman, both of whom cast hard looks at Jennifer when they heard it.

"How often did you see each other?' Griglia asked.

"About once a week."

"And in the course of the relationship, did you and she have further occasion to talk about her marriage?"

"Objection," Ryan said. "Leading his own witness."

"Sustained."

"What did you talk about?"

"A lot of things."

"Can you give me some examples?"

"We talked about her marriage."

"And what did she say about it?"

"Objection. Hearsay."

"I'm only interested in the fact that the statements were made, your honor," Griglia said. "And what they indicate about the defendant's state of mind and her intentions at the time."

"I'll allow it."

"She said she was fed up, she said Ned couldn't keep riding roughshod over her, she said he was worthless, he didn't deserve to live . . . Is that enough or do you want more?" It was all delivered in a flat voice, as if he were denying to himself it had any emotional content, for him or anyone.

"Were these comments general or were they connected to specific incidents?"

"Both. Sometimes there was an incident that triggered it, and sometimes it was just general."

"And can you describe one such incident?"

"There was one time we met and she said she had just been at a party with him and he'd made a pass at a woman there, right in front of her."

"Let me interrupt you," Griglia said quickly as Ryan was getting up to object. "Were you at this party?"

"No."

"And are you testifying as to your knowledge of what happened at the party?"

"No."

"Thank you. I'm sorry for interrupting."

"That's all right. So she said he'd made a pass at this woman. And she said, it's bad enough when he does it behind my back, but if he ever humiliates me in public like that again it's all over for him—the end."

"Let me be sure I understand. She said, 'If he humiliates me in public like that again it's all over for him—the end.' Were those her exact words?"

"Yes. And then she said, I swear, if he pulls that one more time, I'll kill him. I swear I will."

"Thank you, Mr. Maclean. That's all."

Ryan did not move. Corino looked down from the bench and said, "Mr. Ryan? Any questions for this witness?"

"Yes, your honor."

He began with questions about Feed the Children. What it was, what Maclean had done there, what Jennifer had done there. A little back-door character testimony, and it helped him get his bearings.

"You said you and Mrs. Ryan were lovers."

"That's right."

"How long did that last?"

"Six months."

"So it ended six months or so before Ned Ryan was killed."

"Yes."

"Would you say that Mrs. Ryan was an enthusiastic person?"

"What do you mean?"

"Well, did she applaud enthusiastically at the theater?"

"Well . . . yes."

"And did she cry at the movies, show great pleasure with gifts, that sort of thing?"

"Yes, I guess she did."

"And was she impatient with delay? Honk her horn in traffic, that sort of thing?"

"Well, we didn't drive anywhere, not that I remember."

"Would you say that you found Mrs. Ryan to be soft-spoken and mild-mannered and given to understatement?"

Uncomfortable as Maclean was, he could not help an uneasy laugh. "Lord, no."

Ryan did not pause. "This time you were spending with Mrs. Ryan, did your wife know about it?"

No answer.

"Mr. Maclean?"

"No."

"Did that fact produce any particular behavior?"

"I don't understand."

"Did you and Mrs. Ryan go out in public much?"

"No."

"Did the two of you give parties for your friends?"

"Of course not."

"Then let me repeat my earlier question. Did the fact that your wife did not know about the affair produce any particular behavior?"

"Well, we were careful."

"You say we."

"Jen . . . Mrs. Ryan and I."

"You'd say you snuck around."

"I wouldn't say that, no."

"But others might?"

"No." Emphatic.

"You're sure?"

"Well, I suppose . . ."

Ryan let the silence go on a bit before he asked his next question.

"Did Mrs. Ryan express any anxiety of her own on this score?"

Maclean opened his mouth to answer but Ryan cut him off.

"Don't answer quickly if you're not sure. Take your time."

"Well . . . no, not really. I mean, it was a given that we . . ."

"That's fine, Mr. Maclean. Just a yes or no will do. I'll repeat it. Did Mrs. Ryan express anxiety that she might be seen with you and that her husband might object? Yes or no?"

"Well, no. I'd have to say no."

"Thank you. So she didn't seem to care about that one way or the other, with respect to herself."

"I suppose."

"I take that to mean yes."

"I suppose."

"I wonder why that would be . . . not caring whether her husband found out."

"I never thought about it."

Griglia objected loudly.

"I'm sure you didn't," Ryan commented in response to Maclean's answer, and in response to Griglia, "I withdraw the question." To Maclean: "Who broke up the affair?"

Maclean took a breath and shot a quick look at Jennifer. "She did."

"Did she say why?"

Griglia was on his feet objecting. Ryan asked to approach the bench.

"All right gentlemen," Corino said. "What's on your mind?"

"This is hearsay your honor, and it's irrelevant."

"On the contrary," Ryan argued. "All I want is the words the man heard. They're relevant as to having caused prejudice in the witness against Mrs. Ryan, and they may also be relevant as to Mrs. Ryan's state of mind and her intentions, which is why Mr. Griglia called the witness in the first place, if I understand correctly. I'm just trying to get a fuller picture of her state of mind as observed by this witness. A fairer picture, I might add."

"All right, you can go ahead. Mr. Griglia, can I assume you're entering a blanket objection to this whole line of questioning?"

"If the record can indicate it."

"I'm sure it can. All right. Let's go."

Ryan returned to the lectern and glanced at his notes for the next set of questions. "Mr. Maclean. You testified a moment ago that Mrs. Ryan broke up the affair. Did she say why?"

"Something about she didn't think there was any point."

"Is there more?"

Maclean sat motionless, staring at the back wall.

"Mr. Maclean. Is there more?" In a tone that said I know damn well there is.

"She said she saw now what Ned meant when he said it wasn't important."

"It? Did she say 'it'?"

Maclean turned to Jennifer as if to say, do I have to do this?

"Mr. Maclean?"

He sighed and looked down at the floor.

"No, she said 'affairs.' Having sex the way we did, and the way Ned did with other women."

"She said that wasn't important."

"That's right."

"And when she said that, she meant her affair with you, as well, is that right?"

"That's right."

"Wasn't important."

"Yes."

Ryan expected an objection but Griglia stayed in his seat.

"And this happened six months before Ned Ryan was killed, is that right?"

"More or less."

Ryan turned and walked to the defense table. As he sat down he got in a small parting shot. "And that was the last time you saw her . . . ?"

"No, it wasn't," Maclean astounded him by replying.

By reflex Ryan opened his mouth to ask when or why or what do you mean but he caught himself. "No more questions."

He knew that was a mistake, too, as soon as he said it. The right thing to do was to introduce a new line of questions, to bury that tag line in other subjects.

Griglia was already on his feet. "I have some redirect, your honor."

"Go ahead."

The D.A. settled back into his chair. "When did you see the defendant again?" He asked the question mildly. Ryan could not see him beyond Saundra Warneke's broad-shouldered suit, but he guessed that Griglia was fairly vibrating with eagerness.

"A couple of times."

"When were they?"

"Objection," Ryan said to break up Griglia's rhythm, though he had no grounds."

"Mr. Ryan?"

"Irrelevant."

Griglia stood. "Your honor, Mr. Ryan just asked the witness when was the last time he saw the defendant. He didn't seem to think it was irrelevant then."

"Objection overruled. Go ahead, Mr. Griglia."

"When did you see her again?"

"About two months after she broke up with me."

"What did you do?"

"We had afternoon tea, at the Plaza Hotel. I told her I wanted us to be friends."

"And what did she say?"

"She agreed." Maclean looked over at Jennifer. "Grudgingly."

Griglia hurried past the characterization. "And did you see her again, after that?"

He's fishing now, Ryan thought. He has to be.

"Yes."

"When?"

"In June."

"In June?"

Ryan was sure he heard surprise in Griglia's voice. He stood up. "Objection, your honor, the prosecutor is on a fishing expedition here."

"On the contrary, Judge. I'm simply going through the door Mr. Ryan himself opened."

Corino nodded agreement. "Overruled. Go ahead, Mr. Griglia."

"When, exactly?"

"The middle of June."

"Was it before the murder of Ned Ryan?"

"Yes. A few days before."

"And what was the occasion for your seeing her then?"

"It was a celebration."

Griglia was pacing in the small area between the prosecution table and the lectern behind it. Ryan remembered him this way in law school: Franky Griglia as caged tiger. On the edge of a major risk, getting ready to leap.

"What were you celebrating?"

"I had left my wife."

Griglia stopped pacing but he did not turn to face the witness. Instead he looked at the jury. Ryan could not see his opponent's face, but he knew the expression of intensity and portent Griglia would be wearing.

"Really?" Still facing the jury, his voice calm. "And how did you celebrate?"

Maclean seemed to be reaching for an answer. Griglia turned slowly to face him, waiting.

Ryan wished Maclean would just answer the damn question. His reluctance was convincing Griglia to keep pushing.

"We had dinner."

"Where?"

"At the Hotel Parker Meridien."

"Where at the Parker Meridien?" Griglia put an edge on the question, just enough to remind the witness where he was.

Again Maclean looked at Jennifer, a plea in his eyes. For understanding? Forgiveness? Some renewal of their connection? Ryan resisted the impulse to turn and see her reaction.

"Mr. Maclean?" No edge this time. Griglia was being careful.

Maclean's head lifted and his shoulders squared and he took a single long breath. He had made up his mind to answer this question and all the questions that would follow. It was as visible as if he had made an announcement.

"I was staying there. I had left home."

"And where did you have dinner?"

"In my room."

"In your room?" Griglia echoed.

"Yes."

"And is that all you did in your room?"

A brief hesitation. Then, with a slight smile of rueful memory, "No."

"What else did you do?"

"We made love."

It was all Ryan could do to sit there without turning on Jennifer and demanding an explanation. That or get up from the counsel table and walk out.

How could she sabotage them that way? Made adulterous love on the eve of her husband's murder and didn't tell them about it.

But he knew that the real blame belonged to Michael Ryan. To ask a question he didn't know the answer to was bad enough, a violation of the first rule of examining a witness. For the question to be useless, a throwaway, virtually unintended, raised it past the heights of folly. Fitting that the answer should be one that would demolish his client in the jury's eyes—and his own.

He stewed and tried to follow the proceedings through a red haze of anger.

He was dimly aware of activity to his right, Jennifer scribbling frantically on a pad, Miller standing to ask questions on re-cross. It wasn't proper procedure to switch lawyers in mid witness but Corino was not commenting.

Had Maclean seen Mrs. Ryan since then? No. Had they discussed their future together? Maclean said something Ryan did not try to catch about respect and friendship, making him wonder if Maclean put this testimony in the category of respect or friendship.

Griglia's next witness was another friend who had been privy to Jennifer's frustrations and her tendency to exaggerate language when it came to matters of the heart. Jennifer felt trapped and she had no way out. She talked about the relief she'd feel if only Ned were on another planet, or an astral plane.

Ryan scribbled a note to Miller: Take this witness.

At the lunch break he left the courtroom immediately, alone. Reporters crowded him in the hallway, he pushed through not saying a word. Allen Crown loomed in front of him. Ryan turned aside but Crown was still there. Ryan punched at Crown's body, the blow absorbed and deflected by the crush of people. He finally pushed clear and away, past the elevators and into a stairwell. Better to walk the thirteen flights than be trapped by Crown and the others.

More reporters buzzed around him on the courthouse steps, asking questions about Maclean's testimony. He brushed past them and walked through the damp gray noon to a crowded oriental salad bar, enormous steam tables of fried rice and chop suey and lasagna. He walked back out, not hungry.

There was a dim, seedy bar on the next block. He went in and ordered an Irish and a draft beer from a bartender whose whiskey-reddened cheeks sported gray stubble on the left side of his chin but not the right. Ryan swept up the shot glass almost before it hit the bar. He lingered over the beer.

His fault. Whatever damage there was to the jury's image of Jennifer—and it could be fatal—he could blame her only secondarily.

He was berating himself for not keeping his mouth shut, when the full implications of Maclean's testimony burst on him. He swayed on the stool, flattened his hands on the bar to keep himself upright. The bartender, too lackadaisical to shave both sides of his face, still had sharp instincts for his trade. From the far end of the long bar he moved briskly to face Ryan.

"You okay, Mac?"

Ryan nodded and ordered another shot of Irish. The bartender gave it to him and found ways to keep busy at Ryan's end of the bar. Ryan let the shot stand on the bar in front of him while he finished his beer. Proving something. He threw a ten on the bar next to the untouched whiskey and went out into the chill dampness.

He made himself go back to the courthouse. He owed it to Miller not to simply disappear, and there was no point provoking Corino. But now that he had seen the truth it would be hard indeed to sit calmly at the table with Jennifer.

The thirteenth-floor hallway was a smoky throng of people waiting to get back into the courtroom. A rush of excited conversation as he passed. A court officer unlocked the door for him and he went in and sat there alone. After a while Miller sat down next to him.

"It's not as bad as you think," she said.

It brought another pulse of anger. He closed his eyes against the world.

"She's devastated by what happened," Miller said. "And full of remorse that she didn't tell us."

He stared at his co-counsel. Could she be thinking of this only in terms of the testimony, of losing sympathy with the jury? Didn't she see that it was about the baby, about who its father was, about a cruel emotional fraud at the heart of Ryan's choice to represent Jennifer in the first place.

Jennifer came in as the courtroom started to fill. Passing behind him, she put a hand on his shoulder. "I'm sorry."

Her touch made him shudder.

Ryan sat rigidly, his eyes fixed on a spot midway between the judge and the witness box. He vaguely recognized the name of the woman Griglia called next.

She was about forty with a rosy face compliments of the corner drugstore cosmetics counter. Ryan could smell her ten-dollar perfume as she passed by on her way to the witness box. Her blue suit and white blouse were expensive but hung awkwardly, stiff with newness.

Griglia started with the usual biographical data, establishing that the witness was well educated and, by implication, wealthy.

Then he got down to business. Was she acquainted with the defendant? Yes, she was.

"Where did you and the defendant meet?"

"At MacAllister House."

"And where is that?"

"It's in upstate New York."

"And how is it you were there?"

"I had a nervous breakdown."

"Objection!" Miller was on her feet. "Your honor, may we approach?"

Corino had done a mild double take when the objection did not come from Ryan. He motioned her and Griglia to the bench. They were joined by Saundra Warneke. Ryan, a zombie, went, too.

Miller led off. "Your honor, Mr. Griglia is trying to drag in by the back door material that he knows perfectly well is irrelevant and inflammatory."

"This is all a hundred percent relevant, Judge," Griglia argued. "The circumstances under which this witness met the defendant, the surroundings, and consequently this witness's view of their friendship and the weight it had for them, these are not just relevant, they're essential."

"It's a blatant attempt to get before the jury innuendo and inferences the D.A. knows he can't touch with direct testimony because your honor has already ruled that all such testimony is barred from this proceeding."

"I'm going to allow it," Corino said. "With the proviso, Mr. Griglia, that you limit it to the witness. No questions or inferences about the defendant."

"Your honor," Miller protested, "if he gets that much in, the damage is done. No one is going to think Mrs. Ryan was there as a nurse."

"I'm going to allow it, Ms. Miller," Corino said. "Let's move on."

"Could we have the last question and answer please?" Griglia asked.

"Question: And how is it you were there?" The reporter read. "Answer: I had a nervous breakdown."

"And what kind of place was it?" Griglia asked.

"A nuthouse for rich people."

"Objection!"

"Yes, sustained. The jury will disregard the last question and answer. Mr. Griglia, I'm surprised at you."

"I'm sorry, your honor, I must have misunderstood."

"No doubt . . . Proceed."

The rest was predictable, but no less damaging for that. Jennifer had been upset about her marriage. She had said she felt trapped, that there was no way out for her. "She said she wished Ned and her father had never been in business together."

"Did she elaborate on that in any way?"

"Yes. She said it was like a chain binding her to Ned."

"Was there any reason for that?"

"I had the feeling . . ."

"Objection," Miller said quickly.

The witness stopped in mid sentence and glared at her.

"I withdraw the question," Griglia said. "What if anything else did she say on that subject?"

"She said she wished her husband would drop dead."

"Your witness," Griglia said.

"Is MacAllister House the only such place you've been?" Miller asked her, referring to a page she had taken from one of the defense's trial notebooks.

The witness hesitated.

"Is it?"

The witness looked over at Griglia.

Griglia stood. "Your honor, I'd like the record to indicate that the witness looked at me just now and that I made no response."

"Thank you very much, Mr. Griglia."

That was Franky. The Jesuits taught me how to make a profit on honesty, Ryan remembered him saying in law school.

Miller continued with the witness, getting a record of her every commitment and her decades of psychological treatment. She established first that the witness had not seen Jennifer anywhere except at MacAllister House, and there only a few times over a period of one week. Ryan wondered abstractedly if the jury would be able to appreciate the distinction Miller was making between the witness and Jennifer. He thought the opposite was more likely, and the jury would end up having more reason to think of Jennifer as unstable.

Which at the moment did not bother Ryan one bit. Unprofessional as the thought was, all he wanted right now was to see his own client convicted of murder.

13

HE RODE BACK TO THE OFFICE WITH MILLER AND JENnifer because it was the best way to avoid the reporters. No one said a word in the car. At the office he went straight to the bathroom and splashed water on his face and neck. He took his time about re-emerging.

"I sent Jennifer home so we could talk about this," Miller told him.

"I've got nothing to say."

"Well, *I* need some help with it. I didn't get any lunch. How about we have some dinner?"

The night was raw and rainy but, remarkably, there was a free taxi passing as they left the office. She gave the cabbie the address of the Shamrock. Ryan countermanded it and picked a border-Mexican restaurant uptown on Broadway, full of loud young people and louder music.

"I didn't know you had this in you," she said on the way to their table.

"Instant oblivion." He had been there once before, driven out by the pounding noise. This time it was welcome.

They ordered their usual beer and club soda and she said, "Okay, let's talk about how to deal with this."

"You have the floor."

"First of all, Jennifer is *not* a malicious liar. She's confused and frightened and she's sure people are going to turn on her . . ."

"Hold on! I thought this was about courtroom strategy."

Her intense brown eyes held his. "My strategy at the moment is to keep you on the case."

He took a long drink of beer. "You know, it occurred to me on the way here what a good thing it was for Jennifer that the baby got killed."

"Michael!"

"Think about it. The jury would look at her belly every day and wonder who the father was."

"Like you're wondering right now."

"Exactly."

"Maybe we shouldn't talk until we've had something to eat."

Food took away the lightheadedness he had not realized was there. "That's much better. Thanks."

"I'm not done yet. I'm coming home with you so we can talk there."

He could see she was ready for a fight, and he had no spirit for it. It was easier to say yes.

There were cars double parked near his building, and a couple of people leaning against one of them smoking and talking.

"I think we've got company," he said.

"So what? It's not that late. We're having a strategy session."

"Only if you leave at a decent hour."

They no-commented the reporters. Miller surprised him when they got upstairs by asking for a drink.

"Irish courage," she said. "I want to talk about you."

He poured her a drink, nothing for himself. "We can talk about me another time. Unless you want to talk about how I'm going to withdraw from the case." There had to be a way around Corino.

"No, Ryan. We'll do it now. I'm not going to sit by and watch you beat yourself up anymore. I do my homework, remember. I did my homework about you, too. You've done great things in your life, and it's a tragedy that you don't give yourself credit. You put the bad guys behind bars, for heaven's sake. That's the great American myth, the white hats against the black hats, and you lived it. You give yourself grief because of Ned. It's like I said before, you didn't bring him up alone. And suppose you didn't inspire him, what about all the people you did inspire? How about the young lawyers who worked for you and watched you work when you were a U.S. Attorney?''

"Look I appreciate this. I know you mean well, but let's drop it, okay?''

''No, it's not okay, damn it. You're going to sit there and hear me out, because this is important to me.''

He thought: If I push her away, she's going to close herself off, and something important between us will die. Something he sensed he needed more than he would have guessed.

"All right," he said. "I'm listening."

"I asked around about you before we met that first time, and a lot more after. I know you changed people's lives, because I know some damn good lawyers, including a couple who've blown my doors off in court, who use you as a model of how to prepare and try a case. And they're not shy about admitting it. If you want to think your life was a waste, go ahead. But it's bullshit.''

He remembered Jeff Rosen saying he'd learned more watching him prosecute the Klein case than in a year watching his own boss and mentor. Ryan had taken that for polite flattery. This was something different.

"Another thing, Ryan. Self-doubt is great armor against over-confidence, but only if you keep it within limits. We talk a lot about reasonable doubt. That's an idea you should pay more attention to. It has applications outside the courtroom.''

The downstairs-intercom bell rang. The doorman wouldn't bother him for a reporter, and he wasn't expecting anyone.

It rang again. He picked up the receiver. "Yes?"

"Mrs. Ryan here to see you, Mr. Ryan."

He wished he could refuse to see her, but the reporters would have a field day with that.

"Now we can have a real strategy session," he informed his co-counsel. "Jennifer is on her way up."

Miller put her drink down. "You and I talked once about why you took Jennifer's case. I asked you if it was because of the baby. If it was, I can see where you'd be very angry right now. Even so, if you could just give her a chance to explain . . . Sometimes there are reasons." She stood up. "I'm going so the two of you can talk, but I'll be back.''

"Stay, please." He meant it.

"No. This is between you and her."

She was not long out the door when the bell rang. Ryan let Jennifer in.

"I met Kassia in the hall," Jennifer said.

"That's not why you came." Holding his anger in check.

"It's about . . . what happened in court. I tried to call you. I know there's no excuse for not telling you about Nico."

Ryan could not speak.

She shrank from his visible anger. "You hate me. You think I tricked you." She was forcing the words out, holding back tears. "If I did, I didn't mean to. I was so desperate. And I was punished for what I did, wasn't I? I lost the baby. Isn't that enough?" And when he did not respond, "It was Ned's. I know it was Ned's."

"Stop!"

He slammed the heel of his fist against the wall. She recoiled as if he had struck her, then turned with her face to the door. Her shoulders shook; she gulped out wrenching sobs. Despite his anger he thought of the time they had cried together and had a fleeting, absurd impulse to comfort her.

He went into the living room and sat in the easy chair. He would see this through somehow. Miller was probably right: Jennifer was not malicious. Impulsive—out of control, even—but there was a peculiar innocence about it.

She came in slowly, looking lost and helpless.

He motioned for her to sit down.

"All right." He was working hard to appear detached. "You said you were desperate. Desperate to have me as your lawyer, I guess you mean. And that's why you didn't tell me about Maclean . . . because I would think the baby wasn't Ned's?"

"Yes . . ."

"But why were you so desperate to have *me* represent you?" Knowing as he asked that he should have pressed for a better answer long before any of this happened.

He watched the play of emotions on her face: the instinct to give a quick convenient answer banished by memory of what that had led to in the past.

"I was afraid." A small voice.

"Afraid of what?"

"Of the other lawyers."

She sounded like a little girl. Ryan remembered a time in the office, Miller leading Jennifer to a chair like an errant child. This is a thirty-five-year-old woman, he reminded himself.

"I don't understand. What lawyers were you afraid of?"

"All of them."

"All but me. Why?"

Miller's drink was on the side table next to her. She drank it all, shuddering as it went down.

"The people who killed Ned are . . . very powerful. I couldn't trust anyone."

"You know who killed Ned?" He didn't believe it for a minute.

"Not exactly who . . ."

"What does that mean?"

"He was involved with dangerous people. Everybody says so."

"Who? Who says so?"

"You. Kassia. Craig."

"You didn't know that then."

"I knew enough. Enough to be afraid after my lawyers told me to say I was guilty."

"What about it made you afraid?"

"Nothing specific . . . it was only a feeling I had. But I was right."

"So I was the only one you could trust." Playing along.

"You were his father. You wouldn't make deals with them."

"Them?"

"The real killer, or the people behind him."

A certain logic. "And that's why you lied to me."

"No. I didn't lie, I just . . ."

"Held back the truth."

"I was afraid to tell you . . . afraid you wouldn't understand." She started to cry again. He brought her some tissues.

"I gave Nico such a hard time," she said when she had herself back under control. "We were only together about four times in the whole six months. And at the end I was sure I had all the need for revenge out of my system. But then Ned got so weird that last month, distant and moody, and he wouldn't tell me why. I was sure it was me, that he'd found someone else, someone younger. He was busy more than usual, and he looked haunted. And his sex drive was gone—with me, anyway. That's what convinced me there was somebody else. I felt so lost and abandoned. And so angry with Ned. So when Nico called me up and said he wanted to celebrate because he'd finally left his wife for good, I thought, why not . . . I didn't want to sleep with him. Just dinner and drinks and a little comfort. Someone solid to lean on. Someone who thought I was pretty, and desirable."

She stopped for a moment, gathering herself for what came next.

"I got drunk. I won't say I didn't know what I was doing. Somewhere inside I guess I did. We both got drunk and fell into bed and as soon as it was over we fell asleep. I was horrified, in the morning. It wasn't quite the most dangerous time of the month, but I douched and squirted myself full of spermicide—like some kind of ritual cleansing, to wash the whole experience away. To protect myself from my own stupidity. Can you understand? I was so sure Ned was about to leave me for another woman.''

"Was he?'' Being a lawyer in spite of himself. Or maybe just a father.

"No, I don't think so. It was something else. Or, if it was that, he changed his mind. He came to me, I guess it was on the Tuesday before the Friday he was killed. Nico was Sunday, so Ned had to be Tuesday. And he apologized for being so terrible. And I believed him. We made love that night. Wednesday and Thursday, too. Friday he wanted to, before the party, but I said no, let's wait.'' She started to cry again.

His anger was dissolving. He could only think that her mistakes about who to love and trust, who to talk to and how much to say, were not so very different from his own mistakes as a father and a husband. Mistakes he had not let himself see until far too late.

But empathy and understanding could not banish his doubts. He still did not know if in a moment of fury she had killed his son.

He did know that he would not turn his back on this case. Jennifer was entitled to the defense he'd promised. Miller had reminded him of the lawyer he once had been, and in spite of all that had happened since those days he believed that person still existed.

If that Michael Ryan was ever going to be brought back to life, now was the time.

For months now he had been split in two—burying his need for truth and retribution in pursuit of goals that had seemed more important. That would be harder than ever now, but somehow he would do it.

"Relax,'' he told Miller when she came back. "I'm still on the team. I'll give it my best.''

And while he was at it, he might even show Franky Griglia who was really the top gun in town.

14

GRIGLIA'S FIRST WITNESS FOR THE DAY WAS DONALD
Garfield. Griglia presented him as a person who had been having
preliminary business talks with Ned and whom Ned had invited to
Hugo Hill's party. The D.A. got straight to Garfield's going down
in the elevator and seeing Jennifer leaving the building lobby at a
few minutes after nine. Griglia established that Garfield had looked
at his watch before he left the party and again as soon as he got to
his car, leaving only a small window of time when the developer
could have seen Jennifer.

Ryan started with a few questions that partly rehearsed information Garfield had already given Griglia. As he did, he let his
apparent perplexity increase.

"Did you actually see Mrs. Ryan coming out of the stairway?"

"No, sir. If you put it that way, I guess I didn't."

"Then could she have just been standing in that part of the lobby
and decided to leave?"

"I guess maybe she could."

"Could she have come in and gone back out again without reaching the stairway?"

"Yes. I didn't think of it that way."

"So she could have been standing there some period of time and
walked out, or she could have just walked in and turned around and
left. Is that right?"

"Asked and answered, your honor." Griglia was angry.

"Sustained. Do you have a different question, Mr. Ryan?"

"Mr. Garfield, you said you were having preliminary business
conversations with Ned Ryan. Is that right?"

"Yes."

"How were they going?"

"They weren't. They were dead."

"Did you ask people about Ned Ryan?"

"Yes."

"And did you make your decision because of things you heard about him?"

"Yes."

"What sort of things? Good things? Bad things?"

"Bad things."

"Was one of the people you talked to about Ned Ryan at the party you've been testifying about?"

"Yes."

"Do you know his name?"

"Not really. It's hard to remember everybody's name at a party."

"Do you remember what he said?"

"Objection," Griglia quickly said.

"Your honor, we're only interested in the man's state of mind."

"All right, Mr. Ryan, but be careful."

"Thank you, your honor." And to the witness: "You were about to tell us what the man at the party said."

"Well, he wasn't too happy about Mr. Ned Ryan."

"Objection."

Ryan said, "Mr. Garfield, if you could try to tell us his words."

"Oh, sorry . . . He said Ned Ryan had killed his deal, and if he had his druthers he'd have killed Ned Ryan."

"He said he wanted to kill Ned Ryan?"

"Yes."

Ryan was watching the jury. They were all fixed attentively on Garfield except the bus driver, who seemed to be asleep.

"And this was at Hugo Hill's party, the one you've been testifying about here today?"

"That's right."

"Thank you, Mr. Garfield. That's all."

Ryan expected Griglia to try to minimize the testimony on redirect examination, but the D.A. said he had no more questions.

After lunch Griglia called his out-of-town pathologist to the stand and spent the first half hour establishing that he was a world-renowned expert on head wounds and had spoken hundreds of times on the subject before august audiences and testified for prosecution or defense in major trials all over the country.

Griglia took the pathologist through a meticulous description of the scalp wounds and the skull fractures. He paid gruesome attention to the bruising and abrasion of the edges of the scalp wounds, making the point for each wound that although such a wound might look like an incision the pathologist could state with a reasonable degree of medical certainty that the wound was created by a blunt, not an edged instrument: the sculpture, not an axe. Griglia showed his blow-ups of the autopsy photographs of the wounds so the pathologist could point out the marks he claimed had been made by the tiny bumps and ridges of Wingless Bird's rough surface, the marks which led to his certainty that the sculpture was the instrument which had caused the wounds.

Knowing from the pathologist's testimony in other cases that he would be a strong witness, the defense lawyers had debated how to deal with him. Ryan had been all for letting testimony about the wounds go unchallenged. If Jennifer didn't strike the blows, their number and kind did not matter. There was no point in encouraging a repetition of gruesome testimony. It would only intensify the jury's need to convict somebody.

By inclination and experience, Miller was reluctant to let any strong prosecution testimony go unsullied. The area she had most hoped to exploit was the force needed to produce blows to the forehead that killed quickly. The defense pathology experts had reported that people were surprisingly able to survive severe blows to the head. But it would be a risky business to bring that out, because there were too many ways it all depended on the peculiarities of the individual and the event.

Griglia made it harder by anticipating it.

"How much force would it have taken to inflict killing blows in that region of the skull?" the D.A. asked.

"Relatively speaking, a great deal of force."

"How could that force have been applied?"

"Not necessarily by someone very strong. It's more a question of physics than of muscle."

"Can you explain that in greater detail?"

"A lot depends on the speed of the weapon and its weight. Also the motion of the victim." He led Griglia through a simple version of the way force depended on momentum. Griglia drew diagrams and formulas on a big drawing pad mounted on an easel. It was a smooth performance, obviously well rehearsed.

"A roundhouse blow with a long object weighted at one end could easily inflict the damage I observed in this case."

"I show you again defense exhibit eighteen, a piece of sculpture called Wingless Bird. Is this such an object?"

"Yes it is."

"With the court's permission, I'd like to have you demonstrate the sort of blow you mean."

"Objection," Ryan said.

"I'll allow it if the witness can do it sitting where he is."

"Can he stand?" Griglia asked.

"All right, but keep it to a minimum."

A court officer gave Wingless Bird to the pathologist. He stood up and hefted the sculpture while at Griglia's direction the court officer placed a thick chair cushion on the rail of the witness stand. The pathologist held the sculpture out straight behind him and swung it around, overhead and down in a single smooth motion like a tennis serve, his arm more or less stiff at the elbow. Not at all like the motion Jennifer had made, Ryan noted, or Lynn Archbold's demonstration.

He could almost see a bird in motion as the curve of gray metal, more graceful than he had realized, arced through the air with tangible force and slammed down into the cushion with an impressive thud, raising a cloud of dust motes. The rail of the witness stand protested audibly at the blow.

Spectators and jury gasped. The court officer removed the cushion and ran a hand over the rail to see if it had been cracked.

Miller got them up to the bench. "I'd like the record to show that the officer examined the rail in the presence of the jury to see if it was damaged by the blow."

"What's the point?" Griglia challenged.

"I believe it's prejudicial."

Corino glowered at her from under his eyebrows, then turned to the jury. "Disregard anything you saw the officer do." And to an unhappy Kassia Miller: "Let's get back to work."

"Is it your testimony that a blow of that type, struck by a person of average strength, could have inflicted the wounds you observed?" the D.A. asked.

"Yes. Especially a person with relatively long arms. It increases the size of the arc, and that increases the speed, which means greater force."

"When you say a person of average strength, does that include women?"

"Certainly."

If ever there was an expert witness who was better left alone, Ryan thought, Griglia's pathologist was it. He wrote *No* on his yellow pad and pushed it toward Miller. She glanced at the note, stood up and said, "Just a few questions," and then proceeded to get the pathologist to repeat and reinforce many of the things he had already said.

* * *

Ryan tried to keep in mind the principles of constructive criticism he had never completely mastered as unit chief for the U.S. Attorney.

"I'm sure you had something in mind," he snapped. "I'm dying to hear about it."

"You're dying to throttle me," Miller said. "I don't blame you. But I did have something in mind, and I think I accomplished it. I got him to say his demonstration depended on the victim being braced in position or moving toward the blow. And that he had practiced with the Bird to deliver the blow in the most powerful way."

"Well . . ." Ryan said, not quite a concession.

"And I also got him to repeat that he could not tell how tall Ned's assailant was, but that the taller the assailant was and the longer the assailant's arms, the more force the blow would have had, all other things being equal."

"He'd already said it once. The only time the jury needed to hear it again was in our summation. And what good does it do us, anyway? You're not the defendant, Jennifer is."

"Great, Ryan! A short-person joke."

"I just don't see the point."

He was going to say more but backed off. Remember the Gibson case, he told himself. Don't be too critical. Don't give orders about things that can't be undone.

"Look at it this way," she said to him. "The jury was going to be thinking about blows to the head all weekend, anyway. This way maybe they'll think about *unlikely* blows to the head."

15

BEFORE GRIGLIA CALLED THE WEEK'S FIRST WITNESS, he asked for a bench conference.

"Your honor, I don't believe in springing surprise witnesses, and I make it a rule that none of the lawyers who work for me should do it."

Something is coming, Ryan thought. That's the first time he's referred to the fact that he's the District Attorney and not an ordinary prosecutor.

"Unfortunately, I find myself today in the position of having to do that very thing. I have a witness I didn't even know existed until a few days ago. I owe it to the defense for having brought the witness to my attention in the first place."

"Can you favor us with a name?" Corino asked testily.

"Yes, Judge. It's one of the guests at the party. His name is Harry Bundesman, and he's the man referred to in cross-examination as having made threatening remarks about the victim."

There was more, but Ryan heard only the echo of Miller's long-ago warning: *A guy who hates Ned and said so at the party and has an alibi is no use to us.*

He watched Harry Bundesman on his way to the witness box—medium height, thin and looking even more wan and frail than he had in Lawrence's photos.

"Yours," Ryan wrote on his yellow pad.

Griglia went slowly and carefully with Bundesman, first establishing his general business history then focusing in on the part that mattered.

"What, if any, business dealings did you have with Ned Ryan?"

"He arranged a substantial mortgage for an industrial park development of mine."

"What was the tenor of those dealings?"

"They were very unpleasant."

From there, Griglia led his witness up to the night of the party, allowing him to testify that he had attended with a "friend." Did he remember a conversation he'd had there with another businessman? Yes, he did, and he proceeded to describe Donald Garfield far more convincingly than Garfield had ever described Harry Bundesman.

"What, if anything, did you say to him about Ned Ryan?"

"Negative things, I'm sure. I thought Ned Ryan was a bad person to deal with and I said so to anyone who'd listen."

A few spectators thought that was funny. The judge did not. He rapped his gavel at them.

Griglia next had Bundesman testify about the rest of his evening. He had left the party at about seven forty-five, had seen no contact between Ned Ryan and Tina Claire, whom he did not remember, and no argument between Ned and Jennifer Ryan. He had gone to a bar with several people—"six that I'm sure of, and I think there were a couple more who came along but weren't really with us"—and then taken the nine-fifteen New Jersey Transit train, which got him to Rahway, where he was staying with friends. It arrived at nine forty-five, two minutes late, he remembered.

He had flown back to Arizona on Saturday and not heard about Ned Ryan's death until Monday, when the friend he had been staying with in Rahway called to tell him about it. He'd had a mild heart attack later that day.

"Your witness," Griglia said.

Miller started to stand up next to Ryan. He put a firm hand on her arm.

"One moment, your honor."

He scrawled on his yellow pad, "My mess, I clean." Thinking, I'm not going to dump this on her.

"Woman better," she scrawled back.

"Okay." He had disagreed with her judgment about the bandito too often.

She walked to the lectern and took a moment to smile pleasantly at Harry Bundesman.

"Hello, Mr. Bundesman. I'm Kassia Miller. I'm one of the lawyers for Jennifer Ryan."

"Hello." Uncertain.

"We're grateful to you for coming here all the way from Arizona. Was it a difficult trip?"

"Not too bad."

She smiled again, apologetically this time. "I'll try not to keep you up there any longer than I have to. There are just a few parts of your testimony I'd like to understand better."

She waited for him to nod his acceptance. Ryan thought she was playing him just right.

"Mr. Bundesman, when you testified just now that you said negative things about Ned Ryan, isn't it true that your actual words were that you'd like to kill him?"

"They might have been. I said that a lot, too."

"That you'd like to kill him?"

"Yes."

"So you said to a lot of people that you'd like to kill Ned Ryan."

"Yes, I did."

"Did you say you'd like to kill Ned Ryan . . ."

"Objection, your honor! Counsel is repeating the testimony. The question's been answered."

"Sustained. Move on, Ms. Miller."

"For how long a period of time did you tell people you wanted to kill Ned Ryan?"

"Your honor."

"No. Mr. Griglia, I'll allow it. It's a different question."

"Could I have it read back please?" Miller requested sweetly.

The court reporter read: " 'For how long a period of time did you tell people you wanted to kill Ned Ryan?' "

"Ever since that deal I testified about."

"That was more than a year."

"Almost two."

"Are you holding up all right, Mr. Bundesman?"

"I'm a little tired, but I'm okay so far."

"I won't keep you much longer. During these two years you were telling anyone who'd listen that you wanted to kill Ned Ryan, did you make any specific plans to do that?"

He smiled, a pale, thin smile. "No."

She smiled back. In her gentlest voice she said, "Mr. Bundesman, did you in fact kill Ned Ryan?"

The witness blinked rapidly and turned paler. Sweat stood out on his forehead. He grabbed the rail of the witness stand.

One of the court officers took an alarmed step in his direction. For a moment Ryan thought they were going to have a medical crisis in the courtroom, but Bundesman caught his breath and found his voice. "No."

"Thank you, Mr. Bundesman. I have no more questions."

Griglia was standing at the prosecution table staring at her.

"No further questions," the D.A. said, biting off the words.

Griglia's next witness was a police fingerprint expert named Masterson. The D.A. did his usual thorough job establishing the man's credentials, which included analyzing the fingerprints from thousands of crime scenes.

Griglia next had him describe briefly the crime scene unit's dusting for fingerprints at Hugo Hill's and lifting or photographing the impressions. Masterson told the jury about two partial fingerprints that had been identified as possibly having been left in the murder room by the defendant.

Then Griglia asked him, "As a result of your experience and expertise, have you formed an opinion as to the likelihood of finding fingerprints on certain surfaces?"

"I have."

"And does that opinion apply to prosecution exhibit eighteen in evidence?'' Griglia picked up Wingless Bird and brandished it for the jury's benefit while making a show of attempting to read its identification tag.

"Yes, it does."

"And what can you tell us about this exhibit, with respect to fingerprints, with a reasonable degree of professional certainty?''

"I'd say the chances are one in a million you'd ever find a fingerprint on that thing. It's too rough."

"Then you'd say that there's no conclusion to be drawn from the *absence* of the defendant's fingerprints on it?''

"Objection," Ryan said. "He's leading the witness."

"I'll rephrase it. What conclusion, if any, can be drawn from the absence of the defendant's fingerprints on this exhibit?''

"None."

"Is it possible to draw the conclusion from the absence of her fingerprints that she did not handle it?''

"No."

"Objection," Ryan said. "Leading, and it calls for conjecture."

"It's not conjecture, your honor, it's expert opinion."

"May we approach?" Ryan asked, standing, full of fire he had not known was there.

"Your honor," he said when the lawyers were gathered at the bench, "this is meaningless. Based on the witness' testimony it's impossible to say with certainty that *any* person did or did not handle that thing. Singling out Mrs. Ryan among all the people who *may* have handled it is inflammatory and prejudicial."

"Your honor, we have other evidence to present to indicate that in fact she *did* handle it. I am simply trying to make the point here that the absence of fingerprint evidence in no way *excludes* that possibility."

"That's ridiculous. Is he going to put someone on to say that no one saw the crime and therefore there's no evidence to show she didn't do it? Where do we stop with this?''

"I think I'm going to overrule it, Mr. Ryan."

"I'm afraid I've lost my train of thought," Griglia said, back at the lectern. "Can we have the last question and answer, please?''

The court reporter read: "Question: 'Is it possible to draw the conclusion from the absence of her fingerprints that she did not handle it? And the answer was No."

"No more questions."

This was to be Miller's witness on cross-examination. Ryan leaned close to her and whispered, "You know what to do?''

"You bet your ass."

She walked briskly to the lectern.

"Sergeant, based on your last answer, would you say that the fingerprint evidence or lack of it, with respect to prosecution exhibit eighteen, precludes the possibility that Mr. Hugo Hill, whose possession it was, handled that statue?"

"No, it doesn't."

"Mr. Hill might have handled it?"

"He might have."

"Objection," Griglia said.

"I'm just following your honor's ruling," Miller said innocently.

"Objection overruled. Go ahead, Ms. Miller."

"What about Tina Claire, the sculptor who made it and who the jury has heard was present on the night in question. If she picked it up like this"—she grabbed it like a club—"would she have left fingerprints?"

"No, I don't believe so."

The judge got the point. "All right, Ms. Miller, I concede. Ladies and gentlemen of the jury, I'm sorry if this is confusing, but I'm going to ask you to disregard everything you've heard about who may or may not have handled the sculpture based on the lack of fingerprint evidence."

He had the court reporter strike the testimony and then said, "Let me replace this whole line of questions with one of my own. Sergeant Masterson, can you say one way or the other, based on the absence of fingerprints, that *any* person handled or didn't handle prosecution exhibit eighteen?"

"No."

"Thank you. Go ahead, Ms. Miller."

She embarked on the planned part of the defense cross-examination, first an attack on the identification of the fragmentary fingerprints as being Jennifer's, then a tour through the crime scene to determine what other fingerprints had been found in the room and how little success the police had had in identifying the ones that did not belong to Hill or his sometime lover. It was a routine exercise in demonstrating police fallibility. Routine but valuable.

Ryan pulled the fingerprint folder from the crime scene section of the defense file cart. For the moment his thoughts were more on Harry Bundesman and on his own surge of combativeness about Masterson than on the fingerprints found at the crime scene. He flipped in the file to a picture of the crime scene taken after Ned's body had been removed. To help focus his mind on the testimony he set himself the task of finding in the photo each object Masterson mentioned as he referred to his notes in response to Miller's questions.

And saw something he had missed before.

Reining in his excitement, he turned to the police fingerprint report, forcing himself to keep his motions slow, infuriating himself with his inability to get immediately to the information he needed but not wanting to let the jury or Griglia or the witness sense that he was on the track of anything important.

Miller finished her questioning and turned to him to be sure she hadn't missed anything. He shook his head: don't give the witness up.

"Just a second, your honor," she said and came over to the defense table. Ryan got up to meet her, holding the fingerprint report and the crime scene picture.

"Your honor, may we approach?" he said.

Corino waved them up.

"Your honor, I know this is unorthodox, but I've discovered an unexpected line of questions for this witness, and rather than explain it all to Ms. Miller it would be much simpler if I just asked the witness a few questions."

Corino looked skeptical. Ryan took a quick glance at the clock and said, "Your honor, this way we can get it done before the lunch recess. Otherwise we'll have to recess now and call the witness back."

"All right, Mr. Ryan. You're playing on my weakness, don't think I don't know it. But go ahead. Quickly and directly."

He went to the lectern. "Sergeant Masterson, does the list of objects in your official report, which is in evidence, include absolutely every object in the room?"

"I believe so."

"You're sure of that. Everything in the room is on your report." Ryan held up a copy between thumb and forefinger.

"It depends on what you mean by everything."

"Yes or no, please. Is everything in the room on your report?"

"Yes."

Ryan stared at him hard but said not a word.

"Well, no," Masterson amended.

"Which is it?"

"No."

"What objects are not on your report?"

"A few things . . . I don't remember exactly."

"Did the crime scene unit dust everything or otherwise try to develop any latent fingerprints that might have been there?"

''Not on the walls.''

''That's all?''

''I think so.''

''All the small objects people would touch?''

''Not all the books.''

Corino interrupted. ''Quick and direct, Mr. Ryan.''

''I apologize, your honor. I'm almost done.'' And to the witness: ''Let me ask you this—considering only the objects you or the crime scene unit actually dusted or otherwise examined for fingerprints, are all of those on your list?''

''No.''

''Why not?''

''There were no prints on some things.''

''No prints at all?''

''That's right.''

''Isn't that odd?''

''No. Some things don't take prints. Like the murder weapon.''

''Move to strike the answer,'' Ryan said.

''Yes, strike it,'' Corino said. ''The witness will refer to evidence by exhibit number.''

''Some things don't take prints because they're rough,'' Masterson volunteered.

''What about smooth things?''

''They take prints well, in general.''

''And were there any smooth things that were dusted and were not on your list?''

''I don't remember.''

''Let me ask you a hypothetical question, then. If there was a smooth object with no fingerprints, how could that be?''

''A lot of ways. It's decorative or it's out of reach or it's so delicate nobody touches it. Or it gets cleaned, which might remove the prints, or it's just not something people normally handle.''

''Not something people handle?''

''Right.''

''Let me be sure I understand. Smooth things take prints well, but if they're the kind of thing nobody touches and they were cleaned recently they might not have prints.''

''Objection. Counsel is testifying.''

''I'll allow it, if counsel will try to keep his word.''

''Thank you, your honor. Sergeant, I'm going to ask the court officer here to give you this copy of your report marked in evidence and ask you if you see any mention there of a telephone.''

Masterson barely looked at the report. "I don't believe there is."

"In fact you *know* there is no telephone mentioned on that report."

No answer.

"Isn't that true?"

No answer.

"Let me have the officer give you prosecution's exhibit twelve. Can you tell us what it is?"

"It's a photograph of the crime scene."

"And what do you see on the table on the upper right?"

"A lamp."

"Anything else?"

"A note pad."

"Do you see a telephone?"

"Yes."

That brought a satisfying gasp from the gallery, and some widened eyes on the jury.

"Would you describe it?"

"A telephone."

"What kind?" Ryan bore down, remembering his frustration when his own law enforcement witnesses would get their backs up on the witness stand. It accomplished nothing and it made a terrible impression on the jury—and they all did it, Ryan's advice to the contrary notwithstanding.

The reaction he had dreaded then was the one he was hoping for now. So far Masterson was being satisfyingly uncooperative.

"A white Princess telephone." Surly, reluctant. Perfect.

"Sergeant, did you or any member of the crime scene unit dust that telephone for fingerprints?"

Silence. Ryan could almost hear the man's mind grinding . . . admit it had no prints or try to get away with the claim that it had been missed or forgotten in the commotion.

Alert for a reaction from Griglia, Ryan sensed a stir behind him. He turned to see Griglia and Warneke whispering urgently.

"Can we approach, please, your honor?" Ryan headed for the bench, talking as he went. "I have an unusual request but it's important." He ignored Corino's stern look, a warning to wait for Griglia. "If you could make sure no one leaves the courtroom for a few minutes. Otherwise the horse may be gone before we bolt the door."

He turned to face the courtroom on the last words, even before Corino said, "I'd like an explanation, Mr. Ryan."

Detective Garrity was getting up from his seat in the front row and heading up the aisle. Ryan turned pointedly back to Corino, who said again, more severely, "An explanation, Mr. Ryan?" even as he motioned with his gavel to the court officer at the main court-room doors.

Griglia joined them. Before the D.A. could start to bluster, Ryan said, "I'd like to ask you to seal Sergeant Masterson's office and send a court officer over to secure the garbage."

"I don't like this circus, Mr. Ryan," Corino said. The admo-nition sounded real enough, but Ryan guessed that underneath it the judge was enjoying the hell out of himself.

Griglia was as angry as Ryan had seen him in court. "Your honor, Mr. Ryan is using this meaningless so-called discovery to cast the prosecution in the light of concealing evidence. That's pat-ently untrue and unfair and I would ask your honor to admonish Mr. Ryan and bring this whole charade to an end."

"Your honor, I regret the appearance of making the prosecution or the police into concealers of evidence. I'm concerned about losing important evidence. If Sergeant Masterson has notes which he inadvertently did not include in the discovery materials, I'm afraid that by the same sort of inadvertence someone might acci-dentally throw those notes away. And wouldn't it be a shame if by coincidence that happened at the very moment we realize their importance?"

"All right, gents, enough of this. I'm going to call a recess so the jury and anybody else who wants to can get lunch, and so we can send some people around to look through Sergeant Masterson's office."

Griglia's stony expression did not waver. "I don't like the ap-pearance it creates but I won't object, if that's the only way to get past this."

Corino seemed surprised by Griglia's quick acquiescence. Ryan was astonished—Franky should have been protesting loudly against the search.

The judge rapped his gavel. "Ladies and gentlemen . . ."

"Your honor!"

"What now, Mr. Ryan?"

"Can I suggest that we include Mr. Griglia's office in the search?"

"Is that necessary?" Griglia challenged. "It's a big office . . ." Griglia was angry, but still not particularly concerned. Ryan did not like it.

"And Ms. Warneke's," he added quickly.

"Your honor!" This time Griglia was agitated. "Hasn't this gone far enough? We're talking about taking a lot of time, and I don't see what good it will do."

"You didn't feel that way a moment ago," the judge observed.

"That was only one office. By the time you go through all my papers, not to mention Ms. Warneke's . . . She's preparing other cases."

"I think it might be worth it," Corino said.

"A moment please, your honor." Griglia moved away for a colloquy with Saundra Warneke.

He's madder than this calls for, Ryan thought. Maybe he didn't know until now: they didn't warn him about it and now he's stuck with someone else's stupid decision.

Griglia was back quickly. "I think we can save the court some time." He was trying to seem heartily cooperative, but he was rushing it, pushing too hard. "The prosecution will stipulate that someone, Sergeant Masterson or someone in the crime scene unit, examined that telephone for fingerprints and didn't find any prints on it—if that closes the issue."

Ryan was not about to let him off the hook. "Well, your honor, I appreciate Mr. Griglia's candor, but I do need to ask a few follow-up questions."

"As long as you limit it."

Corino rapped his gavel again and explained to the jury and for the record that the prosecution was willing to say that the telephone had been examined for prints and that no prints had been found on it, and that the jury should consider that to be evidence in the case.

"Sergeant Masterson," Ryan said, "in your expert opinion, do people leave fingerprints on telephones of the type and design found at the crime scene?"

"Yes." Still surly.

"On the receiver?"

"Yes."

"On the base?"

"Sometimes."

"On the base of a Princess phone? Would you say more often than not?"

"I suppose so, yes."

"Can you recall any other time in your experience when you dusted a telephone and found it without prints?"

He took the time to think about it, or to give that appearance. "Not that I recall specifically at the moment."

"Was there any evidence that the room had been wiped clean in general?"

"Well . . ."

Ryan picked up a copy of the fingerprint report.

"No."

"But there were no prints on the phone."

"Apparently not."

"None at all?"

"None."

"Thank you, Sergeant, that's all."

When the jury had left for lunch, Ryan made a motion for a mistrial based on the prosecution's withholding evidence favorable to the defendant. He did not expect it to succeed, and it didn't. Still, for a change they were on the offensive.

16

THE DEFENSE TEAM COULD BARELY CONTAIN ITSELF until Corino had left for lunch.

"Let's get out of here," Ryan said. "This is no place to be dancing a jig."

"Ryan, you're wonderful," Miller said. "I told you it's not over till it's over."

"And it's not over yet." He headed out of the courtroom. "We have plenty to do."

The hallway was bedlam, ablaze with television lights, reporters pushing forward shouting questions.

"No comment," Ryan said over and over on the way to the elevator.

Downstairs a phalanx of reporters blocked their way to the car.

"Jennifer Ryan has always maintained her innocence," Ryan said. "We see no reason to be surprised that the evidence supports her."

"What about Griglia?" somebody shouted. "Was he holding out on you?"

"I can't comment on that." Implying he would like to.

"You should have told them Franky's a liar, a cheat and a thief," Miller said on the way to the office.

"Let's not get carried away."

"Yes, let's get carried away. For a few minutes, anyway. You were terrific. Michael Ryan rides again!"

The car pulled up in front of the office. "Inside, everybody," Ryan commanded.

The first thing he did was to call Craig Lawrence. "I need the outgoing calls for the night of the murder from whatever phones are registered to Hugo Hill. If you can, get him to give you the number for the phone in the murder room. That's the one we want. I need it yesterday."

He hung up and collapsed into a chair.

"Would somebody explain this to me?" Jennifer said. "I know you did something good just by how upset the D.A. got, but what does it mean?"

Miller was grinning as she answered her. "We just found out, because you have a very smart lawyer, and the jury found out, too, that somebody wiped the telephone clean in the room Ned was killed in."

"Yes, I got that."

"Well, if somebody wiped it clean, somebody was there who did not want the police to know he was there. So that same somebody must have known that the police were going to be interested in who was there. Which means he must have known Ned was dead or was going to be dead. But he had to use the phone anyway." She stopped and looked at Ryan. "Why? And when? Before the murder? After the murder? After the murder he'd just pick it up with a handkerchief."

"If he had one."

"How else did he wipe the phone clean? Before doesn't make sense. Make a phone call and then kill somebody?"

"Maybe Ned walked in on somebody who didn't want to be walked in on," Ryan speculated.

"But Ned was already there," Jennifer reminded him.

"He could have left and come back, if he was really killed at nine or later," Miller offered.

"Even so, I don't want to get too excited," Ryan said. "We think there was someone in the room. It might have been the murderer. That's all we know now." Unless the person who wiped the

phone off was Jennifer Kneeland Ryan, he thought, and quickly
dismissed it. "Let's get to work. We've got to be back at court in
an hour."

The afternoon session began with a surprise from Griglia.

"I spoke with my associates during the lunch break," he said at
a bench conference before Corino called for the jury. "It seems
they had some material related to Hugo Hill's telephones they
thought was too unproductive to tell me about. It was put in a dead
file and as a result I'm afraid it wasn't forwarded to the defense. It
appears not to contain any material relevant to this trial, but under
the circumstances I want to err on the side of completeness."

He held out his hand to Saundra Warneke, who put a file folder
in it. He handed it up to the judge.

"It's the LUDs for Hill's telephone on the night of the murder."

Corino glanced through it and handed it to Ryan.

"Local call records," Griglia explained. "There was no long
distance after five p.m. We've got those, too, if you want them."

"Please." While Warneke went to get them, Ryan said, "We'll
need some time with these your honor."

"I'm happy to have Mr. Ryan follow this up, your honor, but
I'm confident my people are right and there's nothing here of value."

"How close are you to the end of your case, Mr. Griglia?" the
judge asked.

"We've got one more witness. An expert on blood typing. I
expect to be at least a full day."

"Let's do this: we'll work in the mornings only, the next couple
of days. That way if necessary we can get Mr. Ryan up to the
weekend. That ought to be plenty of time, and if it's not, you'll let
me know why and I'll see what we can do then."

"That's fine with me, your honor," Griglia said, "but my witness is here from California at the people's expense, so any extra
time we take will be quite costly."

"You should have thought of that when you forgot to tell Mr.
Ryan about the telephone."

"But your honor I didn't . . ."

"Never mind, Mr. Griglia. Shall we recess now or do you want
to take an hour or so with your witness today?"

"I definitely want to start with him today."

"Let's get moving, then."

Walter Bailey looked like a cross between Jimmy Stewart and Alfred E. Neumann. He told the jury he had honors degrees from

Harvard and Stanford in molecular biology and he worked at a genetic research company on the peninsula south of San Francisco. Griglia had him detail his publications in scholarly journals on genetic engineering in the years before he took his present job, when his work became trade secrets and he stopped publishing. In the four years since then he had filed forty-two patents, all in the area of analyzing the structure of the basic genetic material called DNA.

His testimony was relaxed and confident, with a faint down-east accent. His goofy smile and jug ears quickly became part of his personality, a humanizing counterweight to his academic vocabulary. He was exactly the kind of expert witness no lawyer wanted to see on the other side.

"Is research the main focus of your work now?" Griglia asked.

"Not anymore. For the past two years I've been the director of our DNA-typing laboratory. My rate of filing patents is way down."

"What are your responsibilities?"

"I supervise the work of eight molecular biologists and technicians who do genetic analysis of blood and tissue samples. I also do some analysis myself, and I participate in developing and testing new techniques."

"And have you ever testified as an expert before?"

He had, twenty-three times in eight jurisdictions, including thirteen times in California and twice before in New York.

"Did you have occasion to examine evidence submitted to you by my office in this case?"

"Yes, I did."

"And what did it consist of?"

"Samples of human blood, hair and tissue."

Griglia established when and how Bailey had received the evidence, and the care he took of it while he had it.

"Did you perform scientific tests on this evidence?"

"Yes."

"And what if anything remained of the evidence after the tests?"

"Nothing. It was consumed in performing the tests."

"Dr. Bailey, I'm going to ask you tomorrow to describe your tests in detail for the jury. Before we close today, can you tell us if the tests you conducted allowed you to reach a conclusion with a reasonable degree of scientific certainty?"

"Yes, they did."

"Would you summarize those conclusions briefly?"

Ryan objected. "There's no foundation for this."

Corino thought a moment. "I'm inclined to allow it, subject to the proper foundation being laid tomorrow."

He was trying to be even-handed, Ryan guessed, giving Griglia something to balance the beating he had taken in the morning. Ryan saw no need to lie down for it.

"Objection, your honor. It means that for almost a whole day the jury will be left with a conclusion whose basis they know nothing about. This is new, unfamiliar technology that relies on delicate measurements. The jury should know that before they hear about results."

Corino was steaming. "Mr. Ryan, I warn you not to make speeches to the jury. Ladies and gentlemen, you will disregard Mr. Ryan's lecture. Will the lawyers please approach the bench."

Corino was playing for time; Ryan could see it. Wanting to let Griglia go ahead but weighing how likely that was to earn Tony Boy Corino one of his rare reversals on appeal.

"Your honor," Ryan said in an apologetic tone, "I didn't mean to seem intemperate. It's a major point. This technology is new, as you know from the pretrial hearing. I don't know which test the witness is going to refer to. It might be the one that your honor ruled could only be used for limited illustrative purposes."

The D.A. grabbed the last part as a way to make a strategic concession. "I'm willing to have Dr. Bailey testify about the novelty of his techniques and make clear which test the findings are based on. But I think the jury is entitled to hear the basic findings."

"Go ahead, Mr. Griglia."

Ryan swallowed his frustration. "I renew my objection."

"Overruled."

Back to the lectern, Griglia asked, "How long have the tests you used been employed for testing human blood and tissue?"

"We employed two tests. One has been in regular use more than five years. The other is less than two years old."

"And is either of them generally accepted as courtroom evidence in this or other jurisdictions, to your knowledge?"

"I'm an expert on DNA analysis, not court rulings, but I have testified in at least ten jurisdictions where the older test is accepted."

"And based on that test only can you summarize your findings?"

"I was given two evidence samples. Sample number one included blood, hair and tissue, sample number two only blood. I was also given two reference standards, called A and B. The blood, hair and tissue in sample number one all matched each other . . ."

Griglia interrupted. "What, if anything, does that tell you about the blood, issue and hair in sample number one, in your expert opinion with a reasonable degree of certainty?"

"It tells me they all came from the same person."

"Thank you. Go ahead."

"Sample number one did not match the blood in sample number
/o. That means they came from different people."

"Objection."

"Sustained. Ask a proper question, Mr. Griglia."

Ryan continued to hammer at Griglia with objections, if only to
∙eak up the flow of information. Inevitably, in the end the D.A.
∙t his point across: blood that matched Jennifer's was at the head
∙d of Wingless Bird's long, narrow neck, opposite the heavy body
∙d tail smeared with Ned's blood, hair and scalp tissue.

It was a rotten way to end what otherwise had been a very good
∙y in court for the defense."

You ready for this guy tomorrow?" Ryan asked when they were
∙ck in the office after the abbreviated court session.

"Based on what I've heard so far. I'm planning to go over my
∙tes again this afternoon and tonight, anyway."

"Good. I'll get Craig started on the phone records." He reached
∙r the telephone.

"Do you need me?" Jennifer asked.

"You're free till tomorrow."

"Okay, see you . . . You did great today."

"And it's about time, too," he said as the door closed. He dialed
∙awrence's number and while the phone rang he said to Miller,
∙Whoever wiped the phone off in the murder room, the big ques-
∙on is why did he use the damn phone in the first place."

Lawrence picked up. He had spoken to Hugo Hill. The gallery
∙wner said the phone in the room where Ned was killed was an
∙tension of his private line, which had five other extensions on the
∙ghth and ninth floors. He did not know if any of the guests had
∙ed the phone. *He* wouldn't do anything that rude in someone
∙se's house, but he couldn't say as much for the people who visited
∙m.

Ryan told Lawrence about the outgoing-call records. "I'll fax
∙em over and you can get started tracking them down."

With that taken care of, Ryan and Miller speculated about the
∙known telephoner.

"He made the call to let somebody know what happened," Ryan
∙gan.

"To ask somebody what to do."

"To get somebody to come and get him out of there."

"To arrange an alibi."

"Ah," Ryan said. "I like that one."

"But why not go to another room?"

"And be overheard? And you wouldn't want to wait any longer than you had to."

"Go downstairs and call from the street?"

"Have you used a public phone lately? Or tried to?"

"Okay. But if he wanted an alibi, why not go back to the party?"

"Good question." He did not have an answer.

"Suppose the call was before the murder, not after," she proposed.

"Okay. Then, why call? And why wipe the phone off if Ned was alive?"

"Suppose you made a call and then killed Ned. Then you might wipe the phone off to keep people from knowing you'd been in the room." She did not sound as if she believed it.

"Franky's going to say it was Jennifer." Now that his first surge of excitement was past, the chances this would lead anywhere seemed slim.

"One way or the other," she said, "we can get some mileage out of it, creating a reasonable doubt."

"I wish I could be so sure."

It was a paradox: this might help them with the jury but in truth Jennifer was the person most likely to have wiped the phone clean, illogical though it seemed for her to have done it. A woman who had just clubbed her husband to death in a moment of anger was not the world's most rational person.

He said, "I'm going over to Craig's and keep tabs on the phone number search."

"Good idea. You'll drive me crazy fidgeting if you stay here."

"Twelve calls between seven-thirty and ten," Lawrence told him. "Not including three to phone-sex numbers."

"You're kidding."

"Me, kidding? Of the twelve calls, three look like people calling home, three are to car services, two are to numbers out of service too long to be traceable, and we're working on the others."

"When were the two you can't trace?"

"Nine thirty-six and eight-oh-nine."

"One's too early, and the other's too late."

"Probably. I can tell you this much about them: nine thirty-six was on the Upper West Side. Eight-oh-nine was probably a mobile phone."

"That's interesting."

''The number was reassigned months ago. The old records were destroyed after six months.''

There would be nothing more for hours. Ryan took a walk. It was one of those April days in New York that feel more like June. The sky was deep blue, the afternoon sunlight so clear it glinted brightly off even the dirt-filmed cars. Walking up the West Side toward Central Park, Ryan could see New Jersey at the end of the cross streets as if it were part of Manhattan.

He had no patience for the beauty of the day. He put his briefcase on a park bench next to him and worked on his plans for the defense.

By evening, Lawrence had accounted for all of the calls except the two to the defunct numbers.

''Nothing even remotely sinister,'' the investigator reported.

''Jennifer swears it wasn't her,'' Miller added.

''That leaves us ten after eight, which is about fifty minutes too early, and nine-thirty, which is a half hour too late.''

''Only by Griglia's chronology,'' Miller countered. ''All we know is that Ned didn't die much before nine. It could have been nine-thirty, just like we tried to convince the jury.''

''I'll keep after the dead phone numbers,'' Lawrence said. He gave them index cards listing the mystery numbers. ''Just in case you get any bright ideas.''

17

THE NEXT MORNING GRIGLIA AND BAILEY PUT ON A show worthy of NOVA. They used color charts with clear plastic overlays, an overhead projector, a slide projector and videotape. Bailey showed his DNA analysis process in operation in the lab, and he described the scientific basis for it. It was not simple material, but he kept it moving right along without losing the flavor of scientific rigor and accuracy. Ryan, making notes for cross-examination, found himself drawn into its substance.

DNA, Bailey explained, is a long sequence of complicated chemicals like beads on a string which, together, make a set of instructions for building a human being. Different lineups of DNA's four basic proteins produce different features of the finished person. Every cell of every person contains DNA which is a duplicate of the same pattern, inherited half from mother and half from father.

In decades of research into the structure of DNA, Bailey testified, scientists had found that certain strings of chemicals in DNA were virtually the same in everyone: the strings for having a right hand and a left, say, or a head or a heart.

But there were some sequences which did not match in that way and whose function was unknown. Some of these, called junk DNA, showed wide variation from one person to another, both in their length and in their arrangement of the four DNA proteins. Because of these, no two people had the same DNA pattern, except identical twins.

Bailey's method, along with others developed since the mid eighties, depended on finding and identifying those unique "junk" sections of the DNA in a sample of tissue or bodily fluid. It was a method of many steps: first isolating the DNA and using special chemicals to cut the long strands of DNA into shorter pieces, then lining up the cut pieces by length on a piece of gel by a process called electrophoresis. Radioactive "probe" chemicals, each with the property of attaching itself to a certain DNA sequence, were then applied to the gel. An X-ray photographic process revealed where the probes had stuck.

The theory was that a given person's DNA always produced the same pattern of probes, looking like a supermarket bar code, but that every person in the world had a pattern different from every other person's.

With that testimony from his expert, Griglia ended the morning.

Lawrence arrived at the office with a package from his favorite deli.

"Any news?" Ryan asked as they ate.

"No positive progress on the defunct phones."

"It looks like we're getting to the end of our rope," Ryan said. "We have what we have. No miracles, no new witnesses, no murderer to pull out of a hat. We can stall a little more to buy time with those two old phone numbers . . . ."

"I don't know if it's worth it." The investigator pulled a notebook from his jacket pocket. "I've been calling all the guests from the party, even the ones who refused to talk to us before. So far everyone I spoke to denies having called either of those numbers.''

''Nobody's going to admit having made those calls,'' Miller predicted. ''Not unless the calls were totally innocent.''

Lawrence put his notebook away. ''You think Griglia is going to put in any evidence about them?''

''If it were my case I wouldn't,'' Ryan replied. ''He knows the calls are all harmless except maybe the two we can't follow up, and he's got to figure we can't do any better finding the missing callers than he can. So it's no real threat to him, because all we can do is make noises about a gap in the evidence. And if we do he tells the jury in his closing that Jennifer wiped the phone off herself.''

''I think the jury will have some doubts about that,'' Miller said as she wadded up the remains of her sandwich in its wrapper. ''I think we're going to get a lot of mileage out of that phone.'' She fired the ball of waxed paper across the room. It missed the wastebasket and bounced off the wall in a scattering of paper, rye crusts and turkey scraps.

For Wednesday morning's court session Bailey provided four-foot-high blowups of the photographs showing the DNA patterns produced by his tests, each a tall column of black bars and blotches. First he showed the results of three separate tests of the same blood sample, used for illustrative purposes.

The three patterns were not exact duplicates: blotches at the same location varied in darkness or thickness from one test to the next. But side by side it was clear that they all matched, especially when Griglia introduced a pattern made from a different person's blood. Its bars and blotches were in completely different locations from the marks on the first three.

Griglia's finale was the patterns from Ned's blood and Jennifer's, and from the samples taken from Wingless Bird. He and Bailey had orchestrated it as a blind test. The labels identifying the patterns were covered until Bailey had made all the matches and explained them.

They ended up with four patterns grouped together at one end of the jury box and two patterns, quite different from the other four, grouped together at the other end.

With a flourish, Griglia revealed the labels. As Bailey had said at the beginning of his testimony, Ned's blood matched the hair, skin, and blood on the gory end of Wingless Bird, and Jennifer's blood matched the small amount scraped from what Griglia persisted in calling the sculpture's handle.

From Griglia's first question of the morning, Ryan objected every time he could think of a reason and sometimes when he couldn't. By eleven o'clock he was getting signs that some of the jurors were annoyed with him, so he slowed down.

The D.A. finished Bailey's testimony just in time for lunch, and Corino adjourned for the day.

Jennifer left for lunch with the friends who were in court that day, part of a group of regular visitors who daily filled the row in the gallery reserved for the defense. The lawyers ordered in, and as they picked at their cold cuts Miller told Ryan what she expected to do in the morning.

"The way I see it, my job is to throw sand in the gears and blow smoke in their faces. I'm going to ask about the sensitivity of electrophoresis to temperature and humidity, and I'm going to go after Mr. Bailey about the poor standards they maintain in that lab of his, because no lab is perfect and every mistake and impurity sounds like habitual filthiness to the jury. Then I'm going to get him to admit that the DNA test that's well accepted requires more blood than they used on the sample they say matches Jennifer's, and isn't accurate on blood as old as the samples were when they tested them. I'm going to try to make him contradict himself or get scientific-haughty or alienate the jury some other way. From what I've seen, that last part probably won't work but I'll try anyway."

"Sounds good," Ryan said. "And that brings us to our big unanswered question—who are we going to put on the stand next week?"

He paced the office. "You're the experienced defense lawyer here, so maybe I should defer to you on this, but I am of the strengthening belief that we shouldn't put in any case of our own."

"None at all?"

"None at all."

"I don't know, Ryan. I don't know about that."

"I owe my reasoning to you."

"Me? I'm always nervous when I don't put in a case, even when I know it's the right thing to do."

"You knew to leave Harry the Bandito Bundesman offstage, for maximum effect. You were right. And now I think the same reasoning applies to our whole case. I've been going back and forth on it for days but that's how it keeps coming up. When we found the telephone, I thought it might make a difference, but frankly I think it's more of the same. We're talking about the Wizard of Oz, here. It looks a lot more powerful if it stays behind the curtain."

"Because you don't believe in it."

"Because I don't believe that Griglia has proved a damn thing except that Jennifer and Ned had a fight and Jennifer's blood is on the murder weapon, which looks bad but actually *proves* nothing. That's one. And two is, there was nothing I liked more as a prosecutor than a puny defense case. I'd always take a weak defense case over no defense case at all any time I could get it. If the defense puts in a weak case, you stand up there and you ask the jury what did the defense show you? What kind of witness did they have? Is that all they can do? Is that their best shot? . . . Whereas, if the defense says, Hey the prosecution case is so empty that we're not even bothering to put in a defense against it, all you can do is stand there with egg on your face."

"You're stacking the deck and you know it."

"Maybe. My problem is, I don't see what we have that's admissible evidence that we can use. We don't have Bundesman. And we can't risk having Lawrence testify that he saw Tina Claire's boyfriend Kenny Peters threaten me with a sculpture exactly like the one that killed Ned, because it'll backfire on us if Peters has an alibi, which he must. If he didn't we'd have heard long ago."

"So we'd end up looking desperate, grasping at straws."

"Right. And without Bundesman or Kenney to blame, all we have is third-party conjecture about drug money, plus hearsay and inference-on-inference about shady business dealings. None of which has anything directly to do with Jennifer's guilt or innocence. And none of which is specific enough to offer a convincing connection between Ned and dangerous illegal activities, much less give us an alternate suspect or theory. And all of which Griglia will do his best to keep out as irrelevant or otherwise inadmissible."

"There's the argument that we should put in some kind of case to give us more time to follow up on the two phone calls," Miller said.

"In the time we can buy, which is not very long, we're not likely to get past what Craig will already have by Friday."

"We have our pathologists."

"And we'll have a very unhappy jury when the two new pathologists don't say anything the jury hasn't heard before."

"I'm smarter than to let that happen," she countered.

"Don't forget Franky. He'll be there to make sure it seems that way."

The phone interrupted them. It was Lawrence.

"The impossible takes a little longer," he began. "We're down to one phone call."

"Is that good or bad?"

"The defunct number that was called at nine-thirtyish belonged to an actress of no particular talent since decamped for L.A. The call was made from Hill's office in the gallery on the ninth floor, not the private quarters on eight."

"I won't even ask you how you did that."

"Blind luck and an honest partygoer. On the other call, we're almost done canvassing the taxi services and the limo companies to see if that mobile phone was one of theirs. No luck at all."

"What about defunct limo companies?"

"Nobody went out of business in the relevant time period."

"Is an extra day or two going to make any difference in this?"

"I doubt it. If we don't come up with anything by the weekend it'll have to fall out of the sky."

Ryan reported the news to Miller. "We're down to the call at eight-oh-nine."

"Then whoever made it, it was almost the minute Jennifer and Ned left the room."

"Unless she was wrong about how long they stayed there. Or unless she's not telling the whole truth, for a change. Which brings us to the final question."

"Do we put Jennifer on the stand?"

"You know how I feel about it," he said.

"You won't get any argument here. The thought of opening up her history for Griglia to poke around in gives me the shivers."

"Not to mention the virtual certainty that he'll provoke her into doing or saying something awful."

"It's her decision in the end."

Ryan took a long breath. "Which is why we have to explain the dangers to her very clearly indeed."

They started by talking to Jennifer about the theoretical pros and cons of having the defendant testify in her own behalf.

She interrupted before they got very far.

"You're saying I don't have to?"

"One way or the other, it's your decision. If you want to you can, even if we advise you against it."

"Is that what you're going to do?"

"Yes." The two lawyers said it almost in unison.

"I don't understand. If that's how you feel, why did we do all that practicing?"

"To get you ready in case we decided you should testify after all. In case you want to anyway."

"I don't."

Ryan was not sure he heard. "Say that again?"

"I said I don't. I don't want to testify."

"You're sure?"

"Yes. I'd be too nervous. I know I'm an actor, and I shouldn't be nervous about it, but this isn't a play and no one will have written any lines for me to say. If I'm nervous they'll think I have something to hide, and if I'm not nervous then Griglia will say, well she's an actor and she must be acting and so nobody will believe me, anyway."

Ryan told himself that he should never have tried to guess what Jennifer would do.

"Before we make this final decision I have to make sure you understand that some jurors may feel cheated if they don't hear you deny in open court that you killed Ned. Even though I tell them and the judge tells them that you have no obligation to testify and they can't weigh it against you."

"I understand all that. But I'd rather take that chance than the other."

"Then it's settled. Kassia and I have some technical things to talk about, deciding what we're going to do next. We'll need to talk to you about them but not right away. After dinner."

They confirmed with Lawrence that he had made no more progress on the one remaining phone call. At dinner they went back over the decision not to put in a case and convinced themselves it was the right way to go.

"It's called a Reasonable Doubt case," Miller explained to Jennifer. "The prosecution has to prove you're guilty beyond a reasonable doubt. What we'll be saying to the jury is, they didn't succeed. And because the best case they can make leaves a reasonable doubt that you're guilty, there's no need for us to put on any witnesses of our own."

Their decision clearly made Jennifer uneasy, but she did not question it.

"You've put up with enough of my misjudgments. Whatever you think is best is all right with me."

Ryan supposed that was as close to informed agreement as they were going to get.

In the morning Kassia Miller confronted Walter Bailey. The cross-examination went as she predicted, except that Bailey proved a tougher witness than he had seemed on direct examination. He resisted her implications that his technicians had been sloppy, and defended as standard procedure their failure to take full bench notes. Her attempts to rattle him were futile. He remained calm and unflappable. His belief in the technology he had developed was clear in every word he spoke.

It was a close decision whether to draw the testimony out until Friday, to give Lawrence more time to track down that last elusive phone call. Ryan decided against it, on the Wizard of Oz principle. Miller asked her last question just after one o'clock on Thursday afternoon.

Griglia had a few questions on redirect, banishing some of the negative impressions created in the cross-examination.

When he was done, he rested the people's case against Jennifer Kneeland Ryan.

The judge dismissed the jury for the day and listened to the defense argue that the prosecution had not presented a case worthy of the jury's consideration. Corino denied the motion for a trial order of dismissal and a renewed motion for a mistrial based on the withheld fingerprint evidence.

"Mr. Ryan, I assume you'll be ready to start for the defense in the morning."

"Your honor, at this time the defense does not plan to put in a case."

Corino did not hide his surprise.

"You've been over this with your client?"

"Yes. She's in agreement."

Corino considered it for a moment. "All right. Today's Thursday. We'll start tomorrow at the regular hour. If at that time you've changed your mind, we can go ahead with your witnesses. If not, I'll expect you to have something for me on my proposed charge to the jury. I'll let the jurors know not to expect to go home from the start of closing arguments until they've reached a verdict. We can start the fireworks at ten Monday morning."

Robertson Kneeland's limousine was idling outside their office. It was not the first time he had been there to pick up his daughter after court, but it was the first time he got out of the limousine when the defense team arrived.

"We need to talk, Ryan," he announced.

Ryan invited him into the office as if he had made the request civilly.

"I'd feel more private in the car," he countered.

Ryan's patience for this kind of treatment was limited, but this was neither the time nor the place for a confrontation. He got into the back of the limousine.

It was as big as any Ryan had been in, upholstered in silky black leather and thick black carpet, with room for five people in spacious comfort. The usual bar and two telephones were augmented by a television and a fax machine, lodged between the two rear-facing seats.

"My daughter tells me you're not going to defend her." The upholstered surroundings softened his voice without dimming the implicit challenge.

"That's a misunderstanding. We've been defending her for months, since before the trial started."

"Don't play games with me Ryan."

"That's not a helpful tone, Mr. Kneeland. Why don't you tell me exactly what's bothering you."

"I hired you because my daughter insisted. I can't say it made me happy, considering your recent track record and the way Ned felt about you."

Ryan reached for the door. Kneeland grabbed his arm, then quickly let go.

"If I'm not being polite, it's because I'm worried about my daughter. I'm not paying you a king's ransom to abandon her when it gets to the tough part."

"You really don't understand. The details of Jennifer's defense have to be my decision. Mine and hers. I believe she's best served if I don't call any witnesses. She hasn't told me she disagrees. Even if she did, I don't believe there is any witness I could responsibly call. Your idea that I'm not defending her is flat-out wrong."

"Maybe I don't understand, but it sounds to me like you've got half the job left to do."

"Mr. Kneeland, I'm going to give you a summary of my reasoning. I hope it satisfies you, because after that there's nothing more to be said."

"I don't know about that, but go ahead."

"In our professional opinion—Ms. Miller's and mine—we found holes in all the major testimony, and we made all our points through the prosecution witnesses. The only witnesses we could put on would just be repeating what the jury has already heard. And we would run the danger that the District Attorney could damage them in the jury's eyes on cross-examination. He's good at that, and it would leave us behind where we stand now. All in all we're better off standing pat. The jury has all the information it needs to acquit."

Kneeland settled back in his seat. "All right. I still don't like it, but all right." As a parting shot he said, "I assume I can come to court now."

The talk in the limousine stuck in Ryan's mind. He had believed his argument when he made it to Kneeland, but in the darkness of the night he wondered if he was not leaving out something important.

18

ALL DAY SATURDAY RYAN BURIED HIS APPREHENSION in work. He drafted and redrafted his closing argument, first ignoring the summations he and Miller had written while they were preparing the case and the notes they had made during the trial, then incorporating them. On Saturday night he did a dry run with her, visualizing twelve jurors where there was one lawyer. He felt stiff and awkward, as if he had never done it before.

They talked about her delivering the summation. He had told himself he would give the trial his best but when it came to the closing argument giving it his best did not necessarily mean doing it himself. Especially not if his uncertainty about Jennifer's guilt or innocence would get in his way.

The more they talked about it the surer he was that having Miller do the closing was the better way to go. They both knew she wanted to, and they were on the verge of locking it in when she said, "We can't do this. The jury is expecting to hear from Michael Ryan. You're not just another lawyer. You're the defendant's father-in-law. You're the victim's father. It's the very things that make it hard for you that make them want to see you do this. If we disappoint them they just might convict out of revenge."

* * *

He worked on his summation all day Sunday and then exhausted himself at the health club pool until closing time. Back home he worked until his eyes began to shut.

Even so he lay awake Sunday night staring at the ceiling. Finally he got up and poured himself a shot of whiskey and raised it in tribute to his dead son. It was his first drink in more than a week and it knocked him out immediately.

He dreamed of Alison and Ned, she young and he grown, the impossible made possible in the way of dreams. In the morning, showering, he thought of them—of how close he felt to them, and how far away.

Shaving, his face magnified in the mirror, he came upon a simple truth that had somehow eluded him before. He could not make peace with the shades of his wife and his son until he first made peace with himself. And he sensed that this was a major part of the process.

Reporters and camera crews thronged the steps to the courthouse but they did not block the defense team's path. It was as if this last, most important day of the trial had brought out some otherwise forgotten civility.

The thirteenth-floor corridor was a mass of people—an even denser than usual group behind the spectators' barricade, a double helping of camera crews and reporters, and a new line of people along the side of the corridor next to the courtroom.

"Who are they?" Ryan asked a court officer.

"More press."

"From where?"

"Everywhere. California, France, Greece—everywhere."

He was sorry he had asked.

He stopped short when they got into the courtroom. Every seat was filled.

The three of them walked to the rail and through the gate to the defense table. Ryan busied himself with his notes and arranged and rearranged the pitcher of water and glasses in front of him and the sharp pencils next to his pad. They had decided not to use any exhibits. It would be Ryan and the jurors. He looked over at the empty jury box, the lectern moved over to stand at its center. No theatrics today, no sound and light, just a man at a lectern and an audience of twelve, plus the four alternates. The judge. Kassia Miller. He did not want to let her down. And Jennifer, about whom he could not afford to think at all.

Maybe the jurors had made up their minds already, the way so many people said. Maybe this was only a question of reinforcing their conclusions, not changing their opinions. Maybe, except Ryan did not believe it.

It was always a race to the wire. Even when you were so far ahead it ought to be a coast home to victory, it didn't feel that way. And for more than ten years of criminal trials and all the civil litigation he had done since then at Pane, Parish—all of his experience in front of juries—he had paced himself in the knowledge that he would have the last word.

Not this time. This time the last word went to Franky Griglia.

That was what it came down to, in the end. Michael Ryan and Francesco Griglia.

Corino took the bench and immediately called for the jury. They came in looking rested and scrubbed and eager, sixteen people comfortably dressed in everything from jeans and T-shirt to a soft orange designer frock. For the first time that Ryan remembered they looked around them as they crossed the well of the court to the jury box.

This was what it was all about for them. They were about to watch the show of their lives, put on just for them. Theoretically, it had always been true, but never like today. Today it was manifest, palpable in the air.

Ryan listened to Corino's preliminary remarks, but he did not hear the words. Corino called his name and he stood up and went to the lectern.

Look at the jurors, he reminded himself. He saw only a blur of colors and shapes.

"Good morning," he said. "It's an important morning for all of us, one we've all been anticipating. We've been through a lot together, and we're coming to the end. Most of my job is done, and the most important part of yours is just beginning. It's customary to thank the jury at this point, and I do thank you, for the attention you've given, and in advance for the work that's still ahead.

"You've been doing a hard job here, listening to all the testimony, trying to make sense out of it, figuring out who's telling the truth and who isn't, whose word you can take, who's mistaken about what they saw or heard.

"It's a hard job and an important one, because another human being's fate depends on your doing it well and honestly."

The jurors were beginning to come into focus. Constable, the retired engineer. The bus driver who slept a lot, the book editor, the art director, the telephone repairman. Sarrubbi, karate muscles striating his T-shirt.

"The good news today is that the hardest part may be over, because the way I read the evidence your decision should be a clear and easy one."

He smiled at them reassuringly: we're in this together.

"I'm going to be talking to you this morning about doubt. That's what it all comes down to. That's the real question. Doubt.

"The prosecutor accepted a heavy burden at the beginning of this trial. He said he would prove the charges against Jennifer Ryan beyond a reasonable doubt. But he has failed to carry that burden of proof.

"I'm going to review the evidence for you. I'm going to put it in perspective, and I'm going to help you see again what you've already seen. Nothing presented to you in this courtroom is enough to remove the doubts we all have about what happened to Ned Ryan on the last night of his life. Doubts we all have that make it impossible to conclude that Jennifer Ryan is guilty of the charge made against her.

"Ned Ryan. As much as this trial is about doubt, it's about Ned Ryan." Saying it, Ryan's throat closed up. He took a drink of water, willing his hand to hold the glass steady.

"There's a famous funeral oration in one of Shakespeare's plays. Marlon Brando gave it in the movies when he was a great young actor. It's hard for me to stand here and not think of him. He was talking about Julius Caesar. Well, Ned Ryan was no Julius Caesar, but he's just as dead, and here I am making a funeral speech about him, in a way.

"The evil that men do lives after them. That's what Marlon Brando said, words by William Shakespeare. I can think of a lot of things that I'd rather do than talk about the evil Ned Ryan did, and how it lives after him. Nobody came in here for the purpose of telling you that Ned Ryan was a liar and a cheat, or that he had enemies on all sides. Ned Ryan wasn't on trial here. But consider what you did hear about Ned Ryan.

"You heard it from the prosecution witnesses, one after the other. It wasn't what they were up here to say, but it's what came out. A married man who slept with women not his wife. You saw for yourself some of the women Ned Ryan slept with, saw them right up here on the witness stand. But you know who wasn't up here? The husbands and the boyfriends and the brothers and the fathers of those women Ned Ryan was having affairs with, and telling people about it. These are men who had reason to hate Ned Ryan.

This is a classic motive for murder. Where were *those* men the night Ned Ryan was killed?

"Who else did you hear from? A man who did business with Ned Ryan just one time and spent the next two years saying he wanted to kill him. Said it over and over again, by his own testimony, *that he wanted to kill Ned Ryan.* But he's not the defendant, even though he was at the party where Ned Ryan was killed.

"You think Harry Bundesman was the only one? These are the prosecution's witnesses. All the testimony I'll talk about is from the prosecution's own witnesses."

Now he was beginning to warm up, getting into the old rhythm.

"There were no defense witnesses. You have to be wondering about that. Why not? Don't we have a case to make? Ladies and gentlemen, we don't need to make a case. The judge will be giving you the law, I can't do that for him. But I can predict some things he'll say, the same things we talked about when we were selecting you to sit here in judgment, selecting you out of hundreds of candidates.

"The judge will tell you that Jennifer Ryan is considered to be innocent unless the prosecution proves that she's guilty beyond a reasonable doubt. *Innocent.*

"He'll tell you that all burden of proving anything in this case is on the prosecution. It's their job to present witnesses, to convince you that what they charge is true.

"We have no such burden. Jennifer Ryan has no duty, no need, to get up on the stand and tell you her version of what happened. The Constitution of the United States tells us that, and so does the constitution of the State of New York. There is no reason for her to do it. She tells you all you need to know when she pleads not guilty to the charges in the indictment. That's all. *Not guilty.*

"Whatever she was doing when Ned Ryan was killed, if she was out for a walk, or at home in bed, or sitting in the stairwell of that building, the details don't matter. I did not kill him, she says and the law says that you *must* presume she is innocent. I'm not telling you that. The judge will tell you that.

"What does it mean when we talk about a burden of proof? How do you know if the prosecution sustained that burden? The judge is going to tell you about that, too, and I'm not stealing his thunder if I predict what he'll say.

"He'll say proof is based on evidence, and there's more than one kind of evidence. There's physical evidence like that piece of sculpture we've seen so often, exhibit eighteen, and there's the testimony of witnesses. And witnesses give two kinds of testimony, as the judge will tell you. They give direct evidence. They tell you what they saw and experienced. If somebody had seen a person hit Ned Ryan in the head, and they came here and swore to tell the truth and said, I saw so-and-so, whoever, hit Ned Ryan in the head, that would be direct evidence about the murder of Ned Ryan. Your job would be to decide if you believed the testimony.

"But nobody came here and said that. Nobody saw this crime, nobody we know about, nobody but Ned Ryan, and he's not here. And the murderer, the murderer saw it, too, but he's not here, either."

The back of Ryan's neck tingled in anticipation of an objection, but one did not come.

"So there will be no direct evidence of this crime. What is there direct evidence of? Some people came in here and said they saw Jennifer Ryan throw a bowl of finger food. That's direct evidence. If you believe the witnesses, you can decide that the evidence shows Jennifer Ryan threw a bowl of finger food.

"There's another kind of evidence—circumstantial evidence. Circumstantial evidence is direct evidence of one thing that permits you to make an inference about something else that there's no direct evidence of.

"Let me try to illustrate it for you. Suppose a witness testifies that she saw a little bird hatch out of an egg one day, and all around it in the nest were other little birds. And along came a duck and fed them all. And suppose the witness testifies that the mother and father duck took care of all the little birds equally, and they were all fluffy and pretty and played together nicely except the one she saw hatch, and that one was scrawny and unattractive and got left out of the other little birds' games.

"If you heard that testimony, and if you believed it, you'd have direct evidence that the scrawny little bird hatched in the nest with the fluffy pretty ones, the mother duck fed it, and the father duck took care of it. You'd have direct evidence that the fluffy little birds left the scrawny one out of their games. That's the direct evidence.

"Taken all together, that direct evidence might be circumstantial evidence. Of what? That the scrawny little bird was the runt of the duck litter. An ugly duckling. You could infer that from the direct evidence.

"Of course, if you watched those ducks for a year or so you might find that there was a beautiful young swan growing up among the young ducks. You might conclude that the witness had not seen an ugly duckling after all. That when you interpreted the circumstantial evidence, you made a mistake, because no one told you about the mischievous little boy who put the swan's egg in the duck's nest.

"The point is that with circumstantial evidence one fact more or less can make a big difference. It's not enough to jump to the first conclusion that comes to mind. Almost always, circumstantial evidence has more than one interpretation. You have to be careful not to see an ugly duckling when what you're looking at could really be a swan.

"In a case like this, where nobody saw the crime, you have to be especially careful not to just let the prosecutor tell you what to think about the evidence.

"That's what he's going to do. He's going to get up here and tell you what he wants you to think it all means. Listen to him, but bear in mind that he's only telling you what he wants you to think. He wants you to think exactly his way and only his way because the minute you start thinking for yourselves, you're going to doubt what he's trying to tell you.

"When it's over, you take the prosecution's claim, and you take the evidence, and you ask yourself, Do I have any doubt that this happened exactly the way the prosecutor said it did? And if you have any doubt, then you have to acquit Jennifer Ryan. Not a big doubt. Just a *reasonable* doubt.

"The judge is going to tell you about that, too. He'll tell you a reasonable doubt is any doubt you can assign a reason to. That doesn't mean a detailed reason like a specific theory of how the crime happened or who did it. It means any reason you might have, to doubt any part of what the prosecution is telling you. To doubt the elements that make up his case, or to doubt the conclusion he wants you to reach. Any reasonable doubt at all. And, ladies and gentlemen, I don't have to tell you this is a case that's full of doubt. Doubt is its middle name."

Ryan stopped. Let the words sink in, roll around in his own mind as he hoped they were in the jurors'. He didn't want this to be a show. He really wanted them to think.

"Before we talk about the evidence, let me say one more thing. I'm not going to cover everything. I'm not going to explain or contradict every piece of evidence, every half-baked motive, every silly intemperate statement by Jennifer Ryan that the prosecution wants you to think of as a threat. Nobody deserves to be convicted of murder for having a fast mouth. It makes lots of people feel good to talk tough when they've got some steam to blow off. It doesn't mean a thing.

"We're not talking about the old-time Mafia here, like in the movies, where people got a fish wrapped in newspaper and the next day they were at the bottom of the river. We're talking about ordinary people—people whose daily life is as far from violence as can be. We're talking about people for whom breaking a dish is a big deal.

"Now we all know the difference between arguing and killing, between throwing dishes when you're angry and bludgeoning a person to death.

"The prosecutor doesn't think you can make a simple distinction like that. His case depends on making you believe that because a person threw a bowl she would also kill her husband. But what evidence has he given you for that outrageous conclusion? And how is he going to use that evidence to convince you to see it his way?

"Basically, he's going to talk about four kinds of evidence. He's going to tell you about the witnesses who testified that Ned and Jennifer Ryan had problems in their marriage. They fought and called each other names and they had affairs. They had a loud argument just before he was killed. None of that is evidence of murder. It's only a smokescreen the prosecutor hopes will hide the holes in the rest of his evidence.

"Another kind of evidence he'll talk about is medical testimony about the murder itself. *When* Ned Ryan was killed. The medical examiner said it could have been almost any time before he was found at nine forty-five. But she said it was most likely around nine o'clock or after nine. It could have been earlier, though, she said that. An in her original notes she thought he might have died at *ten or eleven*.

"Ned Ryan was last seen alive at about eight. His body was found not much before ten. That's almost two hours unaccounted for, and the testimony says he could have been killed any time in those two hours. But the prosecutor will tell you that his witness said the time of death was about nine o'clock.

"Dr. Guevara also testified about how Ned Ryan was killed. And the prosecutor brought in an expert to tell you about that, too. And what did they say? Blows to the head with a piece of sculpture. They also testified that the blows had to be very strong ones, very forceful. The prosecutor may not remind you of that.

"People often live a long time with head wounds from blunt instruments. The prosecution witnesses told us that. Ned Ryan did not live. Ned Ryan died. He had to have been hit *very hard*. The prosecution's witness told us that.

"But the prosecution's witnesses also said that *if* the sculpture was held a certain way and *if* it was swung a certain way and *if* the victim and his assailant were moving a certain way, *then* a woman of the size of Jennifer Ryan *might* have struck those blows. And the prosecutor will try to make that seem like a definite statement instead of what it actually is—a long series of *ifs* and *might-haves*."

He took the time to elaborate on that theme, grateful after all to Miller for having insisted on taking the pathologist through the details.

From there he moved on to the blood evidence. "For that, the prosecutor is going to rely on Mr. Bailey. He'll call him doctor because he has a science degree, but please remember that he is not a medical doctor. Mr. Bailey and the prosecutor showed us a lot of tests. Four separate tests of blood that had nothing at all to do with this case. Why? To get us accustomed to seeing similarities in those strange patterns.

"And when it came to samples related to this case, they showed us four tests of blood and hair and tissue from Ned Ryan to reinforce the idea that exhibit eighteen is the murder weapon. That would be fine, except what they were really doing was trying to lull us into relying on those tests. Why? To take our attention away from the only blood samples that matter, the ones from Mrs. Ryan and from the skinny end of prosecution exhibit eighteen.

"Mr. Bailey admits there was barely enough of that blood to make a test and it was older blood than he liked to have for that kind of test. Not only that, but he could not vouch for the exact temperature and humidity of the gel used in that test, and according to Mr. Bailey, the prosecution's witness, temperature and humidity can compromise the test results. So the test that the prosecutor will claim identifies Jennifer Ryan's blood may not have been as accurate as all those other tests they went to so much trouble to show us.

"And when the prosecutor talks to you about the blood on the statue—blood that *might* be Jennifer Ryan's and might *not* be, though he won't say that—he's going to talk about it as if there's only one way that blood could have got there: in the course of killing Ned Ryan. As if nobody ever had a cut on their hand, and nobody ever had reason to touch a piece of sculpture except if they were using it to kill somebody.

"What else will the prosecutor talk about? He'll talk about Mr. Garfield, who said he saw Jennifer Ryan leaving the building at about nine o'clock. The prosecutor will certainly tell you about that. He may not be so eager to tell you that Mr. Garfield didn't know Jennifer Ryan very well and might have seen someone else. And he definitely won't point out that the woman Mr. Garfield saw was walking out of the lobby, which tells us nothing about where she was before Mr. Garfield saw her. Upstairs? Maybe. Or maybe she was standing in the lobby, or sitting in the stairwell, or maybe she stopped into the lobby for a minute and then turned around and left.''

Ryan stopped again. Took a drink of water and surveyed the jury. They were paying attention. Sarrubbi's mouth was set in a show-me scowl, but the bus driver was awake and Constable looked like he was enjoying himself.

''That's the prosecution evidence. That's all he's going to tell you about, and he'll tell it as if it's all damning evidence, as if it's all proved fact. We know better. We know that every bit of his evidence is riddled with doubt. Not one conclusion is solid. And even if each piece of evidence were solid, what would it all add up to? Nothing.

''Let me summarize it: A man with many enemies was killed with unusually forceful blows from a piece of sculpture, perhaps at about nine o'clock. His wife, who had made commonplace angry remarks about him for months and had argued with him at eight o'clock that night might have been seen in the lobby of the building at nine o'clock. A bit of blood on the sculpture said to have been used to kill him may have been hers, but there is no evidence about how or when this blood got there. And the murder took place in a room to which anyone had access, including dozens of guests at a party upstairs, among whom were people with illegal drugs and loaded guns and at least one person who had good reason to hate the victim and had spoken openly that night about wanting to kill him.

''That's the prosecution's case, ladies and gentlemen. That's all the prosecution's witnesses told us. I submit that it proves nothing about who killed Ned Ryan. It certainly does not prove beyond a reasonable doubt that Jennifer Ryan is guilty of murder.

''I reminded you a moment ago that there were almost two hours during which Ned Ryan might have been killed. Did anyone see Mrs. Ryan in those two hours? She left the party with her husband at eight. Mr. Garfield may have seen her downstairs at nine. That's all.

''Sometimes the most important testimony is the testimony you have not heard or seen. The prosecution witnesses did *not* testify that they saw Jennifer Ryan anywhere in or near the eighth or ninth floor or the roof garden at any time after eight o'clock. No one testified that they heard any noise of arguing from the eighth floor at any time. No one heard blows or a struggle.

"The prosecution wants you to believe the Ryans were arguing the whole time between eight and nine o'clock. That's a long argument. Can you imagine sustaining a violent argument for a whole hour? It's ridiculous. It never happened.

"What's the alternative? She left and came back. How can that be? This woman goes into a place where there are fifty or more people having a party, people coming and going all the time, many of whom know her well, people who have seen her at center stage an hour before, and she sneaks in and no one sees her and she kills a man, and then sneaks out again, and again nobody sees her. The only time anybody sees her is in the lobby, as she leaves. Common sense tells you this never happened."

Ryan stopped for another drink of water.

"Here is what the evidence does show, and here is what happened. Ned and Jennifer Ryan went to a party together. They circulated around separately, the way they were accustomed to, and at some point in the party, Ned Ryan let a vicious, malicious and calculatedly seductive woman get the better of him for a while. Ned Ryan had a weakness for women. His wife had known about it for years. She didn't welcome it, she tolerated it. Sometimes she shouted about it and said foolish things the way people do. You heard Mr. Bundesman. He'd been saying for two years, to everybody who'd listen, I'm going to kill Ned Ryan. Talk like that is empty, it's a figure of speech. Everyone knows that. So now and then over the years Mrs. Ryan says she'll kill her husband, which of course means nothing, and sometimes she yells at him, and once she even has an affair herself, with Nicholas Maclean, who testified here, and what does she say about the affair? That it's meaningless. It's in the record. Meaningless. She said it to Nicholas Maclean and he repeated it to us right here in court.

"We ask about these witnesses: Who do we believe? We don't necessarily belive the ones whose testimony is consistent with some personal axe they may be grinding. We don't necessarily believe the ones who were coked up to the eyeballs during the events they testified about. These witnesses are not the Sunday school choir.

"But when Nicholas Maclean comes in here and he has nothing to gain from saying something that, if you think about it, makes him seem pretty small, perhaps he's a little more entitled to belief, on that point at least. So Nico Maclean says he had an affair with Jennifer Ryan and when it was over she told him it was meaningless to her. And he believed her, too, you could tell. This wasn't some malicious crack she made. Meaningless. That must not have felt great, for him to admit in open court, but he said it. He was the prosecution's witness, with no reason in the world to lie on behalf of a woman who thinks he's meaningless. And what did he tell us she said? That the affair was meaningless *the way Ned Ryan said his affairs were*. So she understood. That was the point. She understood how meaningless her husband's dalliances were, in the context of their marriage.

"That's her state of mind. Not exactly what you would call murderous.

"And here comes Tina Claire, and she's going to play a trick on Mr. Ned Ryan. Why? Because she's nasty, that's why. Some piece of work, that one. You saw her. Guerilla theater. She wouldn't know guerilla theater if it carried her up the side of the Empire State Building. So there she is, making a display of herself, having her fun, showing that Ned Ryan has his sad, blind side, like a lot of human beings do, not all of them as likely to make enemies as poor Ned Ryan was.''

Poor Ned Ryan. The reality of that intruded for a moment. He pushed it away.

"I keep seeing Mr. Bundesman, and how much hate he had. How many more Harry Bundesmans do you think there are? A lot, I'd venture to say. The police didn't bother to check, you heard about that, too.

"So there was Mr. Ryan with this woman who is doing something that looks considerably more provocative than you'd expect to see at a fancy art party, and Mr. Ryan's wife thinks this isn't very nice. To say the least. So she goes over and tells him so. She yells at him. She breaks a dish. Now that's the way people express anger. Boom!'' He slapped the podium. "Break a dish. You feel a lot better. How many people have never broken a dish in anger? Breaking a dish isn't killing anybody. I said it before, there's one of the central questions of this case: Can you accept the difference between arguing and killing, between throwing dishes when you're angry and bludgeoning a person to death? Have you ever been so angry that you've thrown something? If you haven't, you're the exception.

"So she yelled at him and she broke the dish and he left. And she followed him, and maybe they spoke some more, maybe they didn't, and she left and wandered around feeling bad. And maybe around nine o'clock she stopped in the lobby for a moment deciding whether to go upstairs and find him so they could kiss and make up the way they had so many times in the past. And maybe she decided it was better to kiss and make up in private, so she went home to wait for her husband. And meanwhile her husband went to Mr.

Hill's private study and there he encountered somebody who killed him. And who wiped the telephone clean. And left.''

He stopped, let them think about that, started again slowly.

''What about that room? A room *anybody* could get into. A room where Ned Ryan could have let anybody in himself. You heard the testimony about that. Maybe he had a meeting with somebody in there. Maybe a burglar came in. Who knows? Somebody who left by the fire escape, the same fire escape the police never saw until the other day in court. The police didn't see a lot, and who knows what they did see that they didn't tell you about? They didn't tell you about the missing fingerprints on the telephone until I pointed it out. I'm not perfect, ladies and gentlemen, I can't catch them every time. I don't know what else they withheld. None of us does.''

Griglia objected strenuously. His voice tore something in Michael Ryan.

''Mr. Griglia objects! Wonderful.'' The judge sustained the objection, but Ryan kept going as if he had not heard. ''Mr. Griglia objects because I suggest that his police are less than a hundred percent honest and forthcoming.''

''Mr. Ryan.''

''Sorry, your honor,'' he said, but whatever it was that had come loose inside him propelled him onward. ''Mr. Griglia is going to get up here and he's going to brand as a killer a woman whose worst fault according to the evidence was that she got angry sometimes and spoke intemperately. And the prosecutor is going to say these things about her and she has to sit here and listen, and I can't object to that and she can't object to that. A woman whose crime is that someone else killed her husband on the night she argued with him. Can you imagine how that feels? I can, because it happened to me. I fought with my wife, and that same night she drove into a bridge abutment, and somebody said it was my fault. Ned Ryan said it was my fault . . .''

Corino exploded. ''Mr. Ryan! *Mr. Ryan!*''

He froze. Tried to pull himself back under control. For he didn't know how long, it seemed like forever.

''Mr. Ryan?'' Corino's voice, getting through.

He turned to the bench. ''I'm sorry, Judge.'' Meaning it this time. And to the jury: ''I'm sorry ladies and gentlemen. I'm a little tired. I'm under a little strain.''

He took a drink of water and a few steadying breaths. He began speaking again, slower than before.

''But I still know what the evidence says. The evidence says that there are doubts here, and more than doubts. There is no case here, ladies and gentlemen. Jennifer Ryan sits there presumed innocent, and that means she didn't do it, unless and until the prosecution proves different. And they haven't even come close. They have the burden of proof in this, and they haven't held it up, they haven't borne that burden. This trial isn't about name calling or bowl breaking. And name calling and bowl breaking is all the prosecution can credibly claim they've shown.

"It comes down to a question of blood on a statue and a telephone wiped clean of fingerprints. That's all there is. Are you going to brand this woman a killer, a killer of her own husband, *beyond a reasonable doubt*, because some blood which could be hers was found on the instrument of her husband's death? Not knowing how that blood came to be there, with no evidence that it came to be there in a way even remotely related to Ned Ryan's death, a tiny amount of blood on a rough metal object. I'm not going to tell you how that blood came to be there. But I am going to remind you that the prosecution has offered no proof of how it came to be there.

"Make no mistake—we're not talking about fingerprints on the handle of a gun. We're not talking about something that you touch for one reason and one reason only.

"Who knows why a person might grab hold of a piece of sculpture? Maybe it was falling and somebody grabbed it to keep it from hitting the floor. Maybe somebody touched it just to feel the surface, and their hand was already cut. How many ways do we get cuts on our hands in the course of a day or a week? Paper cuts, cuts from kitchen knives, all kinds of cuts.

"And if you go into a museum or a gallery, there are cases and ropes to keep you from touching things. There are signs that say DO NOT TOUCH. Why is that? Because objects like that piece of sculpture call out to us to touch them, to stroke them, to feel their texture. It's human nature to touch something like that.

"We haven't heard how the blood came to be on the statue, because the prosecutor doesn't know, and if he tells you he does, well, he's not talking about any evidence we've seen in this courtroom.

"I'll tell you what we do know: Somebody was in that room who wiped the telephone clean of fingerprints. Now that somebody isn't Mrs. Ryan. How do we know it's not Mrs. Ryan? The prosecutor's witness says her fingerprints may be on other objects in that room. The prosecutor will tell you her blood was in that room. The prosecutor can't have it both ways. It makes no sense at all that she would wipe the telephone clean, and leave everything else.

"Now I'm going to make a prediction, and it's not something

that I have control over, but I'll bet the prosecutor is going to get up here after I'm done and offer some complicated explanation for how it's possible in the heat of whatever imaginary scenario he describes that some person might have thought to wipe the phone off, and nothing else. Well the prosecutor can make up all the scenarios he wants to in his free time, but that's not what he's supposed to do here. He's here to *prove* what happened, not make up stories about what might have happened if you believe everybody acted in one particular and peculiar and hugely unlikely way.

"We have to draw a conclusion from that clean telephone. And here's the only conclusion that makes sense—you wipe the phone off, and you don't wipe anything else off, if you have good reason to believe the phone is the only surface in that room that has your fingerprints on it, and you're desperate to keep people from knowing you touched it, *because you don't want anybody to know you were there*.

"I'm going to take that one step further. There was free access to that room. Anybody at that party could have gone into that room and made a phone call. Anybody at that party, and plenty of people who were not, could have killed Ned Ryan."

He was feeling in control again. And he was feeling in touch with the jury. He did not want to lose it.

"Jennifer Ryan has suffered enough. The prosecutor has brought her in here with an ugly-duckling case that ignores the most important evidence at the scene of the crime, that telephone with the fingerprints wiped off it. You have heard police officers tell you how many ways they did not follow up evidence about Ned Ryan, and you have heard the prosecution's witnesses describe him as intensely disliked, even hated, wherever he went. You don't have to read very far between the lines to imagine how many people there are who might have killed Ned Ryan.

"Is there reasonable doubt here? You bet there is. Reasonable doubt does not begin to express the size and the extent of the holes in the prosecution's case.

"I know that when you go into the jury room and you are free to deliberate on what you have seen and heard that you will see how much doubt you have, you will see that you have no good evidence of what actually happened in that room last June, and you will refuse to return a verdict of guilty in this case."

He paused. "And now I turn you over to the prosecutor, who will try to make you see it his way. I can't rebut what he's going to say. I have to rely on you, as you listen to him, to think: what would

Michael Ryan say about this? What does the *evidence* say about this?

"You won't hear from me again. I don't think you need to. I think you're all more than smart enough to find the holes in what you're about to hear. Thank you."

19

THE WALK BACK TO THE DEFENSE TABLE WAS INTER-minable. Ryan was a hundred feet tall and an inch thick and he felt himself swaying like a skyscraper in a hurricane.

His hand found the back of his chair and he sat down. Miller was watching him, her face determinedly neutral. He turned to see what was happening.

Griglia was standing at the lectern. Ryan heard the D.A.'s voice but not his words. Time now for Ryan to push his chair back to the rail and over to the middle so he could see Griglia, the way he had for the openings. He didn't have the strength yet. He checked to be sure Miller was listening and concentrated on regaining his equilibrium.

He had no idea how he had done, or how badly his outburst had hurt him.

It gets you when you least expect it.

He gradually came back to a mental state approximating normal, and he pushed his chair over to where he could see Griglia better.

The prosecutor was being low-key and straightforward, no great pyrotechnics. This was not the hot-headed, passionate Franky Griglia of the old days. This was a man mellowed and strengthened by experience, confident in himself and his position.

"There is one mistake I have learned not to make," he was saying. "I do not look into the human heart. The argument you just heard rests on the idea that because the defendant told her lover their relationship was meaningless, like her husband's affairs, that because of that one statement you should disregard all the statements she made to others about her desire to kill Ned Ryan. That argument would have you believe that that one statement was pure and true and all the others were empty ravings.

"I don't pretend to have that kind of mental X-ray vision. The evidence shows that the defendant repeatedly spoke of her desire to be rid of Ned Ryan, her wish that he was dead, her intention to kill him. Her anger with him has been described to you. She called his girlfriend to make her threats. I don't know why she told Nicholas Maclean their affair was meaningless. She may have meant it, or she may have said it to hurt him. It doesn't matter. What matters is that this woman saw her husband have affair after affair and according to the witnesses we heard, her response was the same, over and over again. She said repeatedly that she wished Ned Ryan was dead. She wanted him to be dead. She told people she thought about killing him.

"The defendant's lawyer offered you a parody of the evidence. He dwelled on the most minor mistakes and inconsistencies. He tried to build mountains of doubt from dust motes of ambiguity. Don't be fooled. The small mistakes and shortcomings of the human beings who testify on the witness stand should not be confused with weaknesses in the people's case.

"The important evidence that has been presented here is uncontroverted. We have only heard one story from the witnesses, and it is the story of how this sad and violent crime occurred. There has been nothing in this trial to contradict it."

Ryan took note. Cracks about uncontroverted evidence could add up to an improper implication about Jennifer's failure to testify.

Griglia went on: "The defendant's lawyer made many attempts to disparage the witnesses. But he never asked who were these witnesses and why did they come here? Donald Garfield, a businessman from out of state. Nobody said he had a reason to come here and lie. Nobody offered testimony or other evidence that any of the witnesses were here for some ulterior motive. These are people who came here to tell the truth as they saw it that night. People like yourselves, doing their duty as citizens. You have to decide if there's any reason not to believe them.

"Here is what the evidence shows: Ned Ryan angered his wife by having affairs with other women, and by other behavior. She wanted to get out of the marriage but felt trapped in it partly because of her husband's business relationship with her father. She spoke often of wanting to kill him. These were not mild remarks: 'It's all over for him—the end,' and 'If he pulls that one more time I'll kill him.' She called the women he was involved with to make threats: 'If he sees you again, he's had it.' We heard all that from several witnesses, some of them friends of the defendant's, some of them not.

"The evidence shows that on the night of the murder the defendant went with her husband to a party where the guests of honor included the artist named Karen, who the defendant knew was one of her husband's mistresses, and Tina Claire, who flirted with her husband in a way that included overt sexual contact in front of all the guests at the party. We heard this from several witnesses, including Ms. Claire herself. Among the people who saw this display were friends of the defendant's from the charity organization where she is a volunteer. The defendant found this behavior by her husband to be humiliating, as she expressed to people who testified to that effect here in court. She blew up at him. She became so angry she could not contain herself. She said things like, 'You've had it,' and 'I'm not taking this lying down.'

"These are action words, ladies and gentlemen. This is not, You so-and-so. This is, I'm going to make you sorry. I'm going to make you pay. She wasn't just cursing him out, she was making real threats. And when he did not pay sufficient attention, she smashed a serving bowl full of food. The defendant's lawyer would have us believe that was some trivial thing to do. But this was a large serving bowl. That's not throwing a coffee cup or a drink glass. And it was full of pastries, not popcorn. You will have to judge for yourself the kind of anger that moves a person to do an act that extreme in a roomful of people, some of whom were people whose opinion mattered to her.

"And what was the result? Did her husband react in horror? Did he rush to comfort her? Did he yell at her? None of those. He walked out. So far from paying attention to her, he turned his back completely. What could be more infuriating?"

Griglia paused. It was a gesture of pure control. He did not drink: there was no water glass on the lectern, just as there were no notes.

"That's all the direct evidence we have of what happened that night. The rest of our evidence, as the defendant's lawyer pointed out, is indirect. Circumstantial. That does not mean it is without value, or that we can ignore it. If there are inferences to be drawn, we can draw them. Not every inference is an ugly duckling.

"The rest of the evidence is very simple. We heard from the medical examiner that Ned Ryan died sometime between when he left the party at eight and when he was found at nine forty-five. Dr.

Guevara said her autopsy findings, together with her observations of the body and the report of the medical examiner at the crime scene, lead her to believe that death took place around or after nine o'clock. That's her expert opinion.

"We heard from her and from an expert on blows to the head that Ned Ryan was killed by four solid, forceful blows from prosecution exhibit eighteen, a sculpture which had been on a pedestal in the room where Ned Ryan's body was found. And we heard from an expert on analyzing the genetic composition of blood and tissue that on the handle of the murder weapon there was blood that matched the defendant's. And finally we heard from Mr. Garfield that he saw the defendant leaving the building at nine o'clock, the time Dr. Guevara says is the most likely time of death.

"That's the core of it. There's more that's suggestive, like the disappearance of the clothes the defendant wore that night. If we could have known if there were bloodstains on those clothes or not, it would have been a big help to us. But we'll never know if there were bloodstains on her clothes or not, because she gave them away. These were expensive clothes, unique clothes. You heard the witnesses. Shoes that cost six hundred dollars that were specially ordered and that she'd only had for a few weeks. A four hundred dollar blouse. A suit that cost more than a thousand dollars. She gave them away the day after the murder. Was she getting rid of evidence? That's for you to decide.

"It's a minor point compared to the evidence we have. That evidence is very strong indeed. And no evidence was offered that points in any direction but the guilt of the defendant."

Ryan considered objecting but decided to wait for the next time, confident that Griglia would again mention the lack of defense testimony.

"The defendant's lawyer pointed out, accurately, that the people bear the burden of proof in this case, that we have to prove the defendant's guilt beyond a reasonable doubt.

"Judging by his closing argument, he would have you believe that any fairy tale he can invent is enough to create a doubt that's reasonable. I don't think so, and I'd be surprised if you thought so. I'm not going to fall into the trap of responding to all of his fantasies. But I will comment on some of them.

"He was interested in the question of what happened between eight o'clock, when Ned Ryan left the party with the defendant in angry pursuit, and some time shortly before nine when she struck the blows that killed him. The answer is, we have no testimony about that. And another answer is, for our purposes it doesn't matter. All that matters is that the evidence points clearly to her as the murderer.

"He wanted to know why no one had heard the argument that continued after they left the party. They were on the eighth floor. The party was on the roof. And we don't know that no one heard an argument. All we know is no one came forward to report they heard it. Just because Mr. Garfield and the others who came into court to testify are good citizens doesn't mean everyone is.

"But the defendant's lawyer had another interesting speculation. He predicted that I would say the defendant might have left the building and walked around making a murderous plan. That she came back and went upstairs with blood in her eye and carried out her premeditated plan to murder her husband.

"I thank him for the suggestion. It's not what I was gong to say, but it is perfectly possible that it happened that way, and I recommend to you that you give that possibility serious consideration. In fact, I believe it is the most likely scenario for what happened, because it means that the defendant was consciously avoiding detection from the beginning. And that explains why no one saw her. And if someone had seen her on the way in, she could always have changed her plans. As it happened, she was not seen and so she went right ahead with the murder.

"But you don't have to accept all of that, accurate though you may decide it is. The evidence provided by Mr. Garfield proves that the defendant was there at the time specified by the medical examiner as the likely time of death. Either she was there all along, or she left and came back. One way or the other, she was on the premises long after she and her husband left the party.

"Another point the defense made: they were eager to get the medical examiner and the expert pathologist to testify that there was no way to know how quickly or slowly Ned Ryan died, that people often linger with head wounds. But the defendant made no attempt to go for help . . ."

"Objection," Ryan said quietly. "Assuming facts not in evidence."

"He's right, Mr. Griglia," Corino said.

Griglia resumed as if there had been no interruption, elaborating on the pathologist's evidence, bringing out the pictures and the charts of wounds like stars in Ned Ryan's battered head, detailing each blow again as he had during the pathologist's testimony. Counting the blows. This was the first, and this the second, this the third and that the fourth.

He picked up the sculpture. "This, ladies and gentlemen, is the murder weapon, according to the testimony of the expert witnesses you heard here. I ask you to consider the frame of mind of the person who could strike four strong blows, and they had to be strong blows, with this . . . Wingless Bird. The person who did that had only one thing on her mind—crushing and destroying. Do it in the privacy of the jury room and see how it feels.''

He hefted the sculpture and raised it overhead. Brought it down on an imaginary head. ''One,'' he counted. ''Two. Three. Four. Imagine it, feel the intention it must have taken to do that. Feel the weight of it and understand that the person who wielded that lump of metal, smashing it down repeatedly onto Ned Ryan's skull, can have only intended to crush out his life.

''The judge will tell you the indictment charges that the defendant took Ned Ryan's life with the intention of doing so. This is not a question of premeditation. She didn't have to make a plan, though as we've seen she may well have done that. No plan is necessary for murder to be intentional, as his honor will explain. It is merely necessary that at the time the murderous act was taking place the defendant formed a conscious intention to take the victim's life. And I defy anyone to believe that a person could strike four blows with that thing, and see the blood flowing from the wound, and not have the intention of killing Ned Ryan.

''Look at the crime scene photos while you deliberate. See again how much blood there was, not just on the floor but on this exhibit as well. So the killer struck the blows and saw the blood and went on striking blows.

''I defy you to imagine anyone doing that without the intention of causing Ned Ryan's death. I defy you to imagine that the defendant gave so much as a moment's thought to the sanctity or value or fragility of human life while she was striking those four blows.''

''Objection, your honor. We don't know that Mrs. Ryan struck any blows.''

Corino was clearly annoyed at the second interruption and Griglia was livid, but the judge said, ''He's right again, Mr. Griglia. Please be more careful. I know this is argument, but there are limits.''

Griglia's anger worked against his becoming more temperate, but no one could have doubted that he was trying. Even from where Ryan was sitting he could see the D.A.'s face getting red with effort.

The rest was predictable, if no less difficult for Ryan to take.

Griglia emphasized the blood on the statue: ''The defendant's blood to a probability of one in a *billion*. The defense lawyer wants you to think the tests were not accurate but that was not Dr. Bailey's estimony. Have the testimony read back to you if you need to efresh your memory. The laboratory's regular procedures were ollowed. Variations were within accepted limits. Don't be misled y attempts to imply this was some sort of quackery. This is a well-stablished laboratory.

"As for the notion of people running around with cuts on their ands, when was the last time you had a cut on your hand that ontinued to bleed for any length of time without being visible to eople around you? Without its prompting you to put a bandage on t? That's nonsense. It's a fairy tale.

"You heard a lot about a telephone this morning. The defen-ant's lawyer said I would make up a story about why the defendant viped off the telephone and left her fingerprints elsewhere. But I'm ot going to do that. Why not? Because there's no reason for me o do that. There are any number of reasons why she might have viped that telephone clean. And she might have done it for no eason at all. In the heat of passion and the confusion of the moment fter murder we can hardly expect people to behave like computer rogramers.

"But there are other possible reasons for the phone to be without ingerprints that have nothing to do with the death of Ned Ryan. There were drugs found at that party, remember. We don't know vhat kinds of illegal activities might have been going on there. Anybody might have come into the room at any hour of the evening. The party started at five-thirty. And that person makes a call about drug deal. There were guns found there, too. That call could have een about anything. Somebody makes a call and wipes off the hone so no one knows they did it, ordinary caution for people who eddle drugs and carry guns. Bear in mind that the drugs and guns hat the police found were wiped clean, too. So somebody wipes ff the phone and leaves the room. Who knows when that was? At ix o'clock. It could have been any time.

"But to turn that into a phantom murderer who appears from owhere, kills Ned Ryan, makes a phone call, wipes the phone lean and disappears again—that stretches the imagination beyond he tearing point. It's ridiculous. It never happened, as the defense awyer said so often about things that *did* happen.

"Think about it. If there was a phantom murderer, why would e leave his fingerprints on the phone in the first place? He'd have gloves on, or use a handkerchief. Assuming there's any reason in he world why a phantom murderer would make a phone call from hat place at that time. Why? To call mom? A florist, to send flow-rs? Or maybe his car service so they'd come and pick him up? It's all too ridiculous for words. That telephone has nothing to do with this case.

"Ladies and gentlemen, all we have seen in the weeks we have been examining the evidence in this case is a series of witnesses who tell a single story. An enraged woman bludgeoned her husband to death with the first heavy object that came to hand and in the process she cut her hand on the murder weapon just enough to leave behind some of her blood. Then she left and disposed of her clothes, which consequently could not be recovered to test them for blood-stains. That's all there is. There is *nothing* to the contrary."

This time Ryan got to his feet. "I object to the prosecutor's constant improper reference to the lack of defense testimony. I'd appreciate an instruction to the jury, your honor."

"The jury will disregard Mr. Ryan's interruption."

"Your honor!" It was a hell of a time for a joke, however annoyed Corino was with him.

"Sit down, Mr. Ryan. Mr. Griglia, the defense has no obligation to put in a case or to have the defendant testify, as you well know."

"Yes, I know there's no obligation. I'm only suggesting that the defendant's lawyer's stories are entirely without support, and the jury might legitimately wonder why that is. He made comments about the witnesses I didn't put on. I'm returning the favor."

It's not the same, Ryan wanted to say. You've got the burden of proof. I don't have to rebut you with my witnesses if I can do it with yours. But Corino let it go by and Ryan could not afford to seem intemperate in front of the jury, not again.

"Objection," he said, for the record.

Griglia moved on to a look at the law, including the usual prosecutor's point of view on circumstantial evidence and reasonable doubt. "Not a small doubt, not a trivial doubt, not a doubt where the reason is some trumped up theory that could only happen under a blue moon. A *real* doubt. A doubt backed up by a *real* reason. A doubt that makes you think. Not a doubt you fabricate because you don't want to do the admittedly difficult thing and say this woman stands guilty as charged.

"It's a major responsibility to sit in judgment on a fellow human being, and I don't for a minute want to diminish the seriousness and importance and difficulty of what you're all about to do. We're taught about the quality of mercy, and how it falls from heaven like rain. But I would ask you to remember this. Mercy does not extend only in the direction of criminals. Mercy extends to your fellow human who is a *victim* of crime, who deserves the protection of the law and of his fellow citizens. Mercy should have extended to Ned

Ryan. Perhaps he was not the most honorable of men. That does not justify his murder. Ned Ryan got no mercy.

"If murderers are treated lightly in our courts we send a message to the people of this city and this state and this nation that serious crime is treated lightly here. We have a duty to ourselves and our neighbors to see that the laws are upheld.

"It is never easy to pass judgment on another person but sometimes it is necessary and appropriate. You all said when you were selected to serve on this jury that you were willing and able to find the defendant guilty if the evidence warranted it. You cannot now shirk that sworn duty.

"And make no mistake, ladies and gentlemen, the evidence more than warrants your returning a verdict of guilty, as charged in the indictment, of murder in the second degree."

He stood there, full of strength and certainty, thanked them and sat down. He did not look at Ryan.

"Well, ladies and gentlemen," Corino said, "you've been very patient, and I'm sure you're very hungry. We'll break now for a late lunch. We can take an hour, and when you come back I'll give you my charge on the law and you can retire to begin your deliberations. I know that it's tempting, now that you've heard closing arguments for both sides, to talk about the case, but I caution you strongly—now, above all—not to discuss it among yourselves or with anyone else. Not until you've heard my charge and officially begun to deliberate."

Ryan left the courtroom with a woman on each arm—solidarity and support. It was a tight fit going up the aisle. The clamor and tumult in the corridor was welcome because it was so general there was no need to pay attention to any one reporter or camera. They made their way in silence to the elevator and down, and then into the car for the trip to the office.

Corino's charge to the jury was short and crisp and devoid of the Corino-isms that the defense lawyers had expected. He read the indictment, then efficiently summarized the evidence. His description of the standard of proof the jury should apply had more of the feel of cracker-barrel wisdom than a narrow tracking of the law, but it was close enough to Griglia's version to make Ryan wince: "Proof beyond a reasonable doubt is not proof beyond any doubt or proof beyond the shadow of a doubt. A doubt is reasonable if it is a doubt for which a reason can be given, a doubt which a reasonable person would have, acting in a matter of this importance. Not a guess or a speculation, or sympathy for the defendant or a desire to avoid the difficult task of making a judgment. It is an actual doubt, one which you are conscious of having in your mind.'' He paused for emphasis and shifted into his most judicial pose. ''A reasonable doubt is a doubt founded in reason, which survives reason.''

The circumstantial evidence charge was the one Ryan was most concerned about. He had asked for the old form, still favored but no longer required, which would tell the jury that to decide the case based on circumstantial evidence the evidence had to exclude *to a moral certainty* all inferences except the inference of guilt.

Corino hedged, pointing out that if the prosecution case rested solely on circumstantial evidence, then it would have to exclude to a *virtual* certainly all inferences but the inference of guilt. Since there was some direct evidence, he told the jury—evidence, for instance, of the defendant's presence on the premises—they should apply the rule for circumstantial evidence only to that part of the evidence which was circumstantial.

It was a charge that seemed to Ryan to have obscurity as its most salient feature. There was nothing Ryan could do about it but hope the jury would remember ''exclude to a virtual certainty all inferences but the inference of guilt'' and forget the rest. ''Virtual certainty'' was not as strong as ''moral certainty,'' not to Ryan's ears, but the jury would not know that the stronger phrase existed, so maybe it didn't matter.

Corino sent the jury off to deliberate at ten after four. Most of the spectators left, as did many of the reporters. Corino left. The lawyers stayed. Griglia pulled his tie loose and undid his top shirt button. Saundra Warneke got up to stretch.

Ryan put his head in his arms on the defense table.

Miller said, ''I'll man the fort if you want to get some rest.''

''It's okay,'' he muttered into his arms.

Jennifer went to the rail to talk to her father and came back to say, ''My father has a car waiting for us. He wants to take us all out to dinner.''

Ryan's stomach turned over at the thought.

''Thanks,'' Miller said. ''I think we're both too tired for that.''

Ryan dozed briefly, then sat up and stretched and looked around. The courtroom was almost empty. A few spectators read newspapers. Most of the press was gone but their seats held jackets and notebooks and newspapers. They would be out in the hall debating the outcome or downstairs in the press room working on stories.

Saundra Warneke and Kassia Miller went off to the women's

room together. Ryan did not have anything to say to his old drinking buddy and law school classmate Francesco Griglia.

At seven-thirty a court officer informed them that the jury was quitting for dinner, and the night.

20

"I CAN'T BELIEVE IT'S OVER," JENNIFER SAID WHEN they got back to the office.

"All but the waiting and the verdict." Miller dumped a pile of letters and telegrams on her desk.

"At least we don't have to worry every minute something is going to go terribly wrong in court. I mean, it came out okay, didn't it?"

"Ask us when the jury comes in." Ryan was settling into his desk chair, closing his eyes.

"I think we all need some rest," Miller said.

"I can take a hint," Jennifer said. "I guess I haven't been the world's best client."

"No, that's not it," Ryan said. "I really am tired." He wished they would all go away.

"Okay. I'll go. See you in the morning. And thank you. Really. You did a great job."

"Sounds like you have a grateful client," Miller said when Jennifer was gone.

He let it pass.

"So, Mr. Ryan, what do you think?"

"I'm too tired to think."

"And with good reason. You deliver some kind of terrific summation, sir."

"I don't want to talk about it."

"No, Ryan, you're wrong."

"Please." It was not a request.

"Forgive me!" She went into the bathroom for a place to go but came back immediately. "I'm sorry, Ryan. I guess I'm tired, too."

"No apology necessary."

"I thought Corino's charge was okay, on balance. Good on some things, bad on others."

"You know, when Ned was killed, nobody could believe that I didn't want to read the papers or hear about the crime or follow the investigation. But I didn't. Now you're not going to believe that I don't want to speculate about what the jury is doing."

"I believe it. But it's not going make the next couple of days a whole lot of fun."

"I wasn't expecting them to be."

The first full day of jury deliberations Ryan struggled out of bed and went to the health club and from there to the office, where he met his client and his co-counsel for the trip to court.

A messenger from Miller's office brought her a package of work to catch up on. She made a couple of futile stabs at it, then gave up.

At the prosecution table Griglia had been replaced by Joe Becker. He and Saundra Warneke worked busily on other cases. Beyond the rail a few reporters hung out and talked in discreet whispers, and a handful of spectators sat reading. A couple of older men, long-time courtroom buffs, sat in the back corner gabbing quietly. Ryan wondered how his retired engineer was doing in the jury room.

The jury sent out its first note at three ten that afternoon. They wanted to hear some of Walter Bailey's DNA-blood-typing testimony.

The defense team unlimbered its thousands of pages of transcript and hunted up the testimony the jury had asked for, while Becker and Warneke did the same thing. Nobody gave any sign that they were going to fetch Franky Griglia. Ryan guessed he would not be in court again until the verdict.

The courtroom filled quickly with reporters and spectators. From the excited buzz behind him, some of the gallery thought a verdict might be imminent.

The jury marched in, eyes front. They still looked fresh and full of energy. The testimony they wanted involved the scientific basis for the DNA blood-typing. They wanted, too, to hear the theory behind the claimed precision of the tests. Finding, limiting and reading the testimony took more than an hour. For the whole time, ten of the twelve principal jurors kept their eyes firmly on the judge and the court reporter. Only the post office employee and the park maintenance worker, both African-American women, let their gaze stray in the direction of the lawyers and the defendant.

Ryan supposed it would be possible to construct a theory based on that observation. He was not inclined to.

About the testimony the jury had asked for he could not keep his mind so clear of speculation. Intense juror curiosity about the accuracy of the tests that related to Jennifer's blood on the murder weapon was not what he would have hoped for. The testimony they were hearing was likely to dispel doubts, not create them.

The jury left for an hour's dinner at six-thirty, as did the lawyers. As a prosecutor Ryan had hated the suspension of his life during jury deliberations and he did not dislike it less now. Some lawyers got work done during jury deliberations, or recreational reading, or even played cards. Ryan had always ended up with too great a stake in the verdict to be fit for anything but waiting.

Jennifer went off for dinner with the friends who were still faithfully appearing in the courtroom every day.

"How are you doing?" Miller asked Ryan as they walked to a nearby restaurant.

"Lousy. I never had a case I was so involved in and so ambivalent about. I put Franky out of my mind there for a while, but I must admit I really hope we destroy the bastard. About Jennifer, I don't know. I sit there at the table with her and most of the time I'm grateful to have you sitting between us. I go up and down like an elevator about her." He looked at his co-counsel. "What about you? In all this time I've never asked you."

"I wouldn't have told you."

"That's what I figured."

"I keep telling myself not to think about it. Usually I don't. There's nothing worse than truly believing your client is innocent. Suppose she gets convicted because of something you did, or didn't do. For the whole trial you have that hanging over you every minute. How do you live with yourself if you lose?"

"I used to have trouble losing when I was prosecutor, knowing some guilty bastard was getting away with it and maybe going out to do it again. I don't know how I'd feel about an innocent person going to jail because I missed something, did something wrong."

"And you always miss *something*. Everybody does."

Some of us more than others, Ryan thought.

"This time, somehow, I got sucked in," Miller said. "I believe her. I don't know exactly how it happened, or when, but I believe her. It's making me crazy.''

They walked in silence until they turned the last corner before the restaurant and Miller said, ''I have my heart in my mouth the whole time we're in court, not knowing whether to hope they'll hurry or take forever. I didn't like that testimony they asked for.''

''It's too little to base a guess on.'' It was reassurance he himself did not believe.

On the jury's second day of deliberation they asked to hear testimony by the prosecution's head-wound expert. They wanted his testimony on direct examination about the strength of blows needed to cause the kind of injuries Ned has sustained, and the cross-examination relating to the factors that affected the impact, such as the velocity of the head at the time of the blow, the length of the assailant's arms, and the torque factors resulting from the length and weight distribution of the weapon.

Ryan tried to think of a reason this was not bad news again. He could not, and neither could Miller.

At the dinner break they went to a restaurant with Jennifer. Neither of the lawyers could eat.

''Only two days and I'm a basket case,'' Miller said.

''I don't see what they have to talk about for so long,'' Jennifer said, the latest variation on the theme of her comments and questions. Ryan had run out of responses.

The jury worked until ten o'clock.

''I think I'll stop in at the Shamrock,'' Ryan said as he and Miller dragged themselves to the elevator. ''Join me if you want.''

As he set a beer and a club soda on the bar, Kelly said, ''Ms. Miller, do you mind giving us a minute for man talk? I'll keep your place.''

She looked from Kelly to Ryan, who shrugged, mystified.

''If you gents will excuse me . . . '' She headed for the rest rooms.

''What's this about?'' Ryan asked.

''It's about being Irish.''

Ryan knew not to speak.

''That slimeball reporter Allen Crown crawled in here the other day. Before I saw who it was and kicked him the hell out he was talking to some of the regulars. Some bullshit about did they know you were a Russian. You want to tell me about that?''

He didn't want to, and he didn't like the idea of Crown poking around in his family history, but life was full of things he didn't like and didn't want to do.

"My grandfather came from a place called Georgia. You see it in the news now and then, struggling for autonomy from the Soviets. My father was born there, too, but he came over when he was a little kid. My mother was born in Ohio. Her name was Wilson. Saralee Wilson." And she died of heartbreak when I was fifteen, he did not add.

"You're not shitting me." It was a statement. "This is for real." Kelly's big square hands were splayed on the edge of the bar. Ryan saw the muscles bunching in the bartender's forearms and was reminded that Ireland was a place proud of its fighters, where men had once brawled with bare knuckles and stout clubs for the pure joy of it.

"It's for real," he acknowledged.

Kelly did not move, and his eyes did not waver from Ryan's. Deciding how angry to get, Ryan thought.

Some of the tension went out of Kelly's body.

"You could have told me. I feel like a damn fool, all that talk of the Emerald Isle."

"No offense intended, Jimmy. I've been passing since I was a kid."

"Passing?" Kelly didn't get it at first, then he grinned and slapped the bar. "That's the best one I've heard in an age, a man trying to pass for Irish. And it's a fine job you do, too." His hand closed briefly around Ryan's arm. "Sly bastard."

There was a call for service at the other end of the bar. He went to deal with it.

Ryan turned to find Miller at his elbow. She slid onto her stool without comment.

Just before lunch on the third full day of deliberations, the jury sent out a note asking to hear all of the testimony of Nicholas Maclean. Corino conferred with the lawyers and sent back a note asking the jury if they needed all the testimony or if some part of it would be enough.

"This isn't good, is it?" Jennifer asked over lunch.

"It depends on exactly what they want," Ryan told her, "but it's not encouraging."

At two-thirty the jury sent out another note. They wanted to hear Maclean's direct testimony about Jennifer's saying she had to kill Ned to get out of the marriage, the cross-examination about the breakup and all of the redirect about his last night with Jennifer.

The two defense lawyers traded unhappy glances when they heard the request. Jennifer caught them at it.

"That's about as bad as it can be, isn't it?"

"It goes either way," Miller said after an awkward pause. "Either they want to hear it to be reminded how bad it is, or they want to be reassured that it isn't so bad after all."

"Thanks, I appreciate your trying to cheer me up. But I know how it looks—I used Nico until I was bored and then when he was divorced and came looking for me I went to bed with him and then blew him off again. It makes me look selfish and cruel. And it turns me into a homewrecker, too."

"Well . . ." Miller said. "That's stretching it."

Ryan didn't think so. It sounded exactly right.

After the jury retired for the night Ryan and Miller walked to the office and then to a natural-food cafeteria they liked a few blocks into Soho. On the way, Miller stopped short at a newsstand.

"What the hell is this, Ryan?"

BEGORRAH! RYAN'S A RUSSIAN, the headline trumpeted. Only Allen Crown's editors could make a front-page story out of the fact that someone was not Irish.

She was turning pages. "Is this really your name? Rianishvili?"

"My grandfather. Yosef Rianishvili."

"This is what Kelly was upset about yesterday."

"Yep."

"I guess he was disappointed you're not a true Son of Erin."

"He took it pretty well, actually."

"He's a good man." She was skimming the exposé as they walked along. "I can't get over this."

He reached for the paper as they got to the restaurant. "Let me look at it. You might as well get the real story."

Allen Crown certainly hadn't, though as usual he had come close on the major points. Grandpa Yosef, a minor partisan hero whose willingness to inflate his role in creating the short-lived Georgian republic had forced him to flee Stalin's repressive army, had been transformed by Crown into a man with a price on his head. Ryan's father fared better, or worse, depending on whether your criterion was accuracy or respectability. Crown had apparently missed George's mother, the Chirkess, but he was reasonably close on George's life as a sometime con man, the perfect arena for Crown's gift for innuendo, and he had the broad strokes right on the fraud charges that had driven George into the life of an expatriate fugitive.

"Is it true what he says about your father scamming those people out of a million dollars?" Miller asked.

"You read pretty fast."

"It caught my eye."

"It caught mine, too. I don't know if it's true. He's on the lam for it, but I know he claims it was a lot less money and it wasn't really a scam. It has the right touch of Robin Hood to be George's style, but I'm the last person in the world who'd claim to know Gyorgei Rianishvili."

"What about the rest of it?"

"Close enough, I guess. I suppose it must seem colorful."

"It's funny, there's a line in that movie *Anatomy of a Murder*— 'There's only one thing more devious than a Philadelphia lawyer and that's an Irish lawyer.' It never seemed to fit. Now I know why."

"Don't be so sure. There's nobody on the planet more devious than a devious Georgian."

"And that's really what you are?"

"My poor mother keeps getting left out. I'm half pure American Anglo-Saxon. And the other half is only half Georgian. The rest is something even wilder, if that's what you're looking for. Mountain tribes that were part Moslem and part pagan. If I have the story right they assigned thunder, war and justice to the same god."

"A sensible combination."

"They also, it is said, sold their daughters into harems, where they were much prized."

"That's not so terrific."

"One of the many customs of my ancestors I did not adopt. Though they say the young women liked the idea."

"Yeah, right. Who says that, the fathers who collected the money?"

"Deponent knoweth not, as we lawyers say. Let's eat."

As they lingered over coffee she said, "I get the impression you don't love all that about your heritage."

The question pulled the plug on his anger. "Why should I love it? It's full of wrong-headed ideas that make no sense in this time and place. It's no more my heritage than whatever combination of mostly Celtic ingredients went into my mother but never prompted me to paint my face blue. A bunch of hoked up stories about noble thieves. That's what it's about. How do you suppose my father got to be such a prince among men? And the worst part is, he sold it all to Ned. There I was with my life all locked up in setting a good example for my son and Grandpa George swoops in for a couple of well-timed visits playing the dashing brigand, and you see how it all came out.''

21

WAITING FOR THE VERDICT, RYAN COULD NOT KEEP his mind from turning to thoughts of the murder and the murderer. He found it increasingly difficult to imagine that anyone but Jennifer had killed Ned. He had to assume this turn of mind was partly attributable to Franky Griglia's case and summation. It was not a good omen for the verdict.

His outlook did not improve when the jury asked for the medical examiner's testimony about the time of death but not for Miller's cross-examination on the same topic.

Just before dinner, though, the jury sent another note. They wanted the cross-examination testimony, too. It was not worth celebrating, but at least it was not bad news. Ryan took it to mean that there was a difference of opinion on the jury. He knew how dumb it was to try to guess about such things; he was rediscovering how impossible it was to avoid it.

After the testimony was read, Jennifer went to stand by the rail and talk to her friends. Ryan was increasingly glad she had that kind of support; it took the pressure off him and Miller.

"There's something I've been wanting to talk to you about," his co-counsel told him while they sat alone at the defense table. "That conversation last night made it seem more pressing. This is the busybody talking now, so you can shut me up any time."

"What's it about?"

"Your son."

"I don't think I want to hear it. What about him?"

"His good side. The thing is, you've been under a lot of pressure to think about his bad side, so I thought now that we were past that . . .''

"What do you know that I don't?"

"It's not so much what you know as how you look at it. And there are some other things, like what I saw in that trunk."

"Like what?"

"Didn't you read that inventory I sent you?"

"Only looking for evidence."

"Well, there was a person in that trunk. A student athlete who got love letters from girls who liked him and who kept a diary for a few months."

"You read them?"

"Not everything. But I couldn't resist the diary. I said I was a busybody. That's why I'm so good at doing my homework. I like it. And with Ned's trunk I could tell myself I was looking for clues, sort of."

"Did you find any?"

"You'd have known long ago if I did."

"That's right, it's our client who holds things back."

If she noticed the edge in his voice she did not acknowledge it. "You really ought to look through it."

"There'll be time for that. Not yet."

The next morning the jury was beginning to look worn. They came in separately, as if each of them was surrounded by a prickly barrier compounded of fatigue and jury-room antagonism. They requested the testimony of Donald Garfield, on direct and cross-examination, about exactly where and when he had seen Jennifer Ryan.

They sent no notes that afternoon, and none in the evening.

Jennifer was getting more and more nervous. "I thought by now they'd have decided."

Ryan said nothing.

"How can it take so long," she persisted. "It's just guilty or not guilty."

"There's more than one crime for them to decide about," Miller reminded her.

"Murder is what it says in the indictment."

"They don't have to convict you of murder," Ryan said, and thought: We've been over this. Wasn't she listening?

She said, "It's strange, I never believed they would say anything but not guilty."

"There are what's called lesser included offenses," Miller said gently. "Manslaughter in the first degree, manslaughter in the second degree. Criminally negligent homicide."

"It still means going to jail."

"For some of them you might not get any jail time at all. If they convict on anything less than man one it could be a suspended sentence, or probation, or maybe something like six months."

Ryan couldn't believe his ears. This was Hang 'Em High Corino she was talking about. Did she seriously think a judge with his reputation was going to give a minimum sentence to a rich, spoiled dilettante convicted of killing a man in a fit of pique? Because that was what it would amount to, no matter what the jury called it.

He kept his mouth shut.

The jury sent out no notes the morning of their sixth day of deliberation.

"This is getting ridiculous," Ryan heard Joe Becker observe to Saundra Warneke as they left for lunch.

Jennifer went out with her friends. Ryan was relieved. The days of waiting were not improving his reaction to his client. He was increasingly unnerved by her shifts from volubility to moody silence, and by his own uncertainty about her guilt. Feeling alternately warm and cool toward her, he could not find a comfortable way to behave.

Miller commented on it.

"Is it that obvious?"

"You're not Mount Rushmore, you know."

Impatience and frustration were palpable in the courtroom and the corridor that afternoon. Rumors fed on rumors. No one knew what was happening. Everyone believed everything. Ryan could see it just watching the faces of reporters and spectators and even the court officers. He did not need to hear the words.

Jennifer was more on edge than ever, and with no requests for testimony and nothing new to ask about she recycled her old questions and concerns. Ryan took as many walks in the corridor and trips to the men's room as he reasonably could.

With the judge's permission, the jury made Sunday a short day.

As he pushed his chair back and reached for his briefcase, Ryan had a view of Jennifer in an unguarded moment. She looked somehow shrunken—sad and vulnerable—and he felt a rush of sympathy for her.

He realized that his need to avoid her came as much as anything from fear that he had let her down. It was a paradox. Much of the time he thought she was guilty, yet he felt this need to have served her well. To have rescued her from Griglia the dragon. Another unsolved mystery of the human heart.

* * *

In the morning, there was a message on the office phone machine to call the D.A.

"I'm listening in," Miller said.

"Unscrew the mouthpiece."

"Okay, boss."

Ryan made the call.

"Michael," Griglia said heartily. "I was calling to see how you'd feel about a plea at this point."

He was stunned. "What for, Franky? Scared?"

"I thought *you'd* be."

"I didn't expect them to acquit in ten minutes."

"I heard a rumor."

"Oh?"

"They're not off murder."

Ryan looked across the office at Miller. Could that be true?

"So?" he said nonchalantly.

"That doesn't sound so good for your side. If they're that close on murder it's got to be intent that's hanging them up. That still leaves man one as a lesser included. If they had a reasonable doubt she did it, they'd be out of there by now. They'd sure as hell be past intentional murder."

"That's how you read it."

"How the hell else is there?"

"Eleven to one for acquittal with the last one about to see the light any minute."

Miller looked to the heavens. Ryan did not believe it either.

"Dream on, Michael," Griglia said. "Take it from one who *knows*—it's more like the other way around. We're willing to go for man one and dicker about the sentence. Don't fool yourself. You owe it to your client to talk to her about this, and seriously. This offer won't be repeated, and it expires at midnight tonight."

"If the jury doesn't come in today."

"Wait if you want to. You'll still have a couple of hours tonight. But that's it."

Griglia hung up.

"What's he up to?" Miller wanted to know. "If he's right about the jury, why make an offer?"

"To avoid a hung jury, is my guess. No prosecutor wants to go through a retrial. Franky's no different."

"You can bet he won't be the one in court next time."

"No, but it's a lot of money and trial time for his office. They're overloaded and over budget as it is, and the chances of winning usually get smaller the second time around.''

"Maybe not on this one. DNA tests don't lose their memory.''

"Maybe not,'' Ryan conceded, "but there's something else. If Franky gets a hung jury, the public perception is, he didn't win. That's not something he's going to let happen if he can possibly help it . . . I have to admit the bastard's good, though. For a minute there he had me going.''

"You're kidding.''

"I don't mean to take the deal. I mean to give our client a serious talking to about it.''

"That's dumb.''

"I'm not sure it is.'' He thought again of Hang 'Em High Corino. This was not an ordinary gamble they were talking about.

"Okay, you've got to tell her,'' Miller said. "But you don't have to include Franky's rumors.''

"No, ma'am. Not for a minute.'' Suddenly Ryan felt buoyant. "But there sure is something else I can do with those rumors.''

"What?''

"Stick with me, kid, and I'll show you the world. First, we talk to Jennifer.''

The three of them walked to court together instead of taking the car. Ryan explained Griglia's proposal, and his time limit. As he expected, Jennifer rejected the idea out of hand.

The morning in court was like the other mornings in court, and the afternoons and the evenings. The crowds had thinned. The reporters manned their posts stoically, most of them hanging out in the first floor press rooms waiting for the call to come upstairs. The jury sent two notes to the judge, but he dealt with them without coming to the courtroom.

As lunch approached, Ryan said to Miller, "I'm taking a quick trip to the Bar Association. Want to come?''

"You've got something evil on your mind.''

"After a fashion.''

"Okay, I'm hooked.''

At the Bar Association he went straight to the library and pulled down a book of motion forms.

"We filing a motion?''

He was turning pages. When he found what he wanted he showed it to her.

"A mistrial? On what grounds?''

"Violating the sanctity of the jury.''

She laughed. "You sir, are a mad person. You don't have grounds for a mistrial."

"Conduct inside or outside the courtroom that prejudices the defendant's case and makes it impossible for her to have a fair trial. Maybe yes, maybe no. Depends on who Mr. Griglia gets his rumors from, and how. At least I can make him sweat for a while."

"And you used to give me grief for being a trash-and-burn litigator."

The afternoon in court passed without any requests from the jury. The whole courtroom seemed to be in the grip of spring fever on an uncommonly warm day for the tag end of April. Dust motes floated in shafts of yellow sunlight, and no one had much energy even for speculating about the verdict. There was a sense in the air that people had stopped expecting the jury to come to a decision.

Ryan worked on his motion for a mistrial. At dinner time he went for a short walk and then came back to the courtroom to do more work. It was something to focus on, something that seemed like progress.

At eight-thirty the jury sent word that they were retiring early for the night.

"You eat anything, Ryan?" Miller asked as they pushed through the revolving door to the street.

"Nope."

"Me neither. Tell you what—come over to my place and I'll cook you dinner. If you can stand a break from the constant whirl of one restaurant meal after another."

"Thanks, but . . . a rain check, okay? I think tonight I want to be alone. We can go up to Kelly's and I'll buy you a drink."

"Another time," she said stiffly.

"I guess I said the wrong thing."

"Don't worry about it. See you tomorrow."

He skipped Kelly's. By the time he got home, he was feeling desolate. He poured himself a drink and went into the living room to contemplate . . . what?

He called Miller.

"Is that invitation still open?"

A noticeable hesitation. "Yes. Sure."

"What can I bring?"

"Dinner. I didn't shop on the way home."

"We could order in."

"Chinese or cold cuts, like at the office?"

"Never mind."

He did some shopping and then took a taxi across town. In the past he had dropped her off in front of the building and left packages for her, but he had not gone inside.

She answered the door in jeans and a sweatshirt.

"You look about twelve."

"Is that a compliment?"

"I don't know. Isn't it?"

"What's in the bag?"

"Goodies." He followed her into the apartment. And stopped.

"What's wrong?"

"Nothing."

He was in a room at least twenty by thirty, big for New York. The floor was covered with tight-looped gray carpeting and each wall was a different shade of gray, from light to almost black. On the darkest wall was an enormous painting, inspired by a famous NASA photograph: the white-and-brown-marbled blue sphere of the earth shining in a black sky over the bleak horizon of the moon. The only furniture was a long white leather couch, two armchairs from the twenties covered in plum-colored cloth, and a glass coffee table with a Sunday paper strewn on it and on the floor.

"I'm never here," she said. "Kitchen's this way."

He expected a kitchen out of a spaceship and got one out of a French country house.

"Where did you get a kitchen this big?"

"Courtesy of the former owner. It used to be two rooms. Or three."

"This is incredible."

She took the food from him. "What I love about you, Ryan," she said as she unpacked the bags, "is that when you're not grumbling and groaning you're like a little kid."

"Is that a compliment?"

"And *sometimes* you even have a sense of humor. What is this, tomatoes and mozzarella? And fresh basil."

"And champagne. I figured we should drink it before the verdict, just in case."

"Bad joke."

"I hope it's a joke."

"Take off your tie, Ryan. We both need to relax."

They fixed dinner together, drinking champagne as they went. She was right, he needed to relax. He wasn't sure he remembered how.

* * *

'Did we actually kill two bottles of champagne?'' she asked when they were done, lingering at the dining room table.

"Must have. They're empty and there's no one else here. That was great. You make terrific mozzarella and tomatoes.''

"Thank you, sir. You do a pretty good champagne yourself.''

They collected the dishes and brought them into the kitchen.

"Well," he said.

"Bedtime," she said.

"See you tomorrow.''

"Ryan. It's the middle of the night. You want the pajamas or the robe?''

"That was *my* house.''

"You don't think I have pajamas and a robe?''

"You're drunk, Miller.''

"Me? I never get drunk. I'm very temperate.''

"No comment.''

"Bedroom's this way. I have a toothbrush supply, too.''

"So I'm not the only one.''

"I never said you were.''

"And pajamas big enough to fit me.''

"My brother's.''

The bedroom was feminine without being frilly. The bed was king size with a brass headboard. She took the pajamas from a closet. They were navy blue and felt like silk.

"Your brother's?''

"Don't look a loaner in the mouth, Ryan. I'll get your toothbrush.''

"Wait a minute.''

He reached out and she came into his arms. He held her. They held each other. Comfort, friendship, solace. He did not want to let go.

She leaned back to look up at him. He bent and they kissed softly.

"Toothbrush," she said, and disengaged.

He lay in bed with her curled asleep against him, trying not to think about the past or the future, trying to make the regular rise and fall of her body and its warmth the only things he knew.

First light woke him. He lay still, feeling the dawn.

He turned his head. The covers had come off both of them in the night. She was lying next to him, looking at him. She seemed just to have awakened. Her robe was askew, her legs exposed. He stretched and held out an arm and she moved over to nestle against him. She put one leg over his and he felt that she wore nothing under the robe. They lay there together quietly. She stretched enough to kiss the corner of his mouth, then settled back.

He was seized by the desire to taste her. He twisted over and moved her leg aside. She murmured in sleepy surprise but did not resist. He rested his head on the rise of her belly, listening to fluids purling gently within her, letting her scent invade him.

She was sweet and spicy. He stayed longer than he at first intended, until her soft rocking response grew more rapid and angular and she cried out her pleasure.

He rested without moving, turning his head only enough to breathe comfortably, inhaling her, stirring small black hairs when he exhaled.

She stroked his head. Lifted gently to coax him upward so they were again side by side. She licked the moisture from his chin.

He kissed her eyes and her neck and lying back against the pillow fell warmly asleep.

He woke up alone in the bed and lay there until a full bladder prompted him to get up and find the bathroom. He shed the pajamas and showered.

She met him on his way out of the bathroom, toweling himself, and reached up to kiss his cheek. In bare feet she was shorter than he remembered. Tiny and perfectly made.

"Sleep well?" she asked.

"Mmmm . . ."

She cupped him in her hand. "How are you?"

He touched her arm, then leaned down to kiss her.

"I'm fine."

He felt himself stir. Her hand welcomed him. He tingled, but he did not fill to urgency.

He smiled over his sadness. *Sans coitus triste.*

"Coffee?" he asked.

"The coffee's great. Come on in."

He followed her into the kitchen, delighted to watch her bare feet on the carpet, her hips moving under the soft thin robe.

The coffee was rich and dark, the best coffee he ever had. And good crusty English muffins with homemade preserves from some friend's summer house.

"I have an idea," she said. She took his hand and led him into the bedroom, pushed him playfully onto the bed and took away his towel.

"Why should you have all the fun?" she said and lay down with him.

Her hands and mouth were like keys unlocking the tension that bound him. He floated free in a state that was only partly connected to reality. There came a time when he untangled them from each other and retwined them face to face, her legs around him, and remembered how it felt to be a man with a woman.

They showered together and dressed and reconvened in the kitchen for more coffee.

"Well," he said.

"Well, indeed."

"You'll have to excuse me, I'm kind of new at this."

"New? I thought you were married for twenty years."

"I mean new at beginnings. The other, too. I haven't . . . been with a woman in almost five years."

"You must be something when you've had some practice."

She leaned over the table and kissed him lightly.

"You know, Ryan," she said as she got up to brew another pot of coffee. "These days you're supposed to get a person's pedigree." She was puttering with the coffee machine, facing away from him. "I have a friend who says people have developed an ocular exam to tell who's safe." She turned briefly to face him. "You look them in the eye, and you say, is there anything I should know?"

They laughed together and she turned away again.

"I'm thirty-five years old," she said in a flat, soft voice. "I've never been married. I had one major college romance that ended badly. So I came to New York. I was briefly a major party animal, when I was in the glamor magazine business, but I still didn't have much faith in men. I've never had a shortage of guys to go out with, but mostly I just work hard. Three years working days and learning nights didn't help much, and you can imagine how helpful it is getting to know someone if every time you're out on a date the beeper goes off and you have to go down to the courthouse and wait for some client to be arraigned. Or you have to cancel at the last minute, three dates in a row. It doesn't make for much of a stable situation."

"Being a prosecutor had similar problems."

"But you were married."

"That doesn't make it any easier on the other person—never having you around, never knowing when you're going to cancel plans." Twenty-twenty hindsight.

"I never thought of it. Marital problems haven't been a question."

"I don't see why not."

She came to sit next to him. "I have a gift for the inappropriate. I went out with a tennis player, for heaven's sake. And that wasn't the dumbest, either. You missed my intriguing Felon period, and the Dashing Detectives, too. The Older Man and the Younger Man. It's amazing how many mistakes you can make in thirty-five years. And I wasn't even trying."

"What about your doctor?"

"Oh. He says I'm okay. Nothing to worry about."

He reddened. "Not that doctor."

"Oh, the handsome Dr. Kimble. That didn't go anywhere. I went out with him to show myself I wasn't limited to tennis players."

He drank some coffee.

"We still have to decide what to do next," he said.

"Go to court, I'd say."

He stood up in a hurry. "What time is it?"

"It's eight-fifteen. We'll just be okay if we can get a cab."

22

THE SKY WAS A HEAVY GRAY AND THE AIR SMELLED like rain. After ten minutes on the corner with no sign of a free taxi, Kassia spotted a gypsy cab and threw herself into the downtown traffic to get the driver's attention. They dodged over to where the cabbie had pulled up and piled in just as a torrent slammed down from the clouds.

Their car-service sedan was in front of the office. Ryan shoved cash at the gypsy cabbie and they ran over to the sedan, pelted by raindrops the size of marbles. He pulled open the back door and held it for her, then ducked in after her, soaked. Jennifer was already in the backseat, squeezing herself against the opposite door to make room for them.

"Where have you two been?"

"Sorry we're late," Ryan muttered. "Let's go," he told the driver.

The lawyers' clothes gave off a steam of evaporating rain. Ryan could feel the water soaking through from his jacket to his shirt to his skin. His trousers were glued to the underside of his thighs.

"Anybody bring a change of clothes?"

Kassia laughed. "I sure could use one."

"Too bad Daddy isn't here," Jennifer said. "He's always got something in the trunk."

"We can call Craig and ask him to break into our apartments for us," Kassia suggested.

"Now you're talking."

The courthouse atmosphere was as steamy as the inside of the car. Eight days was closing in on the record for a New York murder jury. People were making nervous jokes about the Creation only having taken six.

Ryan deposited his briefcase on the counsel table and went outside to the men's room to wring some of the water from his clothes and dry off.

As he turned to go through the double doors back into the courtroom he thought he saw Franky Griglia down by the far elevator bank.

"Something's up," he said as he sat down at the defense table.

At eleven-ten Anthony Corino entered his courtroom in his robes, scrubbed and clean shaven. There was a tense bustle of activity among the clerks and court officers. The air itself seemed to clear.

"This is it, isn't it?" Jennifer said.

"Looks that way," Ryan said.

A television crew started to set up a camera where the rail met the wall by the jury box. They worked quickly and quietly. Reporters coming up from the press room downstairs stepped carefully over the thick black cables on their way to the four reserved press rows. They were all there, Molly O'Hara and Zeke and Allen Crown and all the others who had been there day after day as the trial unfolded.

Francesco Griglia arrived at eleven-twenty. He smiled broadly at the reporters as he passed them. The smile disappeared as he walked into the well of the court. Joe Becker closed the gate behind his boss and held a chair for him at the counsel table. Griglia gave the judge a small nod of greeting. He did not look at Ryan.

There was a lull as everyone settled into place. The television crew was finishing its work, focusing the camera on the judge and on the defense table.

Ryan felt a movement in his right hand and looked down at it. He was holding Kassia's hand, squeezing tight. Both their hands were slick with sweat.

He let go. "Sorry."

"It's okay."

He wanted to look at her, but it meant turning toward Jennifer and he did not want to do that. He stared straight ahead.

Corino tapped with his gavel. "Ladies and gentlemen, I have had a communication from the jury. They will be here shortly. I will ask you to remain silent now and when they are seated. There is to be no demonstration in this courtroom, and no one is to leave the courtroom until the jury has left."

Everyone sat in damp, uncomfortable silence. Ryan stared at the door the jury used.

The door opened and the jury came in. Slowly, eyes down and ahead, mouths set impassively. They looked tired, ground down. The art director's makeup was uneven for the first time, the book editor looked thinner and paler and older. Even Sarrubbi, whose muscles had always bulged under tight polo shirts, looked slack. Ryan watched Constable cross the well of the court, but the engineer, his white hair askew, did not look up.

They filed into their seats in the jury box and looked at no one. Incongruously, the bus driver twisted in his seat to smile at the television camera. It was focused now on the judge; it had not shown the jury and would not.

The courtroom was quiet. Ryan felt Kassia's hand close briefly over his.

"The jurors are all present, your honor," Corino's clerk said. "Will the foreman please rise?"

Ms. Wu stood up slowly. Like the other jurors, she looked only at the clerk.

"Has the jury agreed upon a verdict?"

Ms. Wu straightened visibly, imbued now with the gravity of her task.

"Yes, we have."

Ryan and Kassia stood side by side. Jennifer stood next to them.

"As to the count in the indictment, charging the defendant with murder in the second degree, how do you find the defendant, guilty or not guilty?''

Ms. Wu took a breath. ''Not guilty.''

Ryan felt the words like a charge of electricity. Kassia's hand squeezed his and he squeezed back. He could sense Jennifer's relief, but he did not look at her.

The clerk was continuing. ''As to the lesser included charge, manslaughter in the first degree, how do you find the defendant, guilty or not guilty?''

This time, the foreman looked at the three standing at the defense table before she said, ''Not guilty.''

Now Ryan's heart was pounding so hard it made him tremble as he stood. Deep in his chest a tiny bubble of elation was beginning to form.

Too soon to be sure, he told himself.

''As to the lesser included charge, manslaughter in the second degree, how to you find the defendant, guilty or not guilty?''

''Guilty.''

There was a moment when Ryan was waiting for the next charge to be read, a suspended instant of silence before he registered what Ms. Wu had said.

All at once he heard Jennifer's single, sharp sob, the hubbub in the court, Corino's gavel.

The clerk polled the jury. Ryan forced himself to watch them. They spoke flatly, looking at the clerk or the floor, except for Sarrubbi, who stared hard at Jennifer as he said, ''Yes,'' and Constable, who answered somberly, then looked up to give Ryan a small, sad smile of regret.

Ryan did not want to look at Griglia but he could not stop himself. The D.A. returned the glance, savage with victory.

Corino thanked the jurors and told them that they had performed one of the most serious and difficult obligations a citizen could be called on to do, and they had done it well in an especially difficult case. He dismissed them with the comment that though they were free to say whatever they wanted to he hoped they would bear in mind his wish that they respect their fellow jurors and be circumspect in discussing the confidences of the jury room and the deliberation process.

Ryan made an immediate motion to have the verdict set aside. He submitted the affidavit of intention to appeal he had prepared in advance.

''Will you be staying on this matter until the notice of appeal is filed?'' Corino asked.

"Yes, your honor, and at this time I'd like to make application for a continuation of bail pending appeal."

Griglia, predictably, opposed it. "Your honor, Jennifer Ryan's incentive to flee is greater than ever. There is no longer the hope of acquittal to bring her back to court. She has nothing to gain from staying, when becoming a fugitive is such an attractive prospect. And even a million dollars bail is no deterrent, considering her father's means."

Chilled by the verdict, Ryan still had fire enough to respond angrily. "Your honor, there is no foundation in fact for a single word that Mr. Griglia has spoken. My client has every reason to hope that her appeal will succeed. There was evidence withheld in this case, by the police and by the D.A.'s office. Mr. Griglia is being vindictive. Jennifer Ryan poses no threat to society, her ties to the community are strong and deep, and she has no prior criminal record of any sort. She has clearly demonstrated her commitment to following this unfortunate matter through the judicial system."

As Ryan paused for breath, Griglia started forward with a counterargument. Ryan cut him off.

"And if Mr. Griglia will allow me another word, I would point out that this application is supported by the family of the victim, whose father stands before you, as you know."

Griglia was not going to give in easily. Corino gave him time to exhaust his arguments and then leaned forward on the bench to glower from under his eyebrows at Jennifer.

"Jennifer Ryan, you have been convicted of a serious crime. I hope that my belief in your commitment to remain in the court's jurisdiction and contest this conviction is not misplaced. I am not inclined to incarcerate you for the lengthy proceedings it will take before the questions your lawyers are likely to raise on appeal are resolved. But I am impressed by the arguments raised by the District Attorney, and I am consequently going to set your continued bail at two million dollars"—there was a susurrus of shock in the courtroom—"the additional million dollars to be deposited in cash within fourteen days."

He set sentencing in six weeks, adjourned, and left the bench.

23

RYAN WAS OBLIVIOUS TO THE CLAMOR AS THE COURT-
room was emptied.

Jennifer was staring blankly in the direction of the empty jury
box. He went to stand by her.

She took a long breath and let it out with a shudder. "It's all
right, Michael, it's not your fault. I brought this on myself." The
words were barely audible. "There was so much I should have told
you and I didn't. But I swear, Michael, I didn't kill him. *I didn't.*"

Somehow they made it out of court and to the office. Kneeland was
there, and some of Jennifer's friends.

Kneeland drew Ryan aside. "I heard you tell the judge that you
would be representing Jennifer until the appeal was filed. We'll
have to see about that."

The world turned red for Ryan. It took all his willpower to keep
from doing or saying something irretrievable. For all his effort to
stifle his reaction, it was visible enough for Kneeland to take a step
back, as if he had been threatened.

"I have my daughter's interests to think about."

"I'm sure you do." Ryan was barely under control. "My remark
in court was *pro forma.* We can talk about what we'll do next,
tomorrow. Today we need to calm down and assess the situation."

Finally, the crowd was gone and only the two lawyers and their
investigator were left.

"I don't know why everyone is so gloomy," Lawrence said.
"Word around the courthouse is we just won a great victory."

"They said guilty," Ryan pointed out.

"Sure they did, but guilty of what? Man two. It could have been
intentional murder. That sounds like a victory to me."

Ryan supposed that by the criminal-defense lawyer's method of scorekeeping this was a victory. But he felt no triumph.

"Tell it to Jennifer," he said.

"I hear she could walk with no jail time."

"With Santa Claus on the bench, maybe." Not Hang 'Em High Corino.

"Don't rub it in, Ryan," Kassia said.

"I'm not." Or was he?

"I think we should all get drunk," Lawrence proposed quickly.

"I think we should get some rest," Kassia countered.

"And I think we should do some work," said Ryan.

"You're outvoted."

"It's not up for a vote. I have an appeal to worry about. And a sentencing report." Until Jennifer fires me, not her father.

But he realized she was right—he was exhausted. He went home and slept until she came over so they could watch the evening news together.

"You're all fired up about this appeal," she said.

"I think we can win. But I'm more concerned about the sentencing report." He turned on the television. "Time for the news."

The verdict was the lead story. Molly O'Hara had cornered a cross-section of the jury for short interviews. She led off with Gail Wu.

"It was a difficult week," the jury foreman said. "It started off very polite and civil, but it got out of control. There were two guys in there, I thought we were going to have another murder on our hands."

"The votes were all over the place," reported the ever-sleepy bus driver. "On one of them, I think it was the fourth day, we almost acquitted her altogether."

The art director said, "I was sorry for Mr. Ryan. He lost his son, and now he lost his big case and his daughter-in-law is going to jail."

"But the verdict was that she killed his son." O'Hara reminded her.

"He doesn't seem to think so."

"But you thought she did."

"There was her blood on the statue, you know? And they didn't really say a whole lot about who else might have done it. They tell you they don't have to, but if they don't it's hard to know what else to think."

"Those fingerprints on the telephone sure bothered me," said the office equipment salesman. "You gotta wonder who wiped them off. But everyone else got so sure she did it. And she had that boyfriend, too . . .''

Sarrubbi was O'Hara's last interview. ''Look, she was guilty, no doubt about it. I think it was the wrong verdict. It should have been murder.''

Ryan turned the set off.

''It looks like Mr. Sarrubbi must have been one of those two murderous guys Gail Wu was talking about,'' Kassia said.

''No question.''

''Who do you think his opposition was?''

''Constable.''

''The engineer?''

''The poet.'' He got up and paced. ''Damn it, I wanted to challenge Sarrubbi. I was sure he was no good for us. But I let you and that idiot Sisley talk me out of it.''

''What does that mean? You blame me?'' Curled on the couch, her legs under her, she watched him stride back and forth. ''Sure you do. But that's not enough. You blame yourself, too, don't you? For not being clairvoyant and superman at the same time.''

''I don't blame you. You made an honest mistake. I'm the one who didn't stand by his convictions.'' He said it calmly, not wanting to expose the emotion behind it to his . . . his what. His co-counsel? The trial was over, and Kneeland had about fired him. His lover? They'd had one mostly half-awake encounter—an encounter that he had no idea how she felt about, however good it had been for him, and that might never be repeated. His friend? He wanted to think so, but it was unexplored ground.

He said, ''If I blame myself, it's with good reason.''

She straightened up and swung her feet to the floor. ''I feel the need to go out for some air. I'll be at the Shamrock when you stop beating yourself up.''

She meant well, he knew that. She was trying to snap him out of it. Protecting herself, too. But when you slapped someone's face to help him, the therapeutic purpose didn't lessen the sting of the blows.

It felt right to be alone now. He began straightening things up around the apartment. Moving piles of papers from one place to another, he came upon a copy of the program from Ned's funeral and memorial service.

He found himself thinking about what Kassia had said about Ned. Maybe she was right. Maybe he had spent too long thinking about the dark side of his son's life. It might help to try to think about the positive.

He scanned the list of eulogizers. Here were six people who had thought well of Ned, or at least spoken well of him. Perhaps he could get them to talk to him, despite the verdict that now stamped him an ally of Ned's convicted murderer. And it would be a good idea to look through Ned's trunk, too. It might be the best place to start. He could have Kaplan send it over.

He closed the program to put it in his To Do box and noticed two phone numbers scrawled on the back, with the message, "If you need anything—HRK." It took him a minute to remember: he had stayed behind after the interment to be alone by the grave. Kneeland, who had made all the funeral arrangements, had made sure a limousine waited. He had left the program for Ryan with the driver.

Ryan looked again at the phone numbers. One, he was pretty sure, was the number for Kneeland's Fifth Avenue apartment. The other looked familiar, too, although he didn't know from where.

When he had a clear space on his desk he sat down with a yellow legal pad and some sharp pencils. He had intended to make a list of issues for Corino to consider in making his sentencing decision. Instead, he began to write down the names of the people who might have been connected with Ned's murder.

The last time he had gone through this he had come up with Ned's interest-skimming and stopped. Maybe there was something beyond that, connections he hadn't reached.

He started with names. Olivera came first. Willy and Kneeland and Jim Morris and Srini Ramanujan, people whose relationship to Ned and the money he had handled were not clear to Ryan. The bandito and others like him Ryan discounted. That kind of theory-spinning was fine to create doubt for the jury, but for all his hopes about Harry Bundesman, Ryan had the feeling old anger like that rarely added up to murder.

Besides the people there were the anomalous facts: the phone call and the fingerprints wiped from the phone. And all the collateral evidence that Ned had been involved with dirty money.

Cui bono? he wrote.

The phone rang. It was Lawrence.

"I just got some news. Nothing that'll help with the appeal, but it closes one of the gaps in what we know."

"I'm listening."

"I put out a feeler a while ago, with this new interagency, superagency lovefest they're trying to put together for big drug cases. Cost me every ounce of professional credit I had left, but I got this computer guy working on Olivera's banking and money handling.

The story is, Willy is one of Olivera's bankers. One of many, but he handles a fair amount of the man's loose change. Has for at least a couple of years.''

Ryan absorbed it. "Well, now we know how Ned met Olivera.''

He moved Willy into the prime category with Olivera. Philadelphia was only an hour and a half from New York. Where was Willy on June 14? Ryan wrote across the pad.

He realized abruptly how long it had been since Kassia had left.

When he got to the Shamrock she was nowhere to be seen.

"The lady got tired and went home," Kelly informed him. "You ought to treat her better.''

"Is that professional advice, or personal?''

"Both. Ah, hell, listen to me. Just what you need tonight—advice from a dumb bartender." He drew Ryan a beer. "All on the house tonight, Michael Ryan, and if you want to drink yourself insensible I'll make sure you get home.''

"I don't, but you're a good friend and I've been an ungrateful pain in the ass lately.''

"Not where I could see you.''

Ryan raised his beer mug. "Confusion to our enemies.''

"Amen, brother.''

"I appreciate your not offering me condolences on the trial.''

"I figured if you wanted to talk about it you would. I also think it was a bum verdict.''

"That it was. What's new in your life?''

"Nothing much. The landlord is still counting the days till my six months are up.''

"How's your cousin the cop?''

"Nephew. He likes being a lieutenant, he tells me. Got transferred to Special Investigations in the Narcotics Division. Swears he's going to make a major collar his first month. He's making my sister crazy with worry. She can't figure out how she went so wrong, that her son grew up so different from what she expected.''

"Tell her for me she's got company feeling that way.''

At the office in the morning Ryan told Kassia about Willy. "It never made sense that Willy didn't know it was dirty money. He was a bigger liar than we thought.''

"My question right now is, how does it help Jennifer?" She fired up her computer. "I thought we were concentrating on the sentencing report and the appeal.''

She went to work, putting up a barrier of concentrated activity he did not know how to penetrate.

Just before noon there was a knock on the front door and Russell Constable peered into the office.

"Mr. Ryan? Russell Constable's my name. Can I disturb you for a minute? I was one of the . . . "

"I know who you are, Mr. Constable." Ryan shook the ex-juror's hand. "Come in. Sit down. You remember Ms. Miller."

"Yes, hello." He sat stiffly on the edge of the one comfortable visitor's chair. "I don't know if this is appropriate, coming to see you. I wanted to talk about the trial."

"I'm glad you're here. What's on your mind?"

"The verdict. The whole process. It gave me a new perspective on my fellow humans."

"It's been known to do that." Not wanting to rush him.

"I don't know who killed your son, Mr. Ryan, but I do know that you made me doubt that it was his wife. I doubted it strongly enough that I did my best to see that she got acquitted."

"I appreciate that, and your telling me about it."

"In the end it all came down to was the doubt reasonable? Ralph Sarrubbi was going to hold out for murder, but he saw that if he did, I would hold out just as strongly for not guilty and we'd end up a hung jury. Nobody wanted that. He let it go, but it was understood that in return the others would vote guilty to one of the degrees of manslaughter. I maintained my position as long as I could, but in the end they persuaded me to think that I wasn't being reasonable. Literally—that my doubt wasn't supported by reason. I wouldn't have believed the amount of sophistry ordinary people are capable of. By the end of it I was exhausted. I gave in. I was sorry as soon as the vote was taken, but they wouldn't let me take my vote back."

"Did you ask to?"

"Yes. They said a vote was a vote and they weren't voting again."

"So it was a compromise verdict." Kassia said. Heading toward grounds for reversal.

"Yes."

"Would you say your vote was coerced?"

"Well . . . I don't know about coerced."

"But you were under pressure from the others to vote against your own judgment?" Ryan followed up.

"Under pressure, yes."

"Would you sign an affidavit about all this?" Kassia asked him.

"Oh." It was not a question he had counted on. "I came by to tell you because I thought you both did such a good job and I felt bad about how it turned out. I don't want to make trouble."

"Jennifer Ryan already has trouble," Ryan said quietly. "Worse trouble than the nuisance of straightening out an improper verdict."

"I have to think about it."

Ryan gave him a card as he left. "Please do think. But bear in mind that the court has time limits for these things."

"You'll hear from me," Constable said on his way out.

"It looks like Griglia was right with that hint about a lone hold-out," Ryan said. "Which means I was right, too—he was getting inside information on the deliberations."

"Don't get all excited. The judge isn't going to change his mind about your motion."

"Probably not."

"Your Mr. Constable is a nice man and he means well, but he won't be back."

Unhappily, Ryan did not think she was wrong. And running after him would not help. You didn't overturn a jury verdict with a single reluctant witness and nothing else.

The alarm woke him early on Thursday morning. He went to the health club and swam ten more laps than usual, then took a long warm shower.

Toweling himself dry, he thought about the phone call from the mysteriously clean telephone, and he saw something he should have seen before. He had been working under the theory that the murderer had made the call, or if not the murderer then someone at the party who was totally unrelated to the murder. Everyone had started with that same premise. The problem with that, a problem they had dealt with by ignoring it, was that the call had been made at almost exactly the same time that Jennifer said she and Ned had finished their second fight.

Assuming Jennifer had left when she said she did, Ned was likely to have still been in the room when the call was made. Why couldn't he have been the one who made it?

If he had, there was a lot of time between ten after eight, when Ned was on the phone, and the apparent time of death at nine or perhaps later. Time for whoever Ned had called to come to Hugo Hill's, perhaps at Ned's invitation. He could perfectly well have summoned his own killer.

Intriguing, but it led nowhere unless Ryan could find out who had been at the other end of the phone call. And why would Ned be worried about fingerprints?

At the office with Kassia, Ryan was feeling increasingly awkward. By mid afternoon, the discomfort overwhelmed his reticence. ''What's going on?''

''Nothing's going on.'' Her tone was sharp. She heard it herself, and sighed. ''I don't know, Michael, I'm confused. I like working with you. I like you. More than like you. And we had . . . a wonderful time together.'' She looked away for a moment. ''But I was going to take a vacation from that, try going without until I had a better idea what I really wanted. I'm too old to fool around . . . I think I may want a kid . . . '' The last part came out in a rush of words, then she slowed down again. ''I guess what it comes down to is I don't think I can mix business with pleasure. Not right now, anyway. I wish I could.''

''Maybe we should just keep working and leave the rest on hold until this is over and our heads are clear.'' He did not know if that was what he wanted. It seemed like something attainable.

''It sounds right, if we can do it.''

He arranged to spend Friday out of the office.

He had an early afternoon appointment with Robertson Kneeland. Jennifer met him at the elevator. Seeing the sweep of the apartment spread before him, with the skyline beyond, he was reminded of the New Year's party. Hard to believe it was more than four months ago.

''I'm sorry Daddy was so rude to you. He was very upset about the verdict.''

''I don't blame him.''

She hooked her arm in his. ''We're going to beat this, aren't we, Michael?''

''You bet we are.''

Kneeland was barely polite. He agreed that Ryan should go ahead with the sentencing report and begin to organize the trial materials that would be necessary in pursuing the appeal.

''But you have to understand that I can't guarantee when you'll get another fee payment. The judge imposed that extra million dollars bail as if I'm a man with unlimited capital. The fact is that I'm overextended. The first million was almost more than I could manage, not to mention the money that's gone into the trial.''

''If you can document that, we can probably get the bail reduced.''

"I don't like to parade my finances in public."

"It's that or put up the money or see Jennifer go to jail."

"There's no need to bully me, Mr. Ryan."

They deferred any discussion about who would work on the appeal itself. Ryan said not a word about its being Jennifer's decision, not Kneeland's, when the time came.

Kneeland showed him out. "This isn't easy for me, Ryan, I'm sure you understand that."

"Nobody likes to see their children hurt."

"I need to be sure she has the right people. As sure as I can be."

When Ryan got home Ned's trunk was waiting in the package room. The porter brought it up in the service elevator and put it in the middle of the living room.

Ryan was not sure he was ready for this. He was too taken up in Ned-the-murder-victim to risk the abyss of emotion that would open when he began to contemplate the real, varied and—in memory—vibrant young man.

Yet here was this antique wood and metal trunk: a long rectangle with a high arched cover, dull gray metal ribbed with strips of polished wood, held closed by an ornate central hasp flanked by two smaller ones. Container for part of a life.

Impossible to ignore it.

The key was in an envelope taped to one side. Ryan worked the stiff old fastenings and swung back the lid of the trunk. Open, it looked like any trunk full of memories. Kassia had replaced the contents neatly; there was no way to know how Ned had arranged them. The trunk was full to the top. It held a removable tray, like a shelf, which he took out, revealing a second layer of clothes and books, a football, other things as yet out of sight. It all tugged at his gut precisely the way he had feared it would. He had a moment of vertigo.

The phone rang.

"Michael?" It was Kassia, sounding agitated. "Have you seen today's paper?"

"No. What?" His mind raced: someone confessed, Jennifer hurt somehow, another murder . . .

"In the Weekend section, page twenty-six, upper right hand corner. Do you have it?"

"No." The Weekend section?

"Can you get it? And meet me at the office. We have work to do."

"You mean now?"

"Yes, I mean now. Get the lead out, Ryan. This is important."

"I'm on my way."

Walking to the subway for the trip downtown, Ryan bought a paper. On the subway platform he turned to page twenty-six of the Weekend entertainment section. Large ads for art galleries covered the page—three across by six down, under a gray banner: SPRING ART SHOWCASE. Top right was a black rectangle with white letters:

HUGO HILL GALLERIES
photoconcepts
patterns in blood—6/14

An ad for Hugo Hill's gallery, no more than that. But Kassia was excited about it. Patterns in blood. The man was bizarre, but they knew that already. Ryan looked at the ad again. The numbers registered: the date of Ned's death.

Patterns in blood.

She was waiting for him at the office.

He put the newspaper on her desk open to the ad. "You think it's evidence?"

"I want us to issue a subpoena and find out."

"Shouldn't we go see it first?"

"It doesn't say when it's going to open. And the gallery's closed today for some reason, so we can't ask. I called already."

"Photoconcepts," he read.

"Right. And Susan Spada, whose work shows at the Hugo Hill Galleries, is what Hugo Hill calls a photoconceptualist. She was at the party that night. Maybe she brought her camera."

"And your bloodstain expert made a fuss about not having all the pictures she needed, so you're all excited about this."

"Seems reasonable."

"June fourteenth is Flag Day. It could be pictures of war heroes."

"You don't believe that."

24

JUST AS THEY WERE FINISHING WORK ON THE SUB-
poena, Lawrence called.

"Where can I meet you?" the investigator asked.

"Anyplace you want." It was clear from the question that the
office would not do.

They agreed on the natural-food cafeteria, an easy walk from the
office. Ryan and Miller resisted the food and took their coffee to a
table in the back corner. Lawrence joined them a few minutes later.

"Nassir found a bug."

They took a moment to absorb the news.

"I guess the important thing is he found it," Ryan said. "We
can be grateful for that."

"Yes and no. He says it could have been there since . . . he
doesn't know when."

"But he just found it."

"This morning." Lawrence spread his hands. "I don't know
why. Limitations of technology. He rigged you up with the best
radio-frequency sweepers there are, so we knew nobody was trans-
mitting anything. He swept regularly with a detector that picks up
passive recording devices. And he did regular visual searches. It
should have caught everything. In fact, it was Nassir's eyeballing
the place that found it. Very clever, latest stuff. The recorder itself
was outside in a janitor's closet with a squirt transmitter tuned close
to WNEW. Hard wired with conducting paint to some pinpoint
mikes in the corridor wall and the partitions. The fidelity can't have
been too good."

"All they need is a few words here and there," Kassia said.
"We're not playing Mozart."

"There's no point blaming anybody," Ryan said. "Let's figure
out what it means."

"It could be the reason for that threat," Lawrence said.

And if it was the reason for the threat it could have been the reason for the shooting, too, Ryan did not say. "Did you get rid of it?"

"No. I figure better the bug you know than the bug you don't."

"We'll have to be careful what we say. We'll need someplace secure, too."

"We talked about Hugo Hill's show," Kassia pointed out.

"Maybe that won't matter if we don't say any more about it." Ryan brooded over the last of his coffee. "I think we should get out of there entirely."

"Even if you do, don't let on to anyone what the real reason is," Lawrence said. "Whoever planted that bug, it's best they think they got away with it."

"They did," Ryan said.

He was not ready to confront his partners, not so soon after the verdict, but under the circumstances there was nothing else to do.

He took Kassia with him to Pane, Parish's new offices.

"The wandering hero," Bob Legler said. "And Ms. Miller. What brings you?"

"We need some office space," Ryan said.

"You have an office, I thought—downtown somewhere."

"We don't need anything luxurious. A place to sit and a couple of desks ought to do it. And a telephone."

"You have an office here, Michael, remember?"

"I wasn't sure I did."

"Is that why we haven't heard from you?"

"My feeling after the executive committee meeting was that I was being told to come back carrying my shield or lying on it. And when I heard Rick Briggs left I didn't see who'd be here to welcome me back if I was anything less than Mr. Victory."

"But you are Mr. Victory. Didn't you get our telegram?"

"We got a bunch of them. I didn't read them. Hate mail gets me down."

Legler turned to Kassia. "I wouldn't ordinarily subject an outsider to these internal misunderstandings, but I want you to know from someone other than Michael that many of us here were impressed with what the two of you did. Not everyone, of course. Speaking for myself, you both handled a difficult situation with remarkable skill."

"Thank you."

"Michael, do you want to look at that office of yours now? We moved in your old desk, but otherwise it's empty. I can have the building staff move in a couple of chairs and bookcases and a small table while we look for an office Ms. Miller can use. You didn't say how long she'd be here."

"It depends on what our status is on the appeal," Ryan said.

"We'll have some motions to file before sentencing," Kassia amended. "Say, six weeks, minimum."

Ryan felt out of place in the firm's new offices. It did not seem to matter that he had been in charge of the planning and the first stages of the construction: it was all alien to him.

"You're staking an awful lot on Hugo Hill and bloodstain patterns," he said to Kassia when they were alone in his office, a wide room with windows on the long wall and his desk planted in its center looking abandoned.

"I'll take it wherever I can get it."

They spent a day downtown stuffing files into cartons.

The next morning Ryan sat at his desk at Pane, Parish building himself up to start unpacking them. Accustomed to the double-height ceilings in Soho, he felt like the one here was pressing down on his head. He found himself gazing across the office at Kassia organizing her small desk.

She looked up and caught him at it. He opened his mouth but there was nothing to say.

The intercom buzzed. Ryan looked around for a button to push. A woman's voice somewhere overhead said, "Mr. Ryan, delivery. Please come to the reception area."

"Expecting something?" he asked Kassia.

"As a matter of fact I am."

There was a large square crate waiting for them. With it was a man in a three-piece suit who introduced himself as Mr. Bruce, Hugo Hill's lawyer. He watched as a handyman carefully unscrewed the front panel of the crate.

There were twelve pictures, each five feet by four feet, in color so glossy and intense it went beyond conventional notions of realism, each signed *spada*. Ryan, who had once dabbled in amateur photography, could not imagine how they had been made.

He and Kassia arrayed them around the firm's large conference room, a dozen images in red-brown and white, some with bright accents, reality as abstraction.

Besides the pictures there were two ragged-edged chunks of plaster, both about two feet by three feet, one taken from a corner, the other from a flat area of wall or ceiling. They were rayed with stains like strings of exclamation points. Ryan was resolutely avoiding thinking of the patterns as his son's blood.

"Lynne Archbold is going to have a field day with these," Kassia said.

The conference room door opened and Legler looked in.

"What's all this?"

"Evidence," Ryan said, wondering if it was.

Ryan met Jennifer in one of the firm's smaller conference rooms. He drew a curtain over the glass walls.

"We have a new lead we hope will make a difference," he told her.

"How much difference can it make, now?"

"I don't know if it will make any." He told her what Kassia had told him: In the best case the bloodstains could point to something about the way the blows were struck or the physical characteristics of the murderer that would cast doubt on Jennifer's guilt or even possibly eliminate her entirely. "It's a real long shot—there's a chance, that's all."

"That's not very comforting."

"If it works out it could support a motion for a new trial."

"No. Not another trial."

"A new trial with stronger evidence. The verdict was very close."

"I couldn't stand it."

"It's not likely to come to that. Griglia isn't going to want to do it again, either—not if we get lucky with this evidence."

"What happens then?"

"They throw out the verdict and you go free."

"But nobody ever says I'm not guilty?"

"No."

"It's not good enough."

"It may be the best you can do."

Lynne Archbold paced back and forth in front of Susan Spada's art, stopping now and then to bend close, or to make a measurement. The two defense lawyers watched her, waiting. Pane, Parish partners and associates passed back and forth beyond the conference room on manufactured errands, peering in as they went by. Mr. Bruce sat glumly on a chair in a corner, protecting his client's property.

"Let's go talk," Lynne Archbold said. In Ryan's office she paced as she spoke.

"Those are the clearest pictures of bloodstains I've ever seen. And to have the plaster, too, is the best, because I don't have to make guesses about the texture. I need to match the stains on those images to the ones on the evidence slides. That tells me where these pictures fit in the real room. That's the hard part. Once I've done that, and assuming we've got pictures here of the bloodstains the cops missed, I can make a model of the room. That's more precise than just calculating from the plans Kassia got from the Buildings Department. It's more visual, too, if I have to testify. Kassia tells me you're trying to reopen the case."

"One step at a time," Ryan said.

Ned's trunk was still in the middle of the living room, where it had been for days. Walking by it Ryan saw Ned's high-school letter sweater and pennants from that championship season when he had captained the team and his father had gone to only one regular season game and missed the county play-offs entirely.

He started to close the trunk. There was only pain here.

Something stopped him. The only place Ned could live now was in memory. It would just compound the earlier sins to deny him that.

Ryan started slowly, handling each sweater or medal or picture but not dwelling on them. The cards and letters in feminine hands he passed by quickly, reading no more than a name here and there. They would contain the victories and disappointments and passions of youth. Someday they would offer him a roundness of detail about Ned's life he could not otherwise have seen.

The audiocassettes intrigued him. There were four of them, with hand-lettered labels—homemade tapes, not prerecorded. The labels were cryptic. Two were marked with pairs of letters Ryan assumed were initials. A third said, "Dawn." The fourth said, "Grateful Dead."

Dawn, it occurred to him, was the name on one of the love letters. He picked up the envelopes, some of them still faintly fragrant with years-old perfume, and shuffled through them. Sure enough, the two sets of initials were there, too.

He remembered the envelope of letters and tapes he had found in Ned's safe-deposit box and went to the study to get it. The tapes were different from the ones in the trunk, all labeled in the same feminine hand as he saw on the accompanying letters, each with the words, "for Ned" and a date. Ned would have been twenty when they were made.

He put one on. "Hi, Ned." A young woman's voice. "It's Ma-

ria, missing you as always.'' Then some noises he took to be sim
ulated kissing and panting. ''I want you, big boy,'' she said. He
turned it off, embarrassed. Remembered that in his own youth com
mitting romantic thoughts to paper was considered reckless, never
mind taking sexy tape recordings.

The tapes in the trunk were labeled in Ned's handwriting. Safer
Ryan thought. He put one on and heard ornate old trumpet music.
He tried Dawn and found more old music: religious chants. Very
different from a panting girlfriend. These tapes would be both a
mystery and a revelation, a way into the unknown person who had
been his son—the music Ned had shared with people he loved.

While Ryan continued to go through the trunk, he put on the
Grateful Dead tape. He knew about the Grateful Dead from his
days as a federal prosecutor. There had been a major marijuana
bust: growers from Northern California come east to make a moun-
tainous sale to avid customers who turned out to work for the government. Grateful Dead was the brand the growers used on their
bales, in homage to their favorite recording artists.

The first song on the tape had been recorded at a concert, complete with a background of cheers and whistles. It seemed to be
about Samson and Delilah. ''If I had my way,'' the refrain repeated, ''I would tear this old building down.'' Ryan could sym-
pathize.

The second song began with an instrumental lead-in and stopped,
music replaced by the hiss of blank tape. Odd. Was something
wrong with the tape player? Ryan went over to check.

''This is Edward Ryan.'' Ned's voice.

Ryan stopped. Wavered, almost lost his balance. It's only a voice
on a tape, he told himself—not Ned returned for their overdue
reconciliation. He reached out to turn it off.

''. . . to bring the original to the United States Attorney's office . . .'' he heard, and stopped again.

''If you are hearing this, I've probably failed. I may have been
murdered. I ask you to please bring this tape to the attention of the
U.S. Attorney.''

Ryan stopped the tape. Sat down. His hands were shaking and
he had sweated through his shirt. He had to know what was on the
tape, but he did not know how he would react to hearing it. And
he could not take a chance on losing this. He would have to record
it as he listened.

He called Kassia and Lawrence and was lucky enough to get
them both. When they arrived, each with a cassette recorder, he
sat them down, braced himself and pressed Play. The innocuous

ong about a Bible story had taken on a sinister tone. The audience
of two listened, bewildered.

"This is Edward Ryan," Ned said again.

Kassia swiveled in her chair to look at Ryan, her brown eyes
wide. Lawrence just shook his head. By the time they had settled
down, Ned was most of the way through his preamble.

". . . recording of a conversation between Edward Ryan and
I. Robertson Kneeland made at Ryan's office on June thirteenth."

Another silence on the tape. No one moved.

The next sound was a voice in mid-sentence, weak at first, grow-
ng stronger as it came closer to Ned's hidden microphone.

". . . know why we have to do this here, but you said come
over, it's urgent, so here I am. Let's get to it and get done. I've got
hings to do."

The voice was recognizably Kneeland's, without the careful
speech and polite phrasing he had used whenever Ryan had seen
him.

"I'll get right to the point," Ned said. "I want out." His voice
was muffled compared to the lead-in, but there was no mistaking
the intensity of emotion the words carried.

"What the hell are you talking about?"

"I'm talking about this deal with the medicine. And I'm talking
about the whole ball of wax. All of your friend Olivera's money
washing."

"If this is a joke, it's a dumb one."

"No joke."

"Then you're high on something. Sleep it off, call me in the
morning."

A sound that might have been footsteps.

"If you leave now, I'm going to blow it all wide open."

"You really are crazy."

Ryan was dizzy, nauseated. He made it to the tape player and
turned it off.

"What are you doing?" burst from Kassia.

"Sorry. This is more than I'm ready to sit through. But I can
read a transcript, and we're going to need one anyway. You two
listen and make your copies. I'll go in the other room and set it up
for us to get a confidential transcript made."

He went into his study, leaving it to them to find the right button.

Reading the transcript gave Ryan less trouble than listening to the
tape, though he could hear Ned's voice in his mind as he read.

"This whole deal has been eating me up for weeks," Ned had

said. "Ever since that meeting we had with your friend Olivera. Okay, I have to make up my mind, and here it is: I don't want this in my life. It isn't worth it, the way it knots up my insides. If this is what it takes to be rich, I'll try being poor."

"You won't like it."

"I'll take the chance."

"Jennifer isn't going to like it either."

"I love Jennifer, and I owe her a lot for how much she's put up with. I'll make this up to her some way. If I can't, I'll deal with it when the time comes."

"It's not so easy getting out from under when you're involved with these people."

"You're the expert on that, aren't you? H. Robertson Kneeland, wholly owned subsidiary of Felipe Olivera."

"I don't need your lip. I don't need any of this. We have a transaction to finish. The trucks start rolling Monday. That means your warehouses have to be ready, and all the rest of it. When we're done with this, you can take vows or whatever you want."

"I'm not doing that deal, and neither are you. If you do, I really will blow the whistle."

"You're nuts. You truly are nuts."

"No. I used to be nuts. I've been doing this for almost two years, hiding the whole time from admitting to myself what I was doing. It was like, at the beginning I thought, hey, maybe this is drug money, you know? Okay, somebody's got to use it, why not me? I told myself it was okay to lend out Olivera's money because money that went into credit for medical clinics or mortgages for industrial parks wasn't going into producing more coke and crack. But then I couldn't get by on that anymore, so I made up stories for myself about how it wasn't really drug money, it was money from your deals. What a joke. Without Olivera you don't have two pennies to rub together."

"Don't start with me. You're what I made you, and no more. When you came to me you were running errands for some old has-been who helped you as a favor to your grandfather."

"I should have stayed there. He's smarter and tougher than you'll ever be. But that's old news. What's on right now is: I tried to tell myself that Olivera was just a different kind of businessman. Well, that's bullshit."

"You think so? You think what he does is worse than dumping oil all over Alaska, or toxic wastes, or the other shit everybody pulls every day?"

"Damn right I do. And this latest is the worst. Taking medicine rom sick starving mothers and children just to pull down some xtra bucks. Who knows how many people it's going to kill? Thou- ands. Just because they're a different color and in a different coun- ry doesn't mean they're not people.''

"Don't be an ass. Do you think they'd ever see those drugs? If ney don't get ripped off at this end by Olivera, they get ripped off ver there by some fat black colonel.''

"That's not my problem. My problem is I won't be part of it, nd I can't let you, either.''

"There are other people in this. You want me to tell them I hanged my mind, I decided it's not nice to take medicine from oor Africans? First they'll laugh at me and then they'll cut my alls off.''

"You do what you have to. I'll do what I have to.''

"You think they'll leave you alone if you try to blow the whistle n this?''

"I'll have to take my chances.''

"You've got to be crazy. You know what you'd be throwing away? set this up. It's my butt if it doesn't work. Everything I have is iding on this.''

"Everything you have. What the hell is that? All you are is a ollow shell for Olivera to fill up. You'd collapse without him. How ong since you made a penny on your own?''

"This whole deal. The whole clinic thing. That's mine. Your right idea, remember? But it would be nowhere if I didn't see that ou needed easy credit to hold your customers, and if I didn't get vou Olivera's money to make it work. I was the one who saw how o use a medical-supplies company to send money out of the coun- ry. That's what sold Olivera and it's what put you in business. It's vhy Olivera came to me with this deal, when he found out he could grab the trucks. The man sells coke and crack—this isn't his busi- ness. We're the ones who know about selling medicine. We're the ones with the warehouses to store the stuff and the distribution channels to unload it.''

"Nobody told you to get into this with him.''

"What is this bullshit? You think those other deals we did with nim were sanctified by the Pope?''

"I have to live with myself. I have to draw the line somewhere. Maybe I didn't see that before.''

"Listen, sonny, this isn't some high school debate. This is real ife. These people start out breaking legs. For fun, for nickels and dimes. And this is no nickel and dime deal.''

"How many people are you willing to kill to do it? Think about it. Your daughter spends her time and your money at Feed the Children, and you're going to steal medicine from African relief."

"Don't talk to me about my daughter. She lives in some other world."

"Then you won't mind if I tell her about this."

"She won't believe you. I'm her daddy and she's the world champion at not seeing the truth if she doesn't like it."

"Nobody's real to you, are they? No wonder you can take medicine from sick babies and send them empty boxes instead."

"How did you get so pure? You think those junkies who buy pills from the clinics you service don't die, doing things you help them do? Overdoses? AIDS? Get smart and forget this crap."

"You don't get it, do you? It's not just this. This is what made me see it. This is what told me how sick and crazy all this shit is. I draw the line here. You're with me on this, about the medicine, maybe we can back away from the rest of it a little at a time. I've learned some things about doing business. We don't need Olivera."

"What you know about business is how to give away somebody else's sixty million dollars. Hans the Counting Horse could do that. And you couldn't even get that straight. You gave terms like you were running a charity until I made you do better. If you learned anything from all that it was because I taught it to you."

"You sure did. You taught me that everything I ever heard about honesty and integrity and keeping your word was a crock, for suckers."

"What matters right now is doing this deal the way I set it up. I told you. They'll feed you your own balls one at a time and make you chew. Nobody backs away from these people. I'll tell you a secret. I'm ninety percent sure my chauffeur spies on me for Olivera. I'm the one who tells the man what's doing at City Hall that matters to him, and I'm his window to the world of legitimate business, and I get driven around by some semiretired thug named Paco. That's how far off the leash Olivera lets me. You need a bodyguard, he tells me. Shit—I need a bodyguard just to protect me from Paco."

"Then you'd really better join me on this because I mean every word," Ned had said, and Ryan could imagine the finality in his voice. "I'm going to blow the whole deal, not just this, everything. I'm the kid who used to visit his father at the U.S. Attorney's office. I know who to talk to and I know what to say. Maybe I'll do some time, but I'll find a way. And maybe then I can start clean again."

"Let's not get carried away," Kneeland had replied—quickly, Ryan assumed, maybe even with a touch of panic. "Let's at least

ink about it for a day. If I can show you some statistics about how
ttle of that medicine reaches the sick people in the best of circum-
ances maybe you'll feel better about just this one, and then we
n both get out somehow. Okay? Just don't do anything crazy. We
n talk tomorrow night. We have to talk tomorrow night. I'll be
a cocktail party and then I'll be at a dinner party but Paco will
now where to find me.''

The transcript ended there.

assia had been sitting quietly in her corner of the office, watching
m read. He looked over at her.

''Do we know anything about this medicine they're arguing
out?'' he asked.

''The news-service database says there was a major hijacking of
edicine destined for the Horn of Africa last year. A whole ship-
ad turned out to be ballast instead of wonder drugs. It was dis-
vered over there last fall when the relief agency checked the
aterfront warehouse. Everyone assumed the substitution was made
that end.''

''But we think it was Olivera.''

''Could have been.''

He hefted the transcript. ''There's a lot here.''

More than he had expected. Small exchanges with large impli-
ations: Kneeland had been behind Ned's business treachery with
eople like Harry Bundesman. How much can you blame a kid in
is twenties for giving in to the older man who's his senior partner
nd mentor? His father figure.

And if Kneeland was the author of Ned's predatory practices,
ad he made up those stories he told about Ned, too?

''Not exactly the Ned we've been hearing about,'' Ryan said.

''What do you think it means?''

''It probably means Jennifer didn't kill Ned.''

''Do you think it was Olivera?''

''It looks that way. Not directly, of course.''

''Where does that leave us?''

''Still relying on your bloodstain expert to get us a new trial.
nd hunting for experts to testify at the hearing when we try to get
at tape admitted as evidence over Griglia's protests and despite
neeland's disavowal. A lot of experts—I'd like to turn authenti-
ating that tape into a national news item. For weeks.''

''You have a nice nasty streak, Ryan. You're going to make a
reat criminal defense lawyer.''

"I've been hating Robertson Kneeland for years. It's nice ▮ finally have a solid reason."

"Jennifer won't be happy about our spreading this all over th▮ front pages. He's her dad."

"Do you think she knows about this?" he wondered.

"Nothing she ever said would make me think so. But as we'v▮ learned she's terrific at hiding things."

"It looks like an inherited trait. Her father's been doing som▮ hiding, too."

"Let's get back to Olivera. Why at Hugo Hill's, and why tha▮ particular Friday night?"

"The timing is easy," he pointed out. "Kneeland talks abou▮ the time limit on the tape."

"Because of hijacking the medicine."

"And he also says that they should talk to each other on Frida▮ and gives Ned his schedule."

"Right. But they didn't talk. Ned got killed first."

"They might have talked anyway, if *Ned* made the phone ca▮ we can't figure out."

Her eyes widened. "You just think of that?"

"The other day, at the health club."

"But why would Ned wipe the phone clean?"

Something was tugging at his mind.

"Ryan, I asked you a question."

"Where did we file those two phone numbers Craig gave us?"▮

"That's no answer."

"It's a question."

"I don't know where we filed them."

He called Lawrence. The investigator was out. Ryan left a mes▮ sage: We need the mystery phone number.

"What's this all about?" Kassia asked him.

"Suppose Ned made the call—to Kneeland. The way they'd ar▮ ranged."

"I still don't see why Ned would wipe the phone off."

"I don't either. That's why I didn't do anything with the ide▮ when I first got it. But let's leave that part of it alone for now▮ Suppose Ned called Kneeland."

"And what? He was at parties all night."

"Right. But he could have gotten a phone call. He told Ned t▮ call."

"Where does that lead?"

"Nowhere that I can see right now, except it might help explain▮

timing. Though I admit it still doesn't explain how or why the
one got wiped off.''

"Like you said, let's give it a rest and come back to it.''

"Right. We ought to get started on the motion for a new trial.
e have whatever your Archbold person comes up with, and we
ve this tape. Which we need to talk to our client about, but not
. There are too many questions to answer, and I'm not ready for
eeland to know we have it.''

25

HERE WAS A MESSAGE FROM LAWRENCE ON RYAN'S
swering machine at home: a phone number, nothing else. Ryan
rote it down and carried it into his study, where he dug through
e To Do box for Ned's funeral program. His hunch had been
ght—the call from Hugo Hill's at nine minutes after eight had
ne to Kneeland's limousine.

Sitting in the spiral-armed chair he'd inherited from his Circas-
an grandmother—Grandpa Yosef's thinking chair—Ryan tried to
agine that night.

He envisioned Ned in the minutes after Jennifer left. What had
en on his mind? The fight and what caused it, without a doubt.
ut why would he call Kneeland at that point? Because he wanted
do something right. The issue of Olivera's money and the hi-
cking would have been on his mind. The tape made that clear—
'd been thinking about it for weeks.

And there was something else . . . something cold and snowy.
snowman. Right—Skippy and Ellis Turner. Ned had been talking
them at the party about the horrors of African plague and famine.
ina Claire said he'd been distracted, his mind somewhere else, on
other planet.

So: you're Ned, you have this major issue weighing on you. It's
en upsetting enough, as Jennifer reported it, to make you distant

and unsexy for weeks. You come to a decision. You're going to g
out of the whole ugly business. Your sex drive comes back. Yo
confront your father-in-law co-conspirator with an ultimatun
You're scared, maybe, high on adrenaline, but you figure you'
getting your life back on track.

You go to a party with your wife. Maybe you don't want to g
but it's been planned for weeks, you urged the host to have it in th
first place, and there are going to be people there you want to tal
to. So you go and you talk to the people you wanted to see, wh
are friends of your wife's, about the way pharmaceuticals are dis
tributed in Africa and how important they are, and how bad it i
when they're unavailable. You're more upset than ever, more cor
vinced that you have to walk away from the deal, whatever the risk
Not just walk away from it—stop it if you can.

The host brings you over to meet the guest of honor, a perso:
you may once have wanted to flirt with, before all this. You've g
bigger things on your mind now, but you're being polite and you'v
had a drink or two and the next thing you know she's all over you
Your body responds on its own, leaving behind your brain, whic
is still mostly in a more serious place.

And then, boom, your wife, whom you love despite your some
times childish and hurtful behavior, descends on you like a banshe
and abuses you as you so richly deserve. You're too caught b:
surprise to respond adequately, so you take off. But she follows an
the fight continues until her irrational, volatile side prompts her t
pick up Wingless Bird and you wrestle it away from her, cuttin
her hand.

She leaves, and you want to follow and make things better, bu
you know she needs time to cool down, and you have business t
finish.

In a way, it's the pivotal moment in your life. You're taking
stand, probably risking your life, and then you're going to star
making it all up to your wife for your bad behavior. Your father-in
law is expecting to hear from you, expecting you'll capitulate. Nov
is the time to tell him you won't reconsider, to let him know how
hard you'll fight. The trucks roll in a couple of days and Kneelanc
will go ahead unless you stop him. This is no time to delay. So you
make the call. And . . .

Ryan thought he was probably overdoing it, making Ned pure
than the reality would support. But maybe not. In any case, it fel
right. It fit everything he knew, and everything he knew had a place
in it.

Up to the point where Jennifer leaves Hugo Hill's. What happens then?

Ned calls Kneeland in the car. He isn't there, so Paco the chauffeur takes the call. Part-time chauffeur, part-time informant for Señor Olivera. And Ned leaves a message? Unlikely, since he knows Paco's other occupation. But at ten after eight Kneeland might have just got into the car after the first party. Say Kneeland takes the call. And Ned tells him forget it, I'm not changing my mind. I'm out of this deal and either you're with me or against me.

Then what? Kneeland says . . . yes, no, maybe . . . and goes to his party, where witnesses said he had definitely arrived by eight thirty-five and possibly earlier. And Ned waits around until someone—Paco?—comes by and clubs him to death at close to nine.

Something was still missing.

Suppose Kneeland and Ned had their conversation and Paco overheard it. That still didn't account for Ned's waiting around. Did Kneeland tell Ned stay there, I'll call you back. Or, stay there and I'll come over. That made sense. He might not want to have such a dangerous conversation over the open public airwaves. A few cryptic exchanges and then: Wait awhile so we can talk this over. I'll call you from a more secure phone. Or, I'll come over and get you so we can talk. And then . . . a call to Olivera? What should I do? Was Kneeland desperate enough for that? And Olivera says stay cool and go to your party. And then he sends Paco, the semi-retired thug, over to ice Ned.

The timing fit, and the players were in character.

What about the phone? Did Paco wipe it clean? Why? Maybe he tried to call Olivera and didn't get through. Or he called and let the phone ring some specified number of times and hung up: a signal that he had accomplished his mission. Plausible reasons for Paco to have handled the phone and wanted to get rid of his fingerprints.

It made a picture Ryan could believe in. A shame there was no evidence. He wondered where Paco was now.

26

KASSIA CALLED IN THE MORNING. LYNNE ARCHBOLD
was putting her report together. She already had a conclusion: Ned's
murderer had probably been more than six feet tall. Almost certainly over five eleven. Definitely no less than five ten.

"Can she really know these things?"

"It's all a matter of geometry, apparently."

"Will it stand up in court?"

"It's admissible in New York. What a jury will think of it I can't
say. Lynne is a good witness."

"Right now I'm more worried about her report writing. We need
to convince Corino to set aside the verdict."

"What about Griglia? Can we get him on our side if the evidence
is convincing?"

"Dream on. His first big case as D.A., and he took the trouble
to try it himself—he's not going to admit he got the wrong defendant . . . Speaking of which, we ought to tell Jennifer."

"She'll want to hear it from you. She needs to know you believe
in her. That she's innocent—no doubts, reasonable or otherwise."

It was only when he heard the words that the realization broke
through—Archbold's conclusions were solid proof that Jennifer had
not killed Ned. Not theory and speculation, and not protestations
of innocence. If you believed in the techniques, and he did not
know enough not to, it meant Jennifer was physically inconsistent
with the murderer, no two ways about it.

But he was already off the seesaw on that subject. Whatever else
Jennifer might be guilty of, he no longer thought she was guilty of
murder. It was implicit in the theory he had spun out the night
before. Still, it was comforting to have evidentiary support.

* * *

Ryan was feeling better than he could remember as he walked to meet Jennifer. A splendid May day, warm with a refreshing breeze, the sky intensely blue.

There was still work to be done, but at least the pieces were there. It was a matter of assembling them in a way that would get the best result.

Right now, he had good news for Jennifer, and he was eager to deliver it.

She met him at the fountain across from the Plaza and they walked in Central Park.

"I told you before there might be new evidence."

"And I might have to have a new trial."

"It looks better than I thought. With luck, we may be able to get you off completely. Get the verdict set aside and the charges dropped."

"You're terrific to say so, but I'm not going to get too excited."

"I can understand that."

"How long will it take?"

"That depends on Judge Corino and the D.A."

"That's why I'm not getting too excited."

They enjoyed the spring greenery and the warm air. Runners passed them on the park paths. Ryan searched for words.

"It's been a while since I said anything about . . . my opinion of what happened."

He could see the question in her eyes.

"I want you to know that I believe you're innocent and I'm sorry it took me as long as it did to be sure."

"I'm sorry about that, too."

"There were times when I wanted to believe it . . ."

"I know. And I didn't make it any easier."

"It's got to have been an incredibly tough time for you. I can't imagine . . ."

She stopped walking and took both his hands.

"Don't try. Life gets very weird when everyone believes you did a terrible thing like that, and you didn't. You begin to wonder, what's wrong with me that people can think of me that way?"

"People don't understand violence," Ryan ventured. "When it happens close by, we've got nothing to relate it to except TV and the movies and the newspapers. Wife kills husband in an argument. It happens all the time, doesn't it? Well, more often the other way around, but either way more often than it should. Often enough that we can believe our neighbors might do it. Or even our friends. Who knows what any other person might be capable of?"

"You're right. We don't even know what we're capable of, ourselves."

They walked awhile in silence.

"I'm curious about your father," Ryan said neutrally. "Do you know much about his business connections?"

"Not a lot. Why?"

Did she stiffen at the question, or was it his imagination?

"Ned did business with people who import illegal drugs. You talked about dangerous people, so I assumed you knew that much."

"I had the feeling there was something but I didn't know it was that."

"It was." Keeping it reportage. "Ned did business with cocaine dealers and he did business with your father."

"This isn't a question. You know something you're not telling."

Ryan hesitated. "Yes."

"What? Tell me."

"Your father is in that business—in it very deeply. He's the one who got Ned into it. They were fighting the day before Ned died."

"You're saying my father had something to do with the murder."

"Only that he may have been connected with the people who did it." Hedging.

She looked away. "Strange how hard it is to hear bad news even when you sort of expected it. I've suspected for a long time that he knew more about what happened than he was saying. I guess that's one more thing I held back. I didn't dare say this to you before but that was really the first reason I thought of you for my lawyer. In the beginning I was so sure I wasn't in any danger. Then, when those two lawyers he recommended said plead guilty and Daddy didn't go through the roof . . . He was very rational about it. He didn't say, do it, plead guilty, but he was acting like it might be a reasonable choice. It scared me. That's when I decided I really needed somebody those people couldn't get to. I told you that part. And that's why I was so afraid to tell you anything that would make you doubt me, or make you angry. Like about Nico. I was terrified you'd quit and then where would I be?"

How busy we all are, making demons for ourselves, Ryan thought. But it was hardly paranoid to see goblins behind every tree if you were falsely accused of murdering your husband and no one seemed to believe you when you said you didn't, and then two lawyers in a row advised you to plead guilty and even your father said you should consider it. All of her behavior took on a very different hue once you saw it in that light.

"Do you know who did it?" she asked him.

"We think so. We think it was your father's chauffeur."

"Manuel? But he's such a sweetie, and he just came to work for Daddy this year."

"The one who was driving him when Ned was killed."

"Paco! That's more like it. He used to look me up and down when he thought I couldn't see him. He gave me the creeps."

"He worked for a cocaine dealer, the same one your father did business with."

"I'd believe anything about Paco."

"I gather he doesn't work for your father anymore."

"No. Not since . . ." She stopped. "Not since about a week after Ned was killed."

"Do you know where he is?"

"I think there was some talk about his going back home."

"Home?"

"Colombia, I think."

"Great."

"We could go down there and get him." Her voice was flat and hard. She was not kidding.

"And get ourselves killed," Ryan said. "These people look out for their own."

"Maybe they'll protect him for now, but I have a long memory. And Ned would have wanted revenge."

Homage to Ned's Circassian heritage. Though clearly she had plenty of that sort of passion all her own.

She walked down a path to a small wooden gazebo by the lake and sat on its rough bench, looking out over the water toward trees and beyond them the towers of apartment houses.

"It's amazing what people can do. That little guy . . ."

"What little guy?"

"Paco."

"What do you mean?"

"He's built like a fireplug—short and thick. Greasy dark hair and one of those Indio kind of faces, square with square features, like his square body. He's really strong, too. I guess that was how he hit Ned so hard. It sure wasn't because he has long arms."

"How short is he?" Keeping his voice level.

"Five four, five five. I don't know exactly."

"You're sure?"

"Of course I'm sure. I had to put up with him often enough."

"Did your father have any other chauffeurs around then?"

"There was a relief guy for Paco's day off."

"Tall, short?"

"I don't really remember. Medium height. He worked on Sunday and sometimes Monday, I think. I didn't see him that much."

Ryan wanted to be out of the park, wanted to hail a cab and get back to the office, do something with this new knowledge that his whole theory of the murder was out the window unless Lynne Archbold had made a mistake.

"Is something wrong, Michael?"

"Everything's fine." Like hell.

They walked back to Fifth Avenue and he tried to concentrate on the conversation. His mind would not leave Paco and Lynne Archbold.

"Something's bothering you."

"You're right. I ought to get back to the office."

"Can you tell me what it is?"

"Not yet."

"Paco is five four," he announced to Kassia as he walked into their office.

It took her a minute. "Oh boy—that's not good. You're sure?"

"Jennifer is sure."

He sat down heavily in his desk chair and leaned back, weary with frustration.

She wadded up a page from a legal pad and lobbed it at him. "Hey! Ryan! It's not the end of the world, you know. We still have Lynne Archbold's evidence that it wasn't Jennifer."

"If we believe her." Unwilling to let go of Paco as the killer.

"I don't see any reason not to believe her. The way she explains it, the tip of the sculpture reached the end of the backswing at no less than seven feet from the ground and two feet behind the point of impact. If you look at her model and her diagrams you'll see how it has to be a tall person."

"I don't like it. My story fits too well not to be true. If it's not Paco we have to rethink it all."

"Why? Keep your story with one difference. Instead of Paco going himself, Olivera sent someone else. It makes more sense anyway. Paco had to stay where he was to drive Kneeland, and Olivera must have a whole battalion of hit men he could have sent."

"Okay, maybe you're right . . . it makes sense. Good. I feel better." But he didn't. "When will Archbold have her report?"

"Monday."

"Tell her to make it as clear as she can. It's all we've got."

"That, and the tape."

Suddenly he sat forward.

"We don't need any extra hit men. There's already a tall person in my scenario."

She looked at him.

"Robertson Kneeland."

"You don't seriously think he did it?"

He wasn't sure. "Let's talk about it."

"He was at one party, then another. There's about a fifteen minute window, maybe as much as twenty-five."

"And he didn't kill Ned without getting some blood on his clothes."

"So he had to get the call, go to Hill's and argue with Ned, kill him, leave—down the fire escape, presumably—clean up and get to the next party, all in that time." She was skeptical.

Ryan could not argue—it seemed hugely unlikely. Still, he did not want to let it go. It's because you hate him, he told himself, because you think he took your place with Ned. And then something stirred in his memory.

"Wait a minute. Didn't Jennifer say something once about how he kept clothes in the car?"

"I don't remember it."

"Sure, that morning it rained so hard." He didn't want to identify it by what else had happened that morning.

"The morning it . . . Oh!" He was amazed to see her blush. "*That* morning. Yes, I do remember. Jennifer did say something like that."

"Okay." He took a breath. "So Kneeland could have changed clothes on the way. But the timing is still wrong. If we split the difference between the parties, he was at Hill's at about eight twenty-five. That's a half hour too early."

"It's not a problem."

He didn't get it. "I thought the murder was nine or later."

"That's what we wanted the jury to keep in mind," she said. "The later the better, from the point of view of Jennifer's defense. Actually, the medical evidence isn't that clear. All the testimony was about the time of death. When he died isn't necessarily the same as when he was hit. People linger with head wounds. Weeks, longer. Ned might easily have lived an hour or more."

"And Franky missed it."

"On purpose. His witness placed Jennifer there at nine, so nine was great with him. He wanted to limit the time window."

"And we wanted to extend it, but in the other direction, toward ten o'clock, to make the case that it happened after she left."

"So neither side wanted to talk much about any time earlier than eight-thirty or so,'' she said. "But he could have been hit at ten after eight, and as he lay dying his life processes continued, so the canapés got digested and there was no pooling of his blood and no rigor mortis, because he was actually alive until nine or ten or whenever.''

It fit. And both sides had turned their backs on the possibility. "Next time I'll pay more attention to the forensic evidence.''

She looked at him when he said "next time,'' but she did not comment.

"So it could have been Kneeland,'' Ryan said.

"Could have been. Not was.''

"Could have been is plenty.''

It opened a whole new line of thought. His theory so far leaned on Kneeland's having called Olivera, or at least having talked in front of Paco, who then called Olivera. But if he was honest with himself he had to admit that either one felt like a stretch. Kneeland's whole argument to Ned was based on fear of Olivera. To call the Colombian for help with Ned's defection might be better than allowing the defection to happen, but it was still dangerous. Kneeland had brought Ned into the operation—Ned was his responsibility. A call to Olivera might be a death sentence for Ned, but it was likely to pull the world down around his sponsor's shoulders as well.

If he didn't call Olivera, what did Kneeland do?

Ryan felt an intense exhilaration, the world focused to a pinpoint. This was what he was meant for, what had made him a top prosecutor. Not just the courtroom skills. It was the ability to see how the pieces fit together, to follow the productive lines building a case and leave the others alone. He could sense how close he was to having it right.

The phone call comes while Kneeland is in the car. He tells Ned let's not talk on the phone, I'll be right there. He doesn't call anyone. This is something he has to do himself. Maybe he still hopes he can talk Ned out of ruining them both. He gives Paco Hugo Hill's address and tells him to step on it. Paco does some fancy driving—Ryan remembered Vladimir on the way to the hospital— and a few minutes later Kneeland is at Hugo Hill's.

"He could easily have been there by twenty after eight,'' Ryan said aloud.

"Kneeland?''

"Right. After the phone call. He goes upstairs the way Ned told him to and confronts Ned. But Ned is primed by what he heard from the Turners and he's feeling guilty about Jennifer, wanting to do the right thing, so he doesn't back down. And either Kneeland

anics or else he goes all cold-blooded, desperate to save himself
from Olivera. One way or the other he grabs the statue and beats
Ned to death and gets out of there down the fire escape. The timing
is close, he'd have to have all the breaks, but with clothes in the car
and Paco's help it's possible.'' More than possible . . .

"And that's why he bugged us," Ryan realized.

"You think he's the one who bugged us?"

"He had the place built for us. Who was in a better position to
install things in walls and partitions?'' He did not tell her the rest
of what he was thinking about the bug, and the shooting.

She nodded. "So he'd know if we were getting close."

Ryan's face was tight. "We don't have a crumb of evidence that'll
stand up in court."

"Unless he confesses," she said.

"Why would he do that?"

"To save his daughter. Until now he must have thought she would
get off."

"He hasn't come forward yet, and she stands convicted of manslaughter, awaiting sentencing by Hang 'Em High Corino."

"The verdict isn't final. Maybe he thinks there's still hope. New
trial, appeals. That's what we're telling her.'' She did not sound as
if she believed it herself.

"It's none of the above," he said. "If Kneeland killed Ned the
reason he's not coming forward is pure self-preservation. He's not
putting himself on the line for anybody. Jennifer just told me he
tried to push her toward pleading guilty."

"He didn't."

"That's what she said. It was one of the reasons she came to
me."

She took a moment to digest it. "What do we do now?"

He went to stand by the window. Shadowed by the midtown
skyscraper forest, the city looked drab and tarnished despite the
perfect day.

"We push him. We confront him with the tape, in front of Jennifer."

"You can't be that cruel to her."

"She already has her suspicions."

He grabbed the telephone and called Kneeland before Kassia
could unearth reasons not to.

"Mr. Kneeland, this is Michael Ryan. We've got some important
new information, and we need to talk to you and Jennifer. It won't
take long."

Kneeland grudgingly agreed to a half hour that evening.

Ryan called Lawrence.

"I need a sound man to wire me and Kassia. Right away."

27

THEY MET WITH JENNIFER AND HER FATHER IN HI§
Fifth Avenue apartment. Kneeland brought them to the library and
seated them by the fireplace.

Ryan propped his borrowed boom box on the mantel. "It'll be
easier if I play this tape for you first, instead of trying to explain."

The room was silent for the entire length of the tape. Ryan's eyes
were locked on Kneeland. The man seemed untouched by what he
was hearing. No tics or mannerisms, his breathing normal, at most
a touch of extra color in his cheeks. Ryan had not done that well
an hour before when he had forced himself to listen to the tape so
this would not be his first full exposure to it. He heard Jennifer
gasp a few times and move in her chair, but he was too intent on
her father to look at her.

The silence continued when the tape ended. Kneeland was the
first to speak.

"If that's a joke it's not funny." There was strain in his voice,
but not much. Ryan thought that ability to maintain his composure
so firmly must have served him well this past year.

His daughter was not so cool. Her teeth worried at her lower lip.
"Was that really you and Ned?" She was at the edge of control.

"I'd rather not do this in front of the whole world, Jennifer."

"These people are my friends. They stood by me all this time."

"And they were well paid to do it."

"That's horrible, Daddy. Apologize."

"Mr. Ryan, my daughter and I have private business to discuss."
Ryan did not move.

"Please leave, Mr. Ryan." A touch of annoyance now.

"No, Michael, don't go."

Kneeland walked calmly to a phone and dialed two digits. "Kevin, there are people here refusing to leave. Call the police and ave security send someone up."

"If they go, I go."

Kneeland smiled reassuringly at her, father to daughter. "It's all lie, sweetheart. They invented it all."

"Why?" She was on her feet, facing him angrily. "Why would ney do that?"

"I don't know." He sounded honestly mystified.

In the silence that followed, Ryan spoke up. "If you don't know nat, maybe you know why Felipe Olivera sent those crackheads to ill Jennifer." A long shot, but it felt right enough to risk, and it night shake Kneeland out of his relentless composure.

He was momentarily speechless.

"At first I thought they were after me," Ryan continued, "but t's too complicated that way. It was Jennifer's house—they were nere to kill Jennifer. I just caught a stray bullet."

"But it was a gang war . . ." Jennifer said, mystified.

"The gang war was real enough. All Olivera had to do was put ressure on the kids so they'd catch you in the shoot-out. Two birds vith one stone, and no one would connect the shooting with the rial."

"That's absurd." The words burst from Kneeland. "Why would nyone do that?"

"To stop the trial," Kassia supplied, her eyes alive with the ealization. "We'd already guessed Ned was involved with Olivera, o as long as the trial continued there was the danger we'd tie you nto it, too, which would have been an awful damn nuisance Señor Olivera."

"Is that *true*?" Jennifer demanded. "Is it?"

Her father returned her stare. "Of course not."

"It *is* true." Cords of muscle stood out in her neck.

"I don't intend to put up with another minute of this," her father aid. He turned to leave the room.

"Bastard!" she whispered, the word more violent for its soft-ness.

She grabbed a thick crystal ashtray and hurled it at him with all he force of her fury. It hit him above and behind the right ear. His nand went to his head and his knees buckled. He grabbed for an upholstered chair to keep himself from falling, then slid to his knees.

Jennifer stood where she was, breathing heavily. Ryan and Kassia were on their feet. No one moved.

An oversize young man in a security uniform came into the room followed at a nervous distance by the maid.

"What's going on here?"

Kneeland pushed himself up to standing. Ryan could see a thin red line of blood running down the back of his neck and spreading into his collar.

"These people were just leaving."

"Door's this way, folks," the security man said.

Kassia glanced at Ryan. He shook his head once: Stay where you are.

The security man shifted his weight. "Time to go."

"Steve," Jennifer said quickly, "my father's not well. He's been saying crazy things . . ."

"Don't listen to her," Kneeland snapped.

". . . and he just fell down and hit his head. I'm going to call a doctor now."

"These people don't belong here. Get them out." Kneeland's voice cracked with strain.

"See?" Jennifer said to Steve. "I told you something was wrong with him. This is my father-in-law and his law partner . . ."

"I said don't listen to her!"

". . . we were talking nicely and Daddy just seemed to go crazy."

Kneeland took a step forward, wavered. Lurched dizzily to a chair.

Jennifer gave Steve a significant look: I told you.

"You don't look so good, Mr. Kneeland." Out of his depth, Steve was backing toward the door.

Jennifer picked up the phone. "I'd like the number for University Hospital, please." And to Steve: "It's okay, we'll be all right. And tell the police we have it under control."

"Yes, ma'am." Relief propelled him from the room.

Jennifer hung up the phone. Looked straight at her father. "You killed Ned, didn't you?" Deceptively calm.

"You're upset, honey. You have to calm down." The form of soothing without its content. "You're not thinking straight."

"You *did*. You killed him. I don't know how, but I know you did."

Kneeland got out of the chair. He was regaining his strength and his control. "You know better than that." And to Ryan, "I hope you're satisfied. You know she's been under a strain. How could you inflict this on her when you knew she wasn't well?"

"I think she's fine," Ryan said. "And I think she's right—you

lled Ned. He called you from the party and reached you in your
r. You changed course and got to him in a hurry. And after you
lled him you wiped the phone clean because you thought that
uld keep people from knowing he'd called you.''

"That's nonsense." Kneeland was glaring at him. "You have no
idence of that. It's all vicious slander.''

"I just played you some evidence. We all heard it.''

"Inventions," he said scornfully. Then: "But suppose for a min-
e what you're saying has some truth in it. Wouldn't that mean I
ve some very dangerous people on my side. And if I did, think
out what might happen if you persisted with these accusa-
ns . . . *If* what you say were true.'' He turned cold with cer-
inty. "Now get out of my house. And take her with you.''

Jennifer rushed for him, terrifyingly silent.

Ryan caught her. She struggled violently in his arms. It was all
could do to hold her. Finally she subsided.

Kassia came over and took her hand and they all left.

How are you doing?" Ryan asked Jennifer when they were in his
ving room.

"Shaky.''

"You want something to drink? Food?''

"Can I take a shower?''

"Make yourself at home.''

"I'll show you where," Kassia said.

Alone, Ryan tried to see the killing from Olivera's point of view.
Kneeland would have wanted to tell Olivera about it right away,
efore Paco had a chance to. Odds were, Kneeland had stuck rea-
onably close to the truth about why Ned had had to go.

Jennifer's arrest had probably given Olivera mixed feelings: glad
wasn't Kneeland but still worried about what the trial would
eveal. There was a lot for Olivera to worry about—Kneeland's
atus as legitimate front and listening post, the medicine hijacking,
e true source of all those millions Ned loaned out.

With every cent of that money subject to confiscation by the
overnment once they connected it to the drug trade, Olivera would
ave had a big stake in following the defense team's progress. Knee-
nd's bug was probably a joint venture, with the tapes going to
livera, too. They might even have gone to Olivera first, or only
Olivera. That explained the timing of the threat, and the shoot-
g . . .

The two women came into the living room. Jennifer's wet hair

was tied back in a pony tail and her face was scrubbed clean ↴
makeup. She looked startlingly young and innocent.

"Feeling better?" Ryan asked.

"I need to talk about this. Otherwise I'll start thinking I'↴
crazy."

"If you're sure you want to."

"First I need to hear that tape again."

Ryan turned the boom box on. Sitting in his grandmother's chai↴
Jennifer listened to the tape three times through, stopping it an↴
rewinding now and then to concentrate on a particular section↴
Then she asked Ryan to tell her everything he could about th↴
murder.

As he described the scenario he had worked out, she sat with he↴
eyes closed. Her fingers traced the spiral-turned wooden arms ↴
the chair, smooth and dark with years of use.

She sat in silence after he finished and then her eyes opened↴
"Yes," she said. "Oh yes—that's my father, right down to wipin↴
off the phone. Careful to the end . . . I kept telling myself he wa↴
avoiding me because he thought I might be guilty. But that wasn↴
it, was it? He was nervous around me because *he* was guilty."

"But he's right that we don't have any hard evidence agains↴
him." Ryan cautioned. "We don't *know* he did it."

"*I* know. I think I always knew. I just couldn't admit it to my↴
self." Seeing it clearly brought her a brief, bitter smile. "Why els↴
was I so desperate to have you as my lawyer, so sure I neede↴
someone uncorruptible, someone to watch over me? If my ow↴
father . . ." She nodded with certainty. "He did it. I know m↴
father. His reaction just now . . . *He did it.*" She sat with th↴
thought for a while. Ryan did not rush her.

"And you think Olivera was the one who turned my doorste↴
into a shooting gallery." She was asking them for confirmation.

"Next to a guilty plea that's the fastest way to stop a trial—fo↴
the defendant to die," Kassia said.

"There was another reason for Olivera to have you killed," Rya↴
said. "As a warning to your father of what would happen to him ↴
he stepped out of line."

"That's how they think, isn't it?" Jennifer said. "People lik↴
that."

"It may have been a kind of disciplinary action, too," Ryan said↴
"To Olivera's troops, killing you—and Ned's unborn child—woul↴
be public retribution for Ned's attempted betrayal."

"Plus if I was dead nobody had to worry Daddy might blow th↴

istle on Olivera to save me," Jennifer said. "Not that he would
ve, anyway."

Another silence.

"We have to do something about him," Jennifer said. "We can't
him get away with killing Ned. Ned, and Ned's child, too. He's
sponsible for that even if Olivera gave the orders."

"Chances are we don't have enough to put him in jail," Kassia
id. "Not even with a tape of what happened tonight. It can help
get you cleared, but it won't convict him."

"I'll kill him myself if that's the only way." Jennifer said it
atter-of-factly but her hands gripped the chair arms with the
ength of her passion.

"Oh, no you won't," Ryan said. "I was your defense lawyer
ce; I don't want to have to do it again. And your father was right
en he said it's not healthy to have Olivera mad at you."

"What difference will it make to Olivera? My father isn't any
e to him now."

It took him a moment to see it. "You're right. That tape of Ned
d your father is going to be all over the place once we file our
pers, and it's going to compromise your father permanently in
the places Olivera needs him . . . He really is useless to Olivera
w." He ruminated on it a moment. "You know, maybe we won't
ve to do anything about keeping your father from getting away
th it. I have the feeling other people may beat us to it. Olivera,
r one."

She thought about that. "Tell me something. When somebody
om the old country takes revenge, do they have to strike the blow
emself?"

"If you're talking about my glorious heritage, you're more of an
thority than I am. I've been trying to ignore it all my life." But
could feel that it still had a hold on him. "I guess it would count
en if you didn't do it yourself."

"I'll bet it's all right as long as you have *something* to do with it
. setting it in motion . . ." Jennifer mused. "And if the person
ho actually did it had reasons of their own for revenge . . ."

Ryan was fascinated.

"Especially if there was a little treachery in the way you set it
. . ."

She could almost have been his Chirkess grandmother, sitting
ere in her chair, straight and strong. The coloring was different,
t the spirit was the same.

She was looking off into a private distance. She pulled herself back and the clear blue-gray eyes fixed on Ryan. "Do you know where to find this man Olivera?"

Ryan thought he might. If Olivera had taken over Irish Viera's empire he was likely to be operating out of Viera's Latin music club, the Tabu, not that far from Michael Ryan's living room. He did not say so.

"You know," he said instead, "talking about Olivera, it would be a big help to us with the court if the police could corroborate any of this. It so happens Jimmy Kelly has a nephew who's looking to make a big narcotics case. I'm sure he'd love to get his hands on our tape. And maybe in return he can find us some solid backup for our theories."

He went to the phone. "I'll call Kelly."

The mill ground faster than he expected.

Detective Lieutenant James O'Donnell came by for a copy of the tape less than an hour after Ryan called Kelly. O'Donnell promised to check out their theory of the January shooting as quickly as he could. "I'll get the word out in the street tonight, what we're looking for."

Early the next morning, on the way home from his daily hour of squash, H. Robertson Kneeland was mugged just behind the low stone wall separating Central Park from Fifth Avenue.

The papers reported that the muggers had struck quickly, getting away with the gold watch Kneeland always wore, said to be worth five thousand dollars, and an undetermined amount of cash. In the course of the crime the muggers stabbed their victim several times and then, for no apparent reason, slit his throat.

He was dead on arrival at Lenox Hill Hospital. His chauffeur told reporters that Kneeland had packed for a long trip and had planned to leave for the airport shortly after returning home from his squash game.

28

RYAN AND KASSIA WORKED STEADILY ON THE PAPERS supporting their motion to set aside Jennifer's guilty verdict. They hired a second bloodstain-pattern expert to bolster Lynne Archbold's analysis, and they retained audio and voiceprint experts to report on the tape of Kneeland and Ned. O'Donnell, happily building his own case based on the tape of Kneeland and Ned and the information it was leading him to, gave them some hints about what corroboration they might get from the Narcotics Division.

With two weeks to go before the sentencing date, Ryan called the judge to tell him he had a motion to submit and that he thought it might be best to do it in confidence. Corino agreed to seal the documents and the proceedings and called an informal meeting with both sides for ten days after Ryan served the papers.

Griglia walked into the room spoiling for a fight. Ryan had hoped the D.A. might yield in the face of the evidence. Clearly that was not to be.

"This is all ridiculous, your honor," Griglia raged. "Not a bit of it is competent evidence. A tape recording supposedly made by two dead men—verified by some mumbo-jumbo comparison with other tapes the defense can't authenticate properly."

"I think they've made an honest effort, Mr. Griglia. If you want to contest it, that's understandable . . ."

"Yes, your honor, I do. And I want to contest the probative value of this bloodstain evidence, too. It's just more of the same. How do we begin to authenticate those photographs?"

"Your honor, I think I've made all that clear in my papers," Ryan said.

"The only thing that's clear, your honor," Griglia stormed, "is that Mr. Ryan, in his desperation, has fastened on the death of

431

Robertson Kneeland as a way to level charges against a man who's hardly in a position to deny them or to defend himself.''

"I see your point, Mr. Griglia," Corino said, "and we have to consider that aspect of it, but right now I'm more interested in the evidentiary weight of the material in Mr. Ryan's motion papers and his exhibits, especially this analysis by his experts in bloodstain patterns. They all seem to say that the murderer was several inches taller than Mrs. Ryan.''

Griglia renewed his diatribe against the reliability of Spada's photographs, making no concession on any point Ryan raised. Mostly, Corino listened in silence, interrupting now and then to ask a question.

Griglia's fervor burned undiminished in spite of clear signs from the judge that he was looking for moderation and logic, not passion.

Ryan's initial dismay at Griglia's forcefulness faded as he saw how desperate Franky had to be to fight so hard with so little eye for whether he was being effective.

Finally, Corino lost his patience.

"In about ten seconds I'm going to schedule a full-scale hearing on all this evidence Mr. Ryan has found that his client did not commit the crime and that others, including people known to the police as dangerously violent, had pressing motives. And I'm going to tell Mr. Ryan that I have no objection to any press conference he might care to call about what he intends to prove at the hearing. That way, Mr. District Attorney, you can get the proper public exposure for your objections to all of this.''

Griglia sputtered a disjointed sentence about maintaining public confidence in the trial process and giving the press premature and misleading information.

"People get public trials here, Mr. Griglia," Corino said. "And public vindications, too. Are you prepared for a hearing or would you like a little more time?''

Griglia stiffened. "I don't appreciate being railroaded.''

"Railroaded, Mr. Griglia? I'll try to overlook the implication. I'm merely seeing to the proper administration of justice. There's a woman here with a substantial claim that she was wrongfully convicted. Perhaps wrongfully prosecuted. We can hardly let that sort of thing go by.''

Ryan could sense Griglia weighing the pros and cons. His face stiffened and without ever looking at Ryan he volunteered to reconsider the new evidence and proposed a press conference to announce new developments in the Ryan murder. He wanted to hold it alone, but Ryan, sensing his advantage, said he thought it would be better if they spoke to the press jointly. It was a bitter pill for Griglia, but he had to swallow it.

The following Friday, the D.A. sat in front of the microphones and cameras with Jennifer at his right and Ryan next to her.

"Ladies and gentlemen," he said to the clamorous crowd of reporters. "I called you here to make an unusual announcement. Members of my staff, at my direction, have petitioned Judge Anthony Corino to set aside the conviction of Jennifer Kneeland Ryan based on new evidence that has come to my attention that indicates clearly her innocence."

Franky's press favorites were ready for it, but among the rest there was a rush of whispered reaction. He kept talking over it.

"I want to formally apologize to Mrs. Ryan for the anguish she has been caused this past year. Given the evidence we had at the time, I believe we took the right course. Fortunately we learned the truth before Mrs. Ryan had to endure any further difficulty.

"About the murder of Edward Ryan, I can only say this: An ongoing investigation has given us convincing proof that the murder was committed by a person who is physically different from Mrs. Ryan. The motive for the crime was a dispute over an illegal transaction which Edward Ryan was threatening to expose."

This brought an immediate shout of questions. Griglia raised a quieting hand.

"I can't comment further. This is part of an ongoing investigation, as I said, and I cannot jeopardize it, or the lives of the undercover officers involved. I can tell you that we do owe some of our information to the efforts of Michael Ryan, the attorney who represents Mrs. Ryan. He has a few words to say."

Ryan could imagine the effort it took Griglia to maintain this generous-losing-warrior pose. He looked out at the densely packed faces, saw friends and enemies and remembered how it had felt in the old days, announcing a victory. On the other side, then, but this felt even better.

"Thank you, Mr. Griglia. My colleague Kassia Miller and I are grateful to the District Attorney for being so responsive once we showed him that Mrs. Ryan could not possibly have committed the crime, and we're grateful for the excellent work of a few officers of the New York City Police Department—which contrasts with the performance of others in this case. We and Mrs. Ryan are also enormously grateful to Dr. Lynne Archbold for her analysis of recently obtained bloodstain evidence from the crime scene.

"Obviously, we wish none of this had ever happened. Under the circumstances we are glad the situation was resolved before further damage was done. I know Mrs. Ryan is eager to resume a normal life. In the past year she has lost a husband, a father and an unborn child. I hope that you will all consider this in the days to come, and leave her in peace.''

His request was followed by a furious barrage of questions. The only word that emerged clearly from the din was *Jennifer*. They calmed down when she started to speak.

''I'm very relieved it's all over. I've always said I was innocent. I'm grateful to all the people who believed in me. Michael Ryan is the greatest lawyer in the world, and there is no way I can thank him enough, or Kassia Miller, either. I know all of you in the press have been enjoying this trial, but I'm actually a very dull person. I hope you'll all find somebody else more interesting than I am to write about soon.''

Laughter and scattered applause. One die-hard shouted, ''Jennifer, did your father have anything to do with it?''

''I have no comment,'' she said quietly, and Ryan turned off the microphones.

Ryan and Miller were organizing the last of their papers. The small extra desk had been moved out of Ryan's office. No sign was left of the past months' work but ranks of file folders on the carpet.

''I got a possible job offer,'' she told him. ''I'm going to take it if they confirm it's a partnership.''

Ryan did not know where to look. ''I'm not surprised. You're a damn good lawyer and you did a great job in a hot case.'' And I should have seen this coming.

''It's not that I didn't enjoy myself.''

''We were done anyway.'' There was something to say now, but he did not know what it was. ''When do you start?''

''They want me as soon as the partner's committee votes, but I said I want a couple of weeks off first, and they said sure.''

''That's great.'' His mouth twisted around the words. ''We ought to celebrate.''

''Champagne?''

''If you want.'' He could not tell if she was taunting him.

''Aren't you going to ask me where I'll be working?''

''I thought I did. I guess not. Where?''

''Pane, Parish, Eisen & Legler,'' she said, grinning.

When he realized what she'd said he grabbed her in his arms and lifted her off her feet.

* * *

They flew to a small tropical island with no casinos and no night-clubs. Ryan swam a lot, and they took long walks in a forest whose eaves were a darker green than any he remembered. In the mornings and evenings he read Ned's diary and letters, including a thick bundle Jennifer had given him, to a background of old trumpet music and medieval chants.

"You know," he said the night before they were scheduled to leave. "I really did let us both down, Ned and me. He was a good kid. He deserved better."

Her eyes narrowed.

"Relax—I'm not going to beat myself up about it. But it's true. I thought being a good father meant being a steady provider and setting a decent example of how to live a responsible life. Making rules for a kid to follow and enforcing them. I missed the most important things. I missed being with him, and listening to him. Listening in a way that would have told me what he was really about."

"He turned out okay," she said. "He went along with the wrong people for a while, but he really knew better."

"He did. Under all that confusion, he had a good heart and he wanted to do good things. Like those medical clinics—that was a good impulse when he started. And he was on the right track, at the end. That's the tragedy—he found his conscience and he died for it."

She sat quietly on the moonlit terrace, leaving him alone with his thoughts. After a time he came to stand by her side.

She took his hand. "It looks like you weren't such a failure as a father, after all."

"Better than I thought, maybe."

"You could always try again."

He opened his arms to her.

"Maybe," he said. "Maybe I could."

ABOUT THE AUTHOR

PHILIP FRIEDMAN, an attorney, is the author of three previous novels, including *Rage,* which was a film starring George C. Scott and Martin Sheen, and *Termination Order,* which the New York *Times Book Review* called "one of the best spy stories of the year." He makes his home in New York City.